"Action-packed, authentic, and altogether satisfying, *Allah's Fire* is a terrific start for what looks to be a great series. Holton and Roper are definitely a winning team!"

JAMES SCOTT BELL, BESTSELLING AUTHOR
OF *PRESUMED GUILTY*

"An action-packed story with real spiritual teeth."

ANGELA HUNT, AUTHOR OF *THE NOVELIST*

"When you pick up *Allah's Fire*, make sure you have a long stretch of uninterrupted time. It's a page-turning thriller as contemporary as today's headlines."

LINDA HALL, AWARD-WINNING AUTHOR OF *STEAL AWAY*

"*Allah's Fire* sizzles with intensity from page one right through to the dramatic conclusion. Military suspense, radical Islam, unexpected romance, and the grace of God all collide into an amazing story. Chuck Holton and Gayle Roper have created a must-read series in Task Force Valor."

MARK MYNHEIR, FORMER MARINE AND
AUTHOR OF *FROM THE BELLY OF THE DRAGON*

TASK FORCE VALOR

ALLAH'S FIRE

A NOVEL

CHUCK HOLTON

GAYLE ROPER

Multnomah® Publishers *Sisters, Oregon*

ALLAH'S FIRE
published by Multnomah Publishers, Inc.
© 2006 by Charles W. Holton and Gayle Roper
International Standard Book Number: 1-59052-405-5

Multnomah is a trademark of Multnomah Publishers, Inc., and is registered in the U.S. Patent and Trademark Office.
The colophon is a trademark of Multnomah Publishers, Inc.

Printed in the United States of America

For information:
MULTNOMAH PUBLISHERS, INC.
601 N. LARCH STREET
SISTERS, OREGON 97759

Library of Congress Cataloging-in-Publication Data
Holton, Chuck.
Allah's fire : a novel / Chuck Holton & Gayle Roper.
    p. cm. — (Task force valor ; bk. 1)
ISBN 1-59052-405-5
1. Religious fiction. I. Roper, Gayle G. II. Title.
PS3608.O4944344A79 2006
813'.6—dc22

                                        2005035663

06 07 08 09 10—10 9 8 7 6 5 4 3 2

To EOD teams past and present, who assume risks in order to reduce them for others. You have my respect and admiration.
—Chuck

For those who serve
For those who have served
And for their families and loved ones who waited and wept
Thank you.
—Gayle

Acknowledgments

A special thanks to Maelle Saliba of Beirut, Lebanon, for reading our manuscript and letting us see her country through her eyes. What a great help! Any errors that may exist are wholly ours.

Thanks once again to Chuck Gordinier for his help in constructing the fire scenes. It is a great blessing to have a firefighter in the family.

Many thanks to our friend Jack, a Muslim-turned-Christian Jordanian who recently married Rowena and moved to England, partly to escape religious persecution in his homeland. He was a big help with Arabic translation.

Thanks to the fiction team at Multnomah: Angela Jones, Sharon Znachko, and especially our editor, Julee Schwarzburg, who with utmost patience has performed miracles for Chuck and me.

"Initial success or total failure."

EOD MOTTO

"If all men were just, there would be no need of valor."

AGESILAUS II

"And we know that in all things God works for the good of those who love Him, who have been called according to His purpose."

ROMANS 8:28 NIV

Map of LEBANON

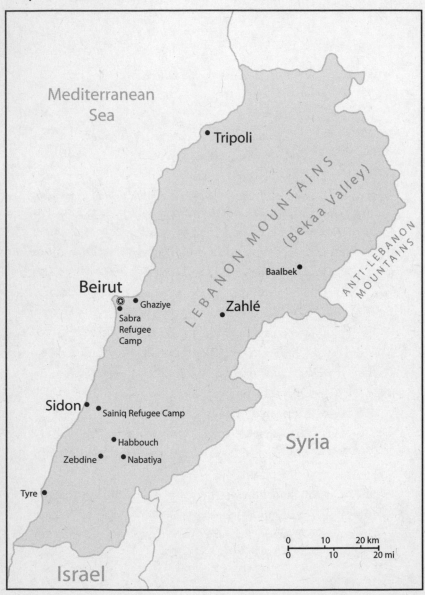

Panama City

FRANJO KAROVIK was smoking a cigarette at a table next to his hotel's brackish pool in Panama City. He was staying at the Hotel Ideal, a dive in the city's Chorillo district, where a room, a meal, and a companion for the night could be easily had, all for less than twenty American dollars. For that reason it was a favorite hangout for ships' captains and other transients.

Franjo enjoyed watching the pretty, young waitress move gracefully from table to table taking drink orders. When a short, jowly man with a thick mustache suddenly sat next to him, he frowned. "This is my table, *señor*."

"You are the captain of the *Invincible*, are you not?"

Franjo regarded the man coolly. "And you are?"

"I am a businessman. I need to get a shipment to Sidon in Lebanon."

The captain had been in the business of shipping long enough to know an opportunity when he saw it. "My ship has a stopover there. But we are on a tight schedule and are very full."

"I know. But my package is not large. It is, however, quite

fragile. Can you handle something like that and keep it confidential?"

Franjo snuffed out his cigarette. "Perhaps. For the right price."

The man produced an envelope and slid it across the table. "This is half of the payment."

After flipping the envelope open with his thumb and glancing inside, Franjo's eyebrows shot up. "Your cargo must be very fragile, indeed."

The next night after she left the Canal, the *Invincible* anchored ten miles offshore. There she waited until almost dawn before a motorboat approached and off-loaded its cargo.

Franjo was amazed at how small the shipment was. Only five metal boxes, each no larger than a small television set. Whatever was in them must be very special, and from the care the Panamanian men took in loading them, very fragile.

But he knew better than to ask what the shipment was. In fact, he didn't really care as long as he got paid. Illicit shipments like this one were the only way a ship's captain could retire in comfort anymore.

Three weeks later he stood on the *Invincible*'s bridge and looked out over Sidon. As he lit his last cigarette of the evening, the city's lights sparkled, and in the distance the Lebanon Mountains were a shadowy backdrop to the port's vibrancy. Had the view changed much over the centuries that Sidon had been a major shipping port for this region? Probably not.

Directly below him were the docks where workers hurried to relieve his ship of her cargo of Central American coffee and sugar.

"Has he arrived yet, Captain?"

Franjo turned to see his first mate, Naeem Bari, step up to the railing and survey the dimly lit docks below. The Pakistani had much less experience with special cargo, and it showed in his abrupt, nervous movements.

"Relax, Naeem. He will not come until the rest of the cargo is unloaded."

He had almost finished his cigarette when Naeem pointed. "Ah, I think our contact has arrived."

Franjo nodded as a dented black Mercedes pulled to a stop on the docks. A tall, thin man dressed in black slacks and a gray sweater climbed out and leaned against the hood of the car, watching as the last of the coffee was unloaded.

"I shall go and meet him." Franjo was eager to take possession of the rest of the payment. "I want you to supervise the unloading of his cargo, but be sure the men are very careful. Whatever it is, we don't want it broken now."

A moment later, the captain walked down the gangplank toward the Mercedes. As he drew closer, he eyed the man still leaning on its front quarter panel. The man had a hawkish nose and a slight build. He tried to appear at ease, but he was coiled more tightly than the great ropes that held the *Invincible* fast.

Franjo didn't trust him. "I assume you've come for the package?" he said in English.

"Yes. And you are the ship's captain?" The man's cold eyes bored into him.

"I am. I understand the cargo is quite fragile. We have been very careful, but would you like to inspect it first?"

The man shook his head. "No."

That surprised Franjo. The customer always wanted to inspect the cargo before making payment, especially with something this valuable. "Are you sure? Don't you want to satisfy yourself that nothing is broken?"

The man smiled without warmth. "If anything was broken, you would already be dead."

Abidjan, Ivory Coast

MASTER SERGEANT JOHN COOPER ran a hand through his sweaty dark hair and wondered if he'd live to see another sunset.

"You're sure this will work, Frank?" he asked the team's dark-haired explosives expert, pushing the negative thought from his mind.

"What I'm sure of, Coop, is that over one hundred children will be forcibly converted into particulate matter in less than an hour if we don't try this. That is, unless someone has a better idea."

John and Sergeant First Class Frank Baldwin both looked across the hood of their Humvee at their commander, waiting to see if he did indeed have a better idea.

Major Louis Williams stared past the two soldiers at the rusty swing set between him and the school compound. His face showed little emotion, except for a firmly clenched jaw. He said nothing for a full twenty seconds.

John's eyebrows shot up. "Well, sir?"

Williams picked up his Motorola radio and growled into it, "What have you got, Dan?"

Dan Daly, the team's sniper, answered from his observation point on the roof of an apartment building across the street from the school complex. "The leader hasn't moved. I can't tell for sure, but it looks like the sick kid they released this morning was telling the truth about the setup inside."

John looked at his watch. *Forty-seven minutes.* "If we're going to try Frank's plan, we'd better make it quick."

Major Williams turned to Frank. "Explain this thing to me again." He gestured to the cylindrical metal object lying on the hood of the Humvee. "It looks like an artillery shell casing."

Frank sighed, then spoke as one would to a slow child. "It's a miniature e-bomb, sir. Basically, it's a small Flux Compression Generator, or FCG, which is a copper tube packed with explosives, surrounded by a coil of heavy copper wire. The wire is charged with electricity just before the explosive is detonated, which creates a ramping pulse of electrical current equivalent to maybe ten or twenty bolts of lightning. That should be enough of an EMP to inhibit the use of the enemy's detonators."

Major Williams stared at him. "You're speaking English, Baldwin. I know you are. It's just not the same English I speak."

John bit back a grin. Granted Frank drove him nuts sometimes with his smarter-than-thou routine, but it had to be hard being a genius.

"I think what he's trying to say is, this thing will create an energy pulse that will toast the bad guys' toys without damaging the building or the schoolchildren. The sick kid said that he saw explosives duct taped to the concrete pillars and wall supports on the first floor, with wires running to a mat the terrorists brought in with them. It looks like the floor mat out of a car, but it has a plate of sheet metal on it. The terrorists are taking turns standing on the plate, never completely stepping off of it."

The major nodded. "So that must be the detonator. And these yahoos are trying to foil our snipers by setting it up so if they get knocked down, the whole place blows. And you're saying this e-bomb will disable their explosives?"

"Not the bombs, sir. Just the circuitry in the detonators."

"What if they have backup methods in place?"

"We have to assume that they do," Frank said. "But this thing will instantly render everything electronic inoperative. Batteries will malfunction, wires will melt, lightbulbs will explode. The only way they could light their demo after the e-bomb goes off is with a manual nonelectric detonator, like a time fuse. Which is why we'll need to assault the building immediately once the FCG detonates."

"And be sure to use a manual detonator for our own breach," John said.

The major rubbed the back of his neck and grimaced. "Have you tested this device?"

John looked at Frank, whose smarts appeared to fail him for a moment as he hesitated, then cleared his throat. "Well, not exactly, sir. The Army successfully used several larger devices like this on bases around Iraq during the initial invasion in 2003. This one is just…um…smaller."

The major, an ex-linebacker from Auburn University, picked up the device and turned it over in his hands like a football. "Where did you get it, Frank?"

He cleared his throat again. "I built it."

Williams nearly fumbled the thing. "You *what*?"

John almost laughed at the major's expression. Frank was an acquired taste, always having a newer and better way of doing things. Sometimes he was even right.

"Well, I assembled it, anyway." Frank stared at the bomb like a man might gaze upon a beautiful woman. "I used the first stage FCG and capacitors from a low-frequency Mark-eighty-four e-bomb the Air Force…um…wasn't using."

The major slapped his Kevlar-helmeted forehead. "I'm going to get fired."

John spoke up. "He didn't steal it, sir. It fell off a forklift at the ammo supply point at Bragg back in January, and they were going to destroy it as potentially damaged. Frank talked them into letting us have it. He's carried it with him on our last two deployments, waiting for an opportunity to try it out."

Williams spat on the ground. "Well, I don't see what other choice we have. If we go in hot and one of the terrorists falls off of his magic carpet, we lose. They've promised to blow the place unless all French and UN peacekeepers leave the country, which ain't gonna happen." He checked his watch. "So in forty-four minutes, we lose. Unless…"

He set the cylinder back on the vehicle's hood and looked toward the high cement wall surrounding the school building. "It looks like we're fourth down and fifteen and plum out of options. But how do you propose getting the e-bomb inside the building?"

"Oh, we don't need to, sir," Frank said. "That's what's so great about it. It can be detonated anywhere within a hundred meters of the school." He hesitated for a moment. "Which reminds me. There might be a few, er, *side effects.*"

The major's gaze narrowed. "Like what?"

John bit the inside of his cheek to keep that smile contained.

"Like anything electronic in the area will also be cooked," Frank said.

"Anything?"

"Pretty much."

Williams didn't immediately answer, and John leaned against the Humvee, scanning the ramshackle neighborhood that surrounded the school. This part of Abidjan was predominantly Christian, but lately Muslim rebels from the north had been sowing terror here. As if these people's poverty wasn't miserable enough.

John'd been all over the world in his years in the Special Forces, and except for the language on the road signs and business signs, this could be any third-world city. They all shared a certain sense of despair, as if the people who labored to construct these rickety dwellings started out with good intentions but at some point were simply overwhelmed by the Law of Entropy and gave up.

The more places like this John visited, the more he appreciated the hopefulness he felt when he was back home. America was the land of optimism, whether its people realized it or not.

He studied the two-story cinderblock homes lining the trash-strewn street in front of the school. Most had corrugated metal roofs and no glass in their windows. Concrete walls around some dwellings showed graffiti in French and Arabic, as well as numerous pockmarks from previous violence.

The French peacekeepers were holding all civilians behind barricades they had set up two blocks away. How many of those people lived in these houses and had children in the school, their kids' lives in the hands of men willing to kill themselves to earn Allah's approval through martyrdom?

How can You let kids be treated like this, God? They're so powerless. You're supposed to protect them, aren't You?

The major nodded abruptly and reached for his radio. "I can handle a few burnt-out lightbulbs if we save the lives of a hundred elementary school kids."

Frank's smile was brilliant.

The major gestured toward the hardened troop transport vehicle the team had brought with them on the mission. "Frank, have the boys put anything that might get wrecked in the back of the Cougar HEV transport over there. Radios, night-vision goggles—everything electronic. Have all other vehicles pull back far enough so their components won't get fried. We might end up buying new televisions for everyone in the neighborhood, but I'm not having the rest of our whiz-bang gear taken out if I can help it. John, keep one radio for yourself in case we have to abort."

Frank scooped up his e-bomb and trotted off toward the

vehicles. The major turned back to the schematics of the school laid out over the hood of the Humvee.

"Okay, John. Get your breach team in position on the south wall. Once we blow that…er…thing, you'll need to hit the school quick before the bad guys figure out what's happened. If they realize we've killed their electronics, they just might resort to blowing this thing the old-fashioned way—if they don't shoot all the kids first, the rotten cowards!" He spoke the last two words with enough volume to be heard across the street.

Cowards was a good word. Grown people who went after kids were cowards. Bullies. What kind of worldview held that murdering a hundred innocent schoolchildren was the path to heaven, but touching a piece of bacon could get you damned eternally? John wasn't even sure he wanted to understand it.

On the other hand, there were people back in the States with similar philosophies—groups who believed that bombing abortion clinics scored them points with God, but owning a Rolling Stones CD was a ticket to hell. Go figure.

John didn't consider himself an expert on the Lord by any stretch, but something inside him knew that a vindictive and unjust God wasn't worth the title.

But those were questions for chaplains and clerics. At the moment, John had time for neither. If God wasn't going to keep kids and the other innocents of the world safe, he and his men would do it.

He consulted his watch again. "We've got fifteen minutes." He keyed the Motorola. "Dan, get ready. We're going for it."

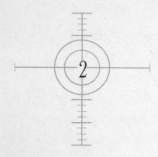

Beirut, Lebanon

"LIZ! SHE WENT BACK!"

Liz Fairchild looked up from her laptop and the interview she was transcribing to see Nabila standing in the doorway, a letter dangling from her shaking hand. "Who went back where?" she asked the family's housekeeper/cook.

"Zahra. To the refugee camp."

Cold coiled about Liz's heart. "Are you sure?"

Nabila waved the letter. "My cousin Hanan has seen her, though she hasn't had a chance to talk to her."

The cold seeped throughout Liz's body, chilling her to the fingertips. It was barely eight o'clock, too early to hear such terrible news. "She'll probably be all right."

But neither of them believed it. Zahra would certainly suffer. The only questions were how much and when.

Nabila read from the letter. "'I worry about her. You know her mother and father. In their eyes Zahra has shamed the family.'"

Liz didn't actually know Zahra's parents as Nabila did, but she knew all about them.

"My aunt and uncle are so ardent, so passionate about the letter of Islamic law." Nabila's face was a study in concern and distress. "My aunt especially is fanatical. I fear her more than my uncle. He is more compassionate by nature, and he is a broken man over what happened to Zahra. That his sons, the future of his family, would rape their younger sister and make her pregnant has shattered his heart. They sit in jail for their crime, and he is shamed. My aunt, on the other hand, is shamed that Zahra got pregnant and had a child outside of marriage. She blames Zahra, not the brothers."

Liz frowned. "I can't understand that thinking. Zahra is the victim. She was only fourteen to the brothers seventeen and eighteen. She needs sympathy, not condemnation."

"You think like an American or a European, not a Palestinian raised in the camps."

Liz couldn't deny that. "Does Hanan specifically say she fears for Zahra's life?"

Nabila shook her head. "Hanan has to be careful what she writes in case a letter is intercepted. No one, not even her husband, knows she writes me."

"Why do you think Zahra went back? She was safe with your relatives in the Bekaa Valley. She could have stayed with them forever. Everyone told her over and over not to go back. She would be putting herself in danger."

Liz knew an honor killing was Nabila's main fear. The crime was not very common in Lebanon anymore, but sometimes in one of the crowded Palestinian camps, where there was essentially no civil law enforcement, terrible things happened in the name of Allah.

"You know the pull of home," Nabila said. "Much as you love living in the United States, you keep coming back to Beirut."

Liz nodded. She had been raised here from thirteen until she went to the States for college. Her parents, Drs. Charles and

Annabelle Fairchild, still lived here and taught at the American University of Beirut. Her sister, Julie, had married a Lebanese and lived here, too.

"And I know how hard it is to stay away." Nabila's voice was low and harsh, full of regret over things she couldn't change and deep in her heart wouldn't change.

She had come from the same camp that her cousin Zahra had returned to, and Nabila knew she could never go back. She, too, had dishonored her family when at eighteen she had walked away from her culture and hitched a ride to Beirut with only the dream of more. It was bad enough that she was getting an education at the American University of Beirut, but she also worked as housekeeper/cook for two American professors.

"Oh, Nabila!" Liz went to her and hugged her. Nabila had been with the Fairchilds for so many years that it was easy to forget she had lived seventeen hardscrabble years in the camp.

"But you left a difficult life, especially for a woman, to seek a better life and your dream of becoming a doctor. Zahra was in such a good situation with people who loved her, and she's gone back to virtual enslavement." Or worse.

"In your eyes. In my eyes." Nabila blinked and brushed futilely at the tears that ran down her cheeks. "I am so frightened for her."

Liz grabbed some tissues from the box on her night table and handed them to Nabila. "When was Hanan's letter written?"

Hanan was the only one from Nabila's family who had kept contact with her after she left. When Hanan went to market in Sidon, she gave her letters to a merchant who sold produce in the souk, and he posted them for her, adding the cost of the stamps to her bill. When Nabila wrote back, the little man wrapped the letter in the papers about Hanan's fruit and vegetables.

"The letter is two weeks old."

"Yikes." So much could have happened in two weeks. "I need

to go see that she's fine. Maybe I can talk her into returning to Nabatiya."

Nabila's face mirrored her relief. "I was hoping you would do that."

"I can't do anything else." Liz Fairchild, would-be Fixer of the Universe. "Zahra's been stuck in my mind and heart ever since you arranged for me to interview her last month." Liz saw the slight girl, swathed in black clothes and head covering, hugging herself as she talked about her despair.

"Who will ever marry me now?" she had asked, dark eyes stark. "I have brought shame upon myself, upon my family, shame so severe I can never recover. I am ruined."

Liz wanted to cry. She leaned forward, note taking forgotten. "Zahra, it wasn't your fault."

But the girl's mother had told her it was. Her culture had told her she was impure, an abomination, a temptress who brought the rape upon herself.

Zahra stared at the floor. "I feel everyone has cast me out. I am all alone," she whispered.

That loneliness was why she had returned, Liz knew. Family ties, no matter how dysfunctional the family, called a siren's song almost impossible to resist, no matter the consequences of listening. Family was security, especially to a traumatized fifteen-year-old.

"I think she misses her baby, though she didn't tell me so." Liz slipped her feet into a pair of Reeboks and tied the laces. Walking around the litter-strewn streets of the refugee camp called for sturdy shoes. "And who knows how much of her despair is postpartum problems."

"There was no way she could have kept that baby girl."

"I agree, and at least some family now has a child they otherwise wouldn't."

Nabila's cell phone rang as Liz made certain her passport was in her purse. She'd need it at the checkpoints.

"Hanan!" Nabila said, shock in her voice.

Liz blinked. Hanan never called. Literally. It was too dangerous. The conversation was short, and Nabila groaned as she hit the disconnect.

"Hanan says my uncle has left the camp on business of some kind. He will be gone overnight. It is only Zahra and my aunt and the younger daughter."

Liz nodded. She understood the danger all too well. She shoved a piece of paper at Nabila. "Directions once I get to the camp."

As Nabila wrote, Liz grabbed her car keys. "Tell my parents that I might not be back in time for dinner."

The road from Beirut to Sidon was good, and Liz drove as fast as she dared.

Heavenly Father, help me get there in time. Please!

The road from Sidon to the Sainiq camp was not as good, and she was forced to slow. She felt the clock ticking, and the sight of the checkpoint outside the camp ratcheted her tension. She rubbed at the base of her sternum, trying to relieve the sick feeling that grew stronger with each moment.

She slowed and held out her passport and journalist's credentials to the young Lebanese soldier who peered in her window. His gun was pointed to the ground, and that's the way she wanted it to stay. She tried to appear calm, to give no hint of the anxiety that drove her or the need she felt for speed.

"Why do you want to go in there?" the soldier asked in fractured English.

"I'm a writer. I'm writing a story about what it's like to be a Palestinian woman today," she answered in Arabic. *And today I'm interested in one small Palestinian.*

The soldier looked at her in surprise and switched to his own language. "An American who speaks Arabic?"

"I lived many years in Beirut. My parents live there still. So does my sister."

"But you now live in America?" His eyes were bright with curiosity.

"I do. In Philadelphia, Pennsylvania."

"My cousin Habib lives in Thorndale, Pennsylvania. Do you know him?"

The question didn't surprise Liz. One of the first things a Lebanese asked when meeting someone was, "What village are you from?" To someone who lived in the small country of Lebanon, the size of the United States, even the size of Pennsylvania, was hard to grasp. "No, I'm afraid I don't know your cousin."

"He is handsome. You would like him. He has a pizza shop."

Liz smiled, though all she wanted to do was hit the accelerator and be gone. "If I ever go to Thorndale, Pennsylvania, I will stop at his shop and say hello to him."

The young soldier looked pleased. He pointed to the camp. "You do not want to go in there. It is dangerous."

"I know, but I do need to talk to the people who live there."

"They don't like Americans."

Another soldier rushed out of the kiosk, shouting and pointing back toward Sidon. The young guard stepped back and frowned down the road.

Liz looked in her rearview mirror and saw three speeding cars, lights flashing on top, bearing down on the checkpoint.

"Go." The young soldier held out her passport, making shooing motions with his hand. "Go!"

As the sound of sirens cut the air, Liz drove the last small distance into the camp, which was not really a camp but a small city. She wanted to pull over, let the speeding vehicles pass, and then follow them to their destination. Stumbling onto fresh news was about as good as it got for a reporter.

But she reined herself in. Today there was something—someone—more important than a scoop. She carefully followed the directions to Hanan's house. She made two turns when she became aware that the speeding cars with the flashing lights and blaring sirens were roaring up behind her. The road was little more than a dirt lane with homes built closely on both sides, and she looked about for somewhere to get out of the way.

A horn blared loudly behind her, a bass to the tenor warblings of the sirens, just as she saw a house set back from the road a few feet. She pulled into a small strip of dirt that was essentially someone's front yard. It was just big enough for her dusty, black rental. She waited as the cars rocketed by, her own car swaying in the air currents of their passing.

She drove back onto the road, feeling somewhat claustrophobic from all the buildings set so closely to each other. There was literally no space between the structures. One house's west wall was the next house's east wall. Women and children stood in doorways to see the passing vehicles.

What did these women think of their lives? Did they harbor the generations-old hatred for Israel, or did they see its futility? Did they meekly accept the fundamentalist interpretation of Islamic law that said they were lesser beings than men, or did they think themselves of value, at least secretly even though they couldn't voice such heresy? Would they see Zahra as the sinner and her brothers as the victims, or vice versa?

To her surprise and growing dismay, Liz found herself making the same turns as the speeding cars. It was like she was deliberately following them.

They couldn't be going where she was going. They just couldn't.

Oh, God, please, no!

She rounded the final corner as the official cars skidded to a halt, and men in uniform jumped out. They raced to a house, nearly pulling the screen door off as they rushed inside. The street was full of people, many of the women crying, most of the men looking pleased. She saw Hanan's home and counted one, two, three more.

It was the home the police and soldiers had entered.

That coil of cold wrapped its hoary arms about her again. Zahra!

"What's happened?" she asked the first man she came to. He looked at her, glanced quickly away, then without a word joined three men standing near Hanan's.

It wasn't bad manners. In her distress she'd forgotten that a lone woman shouldn't talk to a man. She approached a group of women. "What's happened?"

They turned to her, their sad eyes suspicious in spite of the fact that she spoke Palestinian Arabic.

Liz tried again. "Is Hanan here?"

The women's eyes darted to a young woman standing with two little girls hanging on her skirt. Liz approached her.

"Hanan, I'm Liz Fairchild." She dropped her voice to little more than a whisper. "Nabila got your letter today."

Hanan looked at her, dark eyes awash with tears. She was a pretty woman with a strong resemblance to Nabila. "I am afraid it is too late."

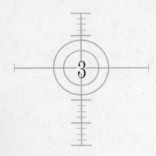

3

Beirut

THE SOFT KNOCK at the door took Jamal by surprise. Panic shot through him as a muffled female voice drifted in from the hallway outside. "Housekeeping. Turndown service."

He dropped his burden, which landed on the floor with a thud, and leapt across the bed toward the door. He heard the maid's electronic master key being pushed into the slot.

He got there just as the handle turned and the door started to push inward. By a supreme effort, he stopped short of crashing into the door. Instead, he eased it closed with both hands and flipped the dead bolt, which he'd foolishly forgotten to turn after the waiter entered.

"La, shukran," he croaked, trying to sound calm. "No, thank you."

The maid mumbled in Arabic that there *was* such a thing as a Do Not Disturb sign. He heard her move away, off to bother some other hotel guest.

Jamal took a deep breath and exhaled slowly. How could he have made such a foolish error? To be discovered now would ruin his entire mission.

He looked at the room service cart by the window. The sight of it appalled him, though not because the man who had delivered it now lay in a crumpled heap between the two double beds, nor because the food on it was bad. In fact, it was some of the best he'd ever tasted. No, what disgusted him was the knowledge that some people thought nothing of paying a third of a working man's daily wage for a plate of stuffed grape leaves.

For four days Jamal had been staying in this luxurious room in the Hotel Rowena, one of the most expensive hotels in Beirut. To him its opulence was nothing short of profane. He thought of his mother and father and their tiny flat in the Sabra refugee camp near Sidon, sixty kilometers to the south. It wasn't much larger than this room. He had lived there since birth, working with his father from the time he was a small boy as they struggled to make a living in their red and white fishing boat.

His earliest memories were of desperation, of warfare. Images were seared into his brain of the 1982 massacre in his hometown, carried out by Lebanese Phalangist Christians out to avenge the assassination of their president.

The screams he had heard and the blood he had smelled as hundreds and hundreds of men and even some of the women and children were murdered rose in his mind's eye as regularly as the sun rose red over the Anti-Lebanon Mountains each morning. His father had been dragged into the street and beaten severely while five-year-old Jamal cowered behind a pile of refuse and watched.

He had nightmares for years, fueled by the fear that the thugs who entered the camp with the permission of the Israelis would come back. This time they would kill his father and maybe his mother, and he would be alone, at their mercy.

Jamal had been powerless then, and even as a child he hated the feeling. He longed to control his own destiny and to have the security to enjoy it. But control was something that did not exist for him or any Palestinian, and security was not to be found, not even in his religion.

No matter how doggedly Jamal pursued his faith, he could not feel safe in it. Islam seemed insatiable, requiring that he forever work to gain Allah's favor. He believed as he had been taught—there is no god but Allah, and Mohammed is his prophet. Jamal prayed without hesitation or regret whenever the muezzin called. He even gave a portion of his meager earnings to the needy, as if he were not needy himself.

But it was never enough. Allah would judge him by his deeds someday, and deep inside Jamal *knew* he could never be good enough to earn Allah's favor. He knew many people in his village saw him as a devout young man, but they never saw his inside. They never heard his thoughts when one of the far-too-plentiful "liberated" Palestinian girls passed him on the street. They never knew the doubts and questions about his faith that he sometimes struggled with. If Allah knew these things, however, he was doomed.

Finally, Jamal had come to understand that there was only one way to guarantee the acceptance of Allah—martyrdom. But coming to that conclusion and actually becoming a martyr were two different things.

He was not a ruthless or violent man. Nor was he brave. On the contrary, he had always been quiet, devout, and thoughtful. When the man had approached him after Friday prayers three weeks ago and asked if he would be willing to accept a mission from Allah, Jamal was taken by surprise. He understood immediately what such a mission would entail, but why did the man ask a nobody like him?

"Let me think about it," he said to cover the fact that he didn't really want to die, not even the glorious death of a martyr. His mother and father would despise the idea, so he shared nothing of the man's offer with them. He could imagine his mother saying, "Your glory will be my pain, and I already have enough pain for many lifetimes and all eternity."

He also knew that if he said yes, his family would be cared for, even richly rewarded, though the identity of the benefactors would not be known. He as a martyr would even be heralded on trading cards—revered as a hero by young boys in the camps.

Silently and alone he weighed the pros and cons. He had just decided to refuse when he learned that Imam Muhammed, the cleric who had taught him all he knew about Allah, had been killed in a roadside bombing. Some said the Syrians were responsible. Others, the Zionists. But whoever was responsible, Jamal could take no more.

He called the number the man had given him and said simply, "I'm ready."

Abidjan, Ivory Coast

Frank squatted next to Sergeant First Class Vernon James, the team's medic. "I need tape."

"Do I look like a tape dispenser?" Doc grumbled as he rummaged in his aid bag. "I'm the medic, not the supply sergeant!" The muscular African-American had been with the unit for three years, and his pet peeve was medical equipment being used for nonmedical purposes.

The team was assembled at the rear of the six-wheeled Cougar HEV. Its armored troop compartment sat high above a boat-shaped undercarriage that was impervious to antipersonnel mines, armor-piercing rifle rounds, and, supposedly, rocket-propelled grenades.

Though no one was excited about testing the Cougar's limitations, it was the preferred mode of travel for this Special Ops Explosives Ordnance Disposal team, code named Task Force Valor. It also made the team something of a hit with the local kids, who came running to see the behemoth anytime it left the

United Nations compound where they were staying.

"Come on, Doc. Hand it over!" Frank was in no mood for verbal jousting.

Bobby Sweeney, a tall Master Sergeant from Alabama, stood watching the argument, chewing tobacco and fingering his new XM8 assault rifle while the other team members made last minute checks of their gear. "So they actually want us to use that thing?" he asked John as they watched Frank feverishly taping the device to a wooden stake.

Frank ignored him, concentrating on connecting the two sets of electrical leads protruding from the device's base to two long spools of electrical wire.

John shrugged. "I don't think they *want* us to use it, but nobody has a better idea at this point."

While Frank continued readying his secret weapon, John looked around the small circle of men that made up the breach team. "We're going to do this just like we've been rehearsing all morning. Breach the wall on the south side, farthest from the cafeteria where they are holding the children. Bobby, Buzz, and I will clear the cafeteria. Dan Daly is on sniper duty—he'll cover the exits to make sure nobody gets out that way. And Sergeant Rubio here—" he patted the former gang member from LA—"will pull rear security. It's a small building, so I don't think we'll have any surprises."

Everyone nodded.

"One more thing," John said. "Put anything electronic in the back of the Cougar. We'll have somebody move it a couple of blocks away so the stuff won't get fried by Frank's little science project. Oh, and Doc, run upstairs and get Dan's electronics. Any questions?"

The team weapons sergeant, Henry "Buzz" Hogan, stroked his heavy beard and voiced the question that was on everyone's mind. "What if it doesn't work, Coop?"

John looked at the ten men surrounding him, all second-enlistment professionals who had seen enough combat to know that he didn't have a good answer to that question. "If it doesn't work, the cowards win."

Buzz slapped a full hundred-round magazine into his heavy-barreled XM8. "Well, we can't have that now, can we?"

A "hooah!" and several grunts of agreement rippled through the team. Sweeney and Buzz slapped each other's helmets. Buzz was also a Southerner, a Texan, and proud of it. "Let's git-er-done!" he drawled.

Seven minutes later, John and the rest of the breach team were in place against the unpainted cinderblock wall at the south end of the building. John ran through the building's schematics in his head. Static crackled in his headset. "One minute."

Fifteen feet in front of him lay the explosive charge that would create an opening into the school building for him and his men and hopefully a surprise for those inside. Once through the breach, it should take them only a matter of seconds to advance through the empty classroom on the other side of the wall and down the hall to the cafeteria to rescue the kids.

"Thirty seconds."

It was a huge risk, and lots could go wrong, but they had little choice. Major Williams had a soft spot for kids, and John wondered if Williams had been thinking of his own seven daughters back at home when he'd decided to execute this mission. John had no doubt that if it were the barrel-chested commander's own girls in that building, he wouldn't hesitate to kill the whole city if that's what it took to free them. But the time for wondering was past. Now it was time to—

"Three...two...one...Execute! Execute! Exec—"

As the commands echoed through his headset, John yanked a wire, and *whoomp!* The wall in front of him vanished in a cloud of debris.

Go, go, go!

Half a second later, Task Force Valor's breach team hurled

themselves through the hole, fanning out to the left and right, their advanced camouflage uniforms disappearing like ghosts into the dust cloud he'd just created.

John charged into the breach himself, the seconds ticking away in his mind as the team exited the first room into a hallway. He could hear the children screaming at the far end of the hall.

From somewhere in front of him came the sound of glass shattering. He sprinted down the hallway on the heels of his men, desperate to get to and through the doorway at the end but afraid that they might be too late.

Gunfire erupted behind him in the hallway, but John didn't stop. He kept his eyes on Sweeney, already pushing the cafeteria door half open. John saw him toss a stun grenade underhanded through the gap and turn away.

Still running, John shut both eyes as the flash-bang detonated, covering the last two steps to the end of the hallway with them closed. No sooner had the stun grenade exploded than Sweeney and Hogan were through the door, one breaking left, the other right.

Without slowing, John cut left through the doorway, his carbine moving with his eyes as he scanned the center of the large room. He could hear his comrades' weapons chattering on either side, but his focus was on the AK-47 in front of him and the terrorist swinging it toward his face.

The assault rifle spat flame, and rounds flashed by John's head as his own weapon coughed twice, guided by a muscle memory born of hundreds of hours in the tire house back at Fort Bragg. The terrorist dropped as if he'd been hit with a falling anvil.

"Clear!" Sweeney called out.

"Clear!" echoed Hogan.

Team Sergeant John Cooper scanned the smoke-filled room, taking in a huddled mass of terror-stricken children who watched him wide-eyed. Then he noticed something wrong in the room.

The lights were still on.

Sainiq Refugee Camp, Lebanon

LIZ AND HANAN WATCHED as the authorities led Nabila's aunt from her home. It was obvious that she was being taken away for questioning, possibly for arrest. Her younger daughter, crying, clung to her mother's skirt.

A soldier reached out and pried the child's fingers off. The little girl let out a thin wail, reaching for her mother who was being put into one of the cars with the flashing lights. Not unkindly the soldier held her hand and looked at all the silent watchers. "Who will take the girl?"

For a time no one moved. The women dropped their eyes. The men looked away.

Liz understood, as did the others present, that "taking the girl" might mean raising her, feeding her, finding her a husband. Depending on her father's response to the new situation in his home, he might not want to be bothered with her, and her mother may or may not be coming home again.

There were two reasons for their reluctance to help. One was purely practical. Another mouth, no matter how small, meant less food for the rest of the family. The other reason was cultural and religious. The women couldn't make such a decision without the approval of their husbands, and the husbands, at least those present, didn't want to add a girl child to their homes. What if she was like her sister and brought trouble with her?

Liz sighed. Had Nabila's aunt even thought about the plight of the younger daughter when she decided to kill the older one?

Hanan was the only one who didn't look down. She turned to a man standing with four others across the road. Her chin was high as she waited for a response from him. He frowned, and Hanan's chin went higher. He glanced at the official, then down at the crying girl. He gave a quick nod.

Hanan smiled at the girl and held out her hand. "Come, Salma."

Uncertain and afraid, Salma reached for her mother who sat in the car, staring straight ahead. Liz's heart broke for the little girl. What had she seen and heard in that dark house? Had her sister pled for her life? Had she screamed for help? Had Salma seen her mother kill her sister?

Hanan took the girl's hand. With a last look over her shoulder at her mother, Salma followed willingly. She stood beside Hanan, tears washing her face though she no longer made a sound.

A stretcher was wheeled out. The sheet covering Zahra's body had been haphazardly thrown over the small corpse, and the tip of the plastic bag still over her head showed. A rope trailed in the dirt, still attached to her wrist.

Liz watched, sorrow for the poor, dead girl a weight pressing on her heart. That such barbaric things as honor killings still happened in the twenty-first century was unbelievable, and she was sickened by all the ruined lives in the needless, sordid tragedy.

At the same time her reporter's mind was recording sights and words for the article she'd write about today's events. She wished she dared take out her digital camera. She should have paid more attention to the ad that kept appearing on her laptop for a camera the size of a quarter.

"Did any of you hear anything?" one of the soldiers asked the crowd. "Can any of you tell me what happened?"

As if by magic, all the women disappeared, Hanan included, fading into their shadowy homes. The men turned and began talking among themselves, backs turned. The soldier shook his head and climbed into his car.

One by one the various vehicles disappeared, the ambulance with its sad cargo last in line, until only Liz was left. She stood in the street, studiously ignored by the Palestinian men.

She walked to Hanan's house and knocked on the battered screen. "Hanan?"

Hanan appeared, her face carefully blank as she looked at Liz without opening the door.

"Is Salma all right?" Liz asked softly. "Nabila will want to know."

"She is fine. She cries. She misses her mother. She misses her sister."

"Has she said anything about what happened?"

"Salma told me that her mother is her hero because she has removed the family's shame."

Liz felt like she'd been struck. "Do you agree with her?"

For a moment Hanan didn't speak. She looked over Liz's shoulder to a man standing two doors away with three others.

Liz followed her gaze. "Your husband?"

"Yes. You are a reporter, aren't you?"

Liz nodded.

"You are going to write about this?"

"I am."

"I cannot stop you even if I plead with you?"

"No." Liz didn't bother to explain that it was her job to tell such stories. It was also the call of her heart to show the narrowness and arrogance of Muslim extremists, especially in their dealings with their women and girls, trying to show by contrast the freedoms women found in a more open society and especially in Christianity.

Hanan sighed. "No, I do not agree."

Hanan's eyes moved past Liz again, and Liz felt a presence behind her. She glanced back and saw the handsome man who was Hanan's husband coming toward the house.

He stopped a few feet from Liz, his expression fierce. "You must go."

The men he had been standing with were now all watching her, their expressions resentful and antagonistic.

Liz nodded. She turned to Hanan. "May I come back to visit you again after things have calmed down?"

Hanan looked again at her husband. Liz saw nothing pass between them, but Hanan gave an abrupt nod, turned, and disappeared into her home.

Her husband watched as Liz climbed into her car, turned in the narrow street, just missing a three-legged dog, and drove away. In her rearview mirror, she saw all the men staring after her.

By the time she got back to her parents' house in midafternoon, Liz was emotionally spent. She wanted nothing more than to go rock climbing to purge the morning's horror. The concentration required would force the scene from her mind.

But first things first. She dragged herself from the car and went inside. She dreaded the conversation she had to have with Nabila who came running from the kitchen as soon as Liz opened the front door.

Liz looked at her hopeful face and felt the weight of what she must say. "I'm sorry."

Nabila started to cry, great wracking sobs. "I knew it. I kept hoping I was wrong, but I knew it."

Liz gathered her close and held her. "I got there at the same time as the authorities. Zahra was already dead." She tried to blank out the picture of the small body on the stretcher, the edge of the plastic bag showing and the piece of rope trailing.

"My aunt?" Nabila managed between rocky breaths.

"The authorities took her away. She is to be tried for murder."

Nabila shut her eyes and took a deep breath. "Good."

Liz agreed as she led Nabila to the living room couch and helped her sit, then sat beside her. "You did the best you could, Nabila. You gave Zahra a chance when you found the family to take her in during her pregnancy. You warned her again and again never to go home. You mustn't blame yourself."

"Maybe if I'd been there…"

"You know that wouldn't have made any difference. Hanan who cared very much was only three houses away, and she couldn't prevent the tragedy."

Nabila wiped her eyes. "I know, but it hurts so much."

Annabelle Fairchild walked into the room. "Oh, good, you're home, Liz." Belatedly she noticed Nabila's distress and stopped abruptly. "What's wrong?"

"My young cousin was killed today," Nabila said, fresh tears streaming.

Annabelle looked pained. "The one who was pregnant?"

Nabila nodded.

"An honor killing." Annabelle made it a statement.

"Liz tried to stop it, but she was too late."

Annabelle stared at Liz, clearly unhappy at that piece of news. "You went into the camp?"

Liz shrugged. "I had to try."

"I don't like your going there. It's dangerous, especially for someone like you."

"Like me?"

"Clearly an American. Clearly uninvited. Obviously a woman." Annabelle shook her head. "You worry me, Liz."

"There were soldiers and police. I was safe."

"This time. What about the next time?"

"I have been invited back." If Hanan's curt nod could be called an invitation.

"And you're going?"

"Of course." Liz gave a small smile. "You know me. I've got to save the world."

"That's the trouble with you fundamentalists, whether you're Christians or Muslims." The deep voice came from the doorway to the hall. Charles Fairchild had come home, and no one had heard due to their intense conversation. "You want to save the world, but strictly according to your view of truth."

Liz looked at her father and forced a smile. How many times had she heard that comment? "Hello, Charles." Somehow calling her father by his first name seemed more eccentric than ever, but he insisted on it, just as her mother insisted on Annabelle.

"Not now, Charles." Annabelle walked to her husband and gave his cheek a kiss. "Liz and Nabila have had a very bad day."

Charles looked at the weeping housekeeper, then at Liz. "What happened?"

Quickly she recounted Zahra's tragic story.

"Nabila." Charles went to her and laid a hand on her shoulder. "I am very sorry."

Nabila tried to smile, clearly moved by his kindness. Charles was the one who had found her wandering about the American University of Beirut campus the day she escaped from the camp. He stopped, spoke with her at length, and brought her home to be their housekeeper/cook.

He treated her with the same benevolent neglect he showed Liz and her sister Julie. He bought her books to help her pass the necessary tests to enter AUB and arranged to pay for her classes. Nabila thrived. She also worshipped the ground Charles walked on.

He squeezed her shoulder, then turned to Liz. "Are you all right?"

Liz shrugged. "I've been better."

"I'll bet."

"All of you stay here while I go get some tea." Annabelle headed for the kitchen with a swish of her long, flamboyantly colored skirt.

Liz watched her go with a small smile. There were rare times when Annabelle acted like a regular mother, and this afternoon was one of them. Even Nabila noticed. She glanced at Liz. "Wow."

"Yeah."

With a small smile Charles left the room, and in a few seconds Liz heard him close the door to his office.

The two women sat quietly on the couch. Liz was still caught in that dichotomy that struck writers, whatever their experience. Her heart ached for Zahra and the woman whose faith was so skewed that she killed her own child in the name of her god. At the same time, her reporter's mind was wondering what would be the best opening lines for her article.

In a few minutes Annabelle came in, carrying a tray with four cups and a teapot, cream, sugar, and lemon. Four spoons clanked gently as she set it down on the coffee table.

Liz stared in amazement at the tray. There were even some small slices of baklava on a plate and four brightly colored napkins. If someone had asked her five minutes ago, she'd have said her mother didn't even know how to make a pot of tea, and here she was with the whole complement of service.

"Annabelle, you have unexplored depths. Shall I get Charles?"

She raised her eyebrow. "Just because I choose not to be domestic doesn't mean I can't be." Annabelle poured a cup and handed it to Nabila. "Go ahead. Drink. The heat will relax your insides." She handed Liz a cup. "The fourth is for your sister, not your father. She said she would stop by if she found time."

Liz settled back in the chair and let the beverage's warmth relax her insides, too.

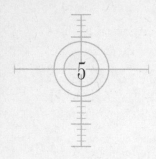

5

Abidjan, Ivory Coast

THE AFRICAN CHILDREN looked as terrified of the hulking American soldiers who had just burst into the room as they were of the terrorists intent on massacring them.

Major Williams spoke from the radio. "Valor One, this is Valor Six, over."

What the…? The fact that the radio still worked hit John like a physical blow, and he flinched involuntarily as it crackled in his ear.

If the radio still worked and the lights still worked, then that meant…

The headset came to life again. "Valor One, do you copy?"

"Whoa, hold up," John said to himself, taking in the room. "We have a problem."

Sweeney spoke from the corner of the large room. "I've got two enemy KIA here."

Hogan sounded bored on the other side of the room. "One dead over here."

John peered at the rumpled form of the terrorist he'd just dispatched. Unseeing eyes stared up at the ceiling from an unshaven

black face that still registered surprise. The man lay on his back
with his legs twisted unnaturally beneath him—exactly on top of
a black rubber mat with a ten-inch square of sheet metal secured
to its center. John saw wires running away from the mat and,
turning, followed them until they disappeared into a large
wooden box against the wall by the door.

The major's voice spoke in John's ear. "Valor One, if you
copy, it appears that the e-bomb failed—I repeat—failed, over.
Since the school is still standing, I assume you somehow disarmed
the explosive yourself. If you can hear me, give me a status, over."

Crack! Crack! Shots rang out somewhere inside the building.
John sprinted out of the room and down the hall toward the
sound. The major would have to wait.

Staff Sergeant Rubio stood at the end of the hall with his
weapon pointed into what looked like a closet.

"What've you got, Rip?"

"One skinny, bro. Unarmed."

John reached the place where Rubio stood. He didn't need to
look into the small room to know it wasn't a closet. The smell told
him it was the toilet even before he saw the filthy hole in the concrete floor. In the far corner crouched a boy who couldn't have
been more than thirteen, with skin so black he was almost invisible
in the dimly lit privy. He was writhing in pain and bleeding from a
gaping wound in his thigh, all the while sobbing and babbling
something John couldn't understand.

"Why'd you shoot him, Rip? He's a kid." They were here to
rescue kids, not shoot them.

"Check the floor next to his left foot."

John squinted. Then his blood ran cold.

A cellular phone.

"When I opened the door, he was dialing it. He might've
been calling his *novia*, but I wasn't taking any chances, you
know?"

The major's voice crackled more insistently in John's ear. "Valor One, this is Valor Six. Give me a sitrep, over."

John picked up the cell phone from the grimy concrete floor. During his three deployments to Iraq, he'd seen too many cell phones used to detonate land mines and other explosives to ever look at a cell phone again and not think *initiator*. And if that was what this phone was meant for, there could be more.

And not necessarily in this building!

"Good call, Rip. Now get this kid out of here before the place blows."

John turned and charged back to the room where the other men were doing their best to calm the children, still staring wide-eyed at their new captors.

"Hogan! Sweeney! Get those kids out of here ASAP! There may be more bad guys off-site who could still blow the building!"

Immediately, a cacophony of voices erupted as his men began herding the children out of the cafeteria.

John snatched up his microphone. "Valor Six, this is Valor One. The building is secure, but the explosives may still be armed. We are evacuating the hostages and need a medic standing by. Do not, I say again, DO NOT send anyone else in, and if you see someone with a cellular phone, shoot first and ask questions later."

It took about three minutes to get the children, their five teachers, and the wounded boy out of the building. Doc James got to work on the boy with the aid of a French peacekeeper acting as an interpreter.

John and Rip watched as Doc knelt over the boy's freshly bandaged leg. He noticed the medic's lips moving silently. Doc always did that when he was working on someone, and John knew he wasn't talking to himself.

"You praying again, Doc?" Sweeney spit a stream of tobacco. "This guy's a terrorist! A minute ago, he was tryin' to blow you up!"

Vernon looked at John. "All the more reason to pray for him, right, Coop?" Doc was always trying to draw him into spiritual conversations. "We can't complain about the evil men do if we act just like the bad guys. You don't beat the terrorists by becoming one."

"Hey, whatever works." John didn't begrudge the man his faith. Task Force Valor didn't have a chaplain of their own, and Doc was often the one who filled that role whenever one of the men needed someone to talk to.

John used to pray quite a bit himself. Since he'd been in the Army, however, he'd begun to wonder if it really mattered. The sum total of the human suffering he'd seen undoubtedly colored his view of God's nature. He'd started to see God more in terms of his own father—an important and semi-benevolent person who wasn't around much, leaving him to fend for himself. It was hard to talk to a God like that.

The peacekeeper/interpreter turned to John. "The boy says that he lives in the north, that these men pay him to come and fight. He fought for them in Burkina Faso when he was a boy."

John snorted. "When he *was* a boy?"

The peacekeeper continued. "He says he has been fighting for five years and is a good soldier. These people offered him a lot of money, but they didn't give him a gun. They gave him a wireless telephone and said, 'Call this number if things go bad.'"

John shook his head. "I bet the poor kid has no idea what he was about to do."

"Master Sergeant Cooper!" Major Williams called.

John turned, expecting a tirade from the stocky commander. The only time he called John "Master Sergeant" was when John was in trouble. He was taken completely off guard when the major grabbed him in a giant bear hug and held him there.

Slightly embarrassed, John halfheartedly patted the back of his commander's body armor. "Um, good to see you, too, sir."

When the major pulled back, John was even more shocked to see a single tear escape the corner of the major's eye. But Williams wore it proudly and didn't wipe it away.

Instead, he quickly regained his composure and said, "Praise the good Lord in heaven. I never thought I'd see you guys again. When that gadget of Frank's failed, I was sure it was game over. How did you neutralize the enemy without setting off the bomb?"

"We got lucky, sir. Plain and simple." John shuddered inside even as he said it. "I somehow dropped the lead terrorist right on top of his prayer mat from hell."

A wide smile split the major's face. "There's no such thing as luck, son."

Beirut

Julie Fairchild Assan hurried down the stairs when she heard Khalil open the front door, announcing his return from work. She had tried hard to look just right for tonight's dinner. The evening was important to her husband professionally, and she was determined to make him proud.

"Khalil! How was your day?" She leaned in and kissed his cheek, a soft, wifely peck. She was feeling very well, not even a twinge of her rheumatoid arthritis. Ah, modern medicine was a wonderful thing. She was actually looking forward to the dinner.

She waited for him to return the kiss, but he took a step back and scowled at her. "That dress is indecent. Change it."

No hello. No how are you. No my-day-was-fine-thank-you-how-about-you? Just "Change it."

She looked down at herself in surprise. The black sequined dress had a modest scooped neck, and the hem fell below her knees. She frowned at Khalil. "But you bought this dress for me at Harrod's." Back when we lived in London. Back when you thought I was wonderful.

His lips tightened. "Too much leg. Too much bosom. And that pendant calls attention to you too much."

Her hand went to the piece she wore around her neck on a slender gold chain. It was an old-fashioned miniature portrait of herself with upswept hair and a blue Regency-style gown. It was a gift her mother had painted and given her on her sixteenth birthday.

She was not taking it off. No other piece of jewelry was as precious to her, except for her engagement and wedding rings and the diamond studs in her ears that Khalil had given her as a wedding present.

After all the time she had spent trying to make certain she was perfect this evening, resentment burned. She glared at him, this man who was becoming more of a stranger every day.

"I'm afraid my formal burqa is at the cleaners, so you're stuck with this." She indicated the dress. "Besides, we're already late. There isn't time to change."

She swept out the door, grabbing her black velvet stole as she went. She draped it over her shoulders. What was happening to him, to her, to them?

When she had gone to America for college, she missed Beirut and the culture she'd grown to love. American things didn't sing a siren's song to her like they did to Liz. Americans were too loud, too greedy, and, well, too American.

She decided to study a semester at Cambridge and see if she could be more comfortable in England. She found herself as lonely and uncertain there as at the University of Virginia, and in England there wasn't Liz's comforting presence.

Then she met Khalil at an international students gathering. She thought him incredibly handsome with his thick black hair, eyes so dark the irises and pupils merged, body slim but strong as he raced up and down the soccer field. She reveled in his fascination with her blond hair, blue eyes, and thoroughly American features.

They talked endlessly about Beirut, spoke Arabic together, shared a yearning for a walk on the Corniche, where the breezes of the Mediterranean blew gently to cool them, or for skiing at the Cedars in the Lebanon Mountains, where the crisp winter air turned their cheeks red.

Sadly, it was now becoming apparent that she had mistaken the comfort of the familiar for love. In turn, she was afraid that Khalil had mistaken her delight in his company and her overeager listening to anything and everything he said as evidence of a sweet, pliant spirit.

"My American Beauty rose," he called her. Rather, he *used* to call her.

They had married in England after a very short courtship, then lived in London for three years as he went to work for the World Bank. Charles and Annabelle Fairchild saw Khalil's religion as an interesting Lebanese/Middle Eastern custom, no more. To them whether you called the deity God or Allah made no difference. They were firm believers in the many paths to God theory, if, that is, someone was weak enough to need religion.

Khalil's parents, Rafiq and Rena Assan, cultural Sunni Muslims, weren't overly happy with their son's Christian wife, but they smiled through gritted teeth. She was pleasant, she was pretty, and she was certainly less embarrassing than the wives some of their friends' sons had picked.

Julie sighed as she and Khalil drove toward the Avenue du General de Gaulle and the hotel where the International Bank for Reconstruction and Development in cooperation with Middle East and North Africa Development Reform was hosting a dinner to open their conference. She hadn't said a word to Khalil since they left the house, and she didn't intend to until she had no choice. This afternoon during her brief visit with Annabelle and Liz, her mother had encouraged her to be gracious.

"You know Middle Eastern men can be overbearing upon

occasion. Just smile and go your own way." Annabelle grinned like a naughty child as she added, "It works with your father."

She and Liz laughed until their sides hurt.

But Khalil's critical attitude showed itself more than just "upon occasion," and Julie was getting sick and tired of being treated like she had no mind or thoughts of her own.

Liz hadn't said anything during the afternoon visit, but she knew her sister hadn't thought she should marry Khalil in the first place.

"He's not a Christian, Julie. You're going to find both faith and cultural differences."

Moonstruck, Julie hadn't listened. After all, she had lived overseas all her life, in Lebanon since she was eleven. She understood cultural differences. With Liz she'd attended the American Community School in Beirut with students of all nationalities. Her parents frequently had students from all over the world at the house.

And on issues of faith, she wasn't as radical as Liz had become. In fact, she had yet to admit to her parents that while in America she had attended a campus Christian organization with Liz and professed faith in Christ.

"Faith, if you have to have it, should be private, nonintrusive," Charles always said. She agreed with him.

Liz didn't. She'd created quite a storm when she confessed her newfound faith.

"What?" Charles bellowed.

"Now, dear," Annabelle said. "Don't worry. She's too intelligent to stay caught in that web of lies. Give her time. It will wear off."

But it hadn't. Liz had built her whole life around her faith, and she wanted Julie to do the same. She probably thought Julie was getting what she deserved in her troubles with Khalil.

Julie caught herself. Such a thought was unfair to Liz. She

had never been anything but nice to Khalil and his family, nor shown any sign she hoped the marriage failed.

Julie sighed as she and Khalil sped through the night toward the Hotel Rowena. She knew that at the dinner she'd have to speak to him, but that didn't count. Her vow of silence applied to their private time.

When that moment of unavoidable social communication came, she'd be coolly elegant and cooperative, just to show him what a treasure he had. She would be oh-so-willing to work to make the evening a success for him. That's what wives did, right? Even wives who were furious at their husbands.

6

Beirut

JAMAL KNEW that a martyr was granted instant access to Paradise, where dark-eyed virgins waited to cater to his every need.

He was already twenty-seven years old, and he accepted the fact that he had little chance of ever finding a bride in the refugee camp. His family's poverty almost guaranteed that no self-respecting family would allow their daughter to marry him, even if he could find a girl who would agree.

A multitude of virgins caring for him in Paradise was certainly enticing, though he wasn't exactly sure how that would work.

While the idea of a blessed Paradise eased his fears and caused his juices to flow, his real reasons for accepting his mission were more nebulous, though no less real. Daily since he said yes, a compelling feeling of purpose and destiny grew in him.

I will not be powerless again. Satisfaction raced through him. *My life will count for something.*

These last four days had only strengthened his resolve. The first night in the hotel he had turned on the television in his room. It was the first time in his life that he'd had a television all to himself, and he hadn't known that there could *be* so many channels. Most of the ones being piped into the hotel were from Europe or America. From his bed he cycled slowly through nearly forty stations, staring bug-eyed, both astonished and sickened by the thinly-veiled pornography that oozed from the screen like untreated sewage.

America called itself a Christian nation, and judging by the American shows he saw that night, he became convinced that Christianity was more perverse and decadent than even Imam Muhammed had said. At least Islam respected women enough not to allow its daughters and sisters to cavort about undressed like animals up for sale in the souks. Revolted, he unplugged the television and turned it around, its dark eye staring blankly at the wall.

Two days ago, Jamal had left the hotel dressed for business and carrying an empty briefcase, just as the man who hired him instructed. He passed the day strolling along the waterfront Corniche, spending some of the money his contact had given him on flat bread, hummos, and a liter of bottled water from a street vendor.

At five o'clock after a short, scripted conversation with another very specific vendor, he purchased three more bottles. These he deposited unopened in his well-padded briefcase. Back in his room at the hotel, he put the bottles into the small refrigerator in the corner by the window for safe keeping.

Yesterday he repeated the process twice, ending with a total of nine liter bottles chilling in the refrigerator. Today he didn't leave the room. Instead, he had waited until evening and ordered in. When the waiter came, Jamal moved behind him as the man lifted the covers from the plates of food. Then he pulled a black plastic bag over the waiter's head. Holding it there until the man stopped fighting for his life had been the most difficult thing Jamal had ever done.

Much more difficult than what would come next.

Quickly he changed into the clothes of the dead man. He walked into the marble-tiled bathroom and looked at himself in the mirror. The waiter's uniform was much too short for his gangly arms and legs, but it would have to do. He ran a comb through his black hair and smoothed his thick eyebrows.

The man staring back at him looked different somehow, not beaten down, not hopeless. For the first time in his life Jamal looked confident. His old life had robbed him of energy, left him devoid of purpose. And he would always be powerless if he went back to living as he had. Powerless against the government of Lebanon, powerless against the soldiers who seemed to be everywhere, powerless against the Christians, powerless against the Israelis.

A picture of his father lying battered in the street flashed before him. His jaw tightened, and a fire ignited behind his dark eyes. Tonight he was in control. Tonight he was full of power. He would strike a blow for his people, for Allah, and for himself. Whatever life came after death had to be better than the one he had been living. With one last resolute look in the mirror, he turned and hurried out of the bathroom.

He cleared the remaining food off of the room service cart and smoothed the white linen tablecloth. He carefully removed all nine water bottles from the refrigerator and placed them on the cart. With one last prayer, he opened the door and carefully backed into the hallway, pulling the cart.

He was halfway out the door when he heard the elevator doors open ten feet to his right. He turned his head and saw—of all things—a large German shepherd, its tongue lolling out the side of its mouth. Jamal froze, terrified of the dog, the fear doubling when he saw who held the leash.

Two soldiers.

They had rifles slung over their shoulders and were coming right for him. His mouth went dry, and his heart crashed against his ribs. He glanced back through the open door of his room and saw the waiter's unclad legs sticking out from behind the bed. That old powerless feeling blew through him with the force of a desert sandstorm, burying all his new confidence. Then he looked down at the nine clear bottles arranged neatly on the tray in front of him, and he remembered.

Power. *Tonight it is mine.*

Jamal glanced back at the soldiers and smiled, pulling the cart into the hall and allowing the door to swing shut.

He held his breath and pretended not to notice the dog sniffing the cart with interest as he pushed it past. The soldiers turned and watched him push the cart into the elevator, but they did not stop. He could hear them snickering as the doors closed. Perhaps they were laughing at the dog, perhaps at his ill-fitting uniform, perhaps at him. It didn't matter.

He allowed himself a weak smile as he realized the magnitude of what just happened. He laid his head back against the burled wood in the elevator and whispered, "Allah ak'bar." *God is great.*

Beirut

Julie Assan was charm itself as she bent her head toward the overweight and graying American economist seated across the dinner table from her. She'd never seen him before in her life, but she was the personification of goodwill and friendship. She would be the most perfect, the most charming wife a man could want, even the retro Lebanese who seemed to have lost his confidence in and affection for her.

"Mr. Romano, I'm delighted to meet you. We're so glad you've come to Beirut."

Paul Romano smiled back. "As am I, Mrs. Assan. We believe in assisting this country's strong economic recovery and keeping the unfortunate events of late from stopping the tide of progress. We

are anxious to meet with your husband and the others of the World
Bank stationed here. We want to learn how much of your fiscal
health is the result of Lebanon itself—its people and their initia-
tives—and how much the result of world monetary circumstances."

In other words, Julie thought, was Lebanon a safe place to
invest his bank's money or not. Khalil would see he decided yes.
After all, Beirut had stringent privacy laws that made banking
here more than merely attractive.

Julie turned to the young woman across from her. "I hope
your visit here will be equally enjoyable, Mrs. Romano. Anything
I can do to help arrange visits to some of our historical sites—"

Mrs. Romano held up a hand. "Please call me Brandy. Mrs.
Romano sounds so old."

Mrs. Romano probably sounded like the first wife.

Julie smiled. "Maybe you'd like to work on your tan, Brandy.
We will provide you with passes to the best beach clubs."

Brandy looked uncertain. "I don't know. I was just going to
stay in our room." She leaned in and hissed, "I mean, terrorists.
You're always reading about them." She glanced around as if she
expected Osama bin Laden himself to be leaning over her shoulder listening. "The Middle East and all."

Julie forced a smile, though what she wanted to do was roll
her eyes. Before she could calm Brandy's qualms, Khalil spoke, his
tone gracious and friendly in spite of the fact that he deeply
resented anyone, especially Americans, who lumped all the countries on the eastern Mediterranean into one feared and fearful
entity, The Middle East.

"Ah, Mrs. Romano, you need not worry about your safety.
Here in Lebanon we are not terrorists. We are a nation that is
friendly to your great nation. We are a people who are understanding and accommodating. Unfortunately, that is rarely the
side of things shown by your media. I daresay that your Miami is
a much more dangerous place than Beirut."

The rest of the table laughed, but Brandy smiled weakly, clearly unconvinced. Why had she accompanied her husband on this business trip if she was so fearful?

"I don't mind staying in my room," she told Khalil earnestly. "I did lots of stuff in London and Paris, so I don't have to do stuff here." She looked at Julie, her face full of sudden enthusiasm. "We went shopping at Harrod's, that store in London that Princess Diana's dead boyfriend's father owns."

Julie, who had shopped at Harrod's more than a few times herself, merely smiled.

"Though I wouldn't mind finding another necklace like yours," Brandy said, staring at the miniature. "She looks just like you, the lady in the painting."

Julie's hand went to the ceramic oval. "It is me. My mother painted it."

"Yeah? My mother painted the living room once."

The girl had a sense of humor! Maybe she wasn't so bad after all.

"Do you think your mother'd do one of me?" Brandy asked.

Julie thought about Annabelle Fairchild and Brandy Romano together, and she couldn't hold back a smile. "Annabelle rarely paints anything but modern abstract works these days, but you can always ask her."

Brandy's eyes shone. "I would be willing to leave my room for something like that." She eyed the miniature with longing.

Julie picked up her glass of water and glanced around the banquet room filled with World Bank personnel and visiting economists from around the globe. If the number of those attending was any indication, the event was going to be a great success. Khalil could relax and enjoy being a host.

In one of those sudden lapses in conversation, Brandy blurted. "Julie, your name is very American. Did you know that?"

Julie nodded. "I am an American."

"You are?" Shocked, Brandy looked from Julie to Khalil. "But you're married to—" Suddenly she saw the faux pas yawning wider than the Grand Canyon. "I mean, Khalil isn't. You know, American. Is he?"

Can you say xenophobic? Julie turned to her husband. "Are you?"

Khalil smiled with all the charm that had caught Julie's attention just as his slim, good looks had caught her eye. "You are right, Mrs. Romano. I am not American. I am Lebanese, raised right here in Beirut. My father is a physician, and my mother is a great benefactress."

Which is what they all wanted Julie to be. It made the family look good, and it was suitable for a woman.

"Then how?" Brandy asked, and Julie saw that the other wives seated at their table were interested, too. Even the husbands looked up from their food. "Where?"

In his perfect British English, Khalil said, "I met my wife at Cambridge. I was taking a master's degree in economics, and Julie was studying there for a semester."

"We met at an international students gathering," Julie said. "Since I had lived for several years in Beirut, I immediately felt at home talking with Khalil."

"You grew up here?" Brandy looked as if Julie had said she was raised by wolves outside ancient Rome.

"My father teaches at the American University right here in Beirut."

"But you didn't meet Khalil until you both went to England."

"That's right."

"I bet it was love at first sight." Brandy poked her husband with her elbow. "Just like us."

Julie nodded. At least love of the familiar if not love of the man. As long as they remained in London, they had done very well together, the fault lines in their relationship holding steady. Julie's independence and individuality didn't seem to bother him.

Nor did the fact that she had started reading her Bible intermittently again, a habit she had originally developed when she was part of the Christian fellowship group at UVA.

Then, after three years in London, came Khalil's present assignment to Beirut. Back on his home turf, the precariously balanced tectonic plates of their marriage shifted, revealing huge cracks that had previously been hidden.

Julie's vivacity and opinions suddenly offended him. No matter how many times he said he was a Westernized man, at some fundamental level, he was all Middle Eastern. Though a thoroughly secular Muslim, not celebrating holidays, not praying when the muezzin called, he still had a cultural mindset that was difficult to overcome. He wanted a properly submissive wife, and she now made him nervous, which in turn made him more critical.

Julie sighed. Too late she had come to understand the dangers of a "mixed" marriage all too well. But such thoughts weren't for Brandy or any of the others at the dinner table. With her hostess smile firmly in place, she kept conversation general for the rest of the meal as others around their table participated. Still, Julie felt on edge, Khalil's tension becoming hers. She needed to escape for a few minutes.

How am I going to ever manage a lifetime with him if I can't manage one dinner?

In the lull after the main course but before dessert, Julie excused herself and headed toward the restroom. As she left the dining room, she saw Brandy was following her. She picked up speed, only to be stalled by the line snaking out the ladies' room door. Too many concurrent events and too few accommodations. Without hesitation she veered toward the escalators, almost tripping over a waiter in an ill-fitting uniform.

"Pardon me," she said in Arabic as she stepped around him. He nodded and kept moving, pushing his cart of water bottles with great concentration. Julie rode down to the ground floor.

With any luck she would both find an under-used facility and lose Brandy. She wasn't sure she could handle a girl-to-girl chat with her emotions so raw.

Glancing back as she hurried across the lower lobby, she saw Brandy looking for her at the top of the escalator. The young woman frowned and moved on, presumably to stand in the long line.

Julie sighed and slowed, allowing herself to enjoy the hotel's opulent, Old World lobby with its cedar walls, palm trees in planters, and four-story atrium with skylights that in daytime bathed the lobby in sunshine but which now with night behind them reflected the lobby. She could see herself when she looked up, all flattened and distorted. She was smiling at the absurd image as she opened the door to an elegant and empty ladies room located off to the side of the lobby.

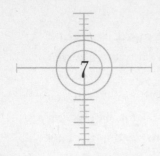

7

Beirut

JAMAL EMERGED from the elevator into the hotel's chaotic, crowded second-floor lobby.

Throngs of men and women attending several concurrently scheduled events gathered in knots around the spacious room, smoking and making small talk. More were visible through the doors to the banquet rooms, already being served their dinners. All were glamorously dressed, and many wore formal attire. Jamal suspected that each article of clothing probably cost more than it took to feed his family for a month, and he gritted his teeth at the unfairness of it all.

Here and there, burly security guards dressed in the same manner as the guests stood with heads swiveling as their eyes roved over the crowd. At each banquet room entrance more guards checked and rechecked the invitations of all. If any of these frightening men took notice as Jamal in his ill-fitting suit hastened across the polished marble floor toward one certain event, they gave no sign.

Maybe they asked a nobody like me to do this mission because they knew I would be invisible. For once his powerlessness was an advantage.

The sound of a crowd laughing drifted out of the double doors to his right, adding to the noise level in the foyer. A printed placard on a stand announced, "World Bank/IBRD—Partnering for MENA Development Reform."

Jamal couldn't remember what IBRD stood for, but MENA was Middle East Northern Africa. And he knew all too well what the World Bank was up to.

Imam Muhammed had often taught that the World Bank was a part of the international Zionist mafia of banks and financial institutions, heavily connected with organized crime and the drug trade. More than once, Jamal heard him rail, "The Jews put on a face of charity to spread Zionist dominance and oppression over the whole world."

Jamal took one look at the keen-eyed guards and knew he had to enter the room by way of the serving area. As he pushed his cart through a door that read Staff Only, he swallowed hard, worried that some employee might notice that he didn't belong. He need not have worried. The bedlam of trying to serve several hundred people at once made the frenzy in the foyer seem as orderly as the row upon row of men at the mosque praying to Mecca.

Waiters and waitresses grabbed dessert plates off the huge carts sent up from the kitchen below, placing them on trays that were then hoisted to shoulders. Others carried silver pitchers full of dark, fragrant coffee.

"Walk!" yelled a man who was clearly the supervisor. "Smile!" The wait staff seemed to ignore him, though they did slow down once they pushed through the curtains that separated the guests from the staging area.

The chaotic scene reminded him a little of the fish market in Sidon on a Thursday afternoon, or the memorial march he had attended two weeks earlier for Imam Muhammed, minus the patriotic slogans and burning Israeli and American flags.

A harried waitress brushed by his cart, nearly knocking over the bottles. *"Shuu! Amya!"* she yelled. *What? Are you blind?*

Unnerved by the close call, Jamal reached to steady his cargo. The woman hurried on, oblivious, tray balanced on her shoulder. He hugged the wall with his cart, suddenly seeing the teeming room much as a child might look at a stampeding herd of cattle.

His mouth went dry as he spotted the Lebanese soldiers with their bright green berets tucked into the epaulets of their uniforms. They stood at the curtained entry points to the dining room, keeping a wary if bored vigil over the activities in the staging area.

You cannot go back now. You have the power!

Taking a deep breath, he approached the curtains slowly, just a poor waiter taking water bottles to the head table.

A soldier raised a hand toward him. *"Wa'ef."*

The hair stood up on the back of Jamal's neck as he stopped as ordered. Sweat rolled down his back. The soldier eyed the bottles without interest. Then he lifted the tablecloth draped over the cart to be certain nothing was hidden beneath its pristine fall. His partner fingered an American-made M-16 and eyed Jamal curiously.

Jamal had seen soldiers like these men all of his life. They might be different militia, but their purpose was always the same. Humiliate the Palestinian. He resented all the different soldiers deeply because they seemed to delight in making him and his friends feel less like citizens and more like prisoners.

Before these men as before all the others he'd ever met, he kept his face carefully blank, letting none of his antagonism show.

The first soldier straightened and nodded at Jamal, who managed to smile thinly and began to push through the curtain when the second soldier stopped him again.

"Wait." The second soldier lifted one of the bottles from his tray. "I'm thirsty."

Before Jamal could protest, the first soldier replied, "Put that back, Yousef. Do you want to get us assigned to guard the street corner? It's cold outside!"

The second soldier shrugged and replaced the bottle. Jamal didn't start breathing again until he was through the curtain and into the banquet hall.

A man was speaking from the podium at one end of the room. "We'd like to thank our distinguished guests for joining us tonight to celebrate the extension of an additional twenty million euros in loans to our Cultural Heritage and Urban Development project."

Loud applause. The man who spoke looked exactly as Jamal pictured a banker to be. He had perfectly combed black hair and a paunchy midsection covered by an expensive double-breasted tuxedo in which the man looked so comfortable Jamal couldn't imagine him in any other attire.

"Some of you were here in 2003 when with the support of UNESCO and the American University's Department of History and Archaeology we launched what has proven to be a wonderfully successful program."

Listening politely were nearly two hundred people seated in groups of eight at round tables packed into the banquet hall. Jamal worked his way down the wall toward the podium, pushing his tray of water bottles. The lights were low enough that he felt certain no one would notice that his pants were four inches too short.

The waitress who had almost knocked his cart over passed him on her way back to the staging area. He felt her look at him once, twice. He stiffened, but she continued on her way.

"And we can't forget the member countries that have made generous financial contributions—France, Italy, and Japan. Each country's finance minister is here this evening, along with representatives from each country in the Middle East/North Africa region. Let's show them our gratitude."

Thunderous applause filled the room again as a handful of men stood, some wearing tuxedos, others in traditional Arabic attire, three wearing the black and white kaffiyeh recognized the world over as a sign of the Palestinians, thanks to the late Yasser Arafat. At the sight of these men, a thought hit Jamal with the force of a brick to the stomach.

I cannot do this! Killing Jews is one thing—but many of the people in this room are my own countrymen!

"We'd also like to extend a special thank you to our newest member, the Israeli Finance Ministry Director, General Yossi Harif."

Jamal stared at the balding Harif. Undoubtedly he was wicked, evil, an oppressor. But killing one Zionist didn't justify killing many Palestinians. Jamal started to turn his cart around and head back toward the staging area. As he did so, he caught sight of the two soldiers who had stopped him earlier. They were moving toward him with the waitress who'd bumped him on their heels.

Jamal froze midstep. Fear and a sense of overwhelming failure stole his breath. Who was he to think that he could please Allah? Nobodies were always nobodies.

Without much hope he looked around for an avenue of escape. There was an emergency exit behind the podium. He turned and ran toward it, abandoning his cart where it was.

The soldiers shouted and broke into pursuit. As one of them passed the cart, he knocked it aside. The bottles crashed to the floor.

The soldier hadn't taken two steps past the cart when a horrendous fireball rocked the banquet hall, sending tables and bodies flying in all directions.

Jamal felt as if a speeding freight train from hell hit him between the shoulder blades and a giant siphon pulled all the oxygen from his lungs. Just before everything went black, one last thought pierced his mind like hot shrapnel, though it wasn't of Paradise or virgins.

What have I done?

Abidjan, Ivory Coast

"Man, I can't wait to hit the showers," Rip said as Task Force Valor arrived at the airfield's front gate.

"I'll second that motion." John smirked. "You smell."

"Yeah, well, in an hour, I'll be clean," Rip shot back over the chuckles of the rest of the team. "And you'll still be ugly, *ese.*"

The chuckles turned to guffaws, but John was too tired for verbal jousting, even if it was all in fun. Looking at his reflection in the side-view mirror, he figured Rip was right. He needed a haircut and a shave, and the blue eyes that so intrigued the locals were bloodshot from lack of sleep. Being team sergeant didn't give him the chance to rest much. What he really wanted to do was get back to Bragg and spend a long weekend doing absolutely nothing.

The major and Doc were in the lead in the team's Humvee, while the rest of the men waited in the Cougar as UN guards performed inspections on those ahead of them. The guards were currently checking an old sedan, its make and model indistinguishable, like most of the vehicles on this continent.

John smiled as he thought of the amazing ingenuity he'd seen exhibited by Africans who made do with whatever they had to keep their cars on the road. Some of the vehicles were held together by nothing more than twine, duct tape, and plastic shopping bags, which Rip called, "The national flower of the Ivory Coast."

"Hey!" Rip pointed out the back window of the Cougar. "Check out behind us. Must be somebody important."

John turned and saw a blue Chevy Suburban pull up behind them. He agreed immediately with Rip because the big SUV was so new it hadn't yet acquired the thick layer of dust that clung to most of the vehicles in this country. As soon as the car stopped, a well-dressed, dark-skinned man of about forty jumped out of the driver's door.

The man ran past their vehicle, waving his arms and shouting frantically at the guards. The man gestured toward his vehicle and babbled excitedly in French. One of the guards attempted to calm the man, then followed him back to the Suburban. The young soldier took one look inside, paled, and walked quickly back toward his post.

As the soldier passed the Cougar, Sweeney opened his door and caught his attention. "*Bonjour, que se produit?*" he asked, his French surprisingly good for someone who, according to Frank, couldn't even speak English properly. "What's up?"

The French soldier gestured toward the man, who was still jabbering away excitedly. "His wife is having a baby right now in his car. He wants to take her to the hospital on base."

"Right now?"

"*Oui.* But he still has to wait his turn."

Sweeney turned to John. "You think maybe Doc could help?"

John nodded. "Probably. You know he never passes up a chance to practice his art." He jumped on the radio and called the Humvee in front of them, informing the major of the situation. Then John opened his door and went forward to see if Doc needed help carrying anything.

Vernon James was grinning broadly as he pulled his aid bag out of the Humvee. "I haven't delivered a baby in years, Coop!"

John had to jog to keep up with the black medic. "You've actually delivered a baby?" Not in the Special Forces he hadn't.

"I helped a woman give birth in the Wal-Mart parking lot in Fayetteville just before I graduated SF medic school. Made me the envy of my class."

Right. "You sure you remember what to do?"

Doc winked at him. "I'm sure it'll come back to me. Besides, the woman does all the work."

Sure enough, the backseat of the Suburban was occupied by a very pregnant woman in traditional dress. She looked young, and she was crying hysterically, rocking side-to-side, arms crossed over her distended stomach. The seat was slick with what John assumed was amniotic fluid.

The husband was now pacing near the front bumper smoking a cigarette. The young UN guard still stood nearby, looking like he was going to throw up at any moment.

John touched Doc on the shoulder. "What can I do?"

"See if there are some blankets or something in the back of this car. We'll start by making her as comfortable as possible." Doc leaned into the Suburban, trying to calm the young mother as best he could, even though he didn't speak her language.

John ran to the rear of the Suburban and threw open its rear doors. The area behind the back seat was completely empty. Not a blanket in sight. In fact, the inside of the vehicle was even cleaner than the outside, and that was saying something.

He frowned and headed for the Cougar, deciding to donate the poncho liner out of his own rucksack to the cause. As he passed in front of the Suburban, he noticed that the driver's hands were trembling. Typical new father.

Only about twenty yards separated the SUV and the Cougar, but in that distance, John realized that something was wrong. It was only the faintest nudge at the back of his mind, but he tried to make a habit of paying attention to that small voice.

But what was the trouble? He made it to the Cougar and started to reach for the door handle when it hit him. *It's too clean.* He'd never seen anything in the Ivory Coast as immaculate as that

Suburban. It looked like it had just rolled off the assembly line. And nobody went anywhere here without at least a bottle of water in the trunk.

John turned. "Doc! Doc! Get out of—"

Hell opened up beneath the Suburban at that second, spitting the seven-thousand-pound vehicle into the air on a fountain of flame. The shock wave from the explosion hit John like a one-ton rodeo bull, and his world went black.

Downtown Beirut

IT WAS A THING OF BEAUTY.

Imad Hijazi stared in awe at the chaos in front of him. A great plume of smoke rose to the heavens, almost completely obscuring the Hotel Rowena. Emergency vehicles roared up with sirens blaring. Flames shot skyward from the place where mere moments before there had been scores of meddling Westerners. People ran screaming in all directions, many covered in blood.

All this was what he had expected to see, only better. What he had not anticipated was the raw power he felt over these people and the sheer pleasure that came with seeing the fear in their eyes. Knowing that he had directed the operation ignited a fire in his breast that rivaled the one currently consuming the hotel.

He pulled his phone from his pocket and dialed a number. To the voice that answered, he said, "Put him on."

A staid, impassive older voice came on the phone. "Is it done?" Abu Shaaban spoke as if asking about nothing more important than a delivery of flowers.

"It is done. You have struck fear in the hearts of the infidel."

But it wasn't only the manifestation of their fear that so

excited Imad. It was the prestige this fear would bring. While it was best to appear humble and let Abu Shaaban believe the plan had been his idea, he would make sure the others knew the truth.

It was Imad who had first heard of this new weapon and approached his leader with the idea of purchasing a small amount to test its effectiveness. At first Abu Shaaban scoffed and would hear nothing of it, but Imad persevered. Finally his leader agreed. Imad then arranged shipment through an arms dealer he knew in Sidon.

Imad had also recruited the now-martyred Palestinian youth from the Sabra camp near that same city in southern Lebanon. He first saw Jamal in tears at the funeral of Imam Muhammad. After watching him for some time, Imad could tell that the boy was smart enough to carry out an assignment of this sort, yet simple enough to be easily persuaded to lay down his life.

All had gone as planned, and Imad smiled at the devastation he'd created. "You may thank Allah for our success," he told Abu Shaaban.

"Very well. We will begin planning for our next operation immediately." The line went dead.

Imad ignored the abruptness of his leader as he basked in the warmth of the flames, which radiated even to where he was standing, nearly a block away.

The beauty of it had been its simplicity. The godless West had devised all sorts of gadgets to stop terrorism, even putting additives in explosives that allowed them to trace manufacturing sources. But this weapon was so fantastic because it was nearly foolproof, and better yet, untraceable.

He looked on, almost giddy, as the emergency personnel ran to and fro, attempting to bring aid to the injured and dying.

Then an unexpected thought hit him.

What if nobody knows it was me? Us?

Imad suddenly knew his job was not yet complete. Attribution in these things was a tricky business. If one made it too clear that his group was responsible, he was inviting the wrath of the government, the military, and possibly his own people once the military began to retaliate. Yet he needed to somehow make it subtly clear that Ansar Inshallah, "The Followers of God's Will," was responsible for this act.

The simplest method would be to call the Arab media and take credit in the name of Ansar Inshallah. But then nothing would stop every other faction in Lebanon from doing the same.

No, he needed something more. Though it was obviously too late for that now, a video of them planning the event, all faces carefully masked, would have worked.. Or maybe…

A hostage!

Yes, that would work perfectly. A hostage clearly tied to this event would provide just the sort of indirect proof needed, and perhaps even provide him with the opportunity to increase his standing within the organization even further! Most important, it would distract attention from their next operation.

A portly man with a head wound brushed by, and Imad briefly considered offering him a ride to the hospital in his Mercedes. That would be the easiest way to secure a hostage. But he thought the better of it. Once the man became aware that he was not being taken to the hospital, he might become belligerent. It would have to be someone who would not be able to resist.

Imad was a leader, not a fighter. He was taller than most but skinny from having grown up in the camps. He had never been physically strong, so he had made up for his body's weakness by learning to manipulate people with his superior mind.

He scanned the teeming crowd before him. Already there were so many emergency vehicles that he began to get afraid there wouldn't be anyone left for him to kidnap.

Then he saw his ideal target, sitting dazedly on a rock near the hotel entrance.

A smile spread across his face.

Perfect.

Outside Beirut

Liz Fairchild jammed her left toe into the small crevice, tested it, then carefully straightened her leg as if she were standing up, balancing her weight on both feet. It was both exhilarating and frightening to rock climb outside. The gym at home was so safe, the routes so easy to discern. The challenge here on the bolted cliffs outside Beirut was to find the best route for her expertise, her strength, and her nerves.

She was still surprised at how much she loved climbing. She loved the stretch and burn of muscles, the challenge to be better, go higher, learn more. Most of all she loved the way it forced her to focus intently to the exclusion of all other problems and worries. After the sad trip earlier today and the distressing visit with Julie that showed more cracks in her marriage than she probably realized, Liz needed release.

She made the short drive outside town where she met some others from the rock climbing club she'd sought out as soon as she got to Beirut. Soon she was scaling a cliff. It encouraged her that she was better than some of the club and challenged her that others were better than she.

When she was sure she was balanced, she released her right hand and reached for the small jam crack higher up, but not too high.

"Trust your legs," her instructor back home had said again and again. "It's all in the legs. They should take your weight, not your arms. Keep both feet attached to the rock."

Even after almost three years of climbing she had to fight the urge to pull herself with her arms. Like most women, she didn't have much upper body strength. Depend on her arms, and the climb would end quickly due to lack of endurance. Use her legs, and she could climb for hours. Carefully she placed her right foot and slowly stood.

When she was stretched against the rock like this, she always felt like some giant bug and half expected an oversized swatter to descend from the sky and get her. Much as she delighted in climbing, there was a certain helpless feeling in this position, in spite of the safety ropes and harness, the climbing buddies. The dangerous thing was the instinctive urge to move quickly to stop feeling so vulnerable.

Don't rush, girl. God's not in the swatting business. He's carrying you.

Some time later she noted with surprise that the sun was going. Elongated shadows distorted the mountainside, and soon it would be impossible to easily judge the options for hands and feet.

After a slow but safe descent during which a pair of Lebanese climbers not from the club called advice to her, some helpful, some suggestive, she waved good-bye and walked to her car. She was sweaty and weary, but in a much better frame of mind than when she came. Endorphins were wonderful things.

Lord, she thought as she drove back to her parents' house, *I need Your help in letting go of what I can't control. Zahra was out of my control. Julie and Khalil are out of my control though where my sister's concerned, it's very hard to remember that. Too many years of watching over her. It's not my job anymore. Still, I'm trusting that all things will work for good for her.*

Liz smiled to herself. In the years since she'd become a believer while a student at the University of Virginia, she'd claimed the promise of that Scripture she was now claiming for Julie. And God had seen that things did work well for her. Liz had been able to get her master's in journalism at the University of Missouri's acclaimed program with a semester at their

Washington, D.C., campus. She'd gotten a great job at the *Philadelphia Inquirer,* seen her byline appear with increasing frequency, and was turning her vacation in Lebanon into a series for the paper on women in the Middle East.

Momentary gloom enveloped her as she thought about how different her piece on Zahra was going to be from the way she first envisioned it. Girl Breaks Free had become Victim Dies at Mother's Hand. How would her apartment neighbors in the renovated factory near the Delaware River react to actions so foreign to American thinking? A mother murdering her daughter in the name of honor.

But the endorphins released by her exercise didn't let Liz stay unhappy long. Her life was good; God was good. She felt blessed because of her faith in the loving and caring Christ who died for her.

As she drove through Beirut, she saw more of the slow but steady recovery from the chaos of the country's civil war that devastated Lebanon in the 1980s. Some day soon she wanted to visit the new downtown area around Parliament and see the new Place d'Etoile.

It had been a sad setback when Rafik Hariri, the man who had been the first premier elected after the civil war, was killed in 2005 in a mammoth car bombing. The backlash from that event had paved the way for the Syrian army's pullout and had brought about changes in the workings of the government. The Lebanese people knew the price of anarchy, and they did not want to pay it again.

When the Fairchilds first moved to Beirut in 1992, right after the ceasefire, Beirut was rubble from the heavy fighting. Sandbags filled doorways, bullet holes and mortar damage pocked buildings, and people flinched at loud noises. The country's international banking industry had been forced to move. Tourists had stopped coming. Shipping faltered. Even AUB had suffered with one president murdered and another kidnapped during the chaos.

Today there was tentative harmony between the Maronite Christians, the Sunni Muslims, the Shi'a Muslims, and the Palestinians who formed the diverse population of the country. Nationalism was encouraged rather than factionalism. All held their breaths, hoping such thinking would continue. As Liz hit her brakes to avoid the car that cut her off, she thought there was a greater chance they'd all kill each other on the highways than in another war. She'd forgotten how chaotic the drivers in Beirut could be. By comparison the drivers in Philadelphia were the very souls of politeness.

You first, sir.

Oh, no, you, ma'am.

Right.

Back at her parents' Liz showered and changed. As she dried her shoulder-length dark hair, she studied the pictures of her and Julie on her bureau. In one taken just before she left Beirut to come to the States for college, she had her arms wrapped around Julie's neck, her head resting on her younger sister's shoulder. Both wore huge smiles. Julie with her long blond hair looked so much like their father, while Liz looked like Annabelle with her dark, mid-length hair.

In the other picture Julie, wreathed in white satin with a veil falling from her upswept hair, stood with one arm looped around Liz's waist and the other around a slim, handsome young Arab. She was smiling with joy as was the young man. It was only Liz who looked less than elated, though no one else who looked at the picture ever seemed to notice her melancholy—which was probably a good thing. Wedding pictures were supposed to be filled with happiness, not doubt.

She and Julie had spent their teen years in Beirut. Julie's very fair blond hair made her look Scandinavian and always drew appreciative eyes, while Liz with her dark hair wasn't nearly as exotic. Maybe it was Julie's physical uniqueness and personal shyness that had made Liz feel so protective of her.

Certainly it was Julie's struggles with juvenile rheumatoid arthritis, its pain and limitations. Then again, maybe Liz was just a little mother at heart—or a bossy kid who liked ordering someone around. Regretfully, it was probably the latter. Whatever the reason, she had always watched out for Julie, loved her as only a big sister could.

Julie had returned the affection until Khalil came along. Not that she didn't still love Liz. There was something about being sisters that forged a bond nothing, not even husbands, could break. But Julie's love centered elsewhere these days.

Liz wasn't jealous of Khalil. She wasn't. A woman was supposed to love her husband more than anyone. It was just that Liz wished she had her own Khalil, only an all-American version, born on the Fourth of July. She thought she had found him once, and she still smarted from the hurt and disappointment.

But all things work together for good, and the perfect man, a better man, was just around the corner. She knew it. He would be a strong Christian as well as an appreciator of the U.S.

A double whammy for poor Charles. He'd certainly done his best to make her and Julie citizens of the world with strong reservations about the United States and Christianity.

"The American system is corrupt," he'd said again and again.

Well, sure, Liz always thought, though she didn't say it. Contradicting Charles wasn't worth the cost. The U.S. had power and power corrupts. Still, it seemed to her that the rule of law kept that corruption in check there much more than in other countries.

"Religion is for the weak," her father also said. "Religion divides. Christianity is full of hypocrites."

When she came home and told her parents she had become a

believer in Jesus, Charles almost had apoplexy. His face got red, and he actually stammered when he growled, "Liz, wh-wh-what have you done?"

"Oh, my dear," Annabelle said, more sorrowful than angry. "You don't need that crutch. You're a strong person."

"And I'm stronger now." Liz spoke calmly though her heart was pounding faster than the beat on her favorite DC Talk track. She'd never stood up to her parents like this before. "You have to take my word for it that my faith has enriched me, not made me weaker."

"It's my fault," Charles said, his head resting in his hand. You'd have thought she'd told him she was about to die. "I should never have sent you to the States for college."

She smiled at the memories as she brushed her hair. She put the brush on the bureau next to the pictures as she heard a phone ring in the other room.

Annabelle answered in Arabic. There was a moment's silence. Then Annabelle screamed, a loud cry of pain.

Liz bolted from the bedroom. As she raced into the living room, her mother sobbed, "No! No! Not Julie!"

Beirut

LIZ AND ANNABELLE sat together through the night, watching the TV, recoiling in horror at the pictures of fire and destruction.

Liz's heart had always broken with sympathy for those caught in terrorist attacks, both the victims and the families left behind. What she hadn't grasped was the depth of the pain for those who waited, for those who lost someone they loved simply because that someone had been in the wrong place at the wrong time.

Oh, God, please! Oh, God, please!

Even as she watched the TV and heard the reports, it was impossible to think of gentle Julie in such a violent setting. Appalling things like this fire happened all the time, but they happened to other people, not to people her family knew and loved.

As windows in the high-rise section of the hotel exploded and rained down on the rescue workers, Annabelle began to shake. Liz wrapped her arms about her mother and held her tightly. She wanted to automatically say, "Shh, it'll be all right."

But it wouldn't be. It couldn't be. Julie had been there with Khalil when the explosion had occurred.

Charles had gone immediately to the scene, and he hadn't

come home. As Liz went to her room around three, unable to watch one more picture or listen to one more reporter, her hope was that when she awoke, he'd have called to say it was all a mistake. Julie was fine. Khalil was fine. Everyone was fine.

Of course, Liz couldn't sleep. Every time she closed her eyes, she saw the raging flames, the crumbling walls, the horror-filled faces of those at the scene. She fell to her knees beside the bed.

"Oh, God, please! Let her be okay!" Over and over and over she repeated the words as tears flowed over her clasped hands, wetting the bedspread, the blanket, the sheets, and the mattress. She couldn't stop begging any more than she could stop weeping.

Sometime just before dawn, she fell into an exhausted sleep. She awoke as light began to fill the sky. For a moment she wondered what she was doing on her knees beside the bed, shivering in the cool morning temperatures. Then memory slammed home, and she couldn't breathe around the pain.

Julie! Lovely, wonderful, beloved Julie. And Khalil.

She pulled her aching body erect and stood, waiting for the pain in her blood-deprived legs to diminish so she could walk.

Was this what it felt like every morning for Julie when she woke? Was this burning, prickling, crampy feeling what rheumatoid arthritis felt like? How had her sister borne such pain for so many years and been able to laugh? To love? To marry?

As the acute aching diminished in her legs, Liz became aware that her face felt hot and swollen from all her tears. She shuffled to the bathroom and ran cold water over a washcloth, and pressed it to her aching eyes. After a few seconds, she rinsed the cloth again in cold water and spread it over her whole face.

She heard no sounds in the house, neither weeping nor rejoicing. Surely if Charles had learned anything positive about Julie, there would be happy sounds. In the pale light of a new morning, the silence meant the worst.

She stumbled into the kitchen. Annabelle, seated at the table with a cup of untouched coffee in front of her, looked up.

"Any word yet?" Liz asked as she sat across from her mother.

Annabelle shook her head. "Nothing. Absolutely nothing. I feel like I'm going to jump out of my skin." And she began to cry, a jagged, raspy sound that tore at Liz.

"Oh, Mom."

Annabelle never cried. When she was upset, she got charmingly, beautifully teary, the moisture resting on her lower lids and making her lovely dark eyes even more luminescent than normal and Annabelle more lovely than ever. But tears? Honest-to-goodness weeping? Charles always gave in before that was necessary.

But Charles couldn't fix this problem.

"Shh, Mom," Liz soothed, feeling helpless and very fragile herself.

"You called me Mom," Annabelle managed through her sobs. "Twice."

Liz blinked. She'd never in her whole life called Annabelle Mom. From the time she and Julie were able to talk, it was Charles and Annabelle. "Well, that's who you are."

"Yes, but don't ever call me that again." The command was stern. Then the crying resumed.

Liz rested her head against the wall, struck by what a contradictory individual her mother was. "Don't cry. Please. It won't help. Besides, it'll make me cry again, too."

Annabelle took a ragged breath. "I don't know how they could have survived."

Liz sagged into the wall. *Oh, Lord, please! They have to have survived!*

"Have you heard anything from Charles?"

Annabelle shook her head, silent tears falling off her chin to drop unheeded into her lap. "He called once, but he had nothing to report. He just wanted me to know he was all right. I asked him to come home, but he can't. He—he can't stay away."

Liz understood. Much as she dreaded what she'd see, she wanted to go there herself. She needed to see the scene and all of its attendant horror to believe Julie and Khalil weren't coming back to them.

She didn't trust herself to drive, so she called a cab. While she waited for it to arrive, she pulled on jeans and a hoodie. She stuck twenty thousand livre in her jeans pocket and her Steno pad, a pen firmly lodged in the coil at the top, in the hoodie's pouch.

She sighed. Here she was, mourning her sister, and she was planning on taking notes for an article. What kind of a person did that make her? It was a given that no one except another writer would understand the compulsion to record what she saw and felt.

"Take me to the Hotel Rowena," she told the driver in Arabic as she climbed in.

He looked at her over his shoulder. "Are you sure?" He turned back and slid into the flow of traffic. "Because it was firebombed last night."

"I know. I still want to go there."

He peered at her in the rearview mirror, obviously intrigued, but he didn't say anything. Her tear-swollen face probably told him all he needed to know. He dropped her off as close to the hotel as the cab could get—which was a block away.

She hurried to join the crowd standing across the street from the hotel at the edge of the area cordoned off by the police and pushed her way forward, ignoring the muttered complaints of those she elbowed aside. She finally reached the front edge of the throng and stared in horror at the blackened destruction. If Julie and Khalil were at a dinner on the second floor of this ruin, how could they have survived?

The answer was simple. They couldn't have.

She stared at the fire trucks, the ambulances, the heavy equipment waiting to move the crumbled and scorched rubble. The stench of wet char hung heavy, and the air was thick with ash.

The hotel's mostly glass front was totally gone, and the roof of the glass atrium had collapsed, leaving nothing but a pile of blackened debris. The back wall and the two side walls still stood, at least partially, though they didn't look particularly stable, seared and damaged as they were.

She scanned the tower rooms where many windows were missing and drapes hung out like lolling tongues. She glanced at the stores and businesses that lined the Avenue du General de Gaulle on either side of the hotel, and many of them were also missing their windows. Some owners had already boarded the gaping holes against looters; others were shoveling or sweeping up the shattered debris. For the first time Liz became aware of the crunch of glass under her feet.

The firefighters, many wearing masks over their noses and mouths, were covered with soot. Liz imagined that most of them had been here since last evening, working all through the night. They had to be exhausted, but they kept moving, dousing hot spots, waiting for things to cool enough for them to examine the remains, looking for evidence about what had happened.

A familiar figure appeared inside the cordoned off area, stepping from behind a police car.

"Charles!" Liz shouted to be heard over the constant noise. "Charles!" She ducked under a sawhorse meant to keep people back and started toward him. A soldier saw her and was beside her immediately, one hand on his rifle. He grabbed her arm. "*Sortez d'ici!*" Apparently he assumed she was European.

"That's my father," she told him in Arabic, pointing to Charles. The soldier looked but shook his head.

"Charles!" Liz shouted again, waving her hands.

Somehow her voice reached him, and he turned. She could see his lips say, "Liz!"

He spoke to the uniformed man beside him. The man, obvi-

ously an officer of some rank if the gold on his uniform was anything to go by, looked toward Liz and gave a signal to the soldier
holding her. The soldier dropped her arm and stepped back. Liz
ran to her father.

"Oh, Charles!" She grabbed him, and they held on to each
other in silence. Liz's throat was too clogged with tears to speak
as she burrowed close. There was something immensely comforting about the circle of her father's arms. Finally he loosened
his grip, and arms still about each other's waists, they faced the
hotel.

"It's hopeless, isn't it?" she managed.

Charles grimaced and rubbed a hand down his face. "I'm
afraid so."

The man her father had been talking to cleared his throat.

Charles stared at the man blankly for a minute, then blinked
to awareness. "Liz, this is Captain Timon Habib. He was one of
my students a few years ago."

Liz wiped her eyes and nodded.

"Timon, this is my daughter Elizabeth."

"I am so very sorry, Miss Fairchild." He spoke in English,
looking toward the chaos and carnage.

Liz managed a small, "Thanks," but his words made her heart
stutter. He had just confirmed that there was no hope, and he
would know, wouldn't he? He'd undoubtedly seen many other
scenes of destruction in his career, perhaps including the scene of
the car bomb that had killed al Hariri.

"Do you know who did it?" She felt a keen need for someone
to blame. "Hezbollah? Al Qaeda? Hamas?" Though why any of
those groups would bomb a group of business people meeting in
Beirut she couldn't imagine.

He shook his head. "We're looking at the groups you mentioned, as well as the Israeli extremists, even the Syrians, as
possibilities, but no group has claimed responsibility yet."

Liz was surprised. "Usually these groups wear their guilt like it was a badge of honor."

Captain Habib nodded. "It will be difficult to cast blame if no one boasts of their cleverness."

A weary-looking man approached Charles and the captain. Tears had carved furrows in the sooty dirt that covered his face. Liz realized with a start that the filthy man was Dr. Assan, Khalil's father.

He wrapped Charles in a fierce hug. "My friend, we have lost our children." He burst into tears.

10

Landstuhl, Germany

SOFT VOICES MURMURED in the blackness inside John's head, at first barely audible, then growing louder, more insistent. Then he drifted until he finally awoke to a gentle voice that, when he opened his eyes, he saw belonged to a pretty red-haired nurse. She was having a hushed conversation with a short, bespectacled man in class-B uniform who wore the rank of major.

I'm in the hospital!

He tried to remember why. He vaguely remembered waking up on a C-17 transport plane with an IV stuck in his arm, but everything after that was like staring through molasses at midnight.

The nurse saw John blinking at them. "Hello, Master Sergeant. I'm Jennifer. I'm glad you are awake because I've brought you something to eat." She set a plastic tray on the table by his bed.

The smell turned John's stomach. "Where am I?" he asked, disgusted to hear a wobble in his voice.

"You're in Germany—at Landstuhl Regional Medical Center. How do you feel?"

John tried to sit up. Why did they always ask that ridiculous question? "Fantastic."

The little nurse smiled at him, and a picture of another woman, moaning in childbirth, overlay the pretty redhead. Then he heard the ka-boom! and remembered flying through the air. "Where's Doc James?"

The nurse gestured toward the major. "This is Chaplain Chad Maxey, the duty chaplain today. He's here to see you."

"Where's Doc James?" John asked again, dread pooling in his chest. The chaplain was a very bad sign, as was Jennifer's refusal to answer his question.

Chaplain Maxey shook his head. "I'm sorry, John. He didn't make it."

John dropped back on the bed, feeling as if he'd just been kicked. He closed his eyes and instantly saw the blue Suburban, riding a fireball high in the air.

Doc never had a chance.

"John, I'd like to pray with you." The chaplain moved close to his bed. "Would you allow me to do that?"

John didn't answer. He threw the tray of food against the wall instead. Nurse Jennifer went scurrying and returned with the doctor, who told John he'd had surgery to remove one fragment of metal from his shoulder and another from his knee. He was also being treated for a level-two concussion, which explained why everything felt so fuzzy.

To his credit, Chaplain Maxey visited again before John was released. Though John refrained from any further outbursts, he hadn't been in any mood to talk to God, or even talk *about* Him, for that matter.

Except for the chaplain, he had no visitors. His godfather, Michael LaFontaine, sent a package with some clothing in it and a note:

"I hear you'll be coming home soon. Those hospital gowns are notoriously drafty on airplanes. Get well quickly. Will call when you get home."

The man was nothing if not generous. John pulled out the striped button-down shirt, khaki pants, and brown corduroy blazer with tan elbow patches. Guess the colonel had sent his secretary shopping for him.

His mother called the day before he was released. "I'm so glad to hear you're alive, John. When the chaplain showed up at my door, I almost fainted."

John could only imagine. "Don't worry, Mom. I've still got all my extremities."

"You really should be more careful, son."

"Mmm…" Yeah, right. If he'd been more careful, maybe Doc would still be alive.

The conversation stalled out after that, and John decided to give her an out. "Well, I bet you're busy there, and it's about time for my supper, so I guess we'll talk later, okay?"

"I love you, honey. No more scares, okay?"

"Love you too, Mom."

"And John…"

"Yes?"

"Your father loves you, too."

John found that hard to believe, but he didn't say so.

"He's locked inside a mountain in Colorado on some training exercise, but he was very concerned about you when he called last night. He talked about ordering a plane so he could come see you in Germany."

"Tell him I'm fine, Mom. I'll be on my way back to the States before he could get here. What he should do is order that plane and take you to the Caribbean."

His mother laughed, though John thought he heard a note of longing in her voice. "That'd be a quick way to lose his pension."

"Tell him he can always come see me at Bragg." But John knew he wouldn't.

"Mmm." She knew he wouldn't either. "Take it easy when you get home. No rock climbing or other crazy things before you're fully recovered."

"Yes, Mother. Good-bye, Mother. I'll be a good boy, Mother."

"Good-bye, John." He heard a smile in her voice.

Before he knew it, he was on a Continental flight home from Frankfurt. He squeezed into a window seat in cabin class and put the window shade down immediately. He looked around for a pillow, hoping he'd be able to sleep for most of the flight.

His shoulder still had a dressing on it, though it wasn't too noticeable under his blazer. Both of his eyes were still a frightening shade of purple mixed with green and yellow, and he had a nasty looking scab on his cheek from where he'd slid along the ground. A butterfly bandage held together the edges of the deep cut just above his brow.

When the flight attendants and other passengers saw him, they quickly looked away, embarrassed somehow at how he appeared. They then avoided him completely. Nobody took the seat next to him.

Frankenstein lives.

John's desire to sleep the long flight away wasn't realized. His mind was too active, and his body too cramped. He itched to do something physical after lying in bed for several days, but he was confined to crossing and uncrossing his legs in the too small space between seats.

He wanted to go climbing, to stretch, to sweat, to conquer.

"No rock climbing." His mother's words rang in his ears. He sighed. Mom was right, much as he hated to admit it. He wasn't physically up to something like that. A walk around the

block would be more his speed for a bit longer.

All too frequently when he thought about climbing, he thought about the girl. Not that he wanted to think about her. In fact, he tried not to think of her. Then, of course, she was all he could think about.

They'd met at a climbing gym at the beach. He was on leave after having passed the Special Forces Qualification course, and she had just finished graduate school. She was vacationing while she waited to hear about a couple of job possibilities. The girl rocked; that was all there was to it. She was smart—really smart. And he'd never forget those limitless brown eyes.

After meeting at the gym he had run into her again that night at a beach club his buddies dragged him to. He'd seen her come in and had made certain he left with her cell phone number. They hung out together daily for the rest of the week. They sat on the beach and watched the waves, talking about climbing and food and anything but their jobs. They'd eaten together at everything from a taco stand to a classy restaurant. He had liked how she didn't care whether it was hot dogs or filet mignon.

Just the opposite of Kim, the girl he'd been "seeing" for three years. With her, hot dogs did not count on the significance scale. It had to be expensive, whether it was dinner or jewelry or any gift. Shallow? Sure. All she wanted to talk about was shopping or some Hollywood hunk or her sorority. But he didn't hold it against her. The relationship had simply been a way to stave off loneliness, at least for him. Not that Kim wasn't nice. She was, and her movie-star looks made John the envy of everyone on the team.

But the brown-eyed girl had a charm, a vitality about her that eclipsed Kim. And it was him, his company, that she enjoyed. She was certainly nice to look at, but John liked the way she stimulated his mind even more—and he found himself feeling guilty for wanting to get to know her better with Kim waiting back home. For her part, she seemed interested, though she never said as much.

It wasn't your typical vacation hookup, the kind people have when they're looking for a bit of romance without commitment. They were friends, plain and simple. He never even held her hand, though he might have if it hadn't been for his loyalty to Kim.

All that week he found himself wrestling with his emotions, something he was not comfortable with. SF guys didn't do emotions. But she was getting to him, and there wasn't a neat little box to put those feelings in.

Three nights before his leave ended, just as he was about to pick her up for dinner, his pager went off.

He left a message on her phone—no details, just apologies. Next thing he knew, he was headed to Iraq. The deployment was a relief in a way. He didn't have to debate with himself about her. Or about Kim. Nine months spent at a remote outpost on the Iranian border meant he hadn't been able to contact either one.

He returned to find Kim married to some guy who sold insurance. One problem solved, and he didn't have to do anything. But the other woman could have been a segment on *Unsolved Mysteries*. She had disappeared as completely as those they searched for on the show. She had gotten a job and moved somewhere, but he had no idea where, and her cell number was no longer active.

He sighed as he lifted the window shade and looked at the Atlantic far below, wondering about what could have been. He crossed and uncrossed his legs another time.

A gangly young private in a class-A dress uniform sat in an aisle seat up a row across from John. It was clear by the kid's dress greens that he had probably been in the Army for less than a year.

Probably going home on his first leave.

A man on his way to the lavatory stopped by the kid and held out his hand. "Thanks."

The kid looked at him blankly.

"For serving."

The kid flushed and smiled.

Several others did the same thing as the flight progressed. About halfway across the Atlantic, the attendant stopped beside the kid. "We're glad to have you on our flight today. We have an extra seat in first class. Would you like to move up?"

The kid was wide-eyed. "Really?"

She smiled sweetly. "It's the least we can do for a soldier who is keeping us safe in the war on terror."

John shook his head, then grabbed at it, a sharp pain reminding him that his brains were still rattling around in there. He wanted to laugh out loud, but that would hurt too much.

Sometimes life had a cruel sense of humor.

11

Downtown Beirut

CHARLES RETURNED Dr. Assan's embrace, and the two men wept. Liz turned away, only to be confronted with the blackened proof of their loss. She put out her hand and steadied herself against Captain Habib's car. Without its support she was afraid her legs would give out.

Dr. Assan pulled back and took a deep breath. "Now I must go tell his mother. Not that she doesn't already know. But I must tell her not to hope."

Liz and her father watched Dr. Assan walk away, shoulders bowed with grief.

"I'd better call Annabelle," Charles said in a weary voice. "She keeps hoping, too. Then we'll leave, Liz."

"Please, Dr. Fairchild." Captain Habib opened the door to his car. "Sit in here. It will be much quieter. And use my cell phone." He held it out.

"Thank you, Timon, but I have mine." Charles climbed in and pulled the door shut, leaving Liz standing in the street.

Captain Habib looked at her kindly. "It would be best if you moved behind the barriers. It's dangerous to stand so close." He pointed to the shattered remains of the hotel's walls. "If they collapse, you could be hit with debris." He looked at her father. "Dr. Fairchild does not need to lose another daughter."

Nodding, Liz took a step back. He was right, but how could she stand behind the barriers? They were too far away, too far from Julie. Still, she had no choice in the matter.

Feeling the captain's eyes on her, she backed slowly toward the watching crowd. At the same time, a section of the far side wall of the hotel began to crumble, sending those standing near it running for safety. Captain Habib bolted for the action, forgetting Liz completely.

She thought of the great lobby of the Rowena as it had been, full of cedar panels and potted palms, carved wooden screens and bamboo furniture, all under that great glass atrium. Talk about flammable! Had it ever been retrofitted with a sprinkler system? Probably not. Add to that the small diameter hoses that were used by European and Middle Eastern fire companies, and you had disaster.

You also had fire-weakened walls like the one finally giving way. First small pieces broke off, then the entire wall began to lean.

She stepped behind a fire truck to watch in relative safety, automatically pulling out her pad and sliding the pen free. She tensed as the wall teetered, seemed to steady, then collapsed in a great cataract of concrete and rebar. The ground shook, and a cloud of pulverized debris rose, billowing outward. She pulled her head back, a turtle hiding from danger as the fog of particulate rolled toward her. She brought the hem of her hoodie to her face and hunkered down by the wheel of the truck.

When the noise and confusion lessened, she stood and dusted herself off. She peered out, taken with her vantage point that allowed her to see but not really be seen. She wrote her observations as well as her thoughts about the vulnerability of the old hotel, thinking like a reporter, not a sister.

She fought the urge to compare this tragedy to the World Trade Centers, but the scope of the 9-11 event made this one pale in contrast. The only similarity, aside from terrorists, was the heartbreak of those bereaved.

She drew a shaky breath. *Julie!*

Liz realized she was near an alley that ran beside the remaining side wall of the hotel, the one farthest from the apparent blast site, from where Julie and Khalil had been eating. But the fire had reached it and blackened it. Still, it looked solid, and since no one seemed interested in this side of the site, it must be stable.

A large, dusty rock, part of what was once lovely landscaping fronting the hotel, sat at the entrance to the alley. She climbed on it and began writing.

Her pen gradually stilled, and she found herself trying to imagine what life would be like without Julie.

Empty, with a hole never to be filled. No one could ever take her sister's place.

Who would she tell about the latest hopeless prospect she'd dated? Who would she brag to about things like an exciting assignment? Who would be interested in the little things—her rock climbing, the singles group at church, the latest movie she'd seen?

Oh, God, I'm so lonely! I want my sister back.

Snapshots of Julie flashed through her mind, a Technicolor collage of their lives together. There was three-year-old Julie with the raggedy haircut she'd given herself. Liz stood beside her with an arm around her shoulder as Annabelle lectured them on the dangers of scissors.

Five-year-old Julie sat in a wheelchair in a Paris hospital, her ankles so inflexible from the juvenile rheumatoid arthritis that she couldn't walk. Liz pushed the chair every time they'd let her.

Eight-year-old Julie was attacked by the school bullies because the JRA made her walk awkwardly. Liz raced to her rescue, giving the older boys bloody noses and getting a few bruises herself in the process.

Fourteen-year-old Julie hid under the covers crying because the boy she liked didn't like her back. Liz sat beside her and rubbed her back, telling her over and over that the boy was an idiot.

Seventeen-year-old Julie cried at the airport as Liz left for college. They e-mailed every day.

Nineteen-year-old Julie said, "Liz, I've become a Christian, though I'm not going to be as outspoken about it as you." Liz rejoiced and helped Julie learn the doctrinal basics.

Twenty-one-year-old Julie stood at the altar, glorious in her bridal white. Liz served as maid of honor in spite of her doubts about the wisdom of the marriage.

Suddenly she couldn't sit still another minute. Clutching her Steno pad, she slid from the rock and began to pace. Into the alley, then out. Into the alley, then out.

Liz stopped her pacing as questions about Julie's last moments struck her. Was death instantaneous? Did she suffer? Did she wake up in the arms of Jesus? At the last thought, Liz looked up toward heaven. She blinked as she saw above her a window with the glass blown out and the wire mesh torn loose.

A wisp of sea breeze floated across the Corniche, across l'Avenue du General de Gaulle, through the soot and dust, and down the alley. Something tinkled above her. She focused on an object caught in the jagged edges of the window's mesh. It looked like a necklace. She stretched for it, but it was just beyond her reach. She jumped and grabbed, but all she got was a scratch from one of the mesh's distorted prongs.

Sucking on the wound, she stepped back and eyed the windowsill above her. Maybe if she could reach it, she could pull herself up high enough to grab whatever it was and jerk it free.

She tucked her pad in her pouch, stuck the toe of one foot into a crevice in the wall, and lunged up and in, grabbing for the sill. Her foot slipped free under the force of her weight, and she plunged down. She managed to stick out a hand just in time to keep her face from hitting the wall. She wasn't so lucky with her knee. She sat on the ground staring at a nasty scrape through the tear in her jeans.

How come stuff like this always looked so easy on TV and in the movies? Then too, she was a climber. She contemplated trying again but decided against it.

She got to her feet and looked around for something to stand on. Deep in the alley near a door stood some boxes. Just what she needed. She ran to them. One crate contained tomatoes. She tried to pick it up, but it was too bulky.

She grabbed one end, slipping her fingers between the wooden slats, and tugged the crate to the window. She climbed on it, feeling the wood bend beneath her weight. She was probably damaging the tomatoes, but who cared? No one would be using them anyway.

She still couldn't quite reach what appeared to be a gold chain caught in the grasping metal fingers at the edge of the mesh. She raced back to what was probably the kitchen door and found another box, this one heavy cardboard with plastic bands around it. The label proclaimed this box to contain grapes grown in Lebanon.

She grabbed the strapping and dragged it to the window where she heaved it up onto the tomatoes. She climbed onto the boxes and reached. Her fingers closed over what was definitely a slim but sturdy gold chain.

She stilled. For a minute there she thought the wall had shimmied. But walls didn't move like that. Her mouth went dry. *Unless they are going to collapse.*

She looked up just in time to see a few bricks from the wall above give way and tumble onto the remaining boxes of produce outside the kitchen. Right where she had been mere minutes ago.

Heart pounding wildly, she struggled to free the chain. She knew it didn't make sense to risk her life for a piece of jewelry, but still she struggled. It became difficult to keep her eyes focused, given the glitter of the chain and the shimmy of the wall.

A low rumble and another section of the wall came crashing down. It became like watching a wave break, the foam curling along the crest as it broke, not all at once but in a progressive line. Another section of wall leaned and fell, followed by another.

Forget being careful with the chain. Liz yanked with all her might. The chain broke and slithered into her hand. She wrapped her fist around it and the locket that hung from it and jumped from the boxes. She raced for the safety of the fire truck and threw herself behind it as the thunder from the collapsing wall chased her out of the alley.

She hugged one of the large wheels, shaking all over at her narrow escape. She pulled her hoodie over her head as the mushroom cloud engulfed her. She waited a few minutes, then peeked out. Dusty, but safe. She opened her hand and stared at the reason she had risked her life.

The chain was lovely but not worth the chance she'd taken. She turned the porcelain pendant face up, seeing it clearly for the first time.

Liz stared in disbelief at the miniature Annabelle had painted of Julie in her blue regency gown.

What was it doing caught in the mesh of a window in the burned-out hotel? And did it mean what she thought it meant?

"Oh, God, she's alive, isn't she? Julie's alive!"

Near Fort Bragg, North Carolina

JOHN COOPER'S FISHING REEL whirred like an angry dragonfly as his sinker traced a lazy arc over Valley Pond. The hook struck the water and disappeared, taking the attached earthworm down with it. The Royalex canoe rocked gently as John leaned back against the thwart to gaze up at the tops of the dark green pine trees that ringed the forty-acre lake. The sky, bright blue above the evergreens, was full of large, puffy clouds, promising a spectacular sunset.

The way I feel, the sky should be black with thunder cracking and lightning flashing. And there should be rain. Lots and lots of rain.

He rotated his stiff left shoulder, grimacing. The doctor at Womack Army Medical Center on Fort Bragg had given John the go-ahead that very day to rejoin his unit after a week and a half of convalescent leave. Since it was already Friday afternoon, John decided to report in on Monday. If he went in today, he'd end up staying all weekend getting caught up. Besides, a couple of extra days to get his head back in the game wouldn't hurt.

After less than a week in Germany, he had been sent back to

Fort Bragg, where his unit placed him on leave until he was again fit for duty. It wasn't until he returned to the States that he heard the full story of what happened the day Doc had been killed.

The Suburban had been packed with an estimated two-hundred pounds of Semtex explosive, and the blast left a crater six feet deep in the road outside the gate of the French compound. Doc, the young U.N. guard, the woman, and her unborn child had been killed along with the driver of the vehicle. The Cougar had held up surprisingly well, with only minor damage to the exterior, which was amazing considering its proximity to the blast. The team members inside were rattled but uninjured. The big vehicle had also shielded Major Williams's Humvee and probably saved his life.

It was rumored that the woman had gotten pregnant out of wedlock, perhaps by one of the U.N. soldiers. Her father had chosen "martyrdom" rather than live with the shame of an illegitimate grandchild fathered by an infidel.

An honor killing of a different sort, John thought sardonically.

He sighed and slowly reeled in his line. His worm was gone, and he hadn't felt a thing. He put the rod in the bottom of the canoe and picked up a paddle. He stroked back toward the center of the lake so the boat wouldn't drift into the weeds near the shallow bank, then rebaited his hook.

Valley Pond and over seven hundred acres of land surrounding it belonged to his godfather, Michael LaFontaine, Colonel, U.S. Army, retired. He had been a cadet at West Point with John's father, William "Buck" Cooper. The LaFontaine family was old Southern money and had owned this farm since it was a plantation in the 1830s. The main house had been used by Confederate forces as a hospital, and General Robert E. Lee himself had visited the place before the Union Army arrived and burned it down.

Today the farm lay just outside the far reaches of Fort Bragg's northern training areas, close enough that John could hear explosions and gunfire from some of the live fire ranges. No one had lived in the rebuilt main house for at least a decade, but the colonel was happy to let John live in one of the dilapidated servant's quarters only a stone's throw from the lake.

In return, John agreed to fix up the cottage as his schedule and pocketbook allowed. It was well worth the thirty-minute drive to work to have some peace and quiet whenever he was given the rare gift of time off.

John threw out his line, and a fish jumped on the side of his boat where the line wasn't.

That figures.

Scowling, he reeled in the hook and cast it close to where the ripples spread across the glassy surface of the water. That he rarely caught any fish hardly mattered. The occasional tug at his line was, if anything, a minor annoyance. It was the exercise itself he was learning to like.

Age twenty-nine might seem a little late for a Green Beret Master Sergeant to develop this new hobby, especially for someone as outdoorsy as John. However, no one had taken him fishing when he was a kid.

Though Buck Cooper had attempted to show an interest in young John's life, the Army always took first place in the man's priorities. John no longer held it against his father as he once did. After his own twelve years of service, he understood the demands that came with a career in the military.

When he joined the Army right out of high school, then Lieutenant Colonel Buck Cooper shook with fury. "Your grandfather, your uncle, and I all went to West Point," he roared. "How can you forsake that tradition?"

But John wasn't interested in following someone else's tradition. If anything, he wanted to make his own. He was young and bullheaded and had no desire to continue his schooling. It was too abstract, too formal for his tastes.

If he wanted to learn something, he did it again and again

until he mastered it. Now he was doing it with his fishing, a skill he wanted to pass on to his own sons someday. He could learn more in one day of actually doing something than he could in a month of reading about it or being lectured on it.

Besides, having something to occupy his hands made it easier for him to think. Or not to think.

John closed his eyes to let the midafternoon sun warm his face, then opened them again immediately. The images around him were much more peaceful than those inside his head. He was enough of a professional to know that he shouldn't blame himself for Doc's death, but he couldn't shake the thought that he should have put the pieces together faster.

That failure would haunt him for the rest of his life.

Vernon's memorial service had been held at the JFK Memorial Chapel on Fort Bragg, a closed-casket ceremony that was one of the most painful things John had ever experienced. Doc's entire extended family had come up from Mississippi. Twenty-one of them in all: parents, brothers, sisters, cousins, aunts, and uncles. His five siblings sang a slow gospel song in honor of their brother.

Thank you for the Lamb,
The precious Lamb of God.
Because of your grace I will soon see His face,
The precious Lamb of God.

John was sure he'd never seen anything as sad as those five brothers and sisters, arms entwined, swaying, singing, and crying. He had to look away, or he'd have cried, too.

He glanced instead across the chapel at Doc's parents. His mother, who was blind, swayed slightly with the music, a look on her face that was both sad and serene as she listened to her remaining children sing. Her hands were raised as if she was soaking up the memory of her son by way of the tearful tribute.

After the ceremony, he tentatively approached Mrs. James,

not really sure what to say but knowing he couldn't leave without expressing his condolences.

He squatted painfully in front of the portly black woman and cleared his throat. "Mrs. James, I'm Master Sergeant John Cooper. I was Doc's, I mean, Vernon's team sergeant. I just wanted to tell you how truly sorry I am for what happened. Your son was…" The words caught in his throat. "He was a good man and very good at what he did. Everyone liked and respected him."

Mrs. James seemed to sense how hard it was for John to talk about Doc. She reached out and touched his face, smiling. "I know, honey. Our Vernon died doing what he was called to do. I truly believe that. And none of us can hope for any better."

She picked up a handkerchief from her lap and dabbed at her eyes. "That boy belonged to Jesus before he belonged to me. And it won't be long before I'll be seein' my son again." She took a deep breath. "God knows best."

Then she looked right at John as if she could see him, or see through him. "God may not give us what we want, Master Sergeant Cooper, but He's always on time with what we need."

John suddenly had to get out of that chapel. "I hope so," he answered weakly. Then he rose and hobbled out of the building as quickly as he could. He didn't voice what he was actually thinking, what he'd been thinking since he learned of Doc's death.

God doesn't care.

The thought didn't come easily to him, even now. He'd believed in God for nearly his entire life, and even attended youth group pretty regularly in high school. But what kind of God would refuse to protect someone like Vernon, someone who believed more fervently than he himself ever had? How could God abandon such a good person?

John leaned back in the canoe and inhaled deeply, pressing his fists into his eyes. He didn't want to consider these questions.

He picked up the paddle again and headed back to the cottage on the west side of the pond. Maybe something on television could help him forget for a while. He stepped stiffly out of the canoe onto the bank, then stashed the boat beneath the deck that formed the cottage's front porch. He'd have to get that fish later.

As he mounted the front steps, John saw a box sitting on his doorstep. He eyed it suspiciously until he noticed the FedEx truck disappearing down the road. He looked again at the white cardboard box. It had originated in Omaha, Nebraska.

Before he could open it, his cell phone rang. He flipped it open. "John Cooper."

"John Cooper himself, in person?"

"Hello, Mr. LaFontaine."

"Oh, John. Must I tell you again? Mr. LaFontaine is my father."

"Sorry, Michael. Old habits die hard."

"As do old soldiers. Speaking of which, I'm terribly sorry to hear about your fallen comrade."

"Thank you, sir."

"And how are you recovering?"

John grimaced and shrugged his sore shoulder. "I'm doing well, under the circumstances. How are things inside the Beltway?"

When Michael left the service, he took over his family's business holdings, increasing their worth significantly. His biggest job, however, was courting prominent politicians to his point of view, and he was extremely good at it. Having a fortune to pump into the reelection campaigns of the favored didn't hurt either.

"Scandalous and two-faced, as usual. These liberal handwringers in Congress will be the death of me. My beagle, Freddy, would be better suited to fighting a war on terror than most of these pacifistic whiners. I spend hours on the phone every day trying to convince these jokers to get their act together, and I always feel the need to shower afterward."

"Wow, sir. Tell me how you really feel."

The older man laughed. "Sorry. You got me on my soapbox. Anyway, I'd much rather have been with you boys in Africa."

John shifted uncomfortably. "You're not supposed to know where we were, Colonel."

"Yes, well, twelve years in Army intelligence does have certain perks."

John grunted. "I suppose so." Still, the leaking of classified information, even to a man as fine as Michael, rubbed against the grain.

"Did you get the package I sent?"

He looked at the box, still sitting on the step. He didn't need to open the package to know that it contained Omaha Steaks. "Yes, I did. You really shouldn't have."

The colonel had sent the gourmet meats to John when he was deployed to Iraq, making Task Force Valor the envy of every soldier on the Forward Operating Base where they were stationed.

"Nonsense. I just wanted to show my appreciation to you and your men. Have a party on me. Feel free to use the pavilion at the main house if you like."

"Thank you, Michael. I really appreciate it, and I know the guys will too."

"So how are you enjoying the cottage?"

"It's fantastic, sir. And I'm earning my keep. I replaced some of that old copper piping under the sink with PVC yesterday."

"Listen, John, you're supposed to be recuperating, not plumbing. I know we agreed you'd fix the place up, but I really only said that to placate my accountant. I don't expect you to be crawling under sinks when you should be resting."

John smiled, appreciating his godfather's concern. "It's okay, really. Makes me feel useful." If only his father had been so attentive...

"Well," the colonel said, "don't feel like you have to do it, okay?"

"Roger that."

"So how's your father?"

John grimaced. "He called the day after I got back to Bragg, but I haven't talked to him since. I think he's still in Colorado involved in some high-level something-or-other." It seemed his dad was always involved in important things. John just wished he had been one of them.

"When you hear from Buck, give him my best. And listen, if you ever need anything, anything at all, you let me know."

"Thanks again, sir. I will." John knew he probably wouldn't. "In the meantime, you keep those politicians in line."

John laughed as the colonel muttered, "Easier said than done."

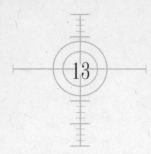

13

Beirut

DAYS LIMPED BY and still no word from or about Julie. Liz clung to the hope the necklace gave her, mainly because she could think of no way it could have gotten caught in that wire mesh unless Julie had somehow been there. But still that told her nothing about what had happened to her sister. If she was alive, why hadn't they heard from her?

Amnesia? But amnesia was for novels and soap operas. Liz knew people rarely got full amnesia. A trauma might be blocked, an accident lost from conscious memory, but total loss of recall was extremely rare.

As the days passed, Annabelle couldn't stop crying, and Charles couldn't stop yelling, his way of dealing with the chaotic emotions of a father who couldn't do anything to help his daughter. He spoke to Timon Habib at least once a day, but the news was always the same.

"We know nothing new."

Liz was exhausted, but she couldn't sleep. She felt disconnected, emotionally vague, and very alone in spite of being with her parents. Her mind went into patches of time best described as absence of thought, not the mental clean slate they told you about in Eastern meditation but a protective blanking from emotions too difficult to deal with.

Julie, where are you? Are you safe? Are you being treated kindly? Are they getting you your medicine?

Liz tried to pray, tried to call on the Lord. He had always been so good to her. Since she had trusted Christ, life had been rich. She had felt blessed, the recipient of God's love.

Now life was hard and full of pain, and it felt like He had withdrawn from her. She e-mailed a prayer request about Julie to all of her friends back in the States, and she received several responses reminding her that God never left His people alone. He was with Julie, wherever she was, whether with Him in glory or somewhere here on earth. And He was with Liz.

But it sure didn't feel like it.

Liz went back to the hotel several times, looking at the space where all those world economists and their guests had been happily eating and talking. Had the monetary centers of the world shuddered with the explosion? Reading the list of the dead or missing and their positions and credentials was like reading a Who's Who of financial geniuses. And each of them had a family who grieved.

Already the rubble was being carted off. Liz understood this clearing had to happen for safety's sake, but it made the deaths of Khalil and all the others seem like something that could be corrected by tidying up the area. The truth was far different.

Soon the site would be ready for rebuilding. Tourism, still recovering from the devastating effects of the civil war, was one of the major sources of economic stability for this nation, and evidence of suicide bombers tended to dampen people's enthusiasm for a destination. Downplay the crime, remove the evidence of danger, and woo the tourists with a new luxury hotel with all the latest everything.

While the front portion of the hotel would play the phoenix, rising reborn from the fire, the tower of rooms had been found stable, and workmen swarmed its walls, removing scorch marks, repairing the cosmetic damage, replacing the broken and blown-out windows. As she stared up at the tower, she wondered which rooms had held the belongings of the many killed.

Then she turned away from the destruction and began her daily regimen.

She held out Julie's picture to anyone who passed by.

"Have you seen this young woman?"

Near Fort Bragg

It was all up to him.

John was sweating buckets under his EOD 9 suit—sixty-five pounds of body armor that would supposedly protect him in case the improvised explosive in front of him happened to go "boom." He would have just as soon taken his chances without the suit. Aside from being unbearably hot even in mild conditions, much less in Iraq, the suit necessarily left his hands unprotected. You couldn't work if you couldn't feel what you were working on.

If there was an explosion, odds were that he'd live the rest of his life without hands, not something he was prepared to contemplate. If it ever happened to him, John hoped the blast would be sufficient to just end it.

They would have sent the robot to disarm the bomb, but so much debris was around the package that the Andros couldn't get to it. So John suited up and waddled over for a look, his teammates watching from a distance.

Rubble littered the street, left after U.S. Marines had called indirect fire in on an insurgent position two days earlier. This unexploded device was reported by a child who saw it while playing in front of his home nearby.

John shook his head at the thought that the kids here could spot IEDs faster than kids in the U.S. could say, "Xbox."

He was still twenty meters from the device, stepping over a large cinderblock, when his heart stopped.

Directly beneath him, taped to the back side of the block, was a cellular phone.

A secondary device! Always check for a secondary!

The phone began to ring.

John turned to run as the cell phone chirped. But the suit was too heavy. He couldn't get away, couldn't run. Couldn't breathe.

He jerked upright, sweating profusely, his heart hammering against his ribs.

His cell phone was ringing on the bedside stand.

He pressed the pads of his palms into his eyes, taking a moment to figure out *who* he was, much less where. Fear still gripped him, the dream far too real.

John flicked on the light on the bedside table and stared at the ringing phone. He finally picked it up just before voice mail kicked in, managing to croak, "Cooper."

Rip Rubio's Latin accent sounded through the phone. "Coop! I hate to tell you this, *bato,* but the weekend is cancelled. We just got alerted."

John groaned.

"Tell me about it. My girlfriend is doing her impression of a Polaris missile right now. See you at the compound."

The call waiting beeped while Rubio was speaking. John hit the button to switch to the other line. "Yeah?"

A gruff voice asked, "How soon can you get back to the company area?"

Major Williams. John probably admired him more than any other man in the world, but that didn't stop him from wanting to throw his phone at the wall. Instead, he sighed heavily. "This isn't a training exercise, is it?"

"Would I do that to you guys?" Major Williams seemed genuinely hurt. "More to the point, would I do that to myself? Get your butt in here, Cooper."

"Roger that." John flipped the phone shut and looked with longing at his pillow. The clock beside his bed read 2:30 A.M.

Welcome back, John.

Fort Bragg

John drove from home to the EOD compound in under twenty minutes, which had to be a new record. As he pulled through the security checkpoint at the Butner Road gate, John flashed his military ID. Had all the money spent on extra security actually made anyone safer, or did it just make people feel safer?

Prior to September 11, Fort Bragg had been an open post. Since the attacks on America, miles of chain-link and barbed wire had sprung up around the installation, many of the roads into the post had been closed, and millions of dollars were spent each year on gate security. All of this mostly added up to a colossal pain in the neck for the forty-two thousand soldiers stationed there.

The compound Task Force Valor occupied was a secluded cluster of corrugated metal buildings set at the very edge of the post, just across from the Macridge Impact Area. Signs along the road near the unit's "shop" proclaimed, "Danger! Unexploded Duds! Keep Out! Trespassing or removal of any items from range is prohibited by law."

Just the kind of place where bomb techs felt at home.

It was obvious something was up by the amount of activity around the small compound in the middle of the night. Men were securing supplies to large pallets, and a flatbed truck idled nearby ready to receive them. Other vehicles were already being lined up for the convoy to the airfield.

John parked his pickup truck in front of the faded yellow

building that held the team room and administrative offices. Every light in the place was on. As he opened the door, he almost got run over by Frank Baldwin, who had his arms full of arcane electronics and slowed only long enough to say, "Hey, John, good to see you."

All of the single men were present, most congregating around the coffeepot or rummaging in their lockers to make sure they had everything they needed for the deployment. They echoed Frank's greeting, waved a hand, or grunted a welcome. Spending such large amounts of time together in very dangerous situations knit them together in a way most civilians couldn't comprehend.

Task Force Valor had been created as a quick-response unit dedicated to stopping the terrorists' supply of explosives by hunting down and eliminating bomb shops and suppliers around the globe. As such, they had to be more than just bomb technicians. They had to be able to shoot their way in, recognize and secure the munitions, and if need be, blast their way out.

They spent an average of two hundred days each year away from Fort Bragg, either training for or performing real-world missions, and John had to admit he preferred being deployed to garrison duty. The team's op-tempo was greater than that of other Special Forces units, since Valor operated worldwide rather than specializing in one particular region of the world as did most. In the last three years, they'd been to both Central and South America twice, Africa three times, and had spent so much time in the Middle East John felt like he should buy land there.

A great sense of purpose went with this job. John had always hated bullies, and his membership in this elite unit gave him a legitimate outlet for those feelings. He understood that the war on terror was, in one sense, about sucking the poison out of the rest of the world by taking the fight to the extremists' home turf so they would be too busy to bring the fight to his homeland.

The long deployments and unpredictable schedule made it all

but impossible to have any kind of social life outside the unit. And since he didn't drink, John ended up getting suckered into being the designated driver more often than he cared to think about.

As for women, he was resigned to remaining unattached for the time being. After he'd returned from that extended deployment to find Kim married to the insurance man, he'd had only a few dates. More often than not, women felt like more trouble than they were worth.

Then there was that brown-eyed girl. He wondered if the long months overseas had caused his memory of her to be more than the reality. Not that it mattered since he'd probably never see her again.

He dealt with his loneliness by throwing himself even more deeply into his job and his joy, rock climbing. He liked the immediacy of climbing. On the rock you just focused on the present. There was always a clear direction—up. And the rock didn't complain if you showed up two days or two months late.

When John entered the room, Hogan and Sweeney were watching Fox News on a television mounted in one corner. John sidled over to them.

The bearded Hogan looked up and smiled. He held out a box of Krispy Kremes. "Doughnut?"

"I'll pass. What's the word?"

Sweeney tugged at his longer-than-regulation mustache. "Shoot, you know nobody ever tells us nothing. Did you meet our new medic?" He gestured to the lanky soldier on the other side of the room, who was at that moment closing his locker.

John recognized the man immediately. "Well, I'll be—that's Joe Kelly! He was in my Assault Climber class last year at Camp Merrill. He and I were the ranking men in the class, so they roomed us together."

Kelly had to be the most optimistic person John had ever

met, and they'd had a great time the previous summer at the two-week course, buddy-climbing on Mount Yonah in the North Georgia mountains.

Staff-Sergeant Kelly spotted John and crossed the room toward him, beaming. "Well, well, John Cooper. I heard someone messed up and put you in charge."

John couldn't help smiling back. No one could ever replace Vernon James, but if John had his pick of men to fill the position, Kelly would have topped the list.

"It beats buddy-rappelling with your fat butt strapped to my back! How are you, Joe? I thought you were getting promoted to Sergeant First Class?"

Kelly laughed. "I made E-7 two weeks ago, pardner. Just haven't pinned it on yet. Been too busy getting moved over here from 5th Group."

At that moment, Major Williams, dressed in black running shorts and a gray Army windbreaker, burst through the door carrying a coffee mug that must have held at least a gallon of liquid. There were two men with him that Cooper had never seen before. They both wore khaki cargo pants and black polo shirts. The major motioned to John and disappeared into his office.

"Who do you suppose they are?" Hogan mumbled through a mouthful of Krispy Kreme.

"I think I'll go find out." John turned and crossed the room to the commander's office.

14

Sainiq Refugee Camp

LIZ DROVE THROUGH the gates in the fence that surrounded the Palestinian camp, her hands gripping the steering wheel, her stomach doing more flips than a gymnast performing a floor routine.

There were no two ways about it: This camp frightened her. She reached up to make certain that the scarf she had tied about her head was still in place. As a disguise, it was elementary, but combined with her fluent Arabic, it should do the trick.

As she once again followed Nabila's directions to Hanan's home, she was appalled at the evidences of poverty all around her: the littered streets; the children's worn clothes, washed so often they'd lost color; the dogs so skinny their ribs looked like fur-covered ladder rungs.

The homes were built of supplies scrounged from dumps, bombed buildings, anywhere there was a sheet of metal, a pile of cinderblocks. Originally meant to be temporary dwellings, they had become home to several generations of refugees. Clustered one upon the other, it was clear no one had bothered with a plumb line in the course of erecting the shelters.

Liz felt hemmed in, claustrophobic. With each breath she tasted the hopelessness and despair carried in the air like a lethal virus. No wonder the *shebab* became terrorists or freedom fighters. What other future was there for them?

And the young men had it good compared to the girls and women. Suddenly Liz saw Hanan's occasional trips to the souks in Sidon in a new light. Relief from the congestion. A temporary feeling of freedom. A change of scenery. By contrast she thought of Annabelle and Nabila going to the modern stores in Beirut any time they wanted.

She thought of herself in Philadelphia, amazed and appalled as she walked South Street, delighted as she toured the historic district or went to a play at the Walnut Street Theater or the Kimmel Center, sated after a dinner at one of the city's multitude of restaurants.

Constraint versus independence.

Scarcity versus plenty.

Limits versus opportunities.

When Liz reached Hanan's, she pulled her car as close as she could to the front wall of the house. When she climbed out, she checked carefully to make certain there was room for another car to pass her. Satisfied, she knocked on Hanan's open front door.

Hanan welcomed her with reserve, obviously not certain what to expect from this American reporter. Liz was struck by how much Hanan resembled her cousin Nabila.

"Please, have a seat." Hanan gestured to the only overstuffed chair in the room. "It is my husband's chair."

Liz was being given the seat of honor, and she took it with a smile. She reached into her bag and got out her Steno pad and pen as well as a small tape recorder she placed on the scarred end table beside the lamp. "May I? I do this so I will not make any mistakes about what you say."

Hanan was quiet for a minute, clearly unsure. Then she gave a quick nod. "May I offer you some tea?"

"Thank you." Liz smiled again, hoping to put Hanan at ease. "I'd love some."

As Liz waited for Hanan to return from the little kitchen added to the back of the house, she looked around the main room and thought that much as Hanan and Nabila looked alike, they couldn't have been living in more different circumstances. Nabila's rooms at Charles and Annabelle's house were filled with light and color, and just steps away was the courtyard with its flowering orange trees and tinkling fountain.

Hanan's place was small, cramped, and dark with electric lights lit even at midday. There was also very little ventilation. Outside Hanan's home were potholed dirt roads, piles of refuse, and festering anger.

"I am sorry about your sister and her husband," Hanan said. "Nabila wrote about the fire."

"Thank you." Liz swallowed back tears. "We have reason to believe that Julie escaped the fire, but we don't know what happened to her."

"The police have not found any clues?"

Liz shook her head. "La. Every day it gets harder, just waiting. Every day I get angrier over the lack of progress."

Hanan sighed. "It seems unreal, I imagine. Like Zahra's death."

Now there was a tragedy. "What has happened to your aunt?"

"She is at home."

Liz made a sound of disbelief.

Hanan held up a hand. "*Wa'ef.* Stop. It is not as you are thinking. She will be tried for murder."

"Good. I was worried there for a minute. How about her little girl? I have thought much about her."

"Salma is at home with her mother and father. For the

moment there is some semblance of normal. But not for long."

There was a knock on the door, and two of Hanan's neighbors came in.

"I never knew an American," one said.

It was obvious that she was disappointed in Liz, so Liz asked her why.

"You look nice, normal." The woman frowned.

"Thank you. What did you think I'd look like?"

The woman shrugged. "I do not know. I have always heard so much about America and Americans, and what I am told is not very nice."

Liz didn't argue the point. "You see pictures of all the worst things. Remember that America is very big, and the pictures you see represent only a very, very small group of people. It's like something bad happening on the other side of your camp. It only involves a few, not the whole camp."

She nodded, accepting the analogy, but Liz knew by her stubborn look that she held deep convictions against the United States.

"America supports the Zionists and Israel." She said it as an accusation.

One of the most difficult things for Liz to adjust to when she became a Christian was the ardent support American Christians gave to Israel. Her whole life she'd been taught to sympathize with the Palestinians, not the Jews, and her outlook had led to many a debate. The establishment of the nation of Israel as a fulfillment of biblical prophecy took her some time to accept, and she still tended to be critical of many of Israel's inciting actions or the overreactions to Palestinian provocation.

"Yes, America supports Israel, but it also supports the Palestinian right to a homeland," Liz said.

"And how can we have a homeland with the Zionists on the land that was our forefathers'?"

Liz had no answer. Her only comfort, warped as it was, was that the politicians of the world hadn't found a workable solution either.

The second neighbor who wouldn't tell Liz her name stepped in front of the argumentative woman and placed a shaking hand on Liz's arm. She spoke in a whisper. "This is more important, what I am about to say."

The arguer snorted but moved aside.

"Please speak for us," the woman said. "We cannot speak for ourselves without endangering our lives and making things worse for our daughters."

"What are your dreams for your daughters?" Liz made believe she didn't see the bruised cheek the woman tried to hide by bringing her head scarf forward.

"That they escape the life I have lived." The woman spoke simply but with tears in her eyes. "I have four girls. The oldest is approaching twelve years, and they follow one right after the other. Eleven, ten, nine. My husband complains all the time about how costly they are. He wants to marry them off as soon as he can. I plead with him to wait. Let them get educated. Let them grow up. Let them pick their own men. He says they do not need an education and we cannot afford to wait."

"What does your husband do for work?"

"Whatever he can."

"He has no regular job?" Liz was careful to keep any kind of censure from her tone. Jobs and Palestinian men were often mutually exclusive, not due to lack of ability or initiative but politics and prejudice.

"Our men are not allowed work permits. Even if he does get a temporary job, he has not the papers to satisfy the soldiers at the road blocks. They humiliate him, sometimes hit him. After all, who can he complain to? Often they will not let him pass to get to the job. Once they stripped him."

The problems in the camps were interdependent, and Liz knew that no work permits meant no incomes which meant no monies for taxes which meant no sanitation services, minimal educational programs, next to no medical care, sporadic electricity, and boredom. Hopelessness.

"I used to think that it was the will of Allah that women are undereducated and kept in seclusion," Hanan said. "Husbands are the masters. They can do whatever they want with their wives. It is what the Koran says. Now I do not think so. I think that is just one interpretation."

"Hanan, do not say such things!" Her neighbor with the bruised cheek was appalled.

"It is only us women." Hanan drew a circle in the air with her finger. "Are you going to tell anyone what I said?" She looked a challenge at both her visitors.

They both shook their heads but continued to look worried.

Fascinating, Liz thought. Women uniting against the men, against the system. Sisterhood in spite of differing opinions.

At the thought of sister, pain squeezed Liz's heart so abruptly, so powerfully that for a moment she couldn't breathe. *Oh, God, please!*

Eyes swimming, she studied her pad like she was reviewing her notes while she waited until she could speak calmly again. "What changed your mind about the place of women?" she finally managed to ask Hanan.

"My daughters." Hanan looked at the two small girls playing with a much used, almost hairless doll and a blanket that had once been pink.

"They are beautiful little girls," Liz said. Their dark hair curled around chubby cheeks, and their eyes sparkled even in the twilight of the room.

"They are smart," Hanan said, making a statement of fact, not a bragging comment. "They ask such questions. Why would

Allah give them clever minds if he did not mean for them to use them?"

"Shh," said the nameless neighbor, her agitation growing. "Someone might hear."

"I do not care," Hanan said, but she looked to see if anyone lingered outside and might have heard her defiant words.

A car pulled up in front of the house, its motor knocking loudly.

Hanan's friends looked at one another, faces filled with alarm.

"Out through the back," Hanan said.

Quickly the women left, shadows disappearing into the gloom.

"Should I go, too?" Liz asked. "I don't want to make things difficult for you."

"Let me see who it is." Hanan walked toward the door. She peeked out, and the tension in her shoulders left. "It is Ali, my husband. He knows you were coming."

Liz rose. "He would probably prefer that I leave now that he's home." She reached for her tape recorder. "May I return another day? I have many more questions to ask you."

"Please. Stay and meet Ali. He is a good man. He does not want to live as he does any more than I want to live as I do. I want you to write that there are fine Palestinian men."

Car doors slammed and Liz heard men's voices. They didn't come closer, so she assumed Ali wasn't coming in this very minute. She checked her list of questions, glad she hadn't turned the recorder off. "How much of your situation or the situation of Muslim women in general is the result of the Islamification of the camps?"

Hanan clapped her hands at her daughters, who grabbed their doll and blanket and ran for a side room Liz assumed was a bedroom.

Hanan frowned as she thought of what to say. "It is true that things here have gotten very strict, but many are cultural Muslims. They say they believe, but they don't practice their faith. They drink if they think no one knows. Or they take a woman who isn't their wife. Can you understand that?"

Liz nodded. "Many in the United States call themselves Christians, but you see no evidence of it in their lives."

"But here even those who do not practice much of anything will use the Koran to keep women subject. It is an issue of control, not faith."

"You're very outspoken, Hanan."

She shook her head, her eye on the door. Was it Ali she didn't want to hear her thoughts or Ali's friends?

"I am rebelling in here." She touched her heart. "It is Nabila who had the courage to actually stand for her convictions." She smiled sadly. "I am afraid to pay the price."

A man in an open-necked, short-sleeved sport shirt entered. A boy of about six followed him. Liz couldn't help compare Hanan in her all-encompassing clothes and head scarf with the man and boy in their much more temperature appropriate dress.

The boy stopped abruptly when he saw Liz. "Is that your car against our house?"

"Yes. Is it in the way?"

"No. It is very nice."

"Thank you." Liz smiled at the boy.

"Mahmad," Hanan brushed a hand over his head, "go play with your sisters."

The boy frowned but went.

Ali nodded to Liz politely. "Welcome to our house."

Liz knew he spoke with pride for somehow he had been able to provide his family a home of only one generation of adults. Many in the camp lived with multiple generations in one dwelling. Some families had built a second story for sons and daughters-in-law. Liz had seen subway cars at rush hour with more space and privacy than many Palestinian homes.

"It is a pleasure to meet you, Ali. I thank you for letting me speak to your wife."

He inclined his head, went to his chair, and sat. Liz recognized his not-too-subtle statement that her time with Hanan was ended.

With repeated thanks, she left, driving carefully through the camp, braking hard a couple of times to avoid the children who ran and played in the street, blinking tears that were for all the women lost in one way or another, Julie included.

Fort Bragg

"Gentlemen, this is John Cooper, Team Sergeant," Major Williams said when John entered his office. "John, these are Special Agents Miller and Sandoval from the FBI Incident Response Team. They are going to explain to us why we're here on a Saturday morning when we should be at home asleep."

John shook hands with the men, then stood next to Williams's desk as Agent Miller pulled a sheaf of papers from a black cordura case.

"Okay, here we go," Miller began, finding the sheet he wanted. "Last month there was a bombing in Beirut that killed one U.S. diplomat and twelve other Americans, as well as scores of other people. Many were economists and bankers attending a World Bank conference." He pushed an information sheet across the desk.

John picked it up and began scanning it. He noted that the incident had occurred during their time in the Ivory Coast. He threw his commander a sideways glance. "You got me out of bed for this?"

"The bombing has the Department of Homeland Security concerned," Miller continued, as if John hadn't spoken. "Agent

Sandoval here was with the forensics team that just returned from the site of the bombing, and he found something quite…disturbing."

Sandoval spoke up. "The explosive that was used appears to be something our forensics team has never seen before. Or rather, we know that it exists as a chemical, but as far as we know, this is the first time it's been used as a weapon."

John was still reading the brief he'd been given. "It says here that the bomber used Iso-Triethyl Borane. I hate to admit it, but that's a new one on me. What is it?"

"It's a colorless, odorless liquid," the agent answered. "It's highly pyrophoric; it reacts very violently with oxygen and packs quite a wallop, almost as powerful as RDX or Semtex."

John rubbed the stubble on his face. "Okay, but why call us?"

"Well," Miller said, "the bomber smuggled this explosive through formidable security at this World Bank event. There were even Lebanese soldiers patrolling the site with explosives-trained dogs. None of them picked up on this stuff. If it can fool the dogs, it may be able to slip past our airport sniffers. You can imagine what will happen if someone gets a bottle of this stuff on an airplane."

The major took a quick swallow from his giant mug. "I recall a few years ago a guy got something similar on a plane disguised as contact lens cleaner. He used his watch for a detonator and set it off in the airplane's lavatory. Killed one Japanese guy, if I remember right."

Sandoval nodded. "Correct. Except in this case, they wouldn't even need a detonator. It appears that all they'd need to do is open the bottle."

"Wait a minute," John said. "If this stuff detonates on contact with air, wouldn't it be pretty tough to make? I mean, you're not going to have some whacko bottling this stuff in his garage, right?"

"Exactly," answered Miller, "and this is why we've come to you. Making this stuff would require a pretty sophisticated lab. Perhaps even something with the backing of a terrorist state. We have people on the ground in Lebanon trying to track down the source of this explosive. When we find it, we're going to need your team to go in and take it out."

John thought about those who orchestrated the murder and mayhem that took place that night, attacking people who not only could not defend themselves, but who were attempting to better the situation in the region. Suddenly, he could feel a fire starting in his gut. These people weren't soldiers. They were thugs, nothing more. "I'm sold. When do we leave?"

"Zero-nine-hundred." The major answered flatly.

"Okay." John dropped the folder back on the desk. "Let's get to work."

The two FBI men picked up their cases and walked out of the office. John was about to follow when Williams stopped him. "Hold it, John."

He turned to face his commander. "What's up, boss?"

"Are you okay to do this? You haven't exactly had a lot of time to heal—and I don't just mean physically. I can't give you the details yet, but some big changes are coming, and we're definitely going to need you to be 100 percent."

"I'm fine, Lou." John put on his best fake smile. "If I have to spend another day in physical therapy, I'm going to kill something."

In reality, he wasn't so sure. Until these past two weeks, as he'd had time to reflect while recuperating, he hadn't realized how much of an effect the pace and work of Task Force Valor had on him.

On one level, John knew that this was where he wanted to be. What he wanted to do. On another he recognized that he was becoming a different person, in much the same way that a career cop becomes embittered by spending too much time with the dregs of society. John was unsure whether he was becoming more jaded or less idealistic, but either way, he had a job to do.

The cowards who bombed that hotel were still out there, most likely planning their next spineless act of violence and murder. These were people who understood no language but that of destruction.

John Cooper and his men were fluent in that language, too, but as those who halted the devastation instead of inciting it. Now was the time to open a dialogue.

He could see no better way to honor Doc's memory.

15

Beirut

TWO WEEKS AFTER Julie's disappearance—Liz couldn't bring herself to think, let alone say, Julie's death—she went with her parents to visit Dr. and Mrs. Assan in their grand house in the Raouche suburbs not far from the Corniche and the spectacular Pigeon Rocks. It wasn't a visit she wanted to make. She knew it would be awkward for everyone with one family buried in grief, the other clinging desperately to hope.

Liz climbed out of her father's car and held her hand over her nervous stomach. Charles pushed back his shoulders as if bracing himself. He took Annabelle's elbow and escorted her to the front door. Liz trailed behind.

Dr. Assan himself greeted them in the *madafah,* the reception room, resplendent with contemporary reproductions of panels of old Lebanese wood carvings and arches painted with beautifully intricate, colorful floral and geometric patterns permitted under Islamic law. The room bespoke the Assans' wealth and position, and on past visits Liz had loved its beauty. Today all she saw was Dr. Assan, his handsome face etched with grief. Though the official Islamic mourning period was the three days after a death, the

Assans would be in mourning for the rest of their lives.

Dr. Assan escorted them to the courtyard, where a fountain played and the sweet fragrance of jasmine and orange trees scented the air. He offered them coffee and tea and struggled to have a conversation, intent on showing them the Arab hospitality that was a legacy of the wandering Bedu.

Liz found it painful to look at him, this man with a broken heart. He had been so proud of Khalil.

"I cannot tell you how sorry we are about Khalil," Annabelle said, her eyes filling with tears. "He was a wonderful man."

Dr. Assan nodded. "I have been thinking that life is indeed strange. During the civil war I worried so about my sons. When we decided to stay in South Lebanon while so many others were emigrating, I moved the boys and Rena to our vacation home in the Lebanon Mountains to preserve their lives. I hired bodyguards who wouldn't let Khalil or Bashir go anywhere alone. I hired tutors to teach the boys, to prepare them for university. I did everything to keep them safe."

He paused, swallowed. "Of course, as a doctor I had to remain here in Beirut to help care for the thousands wounded in the terrible fighting. I had to put myself in danger, but not my sons. Never my sons…".

His voice trailed off, and they sat quietly. Liz tried to imagine what it was like to keep your children safe during the war only to lose one in peacetime through the act of a terrorist.

She looked up and found Bashir Assan, Khalil's older brother, had come into the courtyard. Liz had tried to like Bashir for Julie's sake. He was, after all, her sister's brother-in-law. He was handsome with dark hair and eyes and had a body stronger and stockier than the lean, elegant Khalil. He prided himself on charming the ladies, but Liz thought his eyes were calculating, cold.

He was a newspaper reporter and columnist. "Just like you,

Liz," everyone said, as if this would give the two of them grounds for a fine friendship. It wasn't going to happen.

Bashir was an anomaly, the son of privilege who stood for everything his parents abhorred. He was very anti-American, very pro-Palestinian. Those positions didn't bother Liz because Charles and Annabelle held similar views. What bothered Liz was his involvement with the radical activists who plagued the Middle East. Even her liberal father spoke out against them.

"I admire them for their commitment to their cause," Bashir had told her once. "But they are only sources to me."

Did he admire them enough to help them plan a suicide bombing?

Many considered Hezbollah and the strident and suicidal Palestinians of the Intifada to be heroes, resistance fighters committed to keeping Israel within its own borders and who purposed to one day eradicate that country. She didn't view the radicals in such a fine light in spite of Hezbollah's recent attempts to improve its image by starting schools, building hospitals, and working within the country's political structure. There were even Hezbollah party members seated in Parliament, especially from south Lebanon.

Frankly, all the extreme militants scared and confused Liz. She couldn't comprehend killing yourself and many, many innocent people in the name of your god. It was so antithetical to the biblical call to love your enemies and forgive those who offend. Christianity was about healing rifts and strife, while these Islamic extremists seemed intent on not merely continuing centuries-old vendettas but deepening the divisions and animosity. Their faith was about hatred, not reconciliation.

Not that Christians had always represented themselves well in this part of the world. "What about the Crusades?" That was the question people always threw at her whenever she voiced her abhorrence of vindictive religious warriors.

All she could say was that in their zeal, the Crusaders were often as misguided as the suicide bombers, even though their goal was to keep Europe free from Islam, which already had a foothold in Spain.

"Elizabeth," Bashir said, and Liz realized he was greeting her. She smiled at him and managed, she hoped, to look friendly.

He turned to Charles. "Have you had any word about Julie?"

"Nothing," Charles said, a spasm of pain rippling across his face. "Not one word. I keep thinking today will be the day we'll hear, but each day passes with nothing." He shrugged, and Liz thought he looked too thin, all bones and angles. He'd lost weight over their ordeal.

"I am sorry for your pain." Bashir bowed his head, but Liz doubted he felt anything for any Fairchild except contempt. To him they were rich Americans trying to insinuate themselves into a country that didn't want them or need them.

"You haven't heard anything, have you?" Annabelle asked him.

Bashir blinked. "I beg your pardon?" The words were mildly spoken, but his eyes went hard.

Her mother became flustered. "I'm sorry. I just thought… I mean, I thought you had friends, contacts, sources."

"If I knew anything, I would tell the authorities," he said stiffly. "I know nothing of the bombing."

"Of course not. I–I don't know what I was thinking."

Charles reached out and patted Annabelle's hand. She grasped hold before he could pull away.

Bashir looked at Annabelle and at the clasped hands, no longer bothering to mask his dislike. "Khalil was killed, Mrs. Fairchild. Do you honestly think I would do anything to protect the people who murdered him? He and I might have disagreed in our methods for dealing with Jews and strengthening Lebanon, but he was my brother." His voice blazed with intensity.

Liz watched Bashir, fascinated. He truly was as devastated by Khalil's death as his father. While she still thought it quite possible that he had heard news about Julie from sources unavailable to the rest of them, she no longer wondered whether he'd had anything to do with the bombing. Things might have been strained between the brothers, but family was all to a Lebanese, even one who, like Bashir, had many suspect acquaintances.

Rena Assan appeared, looking as sleek and put together as always in her black dress, hose, and shoes, but she wore that shocked, vulnerable look Liz had seen before on the faces of surviving family and loved ones.

Dr. Assan rose and went to her, taking her arm and leading her to a chair. Her movements were slow and uncertain, and Liz knew she was on heavy tranquilizers.

After a few more awkward moments Charles rose. Annabelle and Liz jumped to their feet, too. The hasty farewells made Liz realize that her parents were as anxious to leave as she was.

Dr. Assan accompanied them to the door. "May you find Julie. May it please Allah to return her to you."

As she walked to the car with Annabelle and Charles, Liz knew that the Fairchilds would not see the Assans again except at Khalil's memorial service next week. The families had nothing in common except their children. If Julie was spared—*please, Lord, please*—the Assans' devastation at their loss while Julie survived would taint any contact. If Julie didn't come home, there would be no reason to seek each other out. Either way, Liz felt wretched.

"You two go ahead," she said when they reached the car. "I'm going to take a walk." To the hotel. The Assans' home was only a matter of blocks from the Corniche.

"Liz." Her mother rested a hand against Liz's cheek. "Don't do this to yourself."

Liz made believe she didn't understand. "I'm just taking a walk."

Annabelle smiled sadly. "Oh. Of course."

"You think you can find her, don't you?" Charles asked, his expression fierce. Liz flinched as she felt the sting of his anger, even though she knew the anger wasn't with her. Poor Charles. Where could he go for comfort?

"I *want* to find her. We all want to find her. Or have her found."

"Obviously. But for some reason you seem to think you can do what the U. S. Embassy and the Lebanese police can't."

Liz shook her head at his accusation, but deep inside, that was how she felt. Somehow, because of her love for Julie, she could find her where others couldn't. "I want a Big Mac." Comfort food. The words just popped out.

Charles opened the car door, ignoring her inappropriate comment. "Come on, Annabelle."

"I keep picturing her wandering around, lost, confused, in terrible pain," Annabelle said through a new rain of tears. She looked at the sky. "Oh, God, please keep her safe, wherever she is. And please let her be alive!"

Liz looked at her mother, moved by her fear and grief while cynical about the sudden calling on God for help. "Or maybe a Whopper."

"I'd gladly give my whole trust fund to get her back," Charles whispered.

Liz shuddered. "With a supersized shake."

"Liz!" Charles pointed at her. "Stop acting like an American!" With that ultimate insult, he slammed his door.

"Or maybe an extra crispy meal at Kentucky Fried Chicken."

Annabelle sighed. "At least that's better for you than the burger."

"I'm so scared for her, Annabelle. Why haven't we heard

anything? What is Captain Habib doing? Sitting on his hands? Why can't they find one blond woman?"

"Oh, sweetie, I wish I knew." She kissed Liz's cheek. "Just don't stay too long at that terrible place."

Blinking back tears, Liz walked to the Corniche, where she stood for a moment staring out at the two great monoliths that were Pigeon Rocks. Why had God dropped them here? It was like He was on His way to put the Lebanon and Anti-Lebanon ranges in place, and when He reached in His pocket to pull the mountains out, two emerged prematurely and fell into the sea, sort of like a pair of pennies falling from a man's trouser pocket. God liked them where they fell so much, giant stony anomalies rising from the blue waters, that He left them there, knowing people would enjoy them as He did.

She smiled to herself. A theologian would probably tell her such an idea was heresy, but she liked it. It gave God a sense of whimsy and joy, and today she needed all the whimsy and joy she could find.

She turned and walked north toward the tourist area and the hotels facing the Mediterranean. She offered her face to the breeze that seemed always to blow over the broad walk beside the sea. Maybe it would blow away some of her mental cobwebs and grief.

She passed the Riveria Hotel and came to what she now thought of as Julie's hotel. She crossed the busy Avenue du General de Gaulle that paralleled the Corniche. She got as close to the hotel as the yellow police tape allowed. Most of the evidence of the disaster was gone. By the end of the week, clean up should be finished. Too bad shattered lives didn't clean up so easily.

She looked up and down the street at the line of luxury hotels and the small businesses. Then she began her mission.

As she did every time she came here, she went to the various merchants, retailers, and servers at the boutiques, cafes, and souvenir stands, even to those sitting at the outdoor cafés enjoying a relaxing drink. To each she showed a picture of Julie.

"Did you see this young woman the night of the fire? No? Have you seen her since?"

The answer was always the same. "She is very beautiful. I would remember. No."

Today Liz approached an old man seated in a white molded plastic chair in an outdoor café two doors from the hotel. His arm was in a sling, and one cheek was black and green and a sickly yellow. His foot in a bright green cast was propped on another chair. A crutch leaned against the wall behind him.

Liz was sure she hadn't seen him before, and hope flared. If, as she suspected, he was one of the old men who sat in the cafés for hours each day, enjoying the sunshine, the coffee, and the people walking by, he might well have been here the evening of the explosion. That would account for his cast and the bruises.

Then again he might have had an auto accident or fallen down the steps.

"Malhaba." Hello. She smiled warmly.

The old man looked up at her and smiled back. At least he smiled until his cheek reminded him that it hurt to smile these days.

"I made it through the war without a scratch." His hand went to his bruised face. "Then I sit here in my chair to enjoy the summer night and boom!" His good hand flew up in the air. "I go to help, but the fire is too fierce. I've never seen anything like it. As I back away, I trip over something and go down."

He had been here! "Oh, I'm sorry." Liz pulled up a chair to sit with him. Her hand was shaking as she held out Julie's picture. "My sister was in the hotel when the bomb went off."

"Ah." He nodded. "She is dead. I am very sorry."

Liz shook her head. "We don't know that. We think she might have escaped."

The old man frowned. "Not many escaped. And wouldn't

you know by now? It has been two weeks."

"I think she was in a room away from the blast."

He gazed at the tower, his head tilting as he looked toward the top floors.

"No, not up there. I think she climbed out a window into that alley." Liz pointed to the opening between the hotel and the boutique next to it.

"Why do you think this?" His voice was gentle.

"I found her necklace there the next day."

The old man turned thoughtful. "So much was happening, you know."

Liz nodded as she put the picture in his hand. "This is Julie. She lives here in Beirut."

The old man reached into his pocket, pulled out a pair of bent spectacles, and slipped them on his nose. He peered at the photo, then looked at the alley. He turned back at the picture, running his finger slowly over Julie's blond hair.

"She is very beautiful."

"Yes." Liz wanted to shake him to make him hurry. "But did you see her?"

"Maybe."

"Maybe?" Hope exploded like brightly colored pyrotechnics lighting a night sky. She dropped to her knees beside him and looked at Julie with him. "What did you see that you think might have been her?"

"I was lying on the ground with my leg twisted and my head throbbing. I think when I fell, I hit my head and knocked myself out for a while. When I woke up, I realized my leg and arm were probably broken. Brittle bones, just one curse of old age. My glasses were missing, too. Lights were flashing and no one paid any attention to me. Everyone ran to the hotel."

He picked up a cup of some brown liquid and took a sip. "I come here every day." He took another swallow. "Since my wife died, I hate my house. I come here, and I watch the people." He held out his glasses, and Liz realized one lens was missing. "It is strange when I look through them now. I will have new ones next week."

"Good. That's good. But what about Julie?"

The old man put his hand over the eye where the lens was missing. "Ah."

Ah? What does ah *mean? Ah, this is better? Ah, I remember her?*

"You're lying on the ground. Your glasses are missing. What happened next?" Her voice shook with tension.

"I felt all around me, and I found the glasses under my shoulder. Even though one lens was gone, I put them on. They did not fit right anymore. That's when I think I saw a woman with this color hair come out of the alley. She was limping. Her dress was torn. I thought maybe she was a—" He cleared his throat. "But I guess she wasn't."

Liz frowned. A what? Then it hit her. The old man had thought Julie was a prostitute! Because she came out of the alley. Because her dress was torn. Because good women didn't limp around at night unescorted.

"No! No! Her husband was killed that night. She was married to a Lebanese man, a banker. And now she's disappeared."

"Ah, well, I think she sat on that big rock by the alley."

Liz looked where he pointed. It was the rock she'd sat on the day she found the locket.

"She sat there and stared at the fire. I lay a short distance behind her and stared, too. I needed a doctor, but not like the people in the hotel. So I waited. She waited. Then a man came up to her. He picked her up and carried her across the street to a car. Two of his friends followed them. It was good to see someone rescued."

He thought someone rescued Julie? But that made no sense. If she was rescued, they should already have her back.

"Who took her? Can you tell me what he looked like?"

The old man closed his eyes and frowned. "Remember I'm lying on the ground with one lens missing, there are people running and screaming, and it's dark."

Liz felt sick with disappointment.

"But I do remember one thing about one of the men."

Hope fizzed through her veins once again.

"He wore a black and white kaffiyeh. And the man who carried her put her into a black Mercedes. An old, very dirty Mercedes."

16

Somewhere in Lebanon

JULIE ASSAN LAY on her narrow bed in the windowless room little larger than a closet, feeling worse than she had ever felt in her life—and that was saying something.

If she lay on her back, her neck and spine throbbed unbearably. If she lay on her side, her shoulders and hips screamed. Her ankles had lost their flexibility, and her knuckles were hot and swollen like an old lady's. Even grasping the blanket to pull over herself hurt.

In short, she was a mess.

When she had first been brought here—wherever here was—she was fed some drug to keep her docile and pliant. She welcomed the soft, cushiony world rather than face the reality she sensed at the edges of her consciousness, ready to pounce like a lioness on a gazelle.

Her rheumatoid arthritis and its attendant pain had been masked, but nightmares plagued her, dark, soul-shattering dreams in which she was trapped in a burning room with no air and no escape or in which she managed to climb out a window only to fall and fall and fall.

Most distressing were the dreams about Khalil. In one he stood in front of her, dressed in morning coat and gray striped trousers, just like he wore at their wedding. Smiling, love lighting his eyes, he held out a single red rose. "An American Beauty for my American beauty."

She smiled back, happiness washing through her.

His smile twisted to a scowl, and the light in his eyes curdled to condemnation. He held not a rose but a scimitar and shouted, "Too much leg. Too much bosom."

Crying, she would wake to darkness and the bitter taste of abandonment.

He was dead. Every time that thought penetrated her haze, a great unbearable weight descended, crushing her chest and making it impossible to breathe. As if it wasn't devastating enough that Khalil was gone, even worse was the knowledge that they could never reconcile, never heal the rift that had separated them.

"I love you," she whispered in the dark, tears wetting her face. "I miss you."

She listened for his answer but never heard it. Instead, she tumbled into another terrifying nightmare.

Then she stopped drinking the coffee they sent each morning with Lebanese flat bread, and the drug haze cleared. While she welcomed the mental alertness, the more aware she became, the more she ached in heart and body. Now it hurt to move at all.

She eased up on her cot. Was it time for Karima to come again? Julie tried to determine how long since her caregiver's last visit, but she couldn't. Her mind was still too sleep-hazed, and the absence of windows kept morning and evening a secret.

She heard the key turn in the door and smiled. Her internal clock and her captors' schedule were meshing. Painfully she swung her legs over the side of the cot. She grabbed the kerchief lying on the floor by the bed and with stiff fingers tied it over her head. Being in the custody of strict Muslims meant she must dress in a long, loose dress and cover her head with the scarf. At least they weren't making her wear a veil.

She wondered what had happened to the clothes she had been wearing the night of the fire. Not that it mattered much. They were undoubtedly ruined beyond repair. It was her pendant she mourned. Annabelle would just have to paint her another when she got home.

The door opened fully, and Karima appeared, tray in hand. She walked to Julie and held it out.

Julie didn't have to look to know what it contained. She had been given *khobez* and *hummos* at every meal for the two weeks she'd been held. She'd always liked the flat bread, and she used to enjoy hummos, but now she'd be happy if she never ate another mashed chick pea in her life. Twice she had been given *kibbe,* and the lamb dish tasted wonderful.

Julie took the tray Karima offered in her swollen fingers, more dropping it than lowering it to her lap.

"Sit." She patted the cot beside her and smiled at Karima.

The young woman had cared for her since the first day, bringing her food, helping her walk to the chamber pot, even lowering her and helping her rise as the RA made it impossible for her to manage by herself. And wonder of wonders, twice Karima had managed to get hold of aspirin for her to help dull the constant aching.

Julie patted the cot again. She'd invited Karima to sit several times before, but always the young woman had taken one look at the guard, standing in the open door, and hurried away. Today there was no guard.

Still Karima looked toward the door, her face uncertain.

"Men fadlik," Julie said in Arabic. "I'm very lonely."

Karima gathered her voluminous black skirts close and perched on the edge of the cot as far from Julie as she could get. She had a black scarf tied over her head, covering all of her hair, and dusty sandals peered out below her hem.

Julie tore off a piece of khobez. She scooped some hummos on it and took a bite. "Did you know that a Mexican tortilla is something like khobez but thinner? So is an American pancake or a French crepe or pita bread."

Karima didn't respond, but Julie thought she was leaning just a bit toward her, like she was interested in spite of herself.

Julie held out her coffee mug. "Did you know that they drink a lot of coffee in America? I know because I went to college there. Then I went to college in England. They drink mostly tea there."

Karima looked at the mug, then at Julie. "I don't know much about England, but I see much about America." Her voice was scornful.

Julie could just imagine. "You mustn't believe all you see. America is a wonderful country, especially for women. We have many freedoms there."

"Indecency," Karima spat. "Immorality. Exhibitionism."

Julie nodded. "Sadly, some of that is true, but most American women aren't like that, Karima. Most are wonderful people who are kind to their families and friends. They work hard and are good citizens. My sister, Liz, lives in a place called Philadelphia where she writes for a newspaper."

"But you live in Lebanon now." Karima said it as if Julie had come to her senses even if Liz hadn't.

"Yes, in Beirut. I'm married to a Lebanese." As the truth struck once again, Julie closed her eyes against the knife thrust. "Or I was."

Karima's face clouded as she looked at Julie. "I-I am a widow, too."

Astonished at the confidence, Julie reached out and laid her hand over the young woman's. "Oh, Karima, I'm so sorry."

Karima lowered her head and nodded.

When the girl said no more, Julie asked softly, "What happened?"

"Rashid was a freedom fighter."

That said it all.

The room fell silent, but the tension between her and Karima had greatly lessened by the acknowledgment of the common bond of widowhood.

"Tell me more about Rashid," Julie coaxed.

Karima didn't need much encouragement. "I fell in love with him when I was fifteen and he sixteen. He was so handsome and strong. He was a good friend of my brother Sami, and he was at our house often. My sister said she couldn't decide whether he came to see Sami or me."

Julie studied Karima. It was difficult to guess her age exactly, but she didn't look all that much older than fifteen now.

"One night Rashid and Sami went with others on a raid against the Israelis, and Rashid was captured. He spent five years in an Israeli prison. I thought my heart would break. I was terrified I would never see him again."

"But you did."

Karima nodded. "When he returned, he was hardened in his resolve and his commitment to our cause. Israel must go. We must have our land back."

Julie sighed inwardly. It was more than fifty-five years since the War of Independence and the establishment of the nation of Israel. The Jews weren't going anywhere. All the world except the extremist Palestinians seemed to understand this.

"When Rashid came home, we married. I was so happy. Then one night he went on another raid. They brought his body back to me, and we buried him in the clothes he wore, like we bury our martyrs."

"Oh, Karima, I'm so sorry."

"Allah ak'bar."

Right. "How long were you married?"

"Two months."

Two short months! Julie's heart shuddered at the girl's loss.

But Karima didn't want sympathy. "I am very proud of Rashid. He sought to regain our homeland and was a brave, bold fighter."

The two women sat in silence for a time. Julie finished off the hummos and held out her water bottle to Karima, who took the bottle and with a brisk, casual flick of the hand loosened the cap.

Julie sighed. Such dexterity! It was all she could do to hold the bottle when Karima handed it back. She allowed herself five swallows, let Karima cap it, then carefully bent to set it on the floor beside the cot. Pulling herself upright again was harder by far than the bending down.

She blinked back tears, uncertain whether they were tears of pain or fear.

Lord, I hate the chronic aching. And I resent my captivity.

A tall, thin man she'd never seen before strode in. He wore olive drab, the sleeves rolled up, the legs tucked into high boots. Even though she didn't know who he was, she knew he was the leader of whatever was going on because of his air of authority. He frowned fiercely at her.

Was he the one who had taken her? The one who was holding her? "Why?" she wanted to ask, but one look at the harsh set of his features dried her mouth. She tried to look unafraid, knowing instinctively he wanted her to quake with dread.

Immediately behind him came two men wearing black ski masks and carrying wicked-looking assault rifles.

One glimpse of the ski masks and the leader got his wish as far as she was concerned. Terror struck deep, making her light-headed.

Lord, how can this be? Help me!

The two masked men rushed at her and grabbed her roughly,

each seizing an arm. They pulled her from the bed and dragged her toward the door. She screamed with fear and pain.

They paid no heed to her cries, not that she thought they would.

Lord, this is it, isn't it? The end. Help me be brave.

She thought of how shallow her faith had been, how cavalier she'd been toward God. Right from the beginning she told Him how much of herself she'd give Him. Then she knowingly disobeyed His Word when she married Khalil. What right did she have to ask God for anything? But plead she did.

Please, Lord, don't let it hurt too much!

She shut her mind to all the terrible things the news carried about the fate of hostages like her. As the men half-carried, half-dragged her from the room, a wisp of thought carved its way through the wall of fear.

I will never leave you or forsake you.

They dragged her down a dark hallway to a dingy room whose walls had once been pastel blue.

Set into one wall was a large window, and the bright light pouring in made her squint and turn her head away. She hadn't seen or felt the sun for so very long. Being careful to keep her eyes closed against the glare, she turned her face to the light, letting the warmth wash over her.

"Over there," the leader barked.

The men turned her from the sun and pulled her across the room. The agony in her shoulder joints brought tears. She stared at the black banner hung on the wall opposite the window. On it was painted a verse from the Koran. *"Slay the infidels."*

That's me. I'm an infidel.

She shuddered.

I will never leave you or forsake you.

The masked men pushed down on her shoulders, forcing her to kneel in front of the banner.

Lord, it hurts so much to kneel! Her stomach reacted and forced her to swallow repeatedly.

I will never leave you or forsake you.

With rough hands the men bound her wrists tightly behind her. The angry man in olive drab strode to the door and barked commands, something about a camera.

Did they know she spoke Arabic? She watched a young man no more than twelve or fourteen enter the room, carrying a tripod and small video camera. He wore the black and white kaffiyeh.

Oh, Lord, ski masks and video cameras. Help!

I will never leave you or forsake you.

The boy erected the tripod in front of the window and fixed the camera atop it. Then he pulled a length of black cloth from a back pocket and passed it to one of the masked men standing behind her. For one second, Julie thought she saw pity in the boy's eyes as he glanced at her before turning back to his camera.

Another man strode into the room as the kidnapper wrapped the blindfold around Julie's head. In the split second before her vision was blocked, she saw the object in the newcomer's hand, and at the sight of it, a stifled cry escaped her lips.

Oh, God, no!

A scimitar!

H-5 Airbase Near Safawi, Jordan.

The C-17 Globemaster III touched down just before dawn, exactly eleven hours after it had gone wheels-up from Pope Air Force Base at Fort Bragg. It taxied to the far end of the runway and stopped. Officially, both the United States and the government of Jordan denied that any American troops were stationed on Jordanian soil, but there had been an unofficial American presence here for years. It now numbered more than six thousand troops. Australian and British forces were also here, as well as personnel from nearly every alphabet-soup government agency in the United States.

Doc Kelly had made a planeload of friends by passing around a bottle of Ambien pills when they took off. The prescription sleep aid was powerful stuff, so John felt as if only an hour or two had passed by the time the tailgate of the hulking aircraft broke open with a hydraulic whine to reveal a collection of hangars on the edge of the tarmac. Some of the buildings were new since 2003, the last time John visited the airfield, also known as Prince Hassan Air Base.

John shouldered his Black Hawk pack and trudged down the ramp onto the tarmac. The temperature was downright chilly. Even in the dark, he could see the miles of nothing but sand surrounding the airfield, dotted intermittently with ankle-high scrub brush. *Hell's parking lot. Welcome back.*

Doc stepped off the plane behind him and inhaled deeply. "Ahhhhhh. I just love the desert. I should buy property here."

John stared at him. "There's lots of it, and you're welcome to it all."

"Yeah, sometimes I think this is where God stores extra dirt until it's needed elsewhere."

John just grunted.

Frank Baldwin walked by in a half daze. "Coffee. I need copious amounts of coffee."

Doc Kelly watched Frank shuffle past. "Note to self. Keep the Ambien away from Sergeant Baldwin."

Major Williams approached the aircraft from the direction of the hangar. John met him halfway. "What's the word, sir?"

Williams pointed back toward the clamshell-shaped aircraft hangar. "We're sleeping in there. Cots are already set up. Not the Ritz Carlton, but you won't be here long. Go get the guys situated, and then get them some chow, which is in that big tent next to the hangar. We can park our vehicles just outside." He glanced at his watch. "It's 0300 hours. The Op order will be at 0700 in the mess tent."

John nodded and set out for the clamshell. "I'm on it."

Four hours later Major Williams raised a hand for silence and got it. "Bring it over here, gentlemen, and listen up."

Task Force Valor quickly found seats on the cots nearest the regional map clipped to a line of parachute cord, hastily strung up clothesline-style behind the major. Until that moment, many of the eighteen men present had been arranging their gear or lounging on aluminum cots spread out along one wall of the hangar.

The team's armorer had set up a television and DVD player to which Rip Rubio had connected his Xbox. He was battling Bobby Sweeney on the latest version of *Halo*. When the major signaled for quiet, they quickly stowed the unit and turned their attention to the briefing. A flash came from Williams's left, and he turned to see Rip with his digital camera, grinning.

"Put that thing away, Rubio! You know that's unauthorized!"

John stifled a grin of his own. Rip was a confirmed gadgeteer. He probably spent a fourth of his paycheck on electronic toys.

"Okay. Here's the rundown," the major began. "Situation: Two weeks ago someone set off an IED inside the Hotel Rowena along the seawalk in Beirut, right in the middle of a World Bank dog-and-pony show. Huge fire. Scores dead. Among the bodies were several Americans, mostly banker types, a couple of wives, an Israeli general, and one state department bureaucrat, to say nothing of finance ministers and influential businessmen from around the world.

"The Lebanese government was on the phone to our embassy asking for our help before the fire was out. They are highly motivated to take decisive action on this one, because until things began heating up recently, tourism in Lebanon had rebounded to the highest point since the early 1970s. Tourism is this country's oil, and they have spent tens of billions of dollars trying to rebuild the industry since the war ended in the early nineties."

John shifted on his cot. The long flight had made him stiff, and he was starting to feel the injuries again.

"Our government also wants this thing resolved," Williams continued. "The State Department scrambled an FBI Rapid Deployment Evidence Recovery Team to sift through the aftermath and try to get a lead on who tossed the bomb. They haven't pinned it on anyone yet, though the Lebanese have some ideas. So far, nobody has claimed responsibility, an interesting fact in and of itself."

The men grunted agreement. They were all too familiar with the lunatics who thought violence against innocents was a badge of honor.

"The FBI zoomies did find something interesting, though. It appears by the residue at the scene that the explosive used was something they've never seen in a terrorist bombing before—a liquid chemical explosive, something called Iso-Triethyl Borane or ITEB."

Williams picked up a sheaf of papers and passed them around the group. "I have here an information sheet on the compound itself. Apparently the stuff resembles water, but it's highly reactive with oxygen. It isn't difficult to acquire, but distilling it down to a level where it becomes a potent explosive and then delivering it in that form would require a sophisticated, high-tech lab. For that reason, the FBI guys believe this attack had to have been coordinated by, or at least supported by, a well-funded, well-connected organization or even possibly a government."

Hogan and Sweeney looked at each other and said simultaneously, "Hezbollah."

Williams shrugged. "We're not going to rule anyone out just yet. But Lebanese Intelligence has other ideas."

As John saw things, Hezbollah would be the logical suspect except for one thing. They were trying to establish themselves as a legitimate faction of Lebanese politics, not terrorists. And with the pullout of Syria and the recent election results, they were poised to do just that. That they would plot such a disaster in Beirut seemed counterproductive to the image they were attempting to create. Now if the blast had been in Israel, it would be different, but Beirut? John didn't think so.

"Anyway, the CIA wants to track down whoever is making this stuff and put them out of business." The major looked at them grimly. "They have requested our assistance in accomplishing this mission, and SOCOM has agreed to task us to them for as long as is necessary."

John's head jerked up. *Did he just say task us to the CIA?* A low murmur rippled through the assembly, and Rip almost dropped his camera.

Williams raised both hands. "You heard me right. You all just became CIA assets. Welcome to Spookville. You will remain attached to them for the foreseeable future. Buckle up, men. This is going to be a bumpy ride."

Frank raised his hand. "Pardon me, sir, but wouldn't that require the personal signature of—"

"The President himself. Yes." The major smiled tightly. "And those of about eight other high-ranking government officials. Washington is highly motivated to nip this in the bud before ITEB starts showing up in water bottles at gas stations in Kansas. If whoever is making this new explosive is allowed to distribute their product around the world, it will wreak havoc. Understand, our present airport technology is unable to detect ITEB. That means anyone could walk on a plane with a bottle of this stuff in his backpack and bring the plane down by simply opening the bottle."

He's not kidding. This is *a big deal!* John shuddered at the mental images that scenario unleashed.

The major continued, "It would cost billions of dollars to

make the world's airports safe again, and who knows how many lives would be lost before that was accomplished. We must find whoever is making and distributing the explosive and give them a terminal case of lead poisoning right fast. In order to do that, we'll have to do things a bit differently than we're used to. And on that note," he put down his clipboard and motioned to the back of the group, "let me introduce you to your new CIA contact, who will continue your briefing."

Heads and eyes turned in unison toward the slender, red-haired woman with a low-slung handgun holstered on her right leg. She strode confidently to the front of the group. The murmuring started again.

John blinked. *Holy smokes. It's Laura Croft! Straight out of* Tomb Raider.

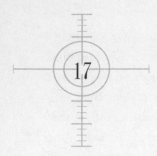

17

Beirut

AS LIZ HURRIED HOME, she thought of Yasser Arafat and the black and white head scarf he had always worn. A black and white kaffiyeh meant Palestinian, just like the red and white one meant Jordanian. She couldn't wait to tell her parents all she'd learned.

"Annabelle! Charles!" She ran from room to room until she found them sitting in the courtyard having pre-dinner drinks. "I found someone who saw Julie after the fire!" She told them about the old man's comments, her voice shaking with excitement. "So we know she's alive!"

"Oh, Liz!" Annabelle began to cry.

Charles seemed unimpressed. He remained cool, his drink held elegantly in his right hand. "Easy, Annabelle. *Probably* alive. And we already agreed with Liz on that point when she found the locket."

Liz would never understand her father. He should be jumping for joy at the new information, grabbing the phone and calling Captain Habib. "But we had no idea what had happened to her before. Now we know. She was kidnapped! We have an eyewitness who saw her being taken by three Palestinians."

Charles held up a cautionary finger. "Three shebab. Isn't that what you originally said? Only one wore a Palestinian kaffiyeh. Maybe he was a Palestinian fighter. Maybe they all were. Maybe they were representatives of their jihad come to watch a triumph. Then again maybe they were tourists, one of whom had bought a kaffiyeh as a souvenir."

"Charles!" Liz scowled at him. "Why would tourists take Julie?"

He waved that very logical question aside. "I'll call Timon Habib and tell him what you learned." He pulled his cell phone from his pocket. "But until we have more information or specific names, what can he do? The Army isn't going to attack the camps and search."

Liz sat on the edge of the chair next to her mother. The two clasped hands as Charles dialed.

"Captain Timon Habib, please." Charles listened, then frowned. "But I have critical information for him about the Rowena fire." The frown deepened. "I don't want to leave a message. I want to speak with Captain Habib. This is Dr. Charles Fairchild."

Two minutes later, after leaving a message, Charles flipped his phone shut with more force than necessary. "He'll call me tomorrow. He cannot be disturbed at the moment."

Liz's spirits lifted at her father's pique. He was more moved by her information than he was willing to admit. "Do you think the authorities are really working to solve this crime?"

"Of course they are. I have every confidence in them." Charles stood and held out a hand for Annabelle.

"Would they tell us if they found anything?"

"I'm sure they would." He laid Annabelle's hand on his arm and started for the door. "We must go. The Gardners are waiting for us."

Well, I'm not as confident as you are, Liz thought as she watched her parents leave for dinner at a restaurant in Parliament Square. As far as she knew, *she* had found the only pieces of information about Julie, not the police.

Well, she'd just continue on her own, though she wasn't sure what the next step should be. She couldn't wander through every Palestinian camp showing Julie's picture any more than the Army could.

She sighed. Maybe her father was right. The old man's testimony was a useless clue, and her determination to find Julie was foolish.

Lord, please! You said You'd give wisdom if we asked. I'm asking. No, I'm pleading!

Before she climbed into bed, she wrote pages in her journal, rehearsing the whole situation. *Dear Lord,* she concluded, *I'm disappointed that You've let this happen to us, to Julie. I know You are God, and You can do anything, but You also promised that everything would work for good. So where's the good? I feel like You've let me down.*

She took a deep breath, then wrote, *I don't want to make You angry, but You could make me feel a lot better by letting Julie be found.*

What she really wanted to write was that God could redeem Himself in her eyes by getting Julie found, but she didn't have the nerve to actually write such a disrespectful thing. And that was stupid because God knew exactly what she was thinking.

She slept poorly, tossing, praying, and crying. When she climbed out of bed at dawn, she had a massive headache and an aching heart. When she came down to breakfast, it was not yet seven o'clock.

Nabila looked up from her place at the sink, surprised. "Liz, it is early for you."

Liz slumped into a chair at the kitchen table. "Bad night."

"I am sorry. I know this is a very hard time."

Nabila's English was precise and quite good. When she had come to Beirut from her home in the Sainiq refugee camp near Sidon several years ago, she knew little English. When she was first hired, the family spoke Arabic with her. Then one day she asked that they speak only English to her so she could become fluent.

When they were in high school, Liz and Julie had been fascinated by Nabila.

"You can never go home?" they asked again and again, having a hard time believing such a thing.

"No," she assured them again and again. "Never."

"You're very brave, Nabila," the sisters told her.

She shrugged. "You came here all the way from the United States. I came less than half a day's journey."

"For you Beirut was many times farther than the United States," Liz said solemnly.

"What made you decide to leave?" Liz asked one afternoon as she and Julie sat in the kitchen after school eating some wonderful baklava Nabila had made.

"An American Red Cross woman doctor came to our camp when measles swept it. She was amazing." Nabila smiled at the memory. "She was educated and trained to help and full of love, not hate. I wanted to be like her. All the other women in my family thought it was scandalous that she was wandering the world alone, uncovered. I thought it was the most wonderful thing I could imagine. From then on, I watched and read everything medical or American I could." She giggled. "I wanted to be an American woman doctor." Her giggle turned into a self-deprecating smile. "I finally decided I would settle for being an Arab woman doctor."

"Your father didn't want this for you?" Liz knew Charles would support her or Julie if that's what either of them decided to become. Not that she would. Science—uhn-uhn!

"My father is very fundamental and rigid," Nabila said. Though she was only four or five years older than Liz, she seemed so mature and adult. "He is bound by the extreme vision of Islam. Women are nothing but slaves. They are not even to be seen, much less educated. My choices were to marry someone he approved, live the life of servitude my mother and aunts lived, or run away. I knew my soul would wither and die if I stayed. I slipped away one day when we were in Sidon. I was wandering the campus at AUB, panicky and wondering how I would ever get the money to eat, let alone study there when I met your father."

"And he hired you to be our housekeeper." Liz enjoyed that part of the story. She was proud of her father for offering help to Nabila.

"And after he caught me up on my studies, Dr. Fairchild got me into university. I might only take one or two courses a semester, but I will get my degree, and I will become a doctor."

"Your father will certainly be proud of you then," Julie said.

Nabila shook her head. "My father will never soften. It would mean admitting that I, a girl child, made a good choice even though it was in defiance of him. I dishonored and embarrassed him. And as if leaving wasn't enough, I work for Americans, and I go to university. I fear he would kill me."

The young Liz and Julie were horrified. Charles might be an unconventional father, but he would die before he hurt them.

Even today, years later, Nabila was still afraid, maybe even more so, of the idea of going home. Zahra's murder had only deepened her apprehension.

Now, the morning after the old man told of Julie's abduction, Liz poured herself a cup of coffee and looked at the woman she so respected. "Nabila, I need your help."

Her friend didn't appear surprised. She nodded her head. "I don't know how you found out, but—"

"It wasn't easy. It's our first clue."

"Yes, it is. And it is a wonderful clue!"

Liz frowned. She wasn't sure *wonderful* was the right word.

Maybe *better-than-nothing*, but not *wonderful*. Charles had killed *wonderful*. "How do you know about the old man?"

"What old man?"

"The one who gave me the clue."

Nabila shook her head. "What clue? I am talking about Hanan's latest letter."

"What letter?"

"The letter that was delivered yesterday. I found it waiting for me when I got home late last night." She held out a much crinkled paper filled with Arabic script.

Liz took the missive and began to read. Several phrases leaped out at her. A Western woman. A blond woman who is sick. A hostage. A secure warehouse in the center of the camp.

Julie!

H-5 Airbase, Jordan

"Good morning," the redhead began, studiously ignoring the surprised looks she was receiving from the men of Task Force Valor. "I'm Mary Walker. My call sign is Phoenix. I run CIA ops here at H-5. I'll be your liaison for the foreseeable future. You all have top secret security clearances, so I shouldn't have to remind you that everything about this mission from now on is highly classified."

As she said it, she walked over to Rip, bent, and looked him in the eye as she took his camera from him.

"Hey!" Rip protested.

Mary deftly removed the memory card, then handed the camera back to the grumbling Rubio.

Sweeney stared at John intently, a "you've got to be kidding me" look on his face. John shrugged. He was as dumbfounded as everyone else.

Major Williams stood next to him, surveying the group with a grin on his face. He was enjoying his men's reactions way too much.

Mary wore tan desert camo pants with an olive drab polo shirt. Her chin-length haircut made her facial features starker than they might have been otherwise, and she had a swimmer's build. She was attractive even though she wore very little makeup. It was probably more the way she carried herself. The woman exuded competence.

John leaned over and whispered to Williams, "Is this for real?"

"You bet your boots it is."

"She won't be going with us on missions, will she?"

The major chuckled. "We'll see. I wouldn't worry about it, though. Word has it she's a former women's featherweight kickboxing champion."

John cocked an eyebrow at his commander, then turned back to the briefing.

Mary continued. "The Lebanese intelligence service suspects a terrorist group headquartered in Lebanon. Here." She pointed to the map, her finger coming to rest on an area east of Sidon and north of Nabatiya.

"The group calls itself Ansar Inshallah, or the 'Followers of God's Will.' They've been around since the early 1990s and have really begun to make a nuisance of themselves lately, assassinating a Muslim cleric and a Lebanese federal judge in the last month and a half. Ansar Inshallah affiliates itself with Bin Laden's stated objective of ridding the Muslim world of Western influences. It also wants to overthrow the Lebanese government."

Ansar Inshallah. John shook his head as he noted the name on his pad. This was a new group to him, and he thought he knew them all.

"The group is comprised of angry Palestinian men, mostly young, and their primary bases of operations are the Sabra and Sainiq refugee camps near Sidon, here and here." Mary pulled a pencil from behind her ear and jabbed at the map with it.

"Lebanese intel says that the hotel bomber lived in the Sabra camp."

She flipped the page on the easel pad, exposing a street map with a building highlighted on it. "They've acquired information from an informant that the group has a warehouse here, inside the Sainiq camp, where it's believed they are stockpiling weapons and explosives for future mayhem. We want you to go in and see if any of the goodies they have stored here happen to be ITEB."

Rip Rubio raised a hand. "Excuse me, ma'am."

"Phoenix."

"I'm sorry?"

"Call me Phoenix."

"Yes, ma'am."

"Phoenix."

Snickers rippled through the ranks. Rip looked flustered. "Right, Phoenix. Sorry. Anyway, so how do we get in to look at this place? I can't imagine the Lebanese government wants an American military unit tromping around its country, not to mention the fact that the warehouse sits in the center of a refugee camp where there are umpteen thousand Palestinians who will most certainly object to our presence."

She nodded. "That is correct. But the plan is for you to be in and out before the Palestinians know what happened."

Sweeney crossed his arms. "And if we're not?"

"You will be."

John liked this mission less and less all the time.

"As for the Lebanese government wanting us there, officially, they don't. Unofficially, a Lebanese military transport plane will be here at 2200 tonight to pick you boys up. The bureaucrats in Beirut feel like they have neither the political capital to poke Ansar Inshallah in the eye, nor the technical expertise to know what they were looking at if they did find something. Besides, they figure that inviting us in under the radar will help them look good to the U.S. and the U.N. They certainly want to at least *look* tough on terror."

Mary stepped to the side, and Major Williams took the floor again. He flipped another page on the easel pad. "Okay, we don't have much time to prepare. So here's the mission: John, I'm going to split the detachment for this one. You will take Baldwin, Rubio, Sweeney, Hogan, and Doc Kelly into Beirut and meet up with a Lebanese Intelligence Service operative who is on the CIA's payroll. The operative's job is to serve as your guide and infiltrate you six into the camp so you can take down the warehouse. You'll be traveling in civilian clothes."

John nodded. *Just the guys I would have chosen.* That said something about what they were likely up against.

Sweeney, looking pleased to be part of the mission, said, "So what kind of security will we encounter once we reach this place?"

Williams consulted his clipboard. "Getting inside the camp will be the trickiest part. It's kind of like a gated community. It might be exclusive, but not in the way you're used to thinking. Checkpoints at each entrance are manned by Lebanese soldiers. It would be tough to get in that way without the residents knowing about it, so you'll have to find another way. Your contact will help you with that.

"Once you reach the warehouse, intel says only one man works the night shift guarding the building. I'd lay odds he'll be asleep when you arrive. As long as you're able to neutralize him without raising the alarm, you should have a good thirty to forty minutes on the objective before anyone realizes something's wrong." He grinned at the men. "Of course, I don't expect you'll need anywhere near that much time."

John agreed. Hit and Git.

"Coop, you'll decide with the Lebanese operative the exact time to hit the building, but I'm thinking sometime late tomorrow night should give you enough time to prepare."

"Sounds good to me, sir." John glanced at his men who all looked happy as squirrels in a bird feeder at the opportunity before them.

Williams glanced at his clipboard again. "If, during your search, you find any signs of ITEB or other terrorist activity, you are to secure a sample if possible and then emplace demolitions on a time delay. Then remove yourselves to this soccer field, two blocks north."

He referred again to the map. "The mission will be timed so your choppers will be inbound as soon as you initiate the raid, so the exfil should go very quickly. A CSAR bird will be on station as backup in case anything goes wrong."

Williams put down his clipboard and gave the team a sober look. "I don't need to tell you that this is unlike any mission we've done before. This isn't like Iraq or Afghanistan. Becoming an operational element of the CIA is bound to have its...er..." he threw Mary a sideways glance, "challenges. So stay flexible. I can't stress enough how politically sensitive this is. The Lebanese government is about as schizophrenic as they come.

"It's a confessional government, meaning that the major offices are held by those who confess a certain religion. The president is by constitution a Maronite Christian, the premier is a Sunni Muslim, and the speaker of the legislature is a Shi'a Muslim. This balance has worked for many years, but it's precarious, especially as the Muslim population grows. In addition, the area around Sidon is still boiling over the assassination of Rafik Hariri."

Doc Kelly grinned. "And you thought the Democrats and the Republicans couldn't agree on anything!"

What a nightmare, John thought. *That would be like having Pat Robertson as President, Hillary Clinton as vice president, and Louis Farrakhan as the Speaker of the House. Yikes.*

How strange that religion determined what office you could

hold. But perhaps it was a way for a very divided country to bring itself together. Well, whatever works.

"The Lebanese want this case solved," the major said. "And they want the perpetrators punished. However—and it's a big however—none of the political factions in the country want to hang any body parts out there that could get lopped off, if you know what I mean."

John shook his head. "Politicians." They were the same everywhere, always protecting their backs, their positions. His aversion to all things political had been one major reason why he'd refused to apply to West Point. He didn't want to play the politics it took to be considered a good officer or to be considered for promotion.

Here in the Special Forces, they were constantly on a real-world footing, and John had learned that when things got hot, the stupid stuff went away. Everyone worked for the good of the team, the good of the mission. He liked that feeling—the do-whatever-it-takes-to-get-the-job-done feeling. Truth be told, he thrived on it.

"You know where the word *politics* comes from, don't you?" Doc Kelly said, still grinning as if they were sitting at a dinner party instead of a mission brief. "It's from two root words, *poly* meaning 'many' and *ticks* meaning 'blood sucking insects.'"

A collective groan arose from the assembled team, and Kelly broke into a loud guffaw even as several hats, wads of crumpled paper, and an empty bottle of Gatorade came flying at him.

The major cleared his throat, and they all turned back to him. "The rest of the team will stay here at H-5 and be prepared to assist if things go badly. John, take your guys over to Phoenix's office, and she'll set you up with a cover story that will get you by for the next thirty-six hours or so. For support, we have three Night Stalker Black Hawks tasked to us, and an unmanned aerial vehicle will be on call."

Hogan raised a hand as if he were still in high school. "What about communications?" The Texan's voice dripped like slow molasses.

"We'll stay in contact by SAT phone as a primary before the mission. Once we go tactical, we'll use the SATCOM radio you will carry with you. Any more questions?"

When there were none, John shut the pad he'd been taking notes in and stood stiffly. The travel was catching up with him. A run would do him good at the moment, but he'd gladly take a strong cup of Turkish coffee instead.

He'd been looking forward to some since they left Fort Bragg. He'd gotten hooked on the cardamom-laced brew on his last trip to H-5. The Arabs had been perfecting the stuff for millennia, and Starbucks had nothing on them.

Unfortunately, the only place that served Turkish coffee was on the other side of the base, so right now he'd have to settle for whatever the chow hall had available, which undoubtedly would taste like lukewarm canteen water with a brown crayon dipped in it, but at least it would have caffeine.

He still had a hard time getting his head around the surprise of having his unit commandeered by the CIA. Civilian clothes? In sixth grade, his teacher had asked him what he wanted to be when he grew up. At the time, he'd been watching all the old 007 movies, so he answered, "James Bond." *Well, John, here's your chance!*

Joking aside, John knew this mission would be different from anything they'd ever done before. But in Explosive Ordnance Disposal, there was no such thing as a routine day. You learned to roll with it, or the job would drive you nuts.

He looked around at his team. Frank, Rip, Buzz, Sweeney, Doc. These men were the brothers he'd always wanted.

What if one of us doesn't come back from this one?

No. I can't go there. I won't go there.

He stowed his notepad and went to find Phoenix.

18

Beirut

THE PHONE RANG as Liz finished reading Hanan's letter.

"Turn on your TV," ordered Bashir Assan without preamble. His voice shook slightly, a fact that terrified her. "But be warned. It's bad. Try to prepare your parents."

But nothing could ever prepare them for the horrific scene being played out before their eyes.

A ski-masked man was reading a proclamation with a blind-folded blond woman kneeling at his feet. A barbaric-looking knife was thrust in his belt.

Julie!

Annabelle made a keening noise as tears poured down her cheeks. Charles seemed frozen.

"Seventy-two hours," the voiceover declared. "All Ansar Inshallah prisoners must be freed."

When the picture changed to an in-studio announcer making comments on the tape delivered to the studio by an unknown person or persons just moments ago, Liz stopped listening

The three-day time frame screamed at her. Seventy-two hours, but seventy-two hours from when? When the tape was first played on the air? When it was made? And did anyone know when that was?

The commentator caught her attention as he said, "Ansar Inshallah is an extremist, anti-Western band led by Abu Shaaban. They are headquartered in Southern Lebanon."

They were still reeling with shock when the doorbell rang, and Captain Timon Habib came in.

"You've seen?" Charles asked, his eyes wide and frantic.

"We are doing everything we can to find her," he assured them.

"But you know where she is, right?" Liz burst out. "She's somewhere in the Sainiq camp near Sidon." The irony of having been there herself just days ago was not lost on Liz.

Captain Habib smiled that condescending smile of his, and Liz wanted to kick him in the shins. "And you know this how?"

"The combination of the old man's testimony and Hanan's letter." She explained again in detail for the benefit of her parents as well as the captain.

Habib looked pained at her vehemence. "May I suggest, Miss Fairchild, that you leave the investigation in the hands of the professionals?"

"But we've only got seventy-two hours! Minus at least one. What are you professionals doing about it?"

"Elizabeth!" Charles's voice was a whip crack.

Liz jerked and looked at her father.

"Get us some coffee." Then as an afterthought, "Please."

"What?" She stared at him in disbelief. Just as anger threatened to consume her, she noticed his shaking hands as he reached for his wife.

Taking a deep breath, Liz went to the kitchen. There she found Nabila already preparing a tray of coffee and cakes. Liz sank into a chair and, elbow on the table, braced her head in her hand.

Lord God, what are You doing?

It felt that every time she turned around, her faith was talking another hit.

Please, God! Help! It seemed certain that Captain Habib wasn't going to. So who would? Who cared about Julie as she did? Sure, her parents were having their hearts torn out, but what were they doing except bothering the authorities? She was the one who had found the clues. She was the one who wouldn't give up.

A feeling of knowing spread through her like liquid soap through hot water.

She *was* the one. It was up to her.

Which was why Liz found herself standing in the foyer of the newspaper office where Bashir worked. As a political columnist for one of Lebanon's major dailies, he saw his mission in life as keeping the coals of dissatisfaction in the Middle East red hot. From Liz's perspective, it was unfortunate that he was so good at his job.

"I'd like to speak with Bashir Assan," she told the receptionist.

"Do you have an appointment?"

Liz mentally rolled her eyes. Receptionists were the same the world over, guarding the office from unscheduled invaders like a jealous girl guarding her boyfriend from flirtatious females.

"No, no appointment."

"I'm sorry." It was clear she wasn't. "He is very busy today. We can make an appointment for the day after tomorrow."

Liz stood her ground. "I must see him today. Now."

The receptionist flipped her appointment book and looked up at Liz, pen at the ready. "Is ten o'clock all right?" Apparently it was two days hence or not at all.

"Please tell him that Elizabeth Fairchild is here." Liz put as much confidence behind the words as she could. "I'm sure he'll see me."

The receptionist's chin went up pugnaciously.

Liz leaned forward slightly. "Elizabeth Fairchild. I am the sister of his missing sister-in-law, the one shown on TV this morning."

The receptionist blinked, clearly surprised, though whether by Liz's tenacity or the mention of Julie was unclear. The woman hesitated another minute, then laid her pen down. She rose and walked up a short hall to a closed office door. She knocked, paused a second, then entered. She returned in a minute. "Mr. Assan will see you. Please follow me."

Feeling that finally one thing was working in her favor, Liz trailed the young woman through the now open door. The receptionist backed out and closed the door behind her, leaving Liz alone with the one person in the world who disliked her, not for anything she had done but merely for who she was. Well, Liz wasn't fond of him either. Something about him raised her hackles every time she was near him.

Now he looked up from his desk, but he didn't stand.

"Elizabeth." His voice was not quite hostile. "I am sorry about Julie."

"I've come to ask for your help in finding her." Might as well baldly state her reason for being here.

Bashir studied her for a long moment. His stare made her fidget with nerves. She forced herself to stand still. He was not going to intimidate her.

"Why should I help find Julie?"

Liz knew her mouth had dropped open. "She's your sister-in-law."

"That is hardly my doing." He turned to the papers on his desk and began to read.

Liz couldn't believe his rudeness, his coldheartedness. His mother would be mortified.

When Liz didn't move, he looked up, first at her, then at the door, his meaning more than obvious.

Two week's worth of tension, fear, and sorrow broke Liz's

composure. "What is *wrong* with you? This is Khalil's wife we're talking about."

He shrugged.

"Surely out of honor for your brother you want to see her safe."

He shifted uncomfortably, and she thought she had scored a hit. Still, he sniffed disdainfully. "She is an American."

"That is hardly her doing."

Bashir gave her a fierce look; Liz met his with one of her own. He blinked first.

"She shouldn't be here to begin with," he said. "Americans belong in America, not Lebanon."

Give me a break! "Bashir! For heaven's sake. She's the daughter of parents who are teaching and working in Lebanon to give the people of the Middle East the best opportunity to accomplish whatever they want in life. She's the wife of a Lebanese who educated himself and worked to better the region economically. She supports the Palestinian cause. Who cares where she was born?"

One look at his face and it was obvious that he cared, and deeply.

"Americans are prejudiced," he finally said in a voice filled with contempt.

"*Americans* are prejudiced?" Can you say pot calling the kettle?

"They are anti-Palestinian, anti-Arab."

"As you well know, it's not so much that we Americans are anti-Palestinian as we are anti-violence as a way to solve problems. We have this little difficulty with taking innocent lives as a way to make a statement."

"They had no recourse but the Intifada. Their lands were stolen by the Zionists who kill them, and it is American money that supports the Zionists."

"I don't want to debate you over this, Bashir, but Israel is over fifty years old."

He looked at her blankly. He didn't see her point. Or he wouldn't.

"The country is here to stay." As a nation, Israel was politically organized, militarily strong, and the people had a sense of nationalism that more than matched the Palestinians. From its very inception at the declaration of the United Nations, Israel had the strongest of allies in the United States and Russia.

It struck Liz as never before how the ramifications of the stories of Isaac and Ishmael were felt right into the present day. Each man's descendents saw the other's in terms of enemy, if not on a personal, one-to-one basis, certainly in the larger political and communal sense. Palestinians saw the Jews as people who came to steal their land, land the Jews saw as rightly theirs, given to them by God millennia ago.

Could such opposing views ever reconcile?

But Liz knew that many of the Palestinians who had been part of the first Intifada back in 1987, largely a civil disobedience movement rather than a violent one as recently, had become pragmatic about the presence of Israel. The general Lebanese population felt a similar weariness with the constant fighting. Bashir's own parents were good examples.

"Bashir," Liz said, the anger suddenly draining. "Today it doesn't matter what I think or you think about politics or terrorism or coexistence." Tears sat in her eyes. "Today Julie is all that matters."

Bashir stared at her, his eyes hot. "What do you expect me to do?"

God, please! Melt his resistance. If he doesn't help, I don't know what I'll do!

Liz shifted her weight from one foot to the other. "Bashir, it's not a family secret that you have contact with some of the more militant Palestinians."

He didn't deny her statement but said in that cold voice, "And?"

"I'm not judging you. I'm stating a fact, okay? I know that your position here at the paper requires that you know all sorts of people."

He nodded. "Many readers see me as espousing violence. I'm not; I am trying to explain it."

Good luck on that one. But Liz nodded.

Bashir smiled thinly. "You must understand that I am not altering my stance, even for Julie. Even in Khalil's memory."

"I'm not trying to change your mind. In fact, I agree with you that something needs to be done to make life better in the camps. But all that's secondary now. I want to find Julie."

He glanced at his computer screen and began to type. She knew he wasn't looking for information to help her but was ignoring her.

Liz took a deep breath and soldiered on in spite of his antipathy. "I have learned two things. One, she was taken the night of the fire by three men, one of whom wore a Palestinian kaffiyeh and drove a black Mercedes. I have also learned that a blond woman is being held by Ansar Inshallah in the Sainiq camp near Sidon."

"How—?"

Liz shook her head and grinned slightly at his amazement. She bet very little caught him by surprise. She cleared her throat and stood as straight as she could. Time to look the very picture of determination in spite of how much she was shaking inside.

"I want you to help me pinpoint where she's being held so I can go into the camp and rescue her."

For once, Bashir, outspoken man of letters, relentless advocate for the underdog, and fierce defender of causes, was at a loss for words. But not for long. "Even you cannot be that foolish."

Tell me how you really feel, Bashir. "If you do not help me, I will go to your father. Because of his mercy trips to the camps, he may be able to provide the information I need."

Bashir leaped to his feet and leaned forward, planting his hands on his desk. "You will leave my father alone. He has more than enough to deal with right now."

"Has sympathy for a potential source ever held you back, Bashir?"

He looked at her like a Newfoundland might look at a miniature poodle that had just bitten him.

She tried not to look too smug. "It's your choice."

Approaching Beirut

"AHHH, BEIRUT! The city that never dies." The Lebanese operative raised his voice over the drone of the airplane.

John turned from the window to look at him across the cramped aisle. The man who had introduced himself as Zothgar directed a toothy smile back at him in the dim light of the cabin's interior.

The operative was a wisp of a man, gnarled in a way that spoke of too many years smoking cigarettes, as he was doing now. John frequently wished that the rest of the world was as smokeless as America had become, but as the pungent smoke filled the cabin, he sighed. Not today.

Zothgar was probably in his midforties, though the outdated European suit made him look somewhat older. But it was the flatness of his intense cobalt eyes that told John this was not someone he'd want working against him.

"This is your first visit to our beautiful country, yes?"

John forced a smile and merely nodded rather than shout. The nine-passenger DeHavilland Dove was the best Lebanon had to offer in the way of VIP private transport, but it wasn't exactly luxurious. With the six men of Task Force Valor, Zothgar, and the two pilots, the plane was maxed out, and the twin-turboprop engines seemed to be straining for all they were worth just to stay aloft. John didn't feel much better when he read the placard above the bulkhead stating that the plane had been built in 1958.

Oh, well, if it's been flying this long, why should it stop today?

He refused to consider the several hundred possible answers to his question, from metal fatigue to engine failure. Instead, he turned and looked out at the bright lights of the city spreading out below him. It didn't look like a war zone, which of course it wasn't any longer. Still, he didn't see the expected black patches amid the light, areas where there would be nothing but bullet-riddled ruins.

"Rebuilt," Zothgar yelled.

John glanced back at him.

"Beirut," Zothgar clarified. "Beautiful buildings downtown, strong and modern. In the Green Zone is much night life. Clubs, cafés, life where there used to be death and destruction."

John understood the Green Zone as the several block no-man's-land that once divided Beirut between the warring Maronite Christians and Sunni and Shi'a Muslims, who in turn fought with each other as well as the Christians. When John was growing up, Beirut had been synonymous with destruction and chaos. He'd been eight when the suicide bombing of the Marine barracks in 1983 killed 241 men.

His father had been outraged, striding through the house as he ranted against those who killed our boys when they were only there to try and keep peace between the warring Lebanese factions. Then followed the years of civil strife complete with vivid TV coverage. Lebanon had not been a nice place at all.

Zothgar was shouting at him again. "Once we land, the plane will drop us at private hangar number twelve. There will be a car that will take us to the terminal. Don't worry about customs—I have already arranged things. You have hotel reservations, yes? Just as I suggested?"

John nodded. "Yes, we do."

"Good. Once we get through the airport safely, you will take a taxi to your hotel. I will meet you tomorrow afternoon at this café." He passed John a business card. "It is not too far from your hotel, so you need not find a taxi. I will have made final arrangements by then for our trip to the camp. You and your men should be prepared to move shortly after we conclude our lunch there."

Actually, Mary had made all of their Beirut arrangements. When they knocked on the door of her office, which occupied a bay in one of the portable barracks-type structures the men referred to as honeycombs, she'd been in the midst of printing their hotel reservations off of her computer. She'd set them up with a cover as a team of German road bikers, coming to Lebanon to compete in an upcoming race.

It was pure genius as far as John was concerned. Three of them spoke passable German, even if Hogan did so with a decided drawl, and they even looked passable once she'd outfitted them with matching navy blue under armor jerseys and baseball caps with *Deutschland* embroidered on them. She outdid that when she brought out a molded plastic, locking bicycle storage case for each of them, just big enough to hold their tactical gear.

"This way, no one will even have to ask you why you are coming to Beirut," Mary said.

John didn't bother to ask how or where she had secured these things on such short notice in the middle of the Jordanian desert. The resources available to the U.S. government never ceased to amaze him.

Mary also gave them German passports and documentation, complete with cancelled boarding passes from an Air France flight that would be arriving in Beirut from Paris at the same time this rattletrap plane sneaked them in from Jordan. Clever, clever girl.

Sweeney, who sat behind John listening to him and Zothgar shout at each other, leaned forward. "Hey, John, why do we need to go through the terminal at all? Why not just have the car drive us straight to the hotel?"

Zothgar gave him a somewhat chilly smile. "I wish that it could be that easy, my friend. But in Beirut, there are still many factions who, if not warring outright, are still doing so secretly. The government only has a few aircraft, and we know that Hezbollah and other groups are very interested to know who is flying on them. Leaving the airport without exiting in normal patterns would certainly make your story for biking here…how do you say…"

"Compromised," John said.

Sweeney pushed back into his seat. "This is stupid. We should have HALOed in."

Hogan, who was sitting behind Zothgar, spoke up. "We're not actually gonna have to ride anywhere, are we? I ain't been on a bike since I was in high school, and it wasn't a good experience."

John chuckled. "What happened?"

"Let's just say that the crossbar wasn't very friendly to me."

Everyone laughed except Hogan and Zothgar, who apparently didn't get it.

John peered out the window again; the plane was lining up on its final approach to the airfield.

From the back of the plane, Rip called out, "Ladies and gentlemen, we are now beginning our descent into Beirut International Airport. Please fasten your tray tables and return your seat belts to the full upright and locked positions."

Doc Kelly continued the fractured litany. "Please keep your hands and arms inside the aircraft at all times until we have come to a complete stop at the terminal."

John looked at Zothgar as hoots of laughter echoed through

the tiny cabin. The man was staring out the window with a sober look, puffing on another cigarette.

"Those things will kill you." John motioned to the cigarette.

"No, my friend," Zothgar said slowly through a cloud of smoke, his gaze not leaving the window. "Beirut will kill me long before the cigarettes do."

Ten minutes later as the team was offloading its gear at hangar twelve, a white box van drove up. A rotund man in a dishdasha emerged and threw open the rear doors. Zothgar spoke to him in rapid-fire Arabic as the men loaded their gear in the van.

Zothgar approached John. "We must hurry. The driver, Mohammed, will take you to the commercial side of the airport, where an Air France jet is now landing. He will open the door to the Jetway, and you will enter the terminal from there just before the doors are opened for the passengers to deplane. This way it will appear as if you are arriving from Paris."

John tossed his duffel into the van. "Whatever you say."

Zothgar smiled thinly. "Mohammed will usher you through customs and make arrangements for your passports and visas. He will also see to your transportation to your hotel. If for some reason I am not at that meeting tomorrow, consider the mission aborted and get out of the country as soon as possible."

The men climbed into the cargo van and sat on their bags.

Zothgar leaned in. "Sleep well, and *insh'allah* I shall see you tomorrow."

John expected to see the man tomorrow whether Allah willed it or not.

Mohammed closed the van doors and climbed into the driver's seat. There was very little conversation on the short ride to their destination, and John used the time to check the Heckler and Koch MK 23 handgun in the hideaway holster at his waist, making sure it was loaded with the safety on.

Then he opened his duffel bag and checked that the clothing

on top obscured the helmet, body armor, night-vision goggles, and ammunition from any casual inspection. His laptop case didn't have a laptop in it. Instead, the XM-8 assault rifle, configured with the compact nine-inch barrel, fit nicely. If need be, he could fire the weapon without removing it from the case, but he hoped it wouldn't come to that. The longer barrel and buttstock were buried in the bottom of his duffel.

When the van pulled up under the Air France Jetway, the flight hadn't yet arrived. As they waited, John decided that Sweeney was right. This was a dumb idea. Walking through an international airport with the amount of military hardware they had was like riding a Harley down the center aisle of the National Cathedral and expecting no one to notice.

Neither Mohammed nor any of the team spoke until the Air France 747 taxied slowly into position at the gate. Then Mohammed said, "Come."

He climbed down from the driver's seat as the team scrambled out. Shouldering their gear, they followed Mohammed up the outside stairs of the Jetway and then inside. He said a few words in Arabic to the gate agent, who was maneuvering the Jetway into place, and then turned and headed into the terminal with Valor in tow.

The concourse was surprisingly full of people given the late hour. Since they had no other luggage, Mohammed led them straight to customs. There he held out his hand. "Passports."

As he collected them, he pointed to the wall on one side of the lines that were forming. "Wait there." Then, papers in hand, he disappeared through a side door. Tension mounted as the minutes ticked by. John hated it when control of his mission was in another's hands.

Mohammed returned and handed back the papers. "All okay. We go." He then led them past the lines of people waiting to have their passports stamped and out of the airport where they were immediately set upon by honking, waving cab drivers. Some even walked up to the group and offered their services.

Mohammed shooed the most aggressive ones off and found a private minibus that would hold the men and their gear. That done, he came and shook hands with each team member, nodding profusely and saying "Welcome, welcome" over and over. Then he left.

The team loaded into the minibus. In his best German accent, he said, "Hotel Berkley, *bitte*."

The driver started his meter and they drove away.

Mohammed nodded at the guard manning the checkpoint as he passed back through security into the terminal and received a similar gesture in reply. Before reaching the door that led downstairs to the tarmac and the white van, he stopped at a pay phone, deposited some coins, and spoke into the mouthpiece.

"Imad, *Wisluu El Gharbiyeen*."

The Westerners have arrived.

20

Downtown Beirut

LIZ SAT AT A SMALL TABLE at an outdoor café on the cliffs beside the Corniche, waiting for Bashir. Yesterday when she left his office, she told him to meet her here with information that could help her. The issue wasn't whether he could find the information. It was whether he was willing to pass it on to her. "Noon tomorrow," she had said.

So here she was waiting, thirty hours of the seventy-two gone. No, make that thirty hours and fifteen minutes.

She closed her eyes in despair. When she opened them, Bashir stood across from her, his eyes hidden behind reflecting sunglasses so that when she looked at him, all she saw was her own squinting face. Not very reassuring.

He was dressed in a navy pinstriped business suit and looked cool and unruffled, totally in control. She, on the other hand, had a dry mouth and a sour stomach, to say nothing of a sun glare headache. In her anxiety over Julie and her hurry to meet Bashir, she'd forgotten her own dark glasses.

He pulled out a chair and sat down. "Please let me say that I am very disturbed about Julie and her danger."

Liz nodded, unable to say anything around the clog of emotion in her throat. Not that she believed in his show of sympathy.

They were silent a few minutes, ordering, then sipping their coffee.

Bashir lifted his hand for a refill. "What you propose to do is very dangerous, very foolish."

Liz nodded.

"Do not even think of going into the camp."

Disconsolate, Liz stared at the Mediterranean. He wasn't going to help. She wasn't surprised, not really.

Bashir took off his glasses and glared at her. "It is suicidal. Not only can it get you killed. It can get me killed if they find out I helped. I do not want to be killed."

Like I do? "I understand." She swallowed her fear. "But I must try. I can't leave Julie there, subject to who knows—" Her voice broke.

"Let the authorities take care of it. It's what they get paid to do."

"I've spoken to Captain Timon Habib. I told him what I told you yesterday. He wasn't impressed."

Bashir nodded as he slipped his glasses back on. "I know Habib." His tone of voice said he didn't think much of the man. "You understand, don't you, that life would be much easier for Habib if Julie were dead? A confrontation with militant Palestinians is the last thing he wants."

Liz's hand went to the pendant hanging around her neck. She'd worn it ever since she found it in the alley by the hotel. "He won't hesitate to let her die, will he?"

"Keeping Lebanon from civil war and keeping the factions quiet are his main concerns."

"Well, Julie is mine."

Bashir leaned back in his green plastic chair and studied her. "So you are riding to the rescue by yourself. Like St. George who

is said to have slain his dragon not far from the place we sit."
Suddenly he leaned forward, reaching across the table and putting
a strong hand on her arm. "Elizabeth, don't."

Surprised, she turned her head and looked at the sea until she
felt she had control of herself. "I don't have a choice. She is my sister."

"You would rather risk that your parents have no daughters
than that they have one safe and well?"

Fear two-stepped its icy dance down her spine. She repeated,
"I don't have a choice. If you won't help me, I will go to your
father. I'll go to whomever I have to."

"You will not go to my father." Bashir slapped the table with
the hand that had just rested on her arm in something like kindness. "I will not have you putting his life in danger. He has
enough to bear without a hysterical American prima donna
putting him in the sights of Ansar Inshallah."

"If you don't want your father involved, then you will have to
help me."

Bashir ignored her comment. "How many times have you
mounted rescue operations? Or tried to sneak through a camp
where Westerners are not welcomed?"

Liz's chin came up. "I have been there before."

"At night? Trying to get a captive out?"

A captive whose unmedicated rheumatoid arthritis would
prevent her from running or moving with any agility. "Do you
have information for me or not?"

"Not long ago they murdered the Palestinian wife of an
American missionary in the very camp you want to infiltrate."

Liz frowned. "I remember hearing about that. She converted
from Islam, didn't she? Upset her family?"

"*Upset* is a mild term." Bashir shrugged. "I know. I play soccer with some men who live in this camp. So did the missionary.
Don't go, Elizabeth."

Again silence fell. Liz was vaguely aware of a man looking through the postcards at the kiosk two doors from the café. When she looked back at Bashir, she said, "I'm going."

He stared at her, shaking his head, obviously convinced she was crazy. Then he surprised her.

Downtown Beirut

Sweat trickled down John's back as he pushed out through the double glass doors of the Berkley onto the sidewalk of the Hamra district of Beirut. The sun was warm, and several blocks away from the sea, the air was relatively still. He quickly donned sunglasses to shield his eyes from the glare. He looked up and down the busy street as Frank emerged behind him.

"Moving," Frank spoke into a tiny Motorola walkie-talkie in his hand.

"German bike team members wouldn't carry military radios," Rip had said that morning as he produced the four standard FMRS radios from his bag. "Of course they don't carry automatic carbines in their shoulder bags either, but we'll just keep that little fact to ourselves."

"Gadget Man to the rescue," Hogan had drawled as he studied his new toy.

To go out today, John had traded his under armor jersey for a lightweight gray crew neck sweater and khakis, clothes he had purchased in Kuwait the previous winter. He almost never bought clothes in the U.S. because they made it more difficult to blend in and not look like an American. Frank wore a sport coat over his turtleneck, which effectively concealed the .45 caliber pistol under his arm.

"Valor Three in position," Rip answered.

"Me too," came Buzz Hogan's reply. He never had been much for proper radio procedure.

John and Frank walked several blocks west, heading for the outdoor café near the Corniche.

John watched a group of young, stylish Lebanese strolling along the avenue. "Is it just me, or are all the women here gorgeous?"

"Quite exotic, yes." Frank nodded.

In fact, John was finding his preconceived notions of Beirut shattered at every turn as he took in the gleaming buildings, the modern shopping boutiques and malls, and the trendy citizens. As much traveling as he'd done, he shouldn't have been surprised.

"I guess I figured they'd all be wearing burqas or something. You know, like in Iraq or even Jordan. Look! There's a Pizza Hut!"

"Wanna stop in for a slice?" Frank's voice was droll.

John laughed. "Not today."

They crossed the Avenue du General de Gaulle and strolled south along the Corniche toward the café where they were to meet Zothgar. Children chased each other along the seaside path, while young men fished with long poles off the seawall.

John spotted Rip looking at postcards in a little newsstand two doors before the café. His black hair and olive skin made him almost indistinguishable from the typical Lebanese.

John had been a bit worried that Hogan, big Texas cowboy that he was, would stand out like a logger at Lollapalooza, but his fears subsided a little when he saw the cosmopolitan makeup of Beirut's people.

"So what kind of a name is Zothgar?" Frank asked. "Is that his first name or his last name?"

"You've got me." John kept walking. "But I trust him about as far as I can throw him."

Rip nodded almost imperceptibly as they passed.

The café was situated on a small flat area of rock on the cliffs on the seaward side of the Corniche, just south of the famed Pigeon Rocks. Several of the tables were occupied with a lunch crowd of college students and workers enjoying the sun. There wasn't anything especially notable about the place, which made it perfect for their meeting.

John slid his six-foot frame into a chair and casually checked the diners out more carefully. His eyes paused briefly on a tall, angry-looking man in a well-tailored suit talking passionately with a woman, whose back was to John. Deciding that the man wasn't a threat, he finished his sweep and settled in to wait for Zothgar.

Frank took a seat several tables over, facing John so he would be able to cover John's back if one of these innocents wasn't so innocent after all. He could also keep an eye out for Zothgar.

John checked his watch. 12:20. The proprietor emerged, and John ordered a bottle of bitter lemon, a drink he'd come to love when he was stationed in Germany but was unable to get in the States.

He waited as the scent of sweet apple *nargileh*, the tobacco smoked in the vastly popular hookahs or water pipes, wrapped around him. The Avenue du General de Gaulle in front of the café offered the competing odor of exhaust. The avenue was absolutely packed with people driving as if they'd just been told to evacuate the city.

A BMW raced by, weaving in and out of traffic with its horn blaring in competition with its radio. Behind it, a young man zipped past on a motorcycle, wearing no helmet and performing a wheelie. Just in case that didn't kill him, a cigarette hung out of his mouth.

John shook his head. Just another of those things no one thought twice about here, but if someone tried it in the U.S., the police—and the lawyers—would have a feeding frenzy.

John sweated and nursed his drink for fifteen minutes, twice having to beg off when the owner came to take his food order.

He had no choice. He would have to pull the plug and abort the mission if Zothgar wasn't here in five minutes.

* * *

"You must wear the proper clothes," Bashir lectured. "Cover your head. Look meek. No respectable Muslim woman should be wandering the streets of the camp at night. Just being there at that time makes you suspect."

She nodded, more than slightly miffed at his condescending tone. "I *know* how to dress." She paused and took a deep breath. He might be irate, but she mustn't react in kind. He might take offense and leave before she had all the information she needed. "But where is she in the camp? Where's the building she's being held in? How many guards does she have? Have they hurt her in any way?"

Until she voiced that question, Liz hadn't realized just how afraid she was for Julie with a fear of things other than death. She had been blocking such thoughts because they were too painful, too devastating. Once more she swallowed against the fear.

"The warehouse where I think they hold her will have a guard."

"Just one?"

He shrugged. "They know she is not going anywhere."

"Does the guard know I'm coming?"

"Of course not." He gave her that superior smile of his.

Well, how was I supposed to know? She forced herself to smile back, her curve of the lips as insincere as his. Over his shoulder she absently watched a little man in an ill-fitting suit approach, then rush past. She eyed the immaculately tailored Bashir. Quite a contrast but proof that clothes did not make the man.

"I must go." Bashir pulled his slim leather wallet from the inside pocket of his suit jacket. He slid a Lebanese ten-thousand livre note onto the table to pay the tab.

"But—"

He reached into his briefcase and drew out an unsealed

envelope. He handed it to her. She blinked. It was stuffed with many Lebanese livre notes of high denomination.

"What—?"

"The guard's name is Azmi. Give him the envelope, and he will see you have entry into the warehouse. After that he cannot and will not help you. And I will not help again in any way."

Liz was still reeling over the fact that he was helping at all. "Why is the guard willing to help me? And where did this money come from?"

"Azmi has a son who has a bad leg as the result of being too near a land mine that exploded. The boy needs surgery to correct his problems, but Azmi hasn't the money." His voice turned harsh. "No one in the camps has the money."

"How do you know this Azmi?"

"Soccer."

"Ah. And the money?"

"Julie is my sister-in-law. I might not have chosen her for Khalil, but she is still extended family whether I like it or not."

Liz was stunned. If she understood what he wasn't saying, the money was from him. *Watch it, Bashir. Next thing you know, I might like you. Or at least tolerate you.*

He pulled a piece of paper from his briefcase and dropped it on the table. "It has been nice knowing you, Elizabeth." With a slight nod that did nothing to negate the acid dripping from his voice, he was gone.

It was clear he expected her to die in this mission.

O, Lord, You have to protect me.

Another thought skittered through her mind. The missionary and his wife had undoubtedly prayed that same prayer, and look how their story had turned out. She swallowed, but the fear continued to sit in her throat.

She unfolded the paper he'd left. It was a map of the camp, with the course she should follow marked on it. A building in the center had an X on it in red ink. As she studied it, she wondered if the X was just for the building, a pretty large one if the map was anywhere near scale, or for that section of the building. She shrugged. She'd find out soon enough.

She closed her eyes and turned her face into the sun.

Lord, what else can I do? She knew the answer was nothing. She also knew that just a month ago she would have expected everything to go well in her rescue venture. She had no confidence that it would go well tonight.

Her faith slipped another notch.

She turned as she heard Bashir summon a taxi. She watched as he climbed in, a slick, overconfident, opinionated, quite nasty man. His driver darted into traffic without regard for the oncoming vehicles.

Then her gaze settled on the athletic man in the gray sweater seated three tables behind her. Those chiseled features looked just like…

John was just about to abort the mission when Frank, digging into a huge plate of hummos, caught his eye and motioned with his head. John turned to see Zothgar threading his way through the traffic and parked cars, wearing the same faded suit as the previous night. He looked as if he hadn't slept much.

When Zothgar spotted John, he headed right for his table. He sat, then called the proprietor over. They had a rapid-fire conversation in Arabic.

"I'll have the same," John said in German. At the proprietor's uncertain look, John pointed to Zothgar, made eating motions, and pointed to himself, nodding. Zothgar translated, and the man brightened and left.

Zothgar settled back and waited until the proprietor returned with the plates of hummos and flat bread and small cups of Turkish coffee.

Zothgar sipped his drink and regarded John calmly. "Did you know that Lebanon is mentioned more than sixty times in your Bible?"

"Er…no." John was startled by the question, which he suspected was exactly what Zothgar had in mind. "I mean, I know it's mentioned, but I didn't know how often. Why do you assume that it's *my* Bible?"

"You are a Christian, are you not?"

He hesitated again. "What leads you to that conclusion?" *Way to avoid the question, Cooper.*

Zothgar shrugged. "Yours is a Christian nation."

John grunted. Hardly. "So if I was born in a garage, would that make me an automobile?"

He could see that his analogy had been lost in the cultural divide, so John grabbed the excuse to change the subject. His thoughts about God were still too confused and full of anger to discuss. "What have you got for us?"

"I have made arrangements for our transportation." Zothgar paused to light a cigarette. "Check out of your hotel and take a taxi to the Moevenpick Hotel where you will secure rooms for the night. Meet me in the hotel lobby at eleven-thirty this evening, prepared to depart."

John tore off a piece of flat bread and used it to scoop up some hummos. "I had ice cream once at the Moevenpick in Frankfurt. It's a pretty classy place. Expensive. What's wrong with the hotel we currently occupy? The rates there are more reasonable."

John suddenly realized that Zothgar wasn't paying attention to him but was staring at another table. His face went suddenly tense. But before John could see what was so distressing, a woman's voice rang out.

"John? John Cooper?"

Zothgar started to stand, but John froze in his seat. What the...? He knew no one in Beirut, no one knew he was here, and no one must ever know. His right hand instinctively slid into the shoulder bag, his fingers seeking his gun as he looked up to face the voice.

"John, it's me, Liz Fairchild!"

John sat paralyzed, staring into those beautiful brown eyes.

21

Downtown Beirut

LIZ FELT THE HEAVINESS in the air that comes when something is wrong, when you've acted in a way you shouldn't, but you have no idea what you've done or why it's wrong. She felt herself flush.

John Cooper didn't move, didn't even blink. He just sat there, handsome as ever, eyes wide, face blank, mouth shut.

What was his problem? Certainly he'd never followed up on what she'd thought might become a wonderful romance after she met him at the beach three years ago, but did that mean he couldn't be polite enough to at least acknowledge her?

Unless he'd forgotten all about her. Unless he couldn't even remember her name.

Now there was a humiliating thought.

She smiled too brightly and began talking in an attempt to relieve the awkwardness. "What a surprise, seeing you here in Beirut of all places."

Had she told him her family lived here? She couldn't remember. Wouldn't it be a real-life fairy tale if he'd come looking for her? Right. And world peace was just around the corner.

"Are you on vacation?" *Like you were when we met?* "I hope you're having a good time."

Talk about inane. What she really wanted to do was ask if he'd like her to show him around since she knew the city so well, but she bit it back. *Dump me once, it's no one's fault. Dump me twice, it's all mine.* It irked her that she still felt that little kick just looking at him. She was pathetic.

She fidgeted uneasily. "So, um…are you still in the Army, or are you a civilian now?"

If only he would respond! Even a blink would be a step in the right direction. She plowed on, not knowing what else to do. Her grin felt pasted on.

"I'm glad you found the Corniche. Walking by the sea is so relaxing."

Suddenly, a muscular arm snaked around her shoulders. She stiffened and turned. The leering face of a man she'd never met hovered much too close to hers.

"Guten abend, Frauline!"

The man was at least eight inches taller than she was, and he was holding her firmly, too firmly, with his powerful right arm. He was grinning from ear to ear. *"Dieses eine gute schauende Frau! He Fritz!"*

She frowned. The man might be looking at her, but he was talking to John.

"Go away! Leave me alone." She tried to shrug the heavy handed stranger away, but he just squeezed her even more tightly.

"Wer ist dieses? Jemand, das Sie gestern bie einen tavern abend aufhoben? Gut ist sie meine jetzt!" He roared with laughter.

Was the man drunk? "John!" She turned to him, desperate. "*Do* something!"

John just sat, looking as if someone had told him he was going to give birth to twins next week.

Liz had heard the phrase "feet of clay" all her life, but this was the first time she'd experienced the pain of someone crumbling before her eyes. The man she remembered was charming, kind, protective, interesting to talk to. He listened like he cared about everything she said. It was only for a few summer days, but he was so attentive it felt like he was courting her. And they laughed together. A lot. The fact that he was a Christian was the icing on the cake.

She'd come home expecting to continue their budding friendship via e-mail and have quick visits when their respective jobs allowed it. Their connection had been so immediate and so deep that she daydreamed about all the foolish things girls yearn for—a first kiss, a ring, a beautiful wedding, a picket fence, two kids, and a cat and a dog.

What she got was one stilted phone message canceling their dinner date, then silence.

It was only in retrospect that she understood he just wanted someone to pass the time with. He'd never said anything that could be misconstrued as romantic. He'd never touched her, not even to hold her hand. He'd never hinted at a future.

Yet somehow in spite of that, or maybe *because* of it, he had remained in her mind as the ideal man by whom she measured every other man. More fool she.

John frowned and looked at Liz's captor, then finally spoke, except it was a curt command and in German! *"Weg. Jetzt."*

"Yavol!" The big blond stranger began pulling her away from the table toward the street. She squirmed and twisted, trying to break free.

"Stop that!" the man suddenly whispered in her ear. "Just keep walking!"

Liz stared. A German who spoke English with a Southern drawl?

All my training is useless.

John had lost track of how many millions of dollars the government had spent preparing him for every eventuality in the field. Well, they neglected to do the "what to say when an old flame walks into the middle of a covert op" drill. For the first time in his life, he was truly speechless. He and Zothgar stared after Liz. Gaped was probably more like it.

And then she was gone, hurrying along the Corniche toward the Hard Rock Cafe. Sweeney sauntered after her, waving his arms and calling, "Come back, beautiful!" in German.

Brown Eyes. She had stopped him in his tracks once before, the first time they'd met at the climbing club in Virginia Beach. Those three wonderful days swirled through his head in an instant, followed immediately by the sting of "if only."

Stifling a sigh, he snapped back to the present and turned his full attention to placating a frowning Zothgar. Thoughts of Liz would have to wait.

The little Arab exhaled smoke and looked around as if he thought someone else might appear to interrupt them at any minute. "This is bad. Very bad."

John agreed but said nothing.

Zothgar produced a Lebanese bank note from his coat pocket. Dropping the money on the table, he stood and crushed out his cigarette. Apparently the meeting was over. Suddenly the little man was in a hurry to be somewhere else.

Not that John blamed him, but he didn't think the security breach was severe enough to abort the mission. It was just a girl mistaking him for someone she knew. Happened all the time.

John stood, aware that too many eyes were still watching him after what had just transpired. He put a hand on the Zothgar's arm as the operative turned to go.

"Whoa, hang on a minute. You haven't told me why we need to move."

Zothgar looked around nervously and hissed, "Because, my friend, your hotel does not have a private marina."

Then he turned and was gone, disappearing into the crowds that walked the Corniche.

Somewhere in Lebanon

Karima held out a hand, a little blue pill sitting in her palm.

Julie reached out aching fingers and took it. It seemed each time Karima came, she brought a tablet or capsule that was a different color. It was as if someone went into a pharmacy and said, "Give me everything you've got for pain." Then he had taken the entire collection, poured them into a big bottle, and shaken them until they were like a colorful collection of medicinal M&Ms.

Not that she was complaining. About now she'd take anything they gave her.

She just wished they'd give her a steroid. That stuff was such a miraculous pain and inflammation reliever. She knew Karima had passed on her request for some. She could only surmise that refusing to honor her request was one more way they sought to control her. Give her enough to keep her relatively healthy but not enough to make her feel well.

But at least they were now giving her something, though she had no idea why. After all, they planned to kill her in two more days.

She swallowed today's offering with the bottled water and lay back, smiling at Karima. It was probably the Stockholm syndrome, but Julie found herself growing fonder of Karima every day. In normal circumstances she and Karima would enjoy being friends. Not that she'd even have met Karima in normal circumstances. Still, something about this young woman was very endearing. Julie felt great pity for her as someone who had no control over her own life and great appreciation for her because she had pushed for the medicine.

"It hurts me to see you hurting so," Karima had said days ago. "I told them that they must get something for you or you will die."

"Thank you." Julie decided that trying to explain that RA wouldn't kill her was more than she was up to. So each time Karima came, she brought a pill that Julie swallowed gratefully.

"What time is it?" Julie asked now.

In this windowless room day and night got confused. There weren't even any clues from her meals, given the fact that they were all hummos and flat bread. Then too she slept as much as she could to counter the exhaustion the RA engendered.

"It's midday."

"Is the sun shining?"

"It is a wonderful spring day. I saw a flower this morning growing in a pile of trash. It was beautiful."

"I miss the sun." To Julie's surprise, tears filled her eyes. "Our house in Beirut has an inner courtyard. Lots of sun and lots of plants and flowers. Fragrance, especially the orange blossoms. Color." She looked at the dirty gray cinderblock walls. "There's no color in here."

Karima ran her hand over the black skirt she wore. "No color here either."

"Don't you ever want to leave and, oh, I don't know, get an education or a job or see the world or something?"

"I am a widow," she said with resignation. "I have gone back to my father's house." She smiled sadly. "He doesn't want me there, but I can't leave. Where would I go and with whom?"

"I would help you." Yes, she could help Karima like Charles and Annabelle had helped Nabila. "You could come to Beirut with me." Assuming she ever got to Beirut again.

Karima looked bewildered. "But this is my home."

Julie nodded. Family, no matter how dysfunctional, was still family. "If you stay here, what will your future be, Karima?"

"A widow is allowed four months and ten days to mourn. Then she may be married to another."

"Your father would marry you off without considering your feelings?"

"I am expensive. He thought he was rid of me." She swallowed and said in a small voice, "I have been in mourning for more than three months, and I know he has already picked my new husband."

"Oh, Karima!" In four months she was supposed to be over Rashid? Become another's wife? Julie wanted to cry for her.

Karima studied her hands, clasped so tightly in her lap that the knuckles paled. "I am only a woman."

Julie forced herself into a sitting position, fighting the nausea that turned her stomach. She placed her hand over Karima's. "You are very special to God."

"To your God maybe, but not to mine."

"Then maybe Allah isn't the all-wise god people say he is."

Karima stared at Julie, clearly appalled. "Shh! Do not let anyone hear you say that! To those in authority here, such words are blasphemy. People have died for saying such things."

"Then he's not compassionate or kind either."

Karima put a hand to Julie's lips. "Please. I don't want anything to happen to you."

"Except my beheading."

Karima jerked, then turned away.

As Julie went back to eating her flat bread, Karima sat at the end of the cot without speaking. When Julie finished, the girl grabbed the tray and left. Julie sighed. She should have kept that beheading comment to herself, but when such a terrible prospect hunkered on the horizon waiting to leap upon her, some reference to it was bound to slip out.

She sighed again and forced herself to her feet. She hobbled back and forth across her little prison. She tried to keep the extent of her increasing mobility, courtesy of Karima's medicine, a secret from her captors. If rescue did come, she wanted to be as mobile as she could, and she was afraid that if Karima knew what she was doing, she'd tell and the medication would cease.

But did it matter if she was mobile? Who was going to rescue her? She spent a lot of time asking the Lord that question. Certainly He couldn't mean for her to lose her life so horribly, could He? If she allowed it, visions of the Iraqi extremists, swords raised, their terrified captives at their feet pleading, filled her mind.

She preferred the nightmares of the burning hotel bathroom. The memories of being trapped in that room became clearer every day, and she allowed herself to relive them because each time added clarity.

She'd been knocked unconscious by the blast and wakened to find herself in a black room, flat on her back on the floor, her head pressed in a vise of pain. She must have struck it when she fell.

As she lay there, disoriented, uncertain how long she'd been out, a whoosh sounded, murmuring, whispering like the susurration of the sea, and a swollen finger of flame appeared in the blackness overhead. Quickly the finger became a writhing dragon, spitting fire and smoke as it slithered through the night to consume all that lay in its path. The room became alive with a fierce, rosy incandescence.

A vicious heat prickled Julie's skin as oxygen rushed in the shattered windows to fuel the conflagration. Frightened, quivering with pain, she crawled to the nearest window, ignoring the glass and debris that cut her palms and knees, and hauled herself to her feet.

Hurry! Hurry!

The glass might be broken from the window, but the wire mesh grating was firmly attached. She looked through it into an alley that ran along the side of the hotel. Safety lay there.

She grabbed the coarse mesh and pushed. Her wrists and hands were weak from her arthritis, and she was terrified she wouldn't be strong enough to dislodge the mesh.

Julie gave a great shove and almost fell out as the grating gave way.

With a shush of sound and a wall of heat, the curtains at the far window turned into a sheet of flames. The dragon was poised to pounce on her.

With a burst of fear-fed energy, she sat on the windowsill and spun until her legs were outside. She twisted, throwing herself forward as she did. Her fingers grabbed desperately at the windowsill as she fell, and her feet dug into the side of the building. She hung there for a moment, took a deep breath, and let go just as the curtains at her window exploded in flames.

The drop seemed to last forever, and the landing jarred her from the soles of her feet up her spine to her already spinning head. That was when she realized she had on only one shoe, a stiletto heel. Thrown off balance, she fell. She lay on the dirty concrete, woozy and shaken, her head a seething volcano ready to explode and splatter what little mind she had left all over the alley.

She rolled onto her back and watched the tatters of curtain flame above her. A flare broke free and floated softly, gracefully down. Hypnotized, Julie watched it until it almost landed on her.

With a start she rolled onto her stomach in the middle of the alley. All she wanted to do was lay her head on her crossed arms and sleep. Her skin prickled like she had a very bad sunburn. She was absolutely devoid of energy. Totally drained.

She began sobbing weakly. She would never have a chance to speak to Khalil again. Ever. If he wasn't already dead, she might soon be. Their marriage, begun in such hope, would end in animosity.

"Julie!"

She raised her head. "Liz?"

A transparent Liz stood at the entrance to the alley. Julie could see a fire truck through her. "Get up, Julie!"

While she knew the apparition was due to her head injury,

she drew strength from her older sister, the one who always cared for her. "Liz, help me."

"You have to help yourself," Liz called as she blew away. "I know you can do it."

Julie forced herself to her feet. She took one step, two, three. Her vision blurred, and her head felt like hundreds of tiny men were inside, all pounding on her skull with their tiny ball-peen hammers.

"Look, Liz," she whispered as she limped toward the street. "I'm doing it."

After an eternity she made it. She leaned against the corner of the building next to the hotel and tried to grasp what she was seeing. The hotel's entry portico and entire four-story façade were aflame. The tower that held the guest rooms and which sat behind all the public areas, looked fine to her, except for some missing windows. At least it was still standing. But the public rooms—lobby, restaurants, banquet rooms, meeting rooms, shops—were all burning.

Julie sank onto a large rock that was part of the landscaping. She watched the firefighters spraying the blaze with their small-flow European hose nozzles. Hopeless. Hopeless. She noted the police and some soldiers holding back the crowd gathered to watch. She felt the searing heat and looked vaguely at the ash that fell like snow.

Khalil! She pressed her hands to her chest and sobbed, her whole body racked with desperate grief, an agony filled with guilt and regret and terrible sorrow. Khalil!

A man with blood running from a wide gash on his cheek walked by, dazed, a limp child in his arms. Another man rushed up to him.

"I'm a doctor. Let me help you."

When would anyone come to her aid? Then a man lay a hand on her arm. Aware that she was fading, she turned her head toward him. "Please..." was all she had the strength to say.

The man lifted her in his arms and carried her away from the noise and chaos, away from the fire.

And brought her here to be held hostage, maybe murdered. Was there ever a clearer example of out of the frying pan and into the fire? Only she had climbed out of the fire and into the frying pan.

God, You helped me escape once. Now please give me Your peace and maybe help me escape again!

I will never leave you or forsake you.

In the time she had been in this windowless room, as uncomfortable as she had become physically, just that comfortable she had become in her conversations with God. There was nothing else to fill the hours, and except for Karima's visits, no one else with whom to speak.

God, she had asked when her mind was first free enough from the drugs to think, *why do things like the fire happen? Why do You let people like the terrorists kill people like Khalil and Brandy and all the others?*

No answers boomed from on high, but Julie didn't expect them to. Why should God give her the answers when He hadn't explained Himself to great men and women of faith through the ages?

Julie knew she was a poor Christian. In fact, she understood that there were those who would probably question her salvation because of her wishy-washy commitment to the One she said she believed in. If her faith meant anything to her, it should show, they'd say.

Well, they were right. Faith should show. Liz's did. And look at what the Muslim extremists did in the name of Allah, killing themselves and others. Talk about visible if misguided faith. Even those Muslims whose faith was quieter and more balanced knelt five times a day facing Mecca and praying. Many days she didn't pray even once to the one true God.

But then, the Muslims *had* to pray like that—they were trying to earn paradise. Julie had been given her promise of heaven for free! And at times in that windowless cell, she wondered how soon she'd see that promise fulfilled.

In college, she had felt a real desire to know God more, though she hadn't been willing to face her parents' disapproval as Liz had. Of course she never was one for rocking the boat. Still, she had meant her profession of faith, and with Liz to encourage her, she had grown in the Lord.

Then had come Cambridge and Khalil. Never would she have recanted for Khalil, but he had never asked. His religion was more cultural than felt, and he assumed hers was too. To her shame, she never corrected him.

Was that my biggest sin, Lord? I was like Peter at the trial of Jesus, claiming I never knew You. Well, maybe not quite like Peter because I never said I hadn't met You. Still, while I never spoke out against You as he did, I certainly never spoke for You. I don't want such spiritual cowardice to mark me ever again.

I will never leave you or forsake you.

Karima came back into the room. "How do you feel this evening? Is the medicine helping?"

Julie nodded. "I don't ache as much, and my ankles and hips don't feel as hot."

She smiled wanly, a brave woman nobly enduring.

"Good."

The door to the room flew open. Both she and Karima jumped at its unexpected and violent slam against the wall.

A man wearing a black and white kaffiyeh strode into the room. Karima jumped to her feet and pressed against the wall, her face white.

"Go," the man said to Karima, pointing to the door.

She ran from the room, never looking back.

"Get up!" the man ordered Julie.

She nodded and rose stiffly.

"Go." He pointed to the door.

Julie stared in disbelief. "I can go home?"

The man threw back his head and laughed.

Julie felt faint as the blood drained from her face.

22

Beirut

AS LIZ CLOSED the front door of her parents' house behind her, her mind whirled. Every time she tried to concentrate on one problem, another jumped up and screamed, "Think of me! Think of me!"

The seventy-two hour deadline with more than twenty four hours gone already.

The fear of what lay ahead—the plan that was forming in her head to find Julie.

The worry about Julie's health and the prolonged time away from her medications.

The warnings and the money Bashir gave her.

John Cooper staring blankly at her and the German with the Southern accent who whirled her away from John. "Get out of here fast," he'd hissed. Then he'd yelled something in German as she ran, something she knew by his tone of voice wasn't complimentary.

The more she thought about it, the more she thought she had somehow stumbled into a covert operation. It was the only explanation. The very thought gave her goose bumps.

She leaned against the door, staring at the floor. She knew John was in the service. Army? Navy? It didn't matter. They both had their Special Forces and covert operations.

What could he and those other men possibly be doing here? Granted things were a bit egg-shelly since al Hariri's assassination, and there was the bombing at the hotel, but black ops stuff? Something involving Syria? Or Israel?

Still, fantastic as such a scenario sounded, she prayed she hadn't ruined something or identified someone who shouldn't be identified or something like that.

Lord, I didn't mean anything bad. Please keep John and the other guys safe. Help them do whatever it is they came to do.

She pushed away from the door and hurried to her room. She heard voices coming from the courtyard, but she didn't want to talk to anyone. She needed to keep her mind centered on her goal.

"You would rather risk that your parents have no daughters than that they have one safe and well?"

Bashir's words roared through her head. How unfair was she being to her parents to go haring off like she planned? She went to her desk, sat, and pulled out a piece of paper. She began writing.

Charles and Annabelle,
   If you are reading this, then I have failed and I have caused you great grief. Please know that that was not my intent, but I cannot stand by while no one goes after Julie.

A sudden thought struck Liz. Could John and his men be here to rescue Julie? Wouldn't that be wonderful! It was just the type of thing special ops guys did, wasn't it? In spite of the U.S. policy of not negotiating with terrorists, they might send in a secret unit, right? It was so cavalry-to-the-rescue, so American.

How would I find out if Julie is their assignment? She shook her head. *I couldn't.* She had no idea where to find John, and even if she did, he probably couldn't tell her because then he'd have to kill her or something. She blew out a breath. She'd have to continue as planned.

She resumed writing.

Going after Julie is probably the result of my watching over her as we grew. I find I can't let go of that habit. I don't want to let go. Please know I love you both.

You are special parents. I know you think my faith is foolish, but let it be a comfort to you now. Both Julie and I are with Jesus. All my love,

She reread the note and could figure no other way to say what she wanted to say. She signed her name, folded the note, and stuffed it in an envelope. Then she went to find Nabila.

"You plan to go into the camp to find Julie?" Nabila was appalled.

Liz shrugged. "No lectures, Nabila. I was hoping you would be able to help me."

"Help you how?"

"Look at this map." Liz spread the map Bashir had given her on the table. "See the X? What is that building?"

Nabila narrowed her eyes as she studied the paper. "I think it's just a big warehouse. Remember, it's been years since I've been there."

Liz nodded. "That confirms what Bashir said."

"Did he also say you're risking your life going in there? They have killed people for far less."

Liz didn't answer. "Do you know anyone named Azmi?"

"Azmi what?"

"I don't know his last name. He has a son who was injured by a land mine explosion."

Nabila shook her head. "That happens too many times. South

Lebanon is littered with land mines left from the civil war and the Israeli and Syrian incursions. They estimate a hundred thousand are still buried. Too often children playing are the victims."

"When you are a doctor, you can help them." Liz smiled. "You will be wonderful."

Nabila merely raised an eyebrow. Hollow compliments were not going to distract her from her disapproval of Liz's plan.

Liz held out the letter she had written to her parents. "If the worst happens, give this to them."

Nabila crossed her arms and just looked at the letter. "I want no part of breaking your parents' hearts again."

Liz kept the letter extended until Nabila sighed and took it.

"I have to do this. How can I let Julie die without trying to find her?"

Tears slid down Nabila's face. "And how can I let you go, knowing you might die, too?"

Liz leaned forward and kissed her friend's cheek. "Thank you for caring so much. Don't worry. I will be back before morning."

As Liz returned to her room, she wished she felt as confident as she sounded. Still, no matter how she looked at things, she had no choice.

She changed quickly into a long, full black skirt, a black blouse, and black flat shoes. She pulled a large black scarf from the closet and draped it over her head. She looked at herself in the mirror. She looked so American! She slouched. Better but still not right.

Makeup! She ran to the bathroom and scrubbed her face clean. That was better. With her eyeliner she drew circles under her eyes, then smudged them, hoping they made her look weary. She was afraid she looked more like a raccoon.

She grabbed her bag, checked to see that she had her passport, Julie's passport, and her medicine. She'd gone to her sister's house after she left the café. Since she wasn't certain what would help Julie most, she took every pill bottle in the house. She put

them all in a sealed plastic bag. She planned to try and bluff her
way past the guards at the gate by telling them she was visiting a
sick friend.

She glanced at her watch. Nine o'clock. Time to go. She hurried through the house, keeping an ear tuned to the voices in the
courtyard. She had to be away before Charles and Annabelle saw
her and demanded to know what she was doing. Without a doubt
they would try to prevent her.

"Liz!"

She turned at the door and with misgivings watched Nabila
approach. The last thing she wanted right now was another lec-
ture about how thoughtless and foolish she was being. She felt
guilty enough as it was. The only thing that kept her going was
the knowledge that she'd feel many times guiltier if she didn't try.

"Here." Nabila held out some tattered papers. "Take these."

Liz took them. "What are they?"

"My old identity papers from when I lived in Sainiq."

"Nabila!" Liz threw her arms around her. "Thank you!"

Nabila hugged her back. "You are going whether I think you
should or not. I offer you this meager protection as a thanks for
what you did for me and tried to do for Zahra."

By the time her rental was on the highway to Sidon, Liz's
tears at Nabila's gift had dried. In their place her shoulders
screamed with tension, and the insane drivers on the road weren't
helping.

Beirut

John stood on the balcony of his room on the fifth floor of the
Moevenpick Hotel, gazing down at the two giant swimming
pools surrounded by imported palm trees. Beyond the trees was
the hotel's private marina where the Mediterranean was a shim-
mering gold as it reflected the setting sun. A few of the yachts

anchored there were probably worth more than some countries he'd visited.

"You're staying where?" Major Williams had practically shouted when John called him on the iridium satellite phone and told him that they were checking into the Moevenpick. The major never shouted.

Even doubling up on rooms, Zothgar's mysterious instructions were no doubt putting a good-sized dent in the credit card the redheaded CIA agent, Mary, had issued him "for emergencies only." John had no idea who got the bill, but whoever it was wouldn't be happy. He just hoped it wouldn't get taken out of his next paycheck. And the one after that. And the one after that.

He couldn't make himself feel too bad, though. A year earlier he had scheduled some leave time and had purchased tickets to Cozumel to do some diving. The day before the trip, Task Force Valor had been alerted, and forty-eight hours later he was defusing a booby-trapped weapons cache outside of Khandahar when he should have been floating serenely above Palancar Reef. He still had the nonrefundable plane tickets in the desk drawer in his office, as if holding them might someday make them valid again.

So maybe this was a little payback.

After they had checked into their rooms, John cut the boys loose for a few hours. Rip and Frank made a beeline for the hotel's business center to check their e-mail. Hogan and Sweeney were working on their tans and gawking at all of the silicon surrounding the swimming pool.

He and Doc Kelly had headed to the fully-equipped fitness center for a light workout followed by a quick swim. They were going to meet at eight for dinner at Hemingway's Grill downstairs.

This place wasn't anything like the Middle East John knew. He recalled his nine months defusing mines around that lonely outpost on the Iraq/Iran border with nothing but camels, bedouins, and super-heated sand for a hundred miles in any direction. His time there had redefined his concept of boredom and misery. That was still the one deployment by which he judged all others.

He smiled. Sitting here on his balcony, letting the light sea breeze dry his bare chest was about as far from the desert as one could get, and it felt good.

Until he thought of Liz.

He ran a hand through his hair. What were the odds of running into someone you had been trying unsuccessfully to find for more than three years while on a covert mission in another country? A million to one? A billion?

God had a twisted sense of humor.

Doc Kelly walked onto the balcony wrapped in a thick, white terrycloth bathrobe. "Dude, this place is great! Maybe we can find a reason to delay the mission for another couple of days. These digs are even better than what the Air Force gets."

John laughed, but the sound was sour.

Doc eyed him. "So who was she?"

"Who?" John asked without much hope.

Doc just looked at him.

John sighed. "Her name's Liz Fairchild. She's—" He hesitated. He certainly couldn't say *the girl of my dreams*, though that's exactly what she was. "An old friend."

"An old girlfriend, you mean." Doc sat in the other balcony chair. "Sweeney said you looked like you'd been shot."

"Sweeney exaggerates."

"He says he saved the mission."

"Mmm." But he was probably right. John didn't think anyone had followed them to the café and thus overheard Liz, but with the crowds it was impossible to tell for sure. He'd briefly considered aborting the mission after Zothgar panicked and left the café so abruptly.

He'd discussed it with the team, and the consensus was that Sweeney's quick thinking diffused the situation enough that whoever observed the exchange would probably pass it off as a case of mistaken identity.

"I hear she's a beauty."

John gave Doc a deadpan stare. The last thing he wanted was this discussion.

Doc just smiled. There was no such thing as slack in this unit.

"So who was she?"

"Just some girl I met at the beach about three years ago." When he'd met Liz, Kim was in Miami shopping with her mother. He was so careful not to "cheat" on her. He never touched Liz, never promised her anything.

Granted he should have been up front with her about Kim. But truth be told, he wasn't sure *what* to say, especially since he knew in his heart that there was a more intense, more personal connection between him and Liz in that one weekend than he'd ever had with Kim.

He swallowed a sigh. The team would have enough fun at his expense as it was. They must never suspect how deeply he really felt, or life wouldn't be bearable.

Just another little sign of how much you care, eh, Lord? You let me find her when I can't explain, apologize, or ask her to dinner so I can find out what she's been doing for the last three years.

John narrowed his eyes at the setting sun. "You hungry, Doc?" He consulted the G-shock on his wrist. "We'd better get a bite to eat before we go."

Doc's eyes brightened. Food was better than stripping a man's heart bare any day. "Is a pig pork?"

"Not in a Muslim country, it's not. Let's get dressed and go round up the others."

Three hours later, John sat alone in a plush leather chair in the tan marble lobby of the Moevenpick. They'd eaten at Hemingway's, enjoying every bite after the fare at H-5. Now the rest of the team was waiting upstairs in one of the rooms with all the gear. John fiddled with the walkie-talkie in his hand.

Let's get on with it!

A wedding party was in full swing somewhere nearby, and the wall behind him reverberated with thumping techno bass. The prettied-up partygoers staggering past him at irregular intervals were clearly part of the country's upper crust, and he was again amazed at the women's style of dress, or lack thereof.

It was much more reminiscent of Los Angeles or London than Beirut, Britney Spears or Madonna than Mother Teresa. What did the hard-core Muslims in the country think of such immodesty? Then he reminded himself that a good portion of the Lebanese people weren't Muslim.

Zothgar appeared through the hotel's revolving front door. He didn't look any more relaxed than the last time John had seen him.

"Ah, there you are. Please, we must hurry. Where are your men?"

John held up the small transmitter. "Right here. Where are you parked?"

"At the marina. Please…" Zothgar motioned to the radio.

John held it to his lips and pressed the button. "We're on. Meet us out back at the marina."

Sweeney's voice came back, "Roger, five mikes."

Zothgar led John to a nearby elevator. It was all glass and looked out on the pools below and the black ocean beyond. When the doors closed on them, John turned to Zothgar. "What's wrong with driving to Sidon?"

"It is safer this way. There are checkpoints on the road, and the traffic is terrible.

"This will be the fastest way for us. Don't worry. It is only forty kilometers, so we should arrive shortly after midnight."

It was the answer John had expected, and it made a lot of sense—except it left them without transportation at the other end. "Once you drop us in Sidon, how do we get to our objective?"

Zothgar smiled again. "I have many contacts. A van for you to use will be parked near the docks. Once you have finished with it, simply lock it and leave it parked near the warehouse. I will send someone tomorrow to retrieve it."

John studied Zothgar. How far could he trust this man? Well, shoot. What choice did he have? "Okay, lead the way."

They exited the elevator and the hotel on the lower level by the pool, which was deserted except for one couple nuzzling each other as they looked out over the beach.

When his men appeared, John waved them over. In silence the team followed the operative to the far end of the docks. The few yachts riding at anchor were dark. Zothgar stopped beside the berth of a somewhat run-down motorboat.

Sweeney eyed the boat dubiously. "You sure this is seaworthy?"

John just looked at him.

Sweeney shrugged and hopped into the boat. He turned and held out his hands for gear.

"Don't forget," Zothgar said. "A boat is harder to follow. I believe someone may have taken an interest in your presence here."

Startled, John asked, "Do you know this for a fact?"

Zothgar shook his head. "Just, how you say, a feel in my gut. It pays to be cautious."

John couldn't argue with that. "Does the boat belong to you or to the Lebanese government?"

"The boat belongs to a friend of my cousin. I borrow it from time to time for fishing." Maybe fishing was a euphemism for smuggling or drug running. Either seemed more in character.

It was the first time John had seen Zothgar smile, and he tried to imagine the little man with a rod in his hand. He failed.

The men quietly passed their duffel bags to Sweeney, then jumped aboard.

John paused with one foot on the gunwale. He glanced at the sleeping yachts, then at the motorboat. "Does your cousin's friend keep his boat moored here all the time?"

Zothgar looked surprised. "Here? Oh, no. It is far too expensive. I had Mohammed drop me off at the slip where the boat is usually kept, and I drove it here. When I return later tonight, he will pick me up at its usual berth and take me home."

Satisfied, John jumped into the boat and watched Zothgar slide into the driver's seat. The engine chugged, paused, then idled somewhat smoothly. Then they were away.

The bright full moon made the sea shimmer like a vast sheet of silver lamé, torn neatly in two by the spreading, frothy wake. John watched the lights of the city recede as they turned south about three miles offshore.

"We shall arrive in Sidon in a little over an hour." Zothgar held up his cell phone. "I just received a text message from a cousin who is waiting at the pier. He says the van is in place. He will call shortly with directions for how to get into the camp by way of a smugglers' route. That way you will avoid the checkpoint."

John cocked an eyebrow. "Smugglers' route?"

"Yes. The government has imposed rules on the settlements that do not allow them to bring into the camps construction materials, even those that would be used to simply maintain the buildings already there." He shrugged. "Men will find a way to get what they need."

John shook his head. "It boggles the mind how ridiculously convoluted the Palestinian issue is. All that's needed is a bit of common sense to fix it."

Zothgar snorted. "If it were only that simple."

Maybe, John thought, but sometimes a big dose of American straightforwardness couldn't hurt.

Zothgar looked out at the black swells sweeping past the boat and sighed. "The Palestinians have a saying. 'Our future is in the past.'"

"What does that mean?"

"It means that they left their future in Israel when they were forced to leave their homes and villages when Israel was born. I knew a man who wore the key to his home in Jaffa around his neck until the day he died. I've been to Jaffa. The door this key opened no longer exists. It was bulldozed in the 1970s to make room for a new Jewish housing development." He shook his head. "The past doesn't exist anymore. Perhaps the future doesn't either."

Zothgar looked strangely unemotional for such a volatile topic, though John wondered if it wasn't so much passivity as numbness wrought by living through so many years of brutal, senseless war.

"Sometimes," John said, "I wonder if the concept of nationalism—on either side—is worth all the hardship and pain it causes."

Zothgar took a long drag on his cigarette, its red tip winking in the dark. "That, my friend, is the wisest thing you have said all evening."

John nodded. "I wonder if there will ever be peace with the Israelis."

The Lebanese operative turned to him with a grave look. "I've heard it said that there will only be peace when both sides learn to love their children more than they hate each other."

And that was by far the wisest thing Zothgar had said, John thought as he joined the team in the shabby boat's spacious galley. His men were busy readying their mission gear. They all wore long-sleeved, dark blue athletic jerseys and navy watch caps with their blue jeans. John dug into his duffel to find his night-vision goggles, mounted on his lightweight Protec helmet.

"Feels strange not to be wearin' a uniform," Sweeney commented as he pulled a 9mm handgun from his bag.

"Yeah," John agreed. "If only First Sergeant Mattison could see us now. He'd have a fit!"

Doc Kelly looked from John to Sweeney. "Where did you guys serve together?"

Sweeney smacked a magazine into his pistol. "Rangers. Same company, different platoons."

Doc shook his head. "Ahhh. Bat boys. I should have known."

John feigned offense. "What's that supposed to mean?"

"Nothin'." Doc held up both hands. "But I heard you guys whined like schoolgirls when they made you start growing your hair out."

Sweeney snorted. "Didn't bother me none. Coop here, on the other hand, kept his high-and-tight until one day during formation Mattison smoked him for it."

John put on his helmet and tested the night-vision goggles. "Hey, hair complicates hygiene. That's in the Ranger handbook. But this—" He tossed the navy blue bike team watch cap at Doc. "This would have made old First Sergeant Mattison have an infarction."

The cloak-and-dagger stuff *did* feel strange. John had chosen the Rangers as the quickest way into the Special Operations community. He'd never doubted that he'd make it through the three-week selection course, though more than 50 percent of those who started were routinely weeded out. John, however, had made the decision that he would succeed or die trying, because failure would only prove his father right, and that wasn't something John could live with.

The Rangers were probably the most disciplined unit in the military. When, after three years in the 1st Ranger Battalion, John put in for the Special Forces Assessment and Selection course, it was something of a shock when he was introduced to the more laid-back, long-haired culture of the Green Berets.

But even there, he normally wore a uniform of some kind. He'd never done a combat mission in blue jeans before, and as he prepared his gear, he couldn't help feeling like a kid out of school.

No question about it. With their assignment to the CIA, Task Force Valor was entering into a whole new level of Special Operations. The thought excited John, and truth be told, it scared him a little, too.

After checking the batteries in his NVGs, he quickly reconfigured his XM-8 assault rifle with the buttstock from his bag. Next came the ballistic nylon vest, filled with magazines for the weapon and several stun grenades and flares.

Rip Rubio tapped him on the shoulder. "Hey Coop, check this out." He held up a small handheld GPS unit. "According to my Garmin here, we are thirty minutes from Sidon, making about twenty knots."

"Roger that. I'd better let the major know what's up."

John's pocket started vibrating. He fumbled for the SAT phone and answered it. "Cooper."

"John, it's Williams." The major had beaten him to it. "What have you got?"

"Speak of the devil. I was just about to turn on the SAT-COM and do a commo check with you. We're about thirty minutes from Sidon, traveling by boat."

"Boat?"

"You heard right. Anyway, I'm estimating our time on target to be about 0100. When we hear from you that the choppers are about twenty minutes out, we'll go in."

"Roger. The birds are standing by at the airfield now. Keep me posted. Out."

John flipped the phone closed and returned it to his pocket. The other men had finished suiting up and were looking at him expectantly.

"Okay, boys, gather round. Let's go over this one more time."

23

Outside Sidon

LIZ HAD NEVER been so scared in her life, and that was saying something. After all, she'd been in the refugee camps before, but tonight the ramifications of her brazen plan not working terrified her.

As she hit the brakes and rolled to a stop before the red and white bunker outside Sainiq, she looked at the young soldier with the rifle pointed in her direction. What would she do if he didn't let her pass through the checkpoint? She had no Plan B.

Oh, Lord, please!

When she had driven down here over two weeks ago in a vain attempt to save Zahra and last week for her interviews, it had been full daylight. The soldiers on duty had identified her as a correspondent with business in the camp, and though they were clearly puzzled why she would want to go there and reluctant to let her pass, in the end they had had no reason to prevent her.

Once she was in the camp, the people might not have been pleased to see her, but no one had threatened her or harmed her in any way. Tonight could be far different. Her stomach cramped, and she regretted the chicken sandwich she'd eaten at the KFC in Sidon.

The young Lebanese soldier wasn't smiling as he approached her car. "You are alone?" He bent to peer into the car.

Liz nodded and handed him Nabila's papers.

"My sister is sick," Liz said, trying to speak with a Palestinian accent. "It is very serious. I went to get her medicine." She held out the plastic bag full of bottles. "Please don't keep me from her. She needs these desperately." She shook the bag, rattling the bottles. "I only hope I don't have to rush her to the hospital," she added, setting up the scenario for leaving the camp.

"Why do they let a woman go for the medicine? Are there no men in your family?" he demanded, but Liz thought his aggressive stance was more from uncertainty than anything. He couldn't be more than eighteen years old, probably newly trained, desperate to do things right.

In spite of his attitude, Liz felt some release of tension. He had lowered his rifle as they talked, so now he would shoot the front tire instead of her if he got a finger cramp.

"Our men are not available." She looked down, as if that fact was distressing. She hoped he thought the men in her family were in Israeli prisons or some such thing.

The young soldier stared at her, clearly weighing whether she was telling the truth or not. Liz stared back, feeling desperate and letting him see it. He opened the papers and began studying them.

Lights appeared on the road behind her, distracting both her and the soldier. A rusty black car swept to within inches of her bumper. Music pulsed from the vehicle and rowdy voices sang along. In the headlight's glare, Liz watched the soldier raise his gun, pointing toward the black car. Another soldier that Liz hadn't even seen stepped from the shadows cast by the checkpoint's lights.

Instantly the music died and the voices stilled.

The soldier, his eyes on the black car, held out Nabila's papers. "Go." Clearly he found the men in the black car more interesting and more threatening than she.

Liz went quickly before he had a change of mind. In her rearview mirror she could see the soldiers making the young men in the black car climb out with their hands raised.

As she drove through the gates into the camp, she felt her heart slide from her throat back into her chest. One possible obstacle was out of the way.

"Thank You," she whispered. "Thank You, thank You, thank You!"

She made her way slowly through the narrow streets past homes that were largely dark. When she saw a group of men laughing and talking in front of a lighted building a block ahead, she quickly turned onto a side street.

Liz held her breath, waiting to see if one of them decided to challenge her. Nothing happened, and she continued on until she came to the very center of the camp and the large warehouse marked with an X on her map. She drove slowly around it, hoping against hope that she'd find a door carelessly left open so she could sneak in and find Julie. No such luck.

The building was almost a block in length with a couple of loading doors on its west side. The doors were firmly shut, and even if she had the strength to lift them, they would make too much noise for a secret operation.

She drove around the building three times, and the only other door she saw was one with a light glowing over it. She grimaced. The thought of walking through that pool of brightness sent her heart back to her throat. She swallowed, then swallowed again. She'd save the heart in the throat for when she had to escape through that with Julie.

Sidon

The men were quiet as Zothgar cut the engine, and the motorboat sidled quietly up to an open berth at the public docks. Unlike at the Moevenpick marina, here their spartan craft was easily the most luxurious in the harbor. Rickety fishing boats painted a faded white looked pale gray as they huddled against the shore. Ramshackle huts draped with fishing nets dotted the waterfront.

Hogan jumped out and secured the lines. John surveyed the pier from the boat. He'd hoped that everything would be deserted at just after midnight, but the area around the docks was still inhabited.

The smell of apple-flavored nargileh wafted from a group of men huddled together a hundred meters down the waterfront, talking and smoking a hookah.

In the other direction, young men and women flirted with each other at a coffee shop that was still open. Fortunately, there wasn't anyone in Valor's immediate area.

"You see the white van—just there." Zothgar pointed with his cigarette. "That is your transportation. The key should be under the front passenger tire."

"Okay." John looked over his shoulder. "Rip, you're with me. The rest of you stay here until I confirm that we've got wheels."

"Hey, Coop." Rip held out a black-and-white checkered scarf. "Cover that big, ugly head, bro."

"A *hattah*? Where'd you get this?"

"In the gift shop at the Moevenpick, only here they call them kaffiyehs. It's kinda like wearin' your colors back on the block in East LA. I just figured it might keep someone from looking twice at us in the dark." As he spoke, he adjusted one on his own head.

"Good thinking, Rip."

"You owe me six bucks."

"Bill me."

Leaving his helmet, vest, and carbine, John stepped off the boat. He and Rip covered the distance to the van in under a minute. It was a white, windowless Citroën and appeared empty. John nodded toward the rear. "Pull security in that direction while I get the key."

"Hold up, boss." Rip was looking at three men who had just crossed to their side of the street. John turned in time to see the men start toward them. He and Rubio exchanged dark glances.

John leaned casually against the van, placing one hand on the butt of the pistol hidden at his back. Suddenly Rip muttered, "I got this. Stay cool."

John pulled one end of the kaffiyeh over his shoulder, so the material partially obscured his face. He hoped that in the darkness, his blue eyes wouldn't be too noticeable. When he looked back at Rubio, the staff sergeant was holding a pack of cigarettes and was in the process of tearing off the shrink-wrap with his back to the approaching men.

John frowned. What the…?

Rip quickly extracted a cigarette from the pack and offered it to John. Realizing what Rubio was up to, John played along. He took one and watched as Rip took one for himself before stuffing the pack into his pants pocket.

As the unknown men drew even with them, Rip produced a Zippo lighter and offered John a light. Hoping he wouldn't start coughing and ruin the whole thing, John ignored the men as he stuck his cigarette in the flame. The men walked past.

Just when he thought they were in the clear, one of the men suddenly stopped and turned back toward them. He walked over to Rip, saying something in Arabic John couldn't understand.

Rip nodded at the man and said, "*Salaam.*"

The man nodded back, then repeated what he had just said, this time gesturing at the cigarette Rip was holding.

Without missing a beat, Rip fished the cigarettes from his pocket and handed the man the entire pack.

The Palestinian scowled and shook his head. Saying something John figured must mean something like, "Oh I couldn't take all of them," he tried to hand the pack back. Rip smiled, held up both hands, and said, *"Hamdulillah, Hamdulillah."*

The man looked at John and Rubio for a tense moment before a smile crossed his face. "Shukran. Shukran." He shook Rip's hand, then placed his hand over his heart before returning to his companions. He handed each of them a cigarette, stuffed the pack in his pocket, then turned and waved. His friends followed suit.

"Shukran!" they called again before disappearing down the dark street.

When they were gone, John exhaled heavily and looked at Rubio who grinned. "That went well," Rip said.

John scowled and dropped his cigarette to the ground, crushing it beneath his foot. "Since when did you start smoking?"

Rip looked genuinely insulted. "You know I'd never use those things. When God gave us nice pink lungs, He didn't plan for us to turn them black with cigarettes. I just thought they might come in handy when I saw how many people smoke in this country. Whatever it takes to get the mission done. Besides…" He bent to pick up the butt John had thrown on the ground. "When did you start littering?"

John grunted. "Touché. Did you get those at the gift shop, too?"

"You got it. Cancer sticks are like universal currency."

"Apparently. What does *hamdulillah* mean, anyway?"

"Oh, I learned that last year in Iraq. It's like 'peace, man, no problem.'"

"Groovy."

Rip just grinned at John's sardonic tone.

The street was now clear in both directions as far as John could tell. While Rip took up a position at the rear of the van, John found the key under the front passenger tire. While he was down there, he looked carefully at the underside of the vehicle. After what happened to Doc James, he was wary of any strange vehicle.

He crossed to the driver's side and unlocked the door. A quick sweep of the interior showed it to be completely empty except for a few plastic water bottles. John then popped the hood and took a quick look at the engine compartment, finding nothing out of the ordinary. "Looks good, Rip. Let's get the boys, and let the major know we've gone vehicular."

Ten minutes later they were making their way through the darkened streets of Sidon, Sweeney driving and Rip riding shotgun with his handheld GPS unit. Even at the late hour, what few drivers were on the road were driving like their hair was on fire.

When a motorcycle without headlights careened through the intersection, Sweeney had to jerk the wheel to keep from hitting him, nearly taking out a light post.

"Sorry, guys," he called when a swell of complaints about the rough ride erupted from the men crammed in the back of the van. "The Lebanese apparently have a death wish when it comes to driving."

John braced himself against the back of the seat and thought about the last thing Zothgar had said to him. *Good luck, my friend, but be careful. Here things are never what they seem. What looks to be an enemy may prove to be your ally, and beware those with whom you make friends.*

Was the man simply voicing a deep-seated skepticism cultivated by living in a country where tensions flourished? Or was he trying to tell them something specific? Well, they'd find out soon enough.

John studied the road map of Sidon by the illumination of

his red LED flashlight. The streets emanated from the port area in no particular order or design, and he had trouble finding their route to the refugee camp, even though it was only a few miles outside the city. Of course they weren't exactly looking for the front gate.

They passed a mosque that looked important, and John pored over the map, hoping to find the landmark there, to no avail.

"Hey, Rubio," John called. "Are you getting a good signal on that GPS unit?"

"Yeah, but it isn't helping much. I figured out the coordinates of the warehouse and plugged them in, but ever since we left that main thoroughfare by the port, my map shows no streets. The best I can do is tell you how close we are to the target as the crow flies."

John gave a puff of laughter. "Modern technology. Data in, data out."

"That's garbage in, garbage out," Sweeney said seriously.

John looked at the big man. For a smart guy, he sure could be dumb. "Thank you, Sweeney. What would I do without you?"

It took another forty minutes of driving around, stopping several times for map checks, to find the smuggler's entrance to the camp. It was just as Zothgar had described. An old chain-link fence stretched behind a dilapidated building that looked like it had once been a service station. One fencepost stood at a skewed angle from the rest, the rusty fence sagging with it. Closer inspection revealed that the post had been broken off at ground level. Tire tracks were evident in the dusty, trash-filled vacant lot beyond the fence.

With a quick check to make sure they weren't visible from the road, John and Doc simply walked up the sagging fence, their weight pushing it to the ground. John then waved at Sweeney, who drove the van, lights turned off, across the flattened chain link.

John and Doc jumped back in, and the van bumped across the vacant lot and onto the deserted street inside the Palestinian camp. A block farther on, Sweeney turned the headlights back on, and the team started breathing again.

"That was fun," Frank deadpanned.

An hour later the team was parked half a block from their objective. John took over the passenger seat and scoped the nondescript warehouse with his night-vision goggles. It looked very old, constructed of stone and built into the side of a hill. The only entrances were two rolling metal doors and one regular door to the left of them. A light shone through a dirty window with metal bars on it like most of the other windows in the neighborhood. The only other visible light on the building was a bare bulb that illuminated the covered entryway in front of the door.

They dropped Rip and Hogan in the unlit alleyway across the street from the warehouse, and Rip began using the scope on his weapon to look for signs of life inside the building.

"What've you got, Rip?" John spoke into his FM radio.

The radio beeped, then Rubio whispered, "Only one man confirmed at the moment. He's watching a John Wayne movie on TV."

John chuckled. "Which one?"

"I think it's *The Shootist.*"

"Sounds like my kind of guy."

"Looks like not much is happening, Coop." Sweeney was observing through his own NVGs, which he balanced on the steering wheel. "We could blow a hole in one of those metal sliding doors and make it more of a surprise than if we went in the front door."

John thought for a moment. "I don't think so. We don't know what the configuration is inside the building. They could have stuff stacked in front of those doors, for all we know. Besides, if they're storing explosives in there, we probably shouldn't be setting off any of our own. The whole place could go up." And us with it.

"So we go in the front door then?"

John shook his head. "Not all of us. Frank and I will go in first with Rip and Hogan. You and Doc stay with the vehicle as outside security. We'll drive past the building again. Frank and I will get out and join Rip and Hogan in the alleyway. We'll approach the building from there when we're ready to execute."

John reached over to Frank and grabbed the SATCOM handset, then updated Major Williams on the situation.

"Sounds like you've got it under control, Coop." The major's voice reflected the anticipation that was rising in John as well. "I'll get the aircraft inbound and will give you a call approximately twenty minutes out."

John checked his watch. "Roger that. Valor One, out." He switched back to the ICOM radio.

Sweeney was looking through the goggles again. "Hold up, boss. We've got company."

Sainiq Refugee Camp

LIZ SAT PARKED in a rubbish-strewn empty lot for over an hour, slumped down in her seat so no one could see her. Never in her life had time passed so slowly, but she made herself wait until she felt the camp was soundly asleep. She checked her watch. 1 A.M. Time to go.

She started the car. The explosion of sound shattered the silence. She cringed and held her breath, expecting doors to fly open and men to rush her, demanding to know what she was doing driving around at this hour. And that would be the question if they bought her masquerade as a Palestinian. She shuddered at what they'd do if they learned she was an American. Beat her? Kill her? Or just kick her out?

As the seconds ticked by and nothing happened, she began to breathe again. It took several minutes for her heart to slow to something remotely like normal.

Slowly, carefully, she pulled onto the dirt street and drove back to the warehouse. Liz drove around it again, hoping to see something she had missed before. Nothing new. She parked in what looked like an inconspicuous place, but one near enough for her to get Julie to the car quickly.

If only she knew what to expect as to Julie's health. Could her sister walk or had the arthritis made her virtually immobile? What was her pain level? Had she been beaten? Or worse? Well, she'd know soon enough.

Liz climbed out of the car, leaving the plastic bag of medicines on the seat beside a bottle of water. Her chest felt as if a great constrictor was wrapped about it, pressing the air from her lungs as it tightened, tightened.

Fear.

She made herself inhale a deep, albeit very shaky breath. The constrictor didn't loosen its coils, but she took the first step toward the warehouse, then the second. For Julie she could withstand the crushing pressure of terror.

As she walked, she dropped the car keys into the deep pocket in her skirt, where they banged against her leg with each step. She'd left her purse and passport as well as Nabila's papers under the front seat because she wanted her hands free. She might need to unlock a cell door. She might need to hold Julie up. She might need to— Her mind froze at the unthinkable possibilities.

Oh, Lord! Help! Help!

She kept to the shadows as much as she could, thankful that Palestinian women wore black instead of white like some of the Maronite Christians or blue like the Druze. She crept to the single window and, standing to the side, peered cautiously in. A man, his back to her, sat in a molded plastic chair that he balanced on its back legs. He was completely absorbed in a John Wayne movie showing on a small TV perched on a rickety TV tray.

She searched for any sign of other guards. Bashir had said there was only one, Azmi, but who knew? All she could see beyond the small circle of flickering light cast by the TV was blackness and more blackness. If there were other guards—*please, God, no*—she would have to deal with them if and when they met.

She stepped back from the window and rubbed her chest, as if she could ease the constrictor's crushing embrace. If anything, it gripped tighter. *Oh, Lord! Please! Please!*

With a final calming breath—Ha! As if she could be calm in circumstances like these—she strode to the front door of the warehouse. She caught herself at such an American movement, horrified at how fast she'd fallen out of character, and tried to scuttle.

As she passed under the light hanging over the door, she felt more vulnerable than she ever had in her life. They could see her clearly, whoever *they* were. They could grab her, shoot her, do whatever it was they did to American women who were where they didn't belong. Still, she made herself continue to move slowly forward.

She grabbed the door handle, turned it, and pushed.

Sainiq Refugee Camp

John was sweating as he keyed the mike again. "What's happening, Rip?"

"It's a woman," Rip said, his voice filled with disbelief. "She peered in the window, and then she went inside. She's dressed in black like a proper Palestinian, but I'm not sure she moves like a Palestinian woman. It sounds weird, but she strides like an American."

Sweeney dropped his goggles and looked at John. "What do you make of that, Coop?"

"No idea. I mean, isn't it odd to have a woman out alone this late, especially here?"

Doc spoke from the back of the van. "Could she be a prostitute?"

John shrugged. "I suppose anything is possible. But it seems pretty unlikely, based on what she was wearing and the fact that we're in a conservative Muslim neighborhood."

"Maybe the guard's wife or daughter?" Frank suggested.

"Not likely."

"So what are we going to do?" Sweeney asked.

"We're going to go ahead as planned. Maybe her being there will distract the guard enough for us to get in before he can sound the alarm."

"Well, let's get on with it, then," Frank said.

"What? You got plans for the rest of the evening that we don't know about?" Sweeney asked.

"Yeah, I was hoping to get back to the hotel in time to catch some rasslin' on tay vay." Frank's simulated Southern accent elicited a laugh from Sweeney.

"Okay, Bobby," John said. "Drop us in the alley with Rip, then take a turn around the block and stop here until we call for the getaway car."

Sweeney grinned. "Hooah. Jeff Gordon, eat your heart out."

"Listen, once we leave the van, I need you to monitor the SATCOM and keep the major up to speed on what's happening. And get those birds inbound. No sense staying here any longer than we have to."

"Roger that, boss."

"Okay. Everyone ready?" As grunts of acknowledgment sounded in response, John keyed his mike. "Rip, get ready. We're coming to you."

Sweeney shoved the van into gear and rolled toward their objective. John snapped the chinstrap on his Kevlar helmet and dropped the night-vision goggles into place. When the van reached the alleyway, Frank slid open the side door, and he and John stepped out, melting into the shadows in the alley where Rip and Hogan were barely visible, even through the NVGs.

The van rolled off down the street with the side door open and turned the corner.

John stuck his head close to Rip's ear. "You cover the rear. I'll go in first this time." He turned to Hogan and whispered, "Stack up on me. Then you, Frank."

At Hogan's nod, John moved quietly to the alley opening, staying in the darkest shadows. Hogan squeezed his shoulder, the signal that everyone behind him was stacked on each other, ready for action.

John keyed the ICOM, knowing that each man would be able to hear him clearly in their earpieces. "Okay, men. Let's do this and get out of here. Bobby, any word from Valor Six?"

Sweeney's voice crackled in John's ear. "Roger. Exfil birds are in the air."

"Copy that. Okay. On my count." John leaned forward, fingering the safety on his XM-8. "Five. Four. Three."

"Abort! Abort!" Sweeney yelled in his ear.

John tensed. "What is it, Bobby?"

"Another vehicle—it just passed me and is headed your way."

"Roger." The four men melted backward into the alley as headlights played on the dirt road in front of them.

Liz found herself in a large room that was empty except for the man watching TV. At her abrupt entrance, he jumped to his feet, his chair going over backward.

She held out a hand like an Indian giving John Wayne the peace sign. "Are you Azmi?" she asked in Palestinian Arabic.

He nodded, looking wary.

"I was told you'd be here."

Azmi took a step back, clearly uncomfortable with this news.

Liz reached into the pocket of her skirt and pulled out the envelope stuffed with money. She held it toward him.

Azmi picked up the chair and held it between them, a flimsy barrier against the unknown threat she represented.

"For your son." Hand still extended, she took a step toward him. "For your son."

He looked at her, then at the envelope. When he glanced back at her, his eyes held both confusion and hope. He turned toward a picture taped to the wall near his chair. A beautiful little boy looked solemnly at the camera, his dark eyes too serious for so young a child.

"Is that your son?" Liz asked. "He's very handsome. How old is he?"

Azmi looked at the picture with a sad smile. "He is six."

"And he was injured?"

He nodded. "We were on a picnic. Don't go away from our blanket, I told him. Land mines. I told all of them."

"You have other children?"

"Six others. All older. I fell asleep in the sun. Working nights, you know?" He indicated the warehouse. "I shouldn't have fallen asleep."

Liz tried to imagine how it must feel when something so terrible happened to a little one you loved, and you blamed yourself.

"The explosion woke me." Azmi put his hand to his forehead and rubbed, as if he had terrible pain even in the recounting of the tale. "My son can walk, but he limps badly and is in pain. The child who stepped on the mine died. We did not know him."

Liz held out the envelope again. "This is for your son. To make him better."

He reached toward her, hope flaring once again. She shook her head and pulled the envelope back. "Tell me where my sister is first."

"Your sister?" His eyes were fixed on the envelope.

"The Western woman who is being held against her will."

Azmi looked up from the money. His eyes flicked to a room that jutted into the main storage area in the far corner.

"There?" she asked as she started across the room. "Julie's there?"

"Not—"

The sound of gunfire filled the room. Liz thought for an instant that it was John Wayne holding off the bad guys. Then Azmi screamed. She spun and watched in horror as he fell, grabbing his leg. The envelope tumbled from her hand as she started toward him, the livre spilling across the dirty cement floor.

Another shot rang out; this one hit Azmi between the eyes. Liz stared at him, trying to comprehend what had just happened.

As three men, two of whom held large rifles of some sort, moved across the room, she spun away from Azmi and screamed, "Julie! Julie, where are you?"

Wild with dread, she sprinted for the little room as one of the men leveled his gun on her.

25

Refugee Camp

"WHAT DO YOU WANT to do, boss?" Rip asked.

John thought for a moment. "They may be here to pick up the cargo we're looking for. If we wait for them to leave, they may take the ITEB with them. But if we go in now, we've got more guns to contend with—and that means more noise."

Frank whispered, "Murphy's Law strikes again."

John fished for his radio. "I'll have Sweeney call the major and get some guidance." But before he could press the transmit button on his radio, a shot exploded inside the building. The sound echoed down the street in both directions. John flinched. Another shot erupted.

Sweeney's voice sounded in his headset. "*What* was that?"

John made a split-second decision. "Whatever's going on in there has compromised our presence. Everyone in the neighborhood has to be awake by now. Let's go."

Task Force Valor was across the darkened street in seconds. They ran one behind the other, looking like a lethal alien caterpillar dressed in black body armor. John didn't bother knocking on the cheap wooden door. Instead, he hit it low with his shoulder and smashed it open, immediately breaking left once inside. Behind him, the rest of the team fanned out left and right to avoid the "fatal funnel" in front of the door.

In a fraction of a second, the scene registered in John's consciousness. Five people, three of them with their backs to the door. As they whirled to meet the unexpected intruders, two of them had Kalashnikov assault rifles. The third appeared to be unarmed. On the ground lay another man in a spreading pool of blood.

One of the armed men had had his rifle pointed at the woman. He spun toward John, but before he could complete his turn, two rounds from John's XM-8 knocked him off his feet. The shock of the weapon firing inside the enclosed space was stunning, even with the hearing protection the team wore.

Then the room broke into chaos. The second armed man's eyes widened with fear, and he dropped his weapon. At the same time the woman screamed, and the taller, unarmed man dove behind a desk that jutted from the corner of the wall and disappeared into the dark, empty space of the warehouse.

"Go! Go!" John motioned to Rip and Hogan to follow the tall man. The two, weapons at the ready, ran up to the corner. They stopped for a split second as Rip carefully rounded the corner. Once certain it was clear, the two men raced off in pursuit of the tall man.

Frank covered the man who had dropped his weapon. When his broken Arabic and hand signals proved insufficient in convincing the Palestinian to lie facedown on the floor, he took two steps closer and swept the young man's legs from under him. He landed heavily on his back.

John pulled a pair of flex cuffs from his vest and tossed them to Frank, who had turned the prisoner over and now had a knee between the man's shoulder blades.

Frank pointed at the fifth man, the one who had been on the

floor when they entered. "Better see if he's breathing."

Cordite smoke curled from the end of John's weapon as he took a step toward the man. The woman had run to him and was kneeling beside him. She kept calling, "Azmi!" again and again.

John decided to see if the woman spoke English. He stepped toward her and said, "Are you okay?" She looked up at him and for the first time, he took a good look at her. Those eyes!

Recognition hit him like a truck.

No…way!

Liz stared in disbelief. "John?"

She was so stunned to see him that she was having trouble believing in him. Even with the black helmet and some sort of binocular-looking goggles covering his face, she knew who he was, though he was the last person she expected to see here.

Then it hit. *They had come to rescue Julie!* She climbed to her feet as relief surged. She wouldn't have to do this on her own.

John looked quickly behind the desk. He frowned at Liz, obviously less than pleased to see her. "What are you doing here?"

At least he talks to me now. "Looking for Julie."

He held a finger to his lips. "Shhh…you're shouting. Your ears are still ringing from the shooting."

"Yours aren't?"

"Earplugs. You mean Julie, your sister, right?"

Interesting that after all this time he still remembered she had a sister.

"She's here?" He didn't sound convinced.

"You haven't been watching the news?"

Recognition splashed across his face. "The hostage? That's Julie?" John frowned. "But she had an Arabic name."

So much for the thought that he was here to save Julie. He didn't even know she was the hostage. "She's married to a

Lebanese man." Liz sighed. "Or she was. He was killed in that hotel bombing a few weeks ago."

John held up a hand, then put it to the side of his head. "Roger that. Two KIA, one enemy captured and one civilian. One escaped. No friendly casualties. Relay to Valor Six that we are searching the premises. And get an ETA from the choppers. Valor One, out."

"Did I mess up your operation?" Liz asked, afraid of the answer.

John shook his head and motioned to the body on the floor. "Who's he?"

"His name is Azmi." Her voice caught, and she couldn't stifle the little tremor. "We were standing here talking, and they burst in and killed him." Tears filled her eyes. "He was going to get help for his little boy so he could walk again."

She looked at the picture taped to the wall.

God, who's going to help Azmi's son walk now? Another chink in her "all things work for good" theology.

John grunted. "So who is he?"

Liz blinked back the tears. "The night watchman, I think. A man who was supposed to be able to tell me where Julie is."

"What made you think he'd know?"

"Someone told me that he might be able to help me find her. John, they're going to kill her soon if their prisoners aren't released." Even saying it made Liz's heart contract painfully.

"I saw that on TV at the hotel." One of John's men looked up from his prisoner, who was crying like a twelve-year-old girl and babbling in Arabic. "The kneeling girl."

"And you came looking for her?" John asked, disbelief written all over his face.

Liz nodded.

"All by yourself? Unarmed? Into South Lebanon? Into a refugee camp? Are you crazy?"

Liz concentrated on the anger his attitude engendered. That way she could forget Azmi lying dead and his son who needed him and the dead Palestinian and the arsenal hanging on John and his men and the still missing Julie.

She scowled. "Well, *someone* has to look for her before she gets killed. No one else seems interested."

John shook his head. "You're lucky you aren't dead, too."

She did not appreciate either his sentiment or his tone of voice. Her nerves were raw enough without his yelling at her. "Well *I* didn't kill anyone!"

She knew the statement was foolish the moment it left her mouth. He was a soldier. Of course he might have to kill people in the line of duty. It was what soldiers did.

And she couldn't help wondering how much of her anger was because he'd hurt her three years ago and ignored her earlier today. Make that yesterday. Foolish as it might be, especially considering the circumstances, seeing him roused all of that old pain.

"Oh, and you're upset because I shot him?" John indicated the dead terrorist. "He'd have happily carved your head off with a dull knife and mounted it on his mantelpiece."

She looked at him defiantly. "Don't commit violence to save me." It was the position with which she had been raised, and she said it to irritate him as he was irritating her.

He tossed her a sarcastic half salute. "Yes, ma'am." Then he brushed past her and into the darkness of the warehouse, barking orders to the other men.

If Liz was honest, she had to admit that her opinions had undergone a sea change in the last few weeks. The transformation had begun with Julie's kidnapping, escalated when she saw the pictures of Julie under the sword, and finished its one-eighty when the assault rifle had been pointed at her. Suddenly she did not want to die, and when the despicable man fell under the bullets from John's gun, she had been very thankful it was him and not her.

Not that she would tell John. He was too full of himself as it was. She looked at Azmi again with genuine sorrow and a growing hopelessness. "He never had a chance to tell me what he knew."

John's man, still guarding his prisoner, looked intrigued. "He didn't say anything at all?"

"He didn't have a chance to say much of anything. He just sort of looked at that room over there." Liz pointed. "He got out 'not' just as they burst in."

"John!" The soldier gestured to the room, then looked at Liz. "Stay here, and if he moves," he indicated the bound man, "kick him in the teeth." He paused, as if a thought suddenly struck him, then smiled at her. "Oh, by the way, I'm Frank."

She glanced at the Palestinian on the floor. *Kick him in the teeth. Right.* Before she could tell Frank what she thought of that idea, he turned and joined John at the faded wooden door.

Liz watched with interest as they kicked in the door and went in low, guns ready. When no shooting erupted, she ran to the room. She had to see for herself what was or wasn't in there.

Frank turned to leave and found her in the doorway. "I thought I told you to stay."

She barely heard him. "No Julie?"

But he was gone. Surprisingly, John took the time to answer. "I'm sorry. The room's empty."

Even though she had known deep inside that Julie wasn't here because there had been no answering cries to her calls, she lowered her head and stared blindly at the floor. John and his men ignored her as they continued their quick and thorough search of the warehouse, and she ignored them.

But hope was hard to kill completely.

So she's not here now. Maybe she was.

Liz peered around the door hanging drunkenly from one hinge. Nothing but darkness. She reached inside the door and felt for a switch. None. Taking a deep breath, she walked into the room, swinging her hand over her head, hoping to find a dangling cord. When she did, she pulled it, and the room was filled with a weak light.

The cell was small, windowless, and chill. A cot was pushed against one wall, and a pot with a lid sat in one corner, obviously the substitute for a commode if the smell was any indication.

She walked to the cot and placed her hand on the thin blanket covering it. "Julie?"

There was, of course, no answer. Liz dropped to the cot, trying to imagine her sister trapped in this anonymous cell, terrified, alone, her arthritis flaring. With a sigh she rose. As she did, she caught sight of some scratches on the wall beside the cot. She bent to them, balancing herself with one hand on the cot. With her free hand she traced the scratchings.

JFA.

Julie Fairchild Assan! She had been here! Liz felt lightheaded at this confirmation. But when? How long?

Was she here when I interviewed Hanan? Probably. Maybe. How ironic to know that she had been so close and not known, not even suspected.

A head poked in the door. "We've got to move, ma'am."

"In a minute." She reached to trace the letters again.

John pushed into the room. "Out, Liz."

"She was here, John! Look. Her initials."

"Liz, we can't stay here. We've kicked up a pretty big anthill. We've got to go." He put a hand in the small of her back and pushed her gently but firmly from the room.

"Hey!" She tried to step away, but he took her by the arm.

"We're leaving."

"So go." She swatted at his hand.

"Fine. Just know that if you stay, you're going to die. We're about to blow this building."

She blinked. Suddenly, she didn't mind tagging along.

"Hey, Coop," yelled one of John's men. "Check this out!"

John went to investigate, and Liz followed. The man moved the beam of a penlight over an empty metal shipping carton, painted green. It was unlabeled. The inside was filled with gray foam padding, with six round holes, each about three inches in diameter, laid out in two evenly spaced rows.

"What do you make of it, Coop?"

John shook his head. "Could be anything. But get pictures. You never know."

One of the men pulled a digital camera from a vest pocket. He quickly snapped several pictures of the padded shipping container.

"Okay, we're out of here!" John ordered as the man stowed his camera back in his vest.

Before she realized what was happening, Liz found herself running out of the building behind John. The other black-clad soldiers followed, two of them dragging the bound terrorist and depositing him unceremoniously in a dumpster across the street.

The last man out the door shouted, "Fire in the hole!"

Everyone scrambled into an old cargo van, and just as the door slid closed, the building behind her erupted in a huge ball of black smoke. Liz flinched instinctively as the concussion rocked the van.

"Wait! My car! And purse. And Julie's meds."

"Forget your car," John growled in her ear. "Think about saving your life instead."

26

Soccer Field, Sainiq Refugee Camp

JOHN KNELT in the bare dirt of what passed for a soccer field in the refugee camp. He had one hand on the rear bumper of the van, the other holding firmly to Liz Fairchild's left arm.

"Exfil three-zero seconds out." Sweeney pressed his finger to his ear to hear his radio better.

"Get ready to move," John ordered her.

"You're hurting me!" Her eyes flashed with anger.

He eased his grip a bit. "Sorry. Just stay close to me." He hated the way she looked at him, as if she'd just found out he was the Unabomber. As if it were his fault she'd been snooping around their objective. Still, he had to admire her courage in coming here, no matter how idiotic the move.

"Hey, Coop, we've got company!" Frank came running from where he had been emplacing infrared chem-lights to signal the choppers. He knelt next to John, panting heavily. "Two vehicles coming down the road in a hurry."

John nodded. "Take Rip and Hogan, and set up over by that stone wall. I'll stay here with Doc and Sweeney." He heard rotor blades thumping in the distance. Then his radio chirped. "Valor One, this is Yellow-three-three, over."

He grabbed his mike. "This is Valor One. Go."

The pilot of the Special-Ops helicopter came back, his voice dispassionate and unhurried, as if he were calling about a misfiled form, not about dropping a multimillion dollar Black Hawk into a hot landing zone. "This is Yellow-three-three. We are on final at LZ football, and have your IR markers, over."

The sound of the rotors came closer, but John still couldn't see the aircraft. He pressed the transmit button in his hand. "Roger, three-three. Be advised, there are two vehicles approaching from the south, possibly hostile. Can you take them out? Over."

"I see them. Stand by."

John watched the wildly bouncing headlights as they sped toward the soccer field. They were less than a hundred meters distant when his radio beeped again.

"Valor One, keep your heads down. We're going to shake them up a bit."

Three seconds later the black helicopter screamed by over their heads, its stubby wing pods sporting barrel-like rocket launchers.

"Get down," John ordered Liz, wrapping a muscular arm around her.

A split second after that, flame spouted from the launchers, accompanied by a loud whoosh.

Liz looked up to see what was happening. In the next instant the lead vehicle disappeared in a ball of flame. Frank let out a whoop. Liz screamed.

"Stay down!" John pushed her back to the ground.

The second vehicle swerved around the fireball and kept coming.

The helicopter pulled up and went around for another pass. It probably wouldn't complete its turn before the car was on them. John watched intently. When the vehicle was only fifty yards away, he raised his rifle and let off a sustained burst, sending several red tracers into the grille of the speeding car. The other members of the team opened up on it as well.

The car skidded to a halt, and four doors flew open. Almost immediately, its occupants returned fire.

John grabbed Liz again and yelled at Doc Kelly. "Get her behind the van!"

The medic took her arm and pulled her around to the side farthest from the incoming rounds.

The helicopter came in for a second pass. This time, however, it hovered sideways directly above John. The minigunner on one side opened up with his 7.62mm Vulcan cannon. A solid line of tracers lit the sky, homing in on the car like a laser beam. Sparks erupted all around the vehicle as hot lead poured into it, ripping the air with a sound like a giant zipper.

John ducked his head as hot shell casings poured down around him. His radio crackled in his ear.

Doc Kelly yelled, "More vehicles coming on this side!"

John jumped to his feet just as one of the rear van windows shattered. Staying low, he charged around the van in time to see men spilling out of the back of a small pickup truck on the north side of the LZ.

He emptied his magazine in their direction, then grabbed his radio to call the chopper. But it had already seen the newcomers. The minigun on that side of the aircraft let loose with a burst that again rained hot brass on his helmet.

Liz made a surprised, frightened sound as shells fell on her, too. And without protective earplugs, the noise forced her to clamp her hands over her ears.

"Under!" John pointed to the van. Liz, eyes wide, slid under the van without a word of protest.

As he slammed home another magazine, a man stepped from behind one of the vehicles and raised a long metal tube to his shoulder.

RPG! John keyed his mike and shouted, "Three-three, pull out, PULL OUT!"

Too late! The rocket-propelled grenade traced a faint line from the end of the tube to the tail of the Black Hawk in a fraction of a second. With a sound like a car wreck in the air, the helicopter lurched and rolled off to one side, its miniguns still spitting flame. As the huge black bird pulled out of its roll and gained altitude, the smoke trailed from its tail section.

Sweeney cursed and dropped the man holding the RPG with a burst from his weapon.

The pilot's voice sounded in John's ear again, unfazed as ever. "This is Yellow three-three. We've taken a hit and are losing hydraulics. Sorry, boys, but we're out of this fight."

John fired a few more rounds toward the vehicles to the north. Then the night fell strangely quiet. There didn't seem to be any more fire from the south, and the men who had come in the second set of vehicles were either out of commission or keeping their heads down. He looked down at Doc Kelly, who was lying along the side of the van, shielding Liz with his body. "You okay?"

The medic got to his knees and reached a hand down to help Liz out from underneath the van. "We're okay. What do you say we leave this little party?"

"You got it. Hold tight for a sec."

Frank, Rip, and Hogan came running from their positions and reported six killed in action from the first set of vehicles.

The major's voice came over John's radio, calling from the airbase in Jordan. "Valor One, this is Valor Six, over."

He keyed the mike. "Go, Six."

"Any casualties, John? Sounds like you all had your hands full."

"Negative friendly casualties. Approximately ten enemy KIA. And we need that CSAR bird in here quick before anyone else shows up."

"There's a problem, John. Your aircraft went down in a field about two miles from your location, and the rescue bird is going in to get them now. You'll need to pull out and proceed to your alternate Pickup Zone, PZ Hockey. We'll have the CSAR bird pick you up there after they get the crew of the Black Hawk on board. It'll be a tight fit, but they should still be able to pack your team on board, over."

"Roger. Pull out to PZ Hockey, over."

"Do it quick, John. The CSAR bird should be there in about one-five minutes. Also, be advised that Phoenix just came in with a report that Washington is getting angry phone calls from the Lebanese government."

Already? John's jaw clenched. Wonderful. "Roger that. Valor One, out."

He quickly looked over the van, noting the broken glass and several bullet holes. "Hey, Bobby, you think this thing still runs? We've got to pull out to our alternate PZ."

"I think so." The blond sergeant yanked open the driver's door. Before he could climb inside, a volley of bullets cracked past their position, one of them starring the front windshield. Liz jumped and gave a little scream. Everyone ducked. Frank, Rip, and Hogan returned fire.

"Go! Go!" John waved Doc Kelly into the van. "And take her with you!"

While Doc pushed Liz into the van and crawled in after her, Sweeny leaped into the driver's seat and fired up the engines. He threw the van in gear and did a hard U-turn back toward the warehouse, spraying gravel.

"Get in! Go!" John thundered at Rip, Frank, and Hogan. As his men climbed in the side door of the van, John emptied his magazine in the direction of the shooters. Just as Sweeney accelerated, he dove through the open side door.

Lebanese Countryside

Liz sat in the van, her back against the vehicle's side. All around her were men in black body armor, each bristling with weapons. She could see the bullet-riddled front window and the missing back window—not that she could actually see something that was missing—and the holes where the gunfire had penetrated the van.

Her nerves crackled and danced like the wildest of dervishes. It was all she could do not to twitch with the potent combination of fear and adrenaline.

She'd lived in the Middle East long enough to have seen the abuse committed by some in the military. She'd seen Israeli and Lebanese soldiers harass Palestinians at checkpoints just because they had the power and Syrian soldiers swagger through Beirut, throwing off authority sparks that would consume anyone who challenged them.

And she'd seen the evidence of the Palestinians' counteroffensive. Ansar Inshallah, Hezbollah, Hamas—it didn't matter. They all used terrorist tactics to exert some leverage in the uneven struggle for clout, for power.

And here she was, surrounded by fighting men. Granted they were Americans, but they were still soldiers.

A fallen world needs soldiers, she reminded herself. Someone has to protect and defend the good guys, or the bad guys would win. It was like the need for police to curtail local lawlessness. The military was to hold nationalistic aggression at bay if at all possible and to stand against that threat when it became uncontainable.

The van screeched around a corner, throwing her against John who sat on the floor beside her.

"Sorry," she muttered as she struggled to regain her balance.

"S'okay." With a gentle push, he righted her.

"The man who escaped the warehouse must have rallied

some of his buddies," Frank said. He was the only one besides John whose name Liz knew. And Doc.

She gazed around the van. One of the men was reloading his weapon. Another was checking the pockets on his vest. She knew from bumping into John that the vest was hard, probably Kevlar. She had dated a guy at UVA who had a Kevlar canoe. Lightweight. Indestructible. She had never imagined being surrounded by the stuff in circumstances like this.

What was she doing here? All she wanted was to find Julie. Instead, she'd seen an unarmed man murdered and a bad guy killed nanoseconds before he was able to shoot her. She'd been in a firefight where several others were killed and red hot shell casings fell on her head. A firefight!

She made herself take several deep breaths.

"You're doing great," Doc said from his seat against the opposite wall. He grinned at her, completely relaxed, one arm draped over a raised knee. "Just think of the stories you've got to tell your grandchildren. It'll all be declassified by then."

"If I live to have grandchildren," she managed as they tore around another corner, throwing her into Frank this time. "Sorry."

But the word *stories* broke through her daze. Yikes! She was riding with a bunch of Special Forces guys as they escaped from terrorists. What a story!

They sped through the darkened camp, bouncing wildly at times, whipping around corners. Liz's teeth rattled as the van lurched and twisted, and she stopped apologizing for slamming against either John or Frank.

"Incoming!" yelled the driver, the blond Southerner. "Hit the deck!" He stood on the brakes.

Before Liz even had time to grasp the news, let alone react, John had her flat on the floor, his arm firmly around her waist as he held her protectively near. She heard a sound like two tractor trailers hitting head on, and this time she knew better than to look. Instead, she burrowed against John and called on heaven with incoherent prayers.

Oh, Lord! Oh, God! Oh, Lord!

The explosion was thunderous. The van rocked and slewed sideways, but somehow the driver kept control, picked up momentum, and sped on.

She felt John lift his head.

"Sweeney?"

"An RPG," reported the driver, who sounded much calmer than humanly possible. "Hit the wall next to us. All clear."

John raised himself to his knees. Liz wanted him back. Having his Kevlar between her and the shooting helped allay her fear.

"Did you see who fired?" he asked.

"Two men down that alley back there. On foot. If they decide to come after us, we'll have plenty of time."

Plenty of time? Liz stared at the hand John extended to her. How long could it take the bad guys to get to a car and chase them? Maybe next time they wouldn't miss. Maybe next time Sweeney wouldn't see them in time to take action.

She took John's hand and let him pull her to her knees. Plenty of time? Sweeney was nuts. They were all nuts. They did this stuff on purpose!

She looked around the van at the men resuming their seats. Doc said something that made one guy laugh. There wasn't one nerve among them, she thought indignantly. Of course she had more than enough to go around, twitching as she was.

"Exit coming up," Sweeney called.

"Hogan, Rip," John said as he settled beside Liz.

"We're on it," the Latino said.

The van slowed, and the two jumped out, leaving the side door open.

In a minute the van passed Rip as he stood on the edge of what looked to be a downed chain-link fence. She assumed Hogan was standing on the fence on the other side of the van. After bumping over the uneven surface, Sweeney slowed again for Rip and Hogan to jump back in.

"Directions?" Sweeney yelled as he drove across scrubby ground.

"In a minute." Rip pulled an electronic gadget from a vest pocket.

She didn't bother to listen as Rip called out instructions for getting to the hockey field. Why should she? She didn't need to know where they were going. Her car was back in the camp, and she wasn't driving it anywhere anytime soon, if ever.

U.S. Airbase, Jordan

MARY WALKER OPENED the door to the air-conditioned clamshell that was Task Force Valor's tactical operations center at H-5. She was running on very little sleep and had been trying to catch a quick nap when the shrill beeping of the secure commlink in her room awakened her. She grabbed the phone and tried to clear the fog from her mind.

The message from her boss had jarred her wide awake. Now it was her job to pass the bad news along to Major Williams.

He was pacing the floor in front of a makeshift table, a radio handset pressed to his ear. The end of a lollipop stuck out of one side of his mouth, the corners of which were firmly set. Word had it the major was trying to give up cigars. "I don't care what your fuel gauge says," he said into the handset. "I want you to remain on station until my team arrives at PZ Hockey. You got that?"

As Mary approached, the major put the handset down and barked to no one in particular, "Someone find me a landing strip inside Jordan as close to the Syrian border as possible. Maybe even the Gaza strip. The CSAR bird may not have enough gas to get all the way back here."

A pair of soldiers jumped up and began surveying the pile of maps lying on the table.

Before Mary could say anything, the major whirled to her. "What now?"

Mary suspected he'd been subsisting on little more than coffee and lollipops since the mission began. She took a deep breath, knowing that given his present mood, he was going to go ballistic.

"Bad news, sir."

His gaze narrowed. "I don't want any more bad news."

Well, you're going to get it. "Langley just got a call from the White House that the Lebanese embassy is screaming bloody murder because U.S. forces are engaged on the ground in their country."

"Why are they screaming? They flew our guys in!"

"Yes, well, we both know the agreement was tenuous at best."

The major grunted. "So you want me to abort pickup?"

Mary ignored the question. "Now that Valor has apparently started a major firefight inside a refugee camp, the agreement is falling apart. It appears that the Lebanese military wasn't informed of our little foray—and they're not happy."

"Of course they're not happy." The major continued to pace. "Reverse situation, we wouldn't be happy either."

"Beirut's afraid the Palestinians will call the skirmish a massacre and blame the government for it. That'd stir up all kinds of old animosities." An understatement if ever there was one.

"Just what we need."

"From what my boss says, the Israelis are calling too, wanting to know what the deal is." She sighed. Such were the joys of instant communications.

"It's got nothing to do with them!" The major's voice betrayed his frustration.

"There's more, sir. Lebanon is demanding that our aircraft withdraw immediately. They're scrambling fighters from Beirut as we speak. Apparently the jets have authority to shoot down any foreign aircraft in Lebanese airspace."

Crunch! Major Williams bit down on what was left of his sucker. He stood silently for a moment, his jaw muscles crushing the remains of the candy. "Wait a minute. I didn't think Lebanon had any operational fighters. And how do they expect us to get our team out?"

"They apparently have three planes that fly, all of them old Hawker-Hunter F-70s made in Britain. As obsolete as they come, but plenty capable of knocking a Black Hawk out of the sky."

She could tell what Williams was thinking. *Welcome to the CIA.* She wished she could tell him this sort of thing never happened, but unfortunately, that wasn't her experience. In the three years she'd been a field agent, she'd never seen a mission come off as planned.

But they had backup plans. They weren't going to leave those men out there all alone. She found it ironic, however, that their ride home would have to bail on them or face air-to-air missiles from an ally who had probably purchased them from the U.S. or its other allies.

To Mary's great surprise, the explosion of profanity she expected from the major at the ruination of his plans never came. Instead, Williams's countenance changed suddenly. The anger vanished, and a thoughtful expression took its place. Since she knew very few in the military who exercised verbal self-control, she looked at him with great respect, not for his rank and the authority it gave him, but for him as a person.

He turned and snatched up the radio handset from one of the operators behind him. "Yellow-three-four, this is Valor Six. Be advised, we have hostile aircraft en route to your location. We need to know the ETA of our team to PZ Hockey, over."

A super-calm voice crackled over the receiver. "Wait one, Valor Six." A tense moment passed during which no one spoke.

Then the radio came to life again. "Valor One estimates seven minutes, over."

The major looked at Mary. "How long till the jets get to them?"

She shook her head. "Less than that. It's only about ten minutes once they're airborne, and they left a few minutes ago. I'd say they have less than five."

Williams looked at his watch and let out a low growl. He yanked the sucker stick out of his mouth and threw it in the trash can. It occurred to Mary that most people would find the major quite intimidating, but he reminded her a lot of her father, a career Marine officer.

The major spread another map out on the table. What Williams said next surprised her even more than the fact he hadn't been swearing like her father always did in a tense situation. "Okay, Lord, it looks like You want our boys to walk. So be it. But please bring 'em all home."

He didn't really say it like a prayer, which to Mary meant folded hands and bowed head. It was more like he was just talking to a trusted superior. The contrast of the gentle prayer with the major's gruff, football-coach exterior stunned her. One thing was certain. Her father would have never done that.

She shrugged. Calling on the Almighty certainly couldn't hurt and was definitely more constructive than a string of cuss words. At least now she had an idea why he reacted as he did. Most senior officers always needed to be in control of the situation, and when they weren't, their personal discipline slipped. Major Williams seemed to be okay leaving those things he couldn't control in the hands of his God.

Mary wasn't sure this worldview belonged in a place like this, but she sometimes wished she could trust in something, in *Someone* like that. Truth be told, the idea fascinated her.

Williams put the radio to his lips once again. "Yellow-three-four, this is Valor Six. Abort pickup. I say again, abort pickup. You and your crew need to get out of Dodge right now, over."

"Roger, Valor Six. Yellow-three-four aborting pickup, returning to base."

Williams dropped the radio mike and picked up a SAT phone. He flipped it open and began to dial quickly and deliberately. "On to Plan C. Granted, our evasion and escape route is a long shot at best. They'll have to implement the plan and head to the coast, where we'll have the special ops guys from the Sixth Fleet come in and pick them up." He finished dialing and put the handset to his ear.

Mary wondered if the situation was already beyond their control.

Lebanese Countryside

"PZ Hockey coming up on the left. Sixty seconds." Sweeney downshifted the van as he prepared to stop.

"Get ready to move," John said.

Liz wilted with relief. They were finally going to get out of here. She couldn't believe that less than two hours ago she had willingly driven into a Palestinian refugee camp, confident that since she spoke the language and knew the culture, she'd be able to handle anything that happened. A little puff escaped her lips as the depth of her naiveté sank in.

"What?" John said.

She shook her head. "Nothing. I just can't believe I'm…here."

It was his turn to huff now, but she noted half a smile on his lips. "Tell me about it. What are the odds?"

The tall commando near the rear door spoke up with an easy Texas drawl. "Lemme get this straight. Y'all know each other?"

Liz looked at John, not sure where to start. He cocked a sweaty eyebrow. "Well, we met a few years ago at the beach…"

John stopped and put one hand to his right ear. The other men seemed to be listening to something as well. Then a collective groan came from all of them, and several muttered curses under their breath. John spun around and knelt next to the driver's seat and appeared to be talking on his radio.

Liz knew she'd missed something important. She grabbed the closest arm, which happened to be Frank's. "What?"

He appeared apologetic, though it was hard to tell in the dark. "The helicopter just radioed that they are aborting our pickup."

A blanket of barely-contained panic settled on Liz. "What? What does that mean?"

The answer she was hoping for, *Don't worry; it'll all work out*, wasn't what she got. "It means this mission just got a lot more complicated." Frank wasn't even looking at her when he answered. He was watching John, now talking on his satellite phone.

Sweeney stopped the van, and it idled quietly by the side of the road as John conversed with the person on the other end of the line, presumably his superior. She didn't understand much of what was being said, which wasn't surprising since they weren't speaking English but acronym-ish.

She heard the term E&E used several times but didn't realize that her confusion was apparent on her face until Frank leaned in and said, "Evade and Escape. In other words, we have to get ourselves back any way we can."

"Any way?" What in the world did that mean?

Frank nodded, his attention back on John, who was saying, "Yes, sir. I understand. Even if they managed to have someone there before daylight, I don't know if we could get there that quick. No, that's okay. We'll just find somewhere to lie low until dark tomorrow, then head back to the coast."

He had a map spread out on the van floor between the two

front seats and was tracing a line on it with a finger. "Okay, I see it. Then once we get there, how do we sig…hello? Can you hear…?" He pulled the phone away from his ear and punched the keypad with an index finger.

Rip spoke from his place in the passenger seat. "Do not tell me the battery just died."

John didn't tell him. Instead, he tossed the phone onto the floor.

The rest of the team got the message. The air inside the van erupted with expressions of frustration and disappointment. Liz never knew there were so many ways to curse one's bad luck.

"Shhh shhh! Hold up!" Sweeney held up a hand for quiet as he cocked an ear out the window. The van fell silent in an instant. Liz strained until she heard what sounded like jets approaching.

"Fast movers," John said.

Sweeney leaned forward and squinted through the shattered windshield. "You think they're looking for us?"

Exactly my worry, Liz thought.

John shook his head. "No, the major said the choppers had to abort because the Lebanese government had fighters up ready to take them out. Apparently somebody forgot to tell them we're supposed to be working together."

Frank said, "That fireball when the warehouse blew probably got them thinking that the Israelis were attacking again."

The rumbling of the jets grew louder. Doc, still sitting on his aid bag, let out a low whistle. "Those jets are a whole lot faster than a Black Hawk. I hope our birds got away safely. Makes me kinda glad to have my feet on the ground."

"Y'all might change your minds about bein' down here pretty quick," Hogan said, focusing on something out the back window. "We got three vehicles coming this way, and it looks like they're in an awful hurry!"

John yelled, "Go, Bobby! Go! Go! Go!"

But Sweeney had already popped the clutch, sending everyone in the back of the van sliding for the rear door. Liz clutched at John as he held on to the front seat. She missed and tumbled headlong into Frank. The scope on his assault rifle caught her squarely in the eye, and she saw stars for a moment. Then Frank pushed her upright. "You okay?"

She held her hand to her eye, trying to stifle tears of pain. "Yeah. Sorry."

Frank braced himself against the side of the van and pulled something, presumably the thing that held the bullets, out of his gun and checked it, then slapped it back into place.

"You better hold on, kiddo," he said to her with a smile. "Things are about to get interesting."

The battered black Mercedes whined and shuddered as Imad Hijazi ground through the gears on the road outside Sainiq. He'd paid off the guards at the checkpoint in order to leave the camp without being hassled, and it had cost him precious time as well as considerable funds. The Americans were getting away, and Imad would not stand for it. They had invaded his home, his domain, and had killed some of his men.

They would pay.

The guards at the checkpoint had confirmed that the infidels had not left the camp by the main entrance. That meant they knew about one of the smugglers' gates, and they would only know that if they had help from Lebanese intelligence. There was one more reason to support the overthrow of the government that was little more than a puppet of the Zionists and Americans anyway.

He was surprised the commandos had come after the girl, but then Americans had a foolishly high opinion of women. It was surely the will of Allah, or perhaps just sheer luck, that they had moved her earlier that day. If they lost her to the American invaders, they would lose their means of distracting attention from their real agenda.

His chest swelled with joy that he had the foresight to suggest they move her as well as their stockpile of this fascinating new secret weapon, what some were calling Allah's Fire, to a more secure location until their next operation. No one needed to know that he'd merely been concerned about petty thieves and collaborators, and that the arrival of Special Forces commandos had never once crossed his mind.

He narrowed his eyes. What if the commandos had been looking for the secret weapon? If that was so, their appearance only confirmed his belief that the exotic material put real fear into the hearts of the imperialist infidels. He smiled. The next time they used Allah's Fire, it would not only strike a blow against the West, it would cause the whole world to tremble at the mention of the name of Ansar Inshallah.

For too long, among those who resisted in the name of Islam, other groups garnered the lion's share of the funding, attention, and respect, while the Followers of God's Will were virtually unknown. Soon, however, that would change. Ansar Inshallah, and by extension Imad Hajazi, would get its deserved recognition.

And the bodies of some American soldiers would only make that recognition sweeter.

Imad had not found it easy to achieve his present position within the camp and within the organization. It had been necessary to show himself zealous, but not so much that he might be asked to martyr himself. He became cunning enough to acquire the good graces of those in power in the camps, especially Abu Shaaban, but ruthless enough to climb a mountain of dead bodies to take that power for himself when the time came. He learned to see opportunity where others saw only tragedy, and that vision was what carried him now.

The loss of the warehouse would most certainly have repercussions with his benefactors. However, if he could capture the American soldiers—they had to be American; he'd heard them speaking English as he fled the building—if he could affect their capture now, he would look like the hero. No one would dare say a word about the loss of the warehouse.

Suddenly jets roared overhead, and Imad laughed. He knew how the politicians in Beirut worked. They would deny knowing anything about the incursion at Sainiq, an incursion they undoubtedly approved, and the jets, all self-righteous about protecting Lebanese soil and airspace, would chase away the American rescue helicopters.

The abandoned commandos were his.

A tune by his favorite musician erupted from his pocket. The car fishtailed a bit as he grabbed for his phone. He hit the on button as he fought to keep the aged vehicle on the road. "Yes? Where are they?"

"We just heard that the white van was seen heading east toward Habbouch!"

Imad hit the brakes and pulled to the side of the road. East toward Habbouch? Why would they go that way? Were they lost? They should be trying to get to the coast since their aircraft had deserted them. Or were they still searching for the blond girl?

"Have someone put up a roadblock on the way to Habbouch, and tell everyone else to meet me at Zaica."

He hung up the phone and pulled the car into a tight U-turn.

They must not escape.

28

Lebanese Countryside

JOHN BRACED HIMSELF between the front seats of the speeding cargo van as it labored up a hill. He hollered back at Hogan, "How we looking, Buzz?"

"They're gaining on us!"

Great. This night just keeps getting better and better.

He didn't bother trying to read the map anymore. It would be impossible inside the lurching van. He looked over at Rip, holding on to the dash with one hand and staring intently at the luminescent screen of his GPS in the other. "Where are we headed, Rubio?"

"Don't know for sure, Coop, but we're headed out into the country going almost due east."

"That's what I thought." Anything uphill in this country was east. While it was more than wise to get away from the city, going east meant mountains and harsh terrain. East meant the Bekaa Valley and then Syria. Not good. "We need to be going west, toward the coast."

Liz was sitting behind him, holding on to the back of the

driver's seat for dear life. Liz! What had he gotten her into by dragging her along? Well, maybe she'd gotten herself into it, but now it was his responsibility to get her out.

Rip squinted at the GPS again. "It doesn't look like there are many roads off of this one, but like I said, the base map in this thing isn't real detailed for Lebanon."

They sped along a road that ran along a ridge, the ground falling away steeply on each side. They passed occasional buildings perched on the crest, and the lights of other villages were visible, probably perched on distant ridgelines.

John turned to Sweeney, who had his eyes glued to the road. "Take the first turn that doesn't look like a dead end."

"What does a dead end look like, boss?" Sweeney's hillbilly accent dripped sarcasm.

"Just turn at the first real intersection you see. We've got to lose these guys." He patted his vest pockets with one hand. "I don't think we have enough ammo left to hold them off for too long. Besides, we need to find a way back toward the coast."

"Roger that. Looks like a little village up ahead. Yep, there's a road going off to the right. Hold on."

John turned and yelled to the guys in the back, "Grab on to something!"

Sweeney barely slowed at all for the turn, realizing too late that it was more than a ninety-degree change of course. John thought the van was going to roll from the centrifugal force and tumble down the side of the ridge.

Liz made a little squeak as she was flung about, but he was too busy holding on himself to help her. Incredibly, the van held the road, swerving at the last moment to miss a parked car, then accelerating.

"Good driving, Sweeney."

"You can tip me later, boss." His voice was calm and totally controlled. Bobby was having fun.

"Okay, looks like we're now headed south toward some town I can't pronounce," Rip said.

John nodded. "South is good."

"No, it's not!" yelled Sweeney. "Roadblock! Get down!" He jerked the wheel to the left, sending everyone sprawling again.

John held on tight as the van sideswiped another parked car just as an RPG streaked by the passenger window, exploding somewhere behind them with a sound like a train wreck. He grabbed Liz, still hanging on to the driver's seat as best she could, pulled her to the floor, and draped himself over her.

Rip yelled, "Left, Bobby! Go left there!"

The van rocked again as Sweeney cut the turn short, skidding around the corner.

It sounded like someone was slamming a pickax into the side of the vehicle as rounds punctured its thin metal flanks.

Liz whimpered, and John pulled her close, burying her head in his vest. He didn't know what else to do. *Please, God, we need some help here!* The thought came so suddenly, so automatically that it shocked him, then disgusted him. He'd wanted to give up on God.

But I haven't given up on you.

The thought threaded its way through the chaos in the van into his heart, but he slammed his mind shut against it. Instead, he concentrated on Liz.

"It'll be okay," he whispered in her ear.

He thought he heard her give a slightly hysterical gasp of laughter, but he wasn't sure.

Hogan knelt at the back window and returned fire with his XM-8. Brass ejected from his weapon and pinged around the inside of the lurching van.

Then as quickly as it began, the shooting stopped. John lifted his head cautiously.

"I think I got at least one of 'em," Hogan announced as he kept watch out the back window.

John pushed off the floor. "Anyone hit?"

"Fine up here," answered Rip.

"Liz?"

"I...I think I'm okay."

"Doc?"

"Good to go."

"Hogan?"

The big man grunted, then said, "Hey, I got an idea." He swung the butt of his weapon and smashed out the other rear window. A chorus of surprised voices erupted inside the van.

Hogan looked at them. "Take it easy. I know what I'm doing. Now we got two firing ports. Baldwin! Get yourself back here and give me a hand."

Frank, who had been sitting on the floor of the van, started to rise. "Okay, you crazy...aaggh!" He clutched his side and sat back down hard.

"Whoa, let me see." Doc Kelly crawled over to him. "You're bleedin', Frank!"

Frank held up a hand and looked at it. John couldn't see any blood in the blackness, but apparently Frank could. "So I am."

"Fix him, Doc," John ordered.

"We've still got jihadists on our tail! About half a mile back!" Hogan hollered.

Things were going from worse to catastrophic. John spun to Rip. "Where are we, Rubio?"

"Still heading south-southwest. Looks like there's a turn east coming up in about a mile."

"We may not make it that far," Sweeney yelled. "The steering is acting squirrelly. I think they may have gotten one of our tires back there."

Figures. But what did he expect? It was obvious they weren't getting any help from above. He might as well have asked the tooth fairy to intervene on their behalf. Whatever happened next would depend on him and his men, on their proficiency, cunning, and skill. It was up to them and them alone. For some reason, the thought was anything but comforting.

Doc had a penlight out and was inspecting Frank's wound. "It got you in the side, just below the vest, but it doesn't look like it hit anything important."

"*Everything's* important," Frank countered, sounding snarly.

John couldn't argue with that. "Is he able to walk?"

"I'll be fine." Frank grunted as Doc poked.

"Hold still. Just let me get a collagen bandage on it."

"Make it quick, Doc!" Sweeney shouted from the front. "We're going to have to bail!"

"There's a T-intersection up ahead," Rip said. "Go left there."

"Left?" John shook his head. "We need to head west."

"Trust me, Coop. I'm on the map."

"Okay." John trusted Rip's judgment. "Hogan, how much of a lead do we have?"

"Thirty seconds, maybe a little more."

"Should be enough," Rip said. "Once you make the turn, there's an immediate right that goes back south. Take that, and we may be able to lose them."

"Can you cut the lights?" John asked.

Sweeney downshifted. "Yep. But the brakes will still light up. I'll try not to use 'em."

"This should be interesting," Frank muttered through clenched teeth as he held his side in anticipation of the jostling.

"Hold on to something!" Sweeney flipped the lights off and downshifted again. He jerked the wheel, cutting the corner tight.

John checked Liz as he braced himself against the passenger seat. She looked scared but didn't say a word, just held on to the back of the driver's seat for dear life. He smiled to encourage her, but he wasn't certain she saw. Maybe now she'd understand why he hadn't called her back three years ago. Not that he thought tonight was doing much to rekindle her feelings for him.

Sparks flew behind them as they rounded the corner on the rim of the left rear tire. The ride immediately got much rougher, and Sweeney fought to keep the van on the road.

"Right! Turn right! Right here!" Rip pointed frantically at the side road. Sweeney used the brakes to make the turn, and John was sure this time the van would topple.

"Made it!" Rip exclaimed when they had all four wheels, or what was left of them, on the ground once more.

"Not for long," Sweeney muttered.

"Okay, we've got to get out," John said. "Frank, how you feeling?"

"I'll feel better once we're walking. Sweeney's driving hurts more than the gunshot."

"Then let's do it."

Sweeney skidded to the side of the road, and every door opened as Task Force Valor piled out with Liz in tow. John quickly surveyed their surroundings. The ground sloped off on either side of the road into what looked like some kind of orchard. "Follow me," John hissed and headed down the embankment.

It was steeper than he originally thought, but the terrain worked in their favor.

They half ran, half slid down the embankment for several hundred meters. Once Liz cried out when she slipped and landed on her backside, but Hogan pulled her back up, not even breaking stride. By the time the ground began to level off, they could hear shouts from above and then a few shots.

"Everybody, keep going!" John waved the men on. "They're firing blind. Rubio, take point."

The group slowed once they reached the bottom of the draw where the vegetation grew more thickly. Shortly they came to a stream, swollen with recent spring rain. John pushed his way through the underbrush until he found Rip. "Can we get across?"

Rip scanned the bank. "Looks like we could get across over there." He pointed downstream.

"Let's do it."

They had to backtrack a bit, but eventually they made it to a place where the stream riffled quickly over a bottom of small stones and sand. Sweeney and Hogan took up positions on the near side pulling security to the rear as John sent Rip across.

When he heard a low whistle from Rubio signaling that the far bank was clear, John tapped Doc's shoulder and motioned for him and Frank to cross. Frank looked extremely annoyed with life as he held a hand against his injury, but he seemed to have no trouble keeping up. Next, John put a hand on Liz's shoulder and motioned her across.

She looked up at him. "Where are...?"

He quickly put a finger to her lips and shook his head— silence was essential. Her eyes held his for a brief moment, and then she stepped into the stream and waded across.

John tapped Sweeney, then turned and followed Liz. Sweeney and Hogan followed him.

Once they were all safely on the far bank, Rip took point again, leading the group away from the road at a right angle. They traveled in single file at a slightly slower pace, and John was glad that clouds were obscuring the sliver of a moon. For the first time in what seemed like hours, he felt like they might actually escape.

After about twenty minutes, the terrain began to rise again. Would Liz be able to keep up as the night wore on? He studied her. If she was feeling fatigued, she wasn't showing it, even as their path grew steeper and steeper.

Rip held up a hand to halt. John made his way forward until he could see what was ahead. A road. He turned and signaled to Doc that a danger area was ahead. Doc passed the signal back.

After watching the road for a few minutes, John decided it was deserted. A couple of houses were just visible off to the west, but no lights were showing. One by one, the team skittered across the road, then continued down the embankment on the other side.

The team plodded past fields of sprouting crops and through stands of olive trees. John worried a bit about being tracked by the terrorists once daylight came. Rip must have had the same concern because he mostly avoided newly plowed fields, sticking to their hard, uncultivated edges as much as possible.

An hour later Rip again signaled a halt. John went to him and whispered, "What've you got?"

"It'll be getting light soon, Coop. We'd better find someplace to hole up." He pointed ahead. "Looks like an old stone house or barn or something. The area is pocked with partially built structures that never got finished because of the war. Most are still uninhabited."

John nodded and motioned for Liz and the rest of the team. After they quietly assembled and crouched in a semicircle around him, he whispered, "We're going to do a quick recon of this building up ahead. If it'll work, we're going to hole up here and get some rest. You all stay here. Rip and I will be right back."

29

Stone Barn, South Lebanon

JOHN WASN'T SO BAD after all.

Liz had to admit that she hadn't been sure there for a while. First he sat in the café, looking like a handsome beached whale. Then he burst into the warehouse, all decked out in body armor and a helmet with night goggles covering his eyes like some ridiculous double periscope. He shot a man dead, yelled orders, practically forced her to go with them whether she wanted to go or not.

Not that she wasn't glad he and the team took her along. If she'd been left behind, she would have been shot as dead as poor Azmi.

Then he'd protected her with his own body those times they'd been in danger. And he asked the men to share a bit of their food with her, which they willingly did, all but the big blond guy, Sweeney. He did it, of course—she figured John's request was really an order—but he hadn't been very gracious about it. The rest of the team seemed to like playing Sir Galahad to her damsel in distress.

Now they sat in the barn, waiting for daylight to go. But since it was nearly summer, the daylight lingered and lingered. Liz was itchy from sitting. She never sat this long unless she was using her laptop or was in front of her PC at the paper.

When they had first arrived at the barn, which looked like it hadn't been used in years, John and Sweeney went off into a corner and had a lengthy discussion in low hushed tones. John produced a map, and the two pored over it. Once they called Rip and his GPS into service.

They were undoubtedly planning their escape route. E&E Frank had called it—she couldn't remember what that meant. Something and escape? Escape and something? Just so they were planning on taking her along. She shivered at the thought of being left here to get herself back to Beirut.

On the other hand, she might be better off on her own than with a band of armed men in flak vests and helmets who, as far as she could tell, didn't speak much Arabic or know much of the local culture.

When John finished his meeting with Sweeney, he went around and briefed the other men. Then he came over to her and went to one knee beside her.

He looked tired, but he radiated an intensity, a confidence that made Liz feel safe. She smiled at him.

"Okay," he began, "here's the deal. As you know, we've lost communications with headquarters, which means that we can't coordinate with them to get out of here. Our backup plan is to head to the coast south of Sidon where a SEAL team can come in and pick us up. We're about twenty kilometers inland, near here." He put his finger on the map just northeast of the town of Nabatiya.

Liz looked at the map. Nabatiya was where Zahra had gone to live while she was pregnant. It was located midway between the sea and Syria, smack in the center of southern Lebanon at the mouth of the Bekaa Valley.

"We'll head back to the beach when it gets dark," John continued. "How are your feet holding up?"

Liz considered her black leather flats. They had held up surprisingly well on the trek last night, but they weren't made for hiking. The walk in the stream hadn't done them any good either, and after their soaking, they chafed. She wished for a pair of heavy socks as a cushion. "I'll be fine."

He wrinkled his brow. "Uh-huh. Any blisters?"

She nodded. "Maybe one or two, but I'll be okay."

"Let's have a look."

She hesitated, embarrassed, then slipped the shoes off.

John cupped her foot in one hand and lifted it to inspect the sole, then the heel.

"Looks like you've got a couple of hot spots here." He then inspected the other foot. His hands felt strong, and his touch brought warmth to her face as well as her feet. "You'd better go see Doc and have him put some moleskin on those places."

"I will." The last thing she wanted was to impede their escape any more than she could help.

He took her chin in his hand and turned her face so he could see her swollen and bruised eye. "While you're at it, have him take a look at this, too. What happened anyway?"

"I ran into Frank's rifle scope during one of Sweeney's fine moments in the van."

John grinned. "Does it hurt much?"

"I wouldn't say hurt so much as feels weird." And it undoubtedly looked great, too.

"Well, Doc can give you one of those instant cold packs to reduce the swelling."

John stood, gave her a brief smile, and went to talk to one of the men standing guard. She watched him, struck by the thought that the qualities that had drawn her to him during their short friendship in Virginia Beach were the very qualities that made him a good leader of men. He was clearly in charge but without being abrasive. He wasn't threatened when one of the others made a suggestion. He shared all the responsibilities and dangers with the men.

Though nothing had developed between them as she'd hoped, she was encouraged in a strange way that she knew how to pick a good man even if he didn't choose her.

The road to true love was littered with potholes deep enough to swallow you if you weren't careful.

She lay down, trying to find a comfortable position, something she concluded was a hopeless task. She ended up on her back with her hands behind her head, feet crossed at the ankles. She was so exhausted that she fell asleep in spite of her discomfort.

When she woke, stiff from sleeping on the ground, she stretched. "I'm going to walk around the barn a few times," she said heading toward the door. She had to work out the nap's kinks somehow.

John moved quickly, stopping her with a hand on her arm. "No. You're not."

She turned, ready to argue, but one look at his face killed her words. Of course she couldn't go outside. It only took one person seeing her to endanger all of them. She nodded, understanding that as long as she was with them, he was in charge of her, too.

John smiled briefly and turned to Sweeney. "I'm going to rest a bit." Sweeney nodded. John lay down and was asleep in a moment.

Liz wasn't sure, but it looked like Sweeney was second in command. She smiled at him as she paced, trying to ease her cramped muscles, but he ignored her.

All around her the men sat or rested as if they had all the patience in the world. Liz supposed this was the result of their training. A large part of any military operation had to be waiting for exactly the right moment and then being smart enough to know when that moment came.

Two of the men were on guard at all times, one near the crumbling wall where there had once been a door, the other up in the loft, watching over the scrubby valley through an opening where the roof had collapsed. All in all she felt very secure.

When she tired of stepping over or around sleeping men, she slid down the wall, sitting near Rip who was on guard duty at the missing door.

"Hi, I'm Liz Fairchild."

He smiled at her. "I know. I'm Rip Rubio."

She smiled back. "Mr. GPS. How'd you get the nickname Rip?"

"It's just the shortened form of my name. Like Rob is for Robert."

"Really?" Try as she would, Liz couldn't come up with anything that produced the name Rip as its shortened form. "I give up."

"Euripides."

She stared at him. No wonder she had drawn a blank.

"But nobody calls me that anymore, you know?"

"No?" She just bet they didn't.

"No, ma'am. The last guy who did ended up in the hospital."

"Used all your special training on him, did you?"

Rip laughed quietly. "Nope. That was, like, fifth grade or something."

Liz laughed, then with a glance at the sleeping men, clamped a hand over her mouth. "So where are you from?"

"East LA. I grew up in the barrios. A whole lot different than this place." He gestured outside, where scrubby hills stretched to the horizon. A flock of goats dotted a far off ridgeline.

"I bet." That explained the Latino accent. "Probably not a lot of goats in Los Angeles."

He shook his head. "I never saw a goat up close until we had to kill and eat one in Special Forces Selection."

She looked out at the goats. "They say there are more goats here than people by a large majority."

"There certainly aren't many people. We haven't seen a soul all day. But it sure is pretty here."

"The Lebanese love the Bekaa Valley." Liz gestured to the north. "It's the fertile area of the country and produces wonderful crops. They're developing an increasingly successful wine industry because the climate's perfect for the grapes. It doesn't look it, but it's actually below sea level, hemmed in by the Lebanon Mountains on the west and the Anti-Lebanon Mountains over there." She pointed toward the east.

"People vacation in the Bekaa. They go to see the scenery, enjoy the temperate climate, and bask in the beauty and history. You should see the ruins at Baalbeck. Fantastic."

Rip looked slightly overwhelmed.

Liz smiled ruefully. "Sorry. That was my travel agent spiel."

"So you've lived in Lebanon how long?"

Liz jumped on the question. "I don't live here anymore. I was just coming over to…well…I was going to research a story on Lebanese women, but then my sister…" Her voice trailed off, and she had to look away. *Julie.*

Oh, God, please take care of her!

Rip sat quietly and let her compose herself.

Liz took a deep breath. "I was trying to find her last night when you guys arrived." She looked up at him. "Why were you guys there?"

He looked pained. "Sorry, *chica*. We can't talk about that stuff, you know."

"If you tell me, you'll have to kill me?" The old joke came out sounding flat rather than funny, but then Liz no longer felt funny.

"I can say that I hope your sister gets out okay."

Tears welled in Liz's eyes at his kindness, and she suddenly didn't feel like talking much anymore. She managed a weak

"Thanks, Rip" before she moved off to another part of the crumbly old barn.

She passed the time by trying to compose the lead for her story about Zahra and the women she'd interviewed, but worry about her sister constantly intruded. Compounding her distress was the guilt that struck every time she thought about her parents. They must be going crazy about now, knowing that not one but two daughters were missing.

An hour later, the sound of a plane flying over caused John to sit up, instantly and completely awake. He rose and walked to the window. When he returned, he sat beside Liz, stretching out his legs and crossing them at the ankle. Apparently the plane had nothing to do with them because he looked completely relaxed.

"You're doing a good job at waiting." He smiled down at her.

She rolled her eyes. "This is very hard work, sitting here like this."

"Actually it is."

Feeling inordinately pleased at his approval and more than a bit self-conscious, she grabbed at the one interest she knew they had in common. "You been climbing much lately?"

"I wish."

"What's the matter? Did you scare off all of your climbing buddies?"

He gave a half-laugh. "No, nothing like that. I...I'm recovering from an injury."

Her heart tripped. "What happened? Are you okay?" Dumb question. Of course he was okay, or he wouldn't be on this mission. But an injury! Was he shot in the line of duty?

"How'd you...?" She caught herself. "Never mind. You probably can't tell me because of national security or some such thing, right?"

He laughed quietly. "Something like that."

The thought of him shot and in pain hurt her more than it

should. He was, after all, just a guy she hadn't seen in three years, a guy who had essentially stood her up.

"What happened three years ago, John?" The question slipped out before she could bite it back, and she flushed.

He looked at her for a moment, then lifted his hand and indicated the barn and the men. "Only then I was gone for nine months."

Nine months? With not one word? "I guess calling someone while you're on a secret mission sort of ruins the secret part of it, huh?"

He grinned. "Ever so slightly, though it wasn't quite like this. I was stuck in the desert near the Iranian border, tracking down a man who was mass-producing car bombs."

"Yeah, sure." Liz chuckled. "That's what they all say."

They sat in companionable silence for a few minutes. Liz didn't know what he was thinking about, but she was wondering how a woman dealt with her man disappearing for uncertain lengths of time for the most dangerous spots on the globe.

"Just what exactly do you guys do? Besides keep the world safe for democracy, I mean." She was half afraid of his answer. "In general terms I can understand, please."

"We're explosive specialists."

She stared at him, aghast. "You mean like, you're human mine sweepers?"

He grinned. "It's a bit more complicated than that, but sorta."

"You're nuts, all of you!"

"Believe it or not, you're not the first person to say that. But we're also intelligent, charming, and dynamite to look at in our uniforms."

She leaned back and eyed his dirty jeans and T-shirt. "So I see. Tell me, if you're such a wonder, how'd you reach the age of what? Twenty-nine? without getting hitched?" He wore no ring on his left hand, but maybe it wasn't allowed for some reason. She was somewhat mortified at how much she wanted him to still be single.

"I almost made that mistake once. Her name was Kim. We dated for three years."

When he didn't say any more, Liz couldn't stand it. "So what happened?"

He studied his hands, as if what he was going to say made him nervous. "You and that nine month deployment." He glanced at her to see her reaction.

"Me?" she squeaked.

"And the nine months. When I came home, I found Kim had decided I wasn't worth waiting for and had married an insurance salesman."

Foolish, foolish woman. "I'm sorry. It must have broken your heart."

He gave a snort. "Not hardly. It was a relief. What really hurt was that you had disappeared." He looked her right in the eye as he told her that.

Oh, my! Her pulse went from normal to overdrive in one second flat.

"I want all of your latest contact info." He pulled a piece of paper and a pen from his vest. "So I don't lose track of you again."

"Now?"

"Why not? Later there might not be time."

As she reeled off her e-mail address and her various phone numbers, she wondered what his last comment meant. Whatever, it didn't sound good. "Do you get shot often?"

"Nah. I've never been shot. Shot at, yeah. Shot, no."

She was confused. "Then your injury?"

"We're an explosives disposal team, remember?"

"You got blown up?" Horror chilled her to the bone.

Suddenly he looked full of sorrow. "No, I didn't get blown up." He frowned. "I...I can't talk about it."

Can't or won't? Liz got the feeling it wasn't because the mission was all *that* secret.

"Well," she said, making her voice light, wanting to draw him back to the moment, away from his pain, "if we ever get out of here, I'll show you this sweet limestone overhang I found north of Beirut. It's only a five-seven, but it'll curl your toenails."

"Yeah?"

She nodded. "I've met some really nice climbers here that we can go with." If he was thinking they would never get the chance, he didn't show it. He was grinning at her.

"That would be great, Liz. I'd really like that."

Me, too. Oh, yeah, me, too. "Since you couldn't climb while recuperating, what did you do?"

"Fishing's my current way to unwind."

"Fishing's manly enough for a Special Forces guy? After all, it's kind of passive compared to climbing."

He nodded. "Anything that involves worms and fish guts has to be manly."

"Point taken. Well, I can certainly see the need for you guys to have relaxing hobbies. Many nights like last night, and I'd be dying for something to calm me down, too."

"Thankfully there aren't that many nights like last night. Ninety percent of Army life is training and waiting."

She eyed him. "What made you decide on the dull life of the Army?"

"Two things." He grinned at her, the full power of his personality concentrated on her. She blinked. *Wow!* "One, I realized I had no talent worth speaking of."

"Wait a minute there." Liz held up a hand. "I find that hard to believe."

"Well, I was a highly skilled pool player, but somehow I think my father would have had a coronary if I announced I was going to become the next Minnesota Fats."

She laughed. Charles would have responded the same way. "What was the second reason?"

John pressed his lips together, the laughter gone. "My father came home from an extended tour."

Liz waited for more. When he said no more, she finally asked, "And?" She could see she had a lot to teach him about sharing.

"And we didn't get along too well." The flat tone in which he spoke said far more than the words.

"Ouch."

"Yeah. Ouch." John leaned his head back against the wall. "That's when I decided I was not going to West Point. I was not going to be my father."

"So where did you go to college?"

"I didn't. I enlisted the day after high school graduation." He smiled grimly. "I thought Dad would have that heart attack after all."

"My father almost went into cardiac arrest when I told him I had become a Christian."

He looked at her as if he doubted she was serious. "Now there's a rebellious action if I ever heard one."

"It is if you're Charles Fairchild's daughter. 'Elizabeth Fairchild, have you lost your mind?'" She deepened her voice in imitation of her father. She gave John the short version of her experiences at UVA, certain she'd told him the long version before. He nodded as if he remembered the story. "Charles saw and still sees all religions as divisive and suitable only for weaklings. We never went to church."

"I remember you telling me that before."

"And I remember that you went to church your whole life."

"I did."

"How did a goody-goody church kid become a Special Forces guy?"

"Who said I was good?" His sly smile made her laugh.

"I think I was probably the goody-goody kid." She wrinkled her nose as she thought of herself growing up. "I was always trying to impress God."

"Well, if you have to impress someone…"

She grinned. "Even though Charles told us God wasn't there, I spent a lot of time bargaining with Him. I'll be good—or get great grades or clean my room or feed the poor—if You make Julie well. I kept bargaining even when the results were less than stellar."

"She didn't get well?"

"She didn't, and eventually I decided my father must be right. Better not to believe in God than be disappointed that He didn't come through. Julie still struggles with RA. I can't imagine what this captivity is doing to her without her meds." Liz's voice was harsh with emotion.

"So how do you reconcile your sister's plight with God's supposed 'loving nature'?"

He spoke with an edge that made Liz realize something more than mere curiosity was behind his question. She decided to risk big in revealing a deep place within. She felt she had no choice, both for herself and for him.

She started drawing with her finger in the barn's dirt floor so she wouldn't have to look at him. "I've got to admit, I'm having a hard time not being mad at Him right now."

"Hmm…" He wasn't looking at her, either. His voice held concern, but something deeper, darker was there, too.

"You know that verse, 'All things work for good'?"

He gave a single nod that she saw peripherally.

"Things aren't working for good." Liz swallowed her tears. No crying allowed in Lebanese barns. "Khalil's dead. Julie's missing. I'm stuck here, who knows where, messing up things for you guys."

Sweeney climbed the ladder to the loft to take over guard duty, relieving Hogan who joined Doc in taking a nap. Frank was awake now, busy disassembling his weapon.

John sighed. "Makes you wonder just what *good* means to God, doesn't it?"

Liz blinked. Good means good. Nice. For my happiness. What else could it mean? She turned to him, ready to tell him that, when Sweeney called, "Coop, get over here!"

John was on his feet and up the rickety ladder in an instant.

"What have you got, Bobby?" John crouched beside Sweeney who had his eye pressed to the scope on his XM-8.

"Coming this way."

John shielded his eyes against the glare of the setting sun. Then he saw her, a little girl, no more than nine or ten, swinging a plastic bucket and skipping toward the barn. She was obviously oblivious to their presence, and they had to keep it that way.

"Wouldn't do any good to shoot her," Sweeney said as if Valor shot little girls all the time. "The noise would give us away. What if we wait until she gets here and then grab her?"

Sometimes John wondered about Sweeney. "Of course we're not going to shoot a little girl." The very thought put a bad taste in his mouth. "We aren't going to grab her either. Sooner or later someone's going to come looking."

They watched the girl, barefooted and bareheaded, as she skipped closer to them. Her mouth was moving, and John imagined her either having a conversation with herself or singing some favorite song. When she threw her arms wide and spun around, he decided she was singing.

"Well, we'd better think of something quick," Sweeney said.

The girl was only about a hundred yards away from the barn now. She stopped momentarily and picked a flower, sniffed it, then stuck it in a buttonhole on her purple blouse. Then singing to herself again, she continued walking closer.

John patted Sweeney's shoulder and whispered, "I have an idea. You stand fast. I'm going to get Liz and have her talk to the kid. She can pretend she's lost or something."

Sweeney looked at him as if he were nuts.

"You got a better idea?" John challenged. "We've got to keep her from seeing us."

"I didn't say anything," Sweeney protested.

John turned back toward the ladder. Before he reached it, however, one foot broke through the rotten boards of the loft with a loud crash. John caught himself with one leg dangling through the broken planks and froze, hoping for all he was worth that the sound hadn't traveled outside the barn.

It had.

Sweeney cursed. "She's turned tail and is running back toward wherever she came from!"

John pulled his leg free, taking care not to come in contact with a couple of lethally pointed floorboards. He checked for any puncture wounds. None, though there would probably be a nasty red gouge along his inside thigh. *Thank goodness for denim!* He stepped gingerly to the ladder.

"John, are you all right?"

He glanced down to see Liz's concerned face. He winced as the setting sun cut through the doorway and across her face, highlighting her swollen, discolored eye. Sitting with her in the gloom of the barn, he hadn't realized it was so bad.

"Fine," he mouthed, then turned and started down. "Come on, Sweeney. We've got to get out of here while we still can."

30

Lebanese Countryside

IMAD HIJAZI STOOD on top of his aging Mercedes and scanned the surrounding hillsides with high-powered binoculars, looking for any sign of the American soldiers.

They were out there; he knew it.

When his men found the abandoned van the night before, its insides stained with spilled blood, he knew he would win. He had been able to muster ninety men from their homes, nearly one-third of the total membership of Ansar Inshallah and a testament to his power in the camp.

"We must find them!" he told the men, his voice ringing with intensity. "They have come uninvited into our homes. Our women and children must be protected! Islam must prevail!"

He was tempted to rally the men with tales of the coming Great Fire Storm, but he reined in the impulse. The fewer who knew of it, the greater the chance for its success. Besides, his gifted rhetoric had accomplished what was needed.

The men searched all night and into the morning with great diligence, but they found nothing.

Still, he was a man of great cunning. He would outthink

these weakened Americans. They had to be headed for the coast, hoping to somehow be rescued by the American Navy. East toward Syria would not be an option for them, and it would be insane to attempt to cross into Israel, even with the help of the Israeli Defense Forces. It had to be west toward the water.

Imad left nothing to chance, so he stationed a man on each road leading to the coast. He also dispatched several men to drive around and ask the locals if they had seen a troop of highly armed American men with a dark-haired woman in tow. So far, nothing, and now it was getting dark again.

His superiors had argued among themselves about whether or not to involve Hezbollah in the search. That organization had many thousands of men who could respond to the call and hunt down the Americans. In the end Hezbollah's leadership made the decision that with the Syrians now gone, it was best for their image as a legitimate political party not to do anything that might make it look as if they were terrorists.

That was fine with Imad. He smiled as he savored the thought of the invaders' capture. It must happen soon for the timing of the Great Fire Storm, and he was the one who would make it happen. He was the one who would get the credit. Delivering the Americans' heads on a platter would ensure his position within the movement. Between the capture of the Americans and the success of Allah's Fire, he would be lauded throughout all of Islam.

His favorite tune played again from his jacket pocket. He fished for the phone and flipped it open. *"Naaem?"*

The rapid-fire Arabic voice on the other end was filled with excitement. "A man in the valley says his daughter heard someone in their barn not thirty minutes ago. He thought she was imagining things until we came asking questions."

"Excellent. Where are you?"

"On the road to Bfaroua."

"Stay there. I will arrive with twenty men as soon as possible. Watch for the Americans."

He slapped the phone shut. Warmth spread through Imad's chest.

I have them.

Southeast Lebanon

Julie lay on the cot in her new cell, its stone walls looking like they were hewn out of rock. This room was smaller than the first one, and the care she received here, wherever here was, was far poorer than at the first place. A lumpy mattress, a shaggy blanket, and no pillow. Food once a day, twice if she were lucky, and never enough to satisfy her hunger. The only thing she got on any schedule was her medicine.

It made no sense. Why did they threaten her life on one hand, then give her medicine on the other? If they planned to kill her as they said, why ease her pain?

And why wait? Why not just drag her out and do the deed?

What's going on, dear God?

How she had gotten to this new prison, Julie wasn't certain. The man had grabbed her and forced her from her old jail, but after that she remembered nothing until she woke up here.

A drug of some kind, she assumed. Vaguely she remembered the prick of a syringe. Well, she had to live with the painful flare up from the rough treatment, but at least she hadn't suffered at the time it was inflicted. If she only had a pillow to ease the pain in her neck and upper spine, she'd feel much better.

To her surprise she missed Karima. Here she saw no one. The door was opened, a tray was shoved in by unseen hands, and the door was shut. No one said a word to her.

Except the Lord. He spoke comfort to her, easing her fears, filling her with hope in the middle of her despair. She talked to

Him out loud. He answered with whispers to her heart.

"I ask your forgiveness for being so shallow in my love for You."

How great is the love I have lavished on you that you should be called My child.

"But why, Lord? Why would You love someone like me?"

I am love, and I have loved you with an everlasting love.

The comfort she received from these conversations was beyond her understanding. She just knew it was so. The sad thing was that she'd had to be in such a terrible situation before she called to Him with any real yearning, any real heart.

"I am so alone and afraid!"

I will never leave you or forsake you.

One of the deep desires of Julie's heart became the wish to tell Liz what the Lord now meant to her. She knew her sister worried about her lack of spiritual depth and about her deliberate choice to marry Khalil in spite of the large religious differences between them. How wonderful it would be to say, "Liz, I love the Lord deeply now. I understand what you used to try to tell me."

And she wanted to tell Charles and Annabelle that she was a follower of Christ.

"I want to confess You before men, Lord."

If you confess Me before men, I'll confess you before My Father in heaven.

"I will. I'll do it if I get the chance. I promise."

She was talking aloud when the door to her cell suddenly crashed open. She spun, heart pounding. They had come for her. It had to be that. She'd had two meals today, two bottles of water, and her full regimen of medicines. There was no reason for anyone to come again until tomorrow.

"Oh, Lord, don't let it hurt too much. And take care of Liz and Charles and Annabelle."

Karima walked into the room, a tray in her hands.

"Karima!" Julie wanted to throw her arms around the young woman, but she wasn't certain how Karima would react. She was still the infidel, after all. Still, she couldn't stop smiling. "What are you doing here?"

"I have your dinner," Karima said stiffly, walking across the room.

The door shut behind her, and suddenly Karima was smiling also. "I told them they had to bring me to care for you." She put down the tray on the cot. "I told them only I could keep you well."

Julie threw her arms around her friend, for that's what Karima had become. Karima held herself aloof for a few seconds. Then she softened and hugged Julie back. The women sat next to each other on the cot.

"Where am I?" Julie asked, hoping she'd finally get some answers.

Karima shook her head. "Please do not ask me. I cannot tell you."

"What is this building?"

"It is a ruined fort, maybe from the time of the Crusaders, maybe from the time of the Turks." Karima shrugged. "It is being used for a special project."

"What's the project? Me?"

"I do not know. No one knows. But somehow you are vital."

Julie frowned. No matter how hard she tried, she could think of no way that she was vital to anything these terrorists would do.

Karima studied her. "They give you medicine?"

"They do. I have no idea what it is, but I don't care. It helps." What it might be doing to her liver or her stomach lining she refused to consider. If they were going to kill her, what did it matter anyway?

Karima studied her hands. "They play that tape of you on TV all the time."

Julie tried to speak, but the thought of her parents having to watch her bound and on her knees gave her a lump in her throat too large to get words around.

"I have been worried about you." Karima looked away as she said it. "Afraid they had hurt you."

That was a costly confession for the young woman to make. It was well on the way to wondering whether those who held Julie might be wrong. She tried to hide her excitement. If Karima could question one thing, she might well be able to question others. She might actually wonder if the legalistic subjugation to Allah was also wrong.

"Thank you. You are a good friend." She laid her hand on Karima's.

"No!" Karima stood and ran the six steps to the other side of the room. "I am not a good friend." She spun to Julie, her hands shaking. "Always remember that if I must choose, I must choose Allah. I must choose my people. I must make certain that Rashid's death was not in vain."

With that she walked to the door, rapped on it until it was unlocked, and left without a backward glance.

Southeast Lebanon

If only these guys didn't have such long legs! They were moving through the night at a brisk pace. Though it probably felt like a walk in the park to them, to Liz it was too fast for a walk and too slow for a jog. So it was walk, walk, jog, walk, walk, jog.

Or, her personal favorite, walk, walk, jog, step in a hole. It was a good thing she had strong ankles, or they'd be carrying her.

They walked single file with about ten feet between them. She was assigned to walk behind John and in front of Sweeney. She felt the daggers the tall Southerner tossed at her back. What was his problem? All women? Just her? Or was she receiving the venom he felt for reasons she knew nothing about?

Maybe he got left at the altar. Maybe he'd just gotten a Dear John letter. Maybe his mama ran away from home when he was just a little boy wandering barefoot in the Alabama heat. Of course, if Sweeney's father was anything like Sweeney, no wonder the woman ran.

Misogynist! She'd tell him that's what he was, but he'd probably take it as a compliment.

At least the mental griping about Sweeney took her mind off the blister on her right foot for a while. Doc had put ointment and moleskin on it, but with every step, it still shrieked at her.

John held up his hand, and everyone stopped. Liz sank to the ground. To her surprise, so did John and Rip. She watched as they lay on their stomachs beside each other.

A soft flutter made her glance up, and there was Doc, shaking out an emergency blanket he'd pulled from a vest pocket. He let the blanket fall over John and Rip, covering them from the hips up. Then Doc, Hogan, and Sweeney stood guard, forming a perimeter of sorts around the men on the ground.

Frank lowered himself gingerly to the ground next to Liz. Aside from moving a bit carefully, he gave no sign of having been shot. His endurance seemed as inexhaustible as the others'.

"You okay?" she whispered as softly as she could. He obviously wasn't, or he would be standing guard with the others.

Frank nodded and took a drink from his canteen.

She pointed to the blanket and the four legs sticking out. Then she spread her hands in the universal what's-up gesture.

Frank leaned toward her. "Reading the map."

Liz blinked. "GPS?"

"Too much light." He pointed to the small LED penlight clipped to his vest, then to the huddle.

Liz nodded. The night was black, the moon a mere crescent so dim it shed little illumination. A light, no matter how small, would stand out clearly. The green illumination of the GPS would advertise their location as clearly as if she stood on a rock and yelled, "Over here, boys!"

Route established, John and Rip got to their feet. John pointed to the right. The men fell into position, Frank grunting as he rose to take his place. Rip continued on point, and Hogan brought up the rear. Liz fell in behind John again. They walked for about an hour in the direction that Liz thought was south, then turned right again. If she was right, they were heading for the coast now.

They trudged—well, the men walked, she trudged—up a rocky hillside. At the top they found a road. They hadn't gone more than a few yards on it when the headlights of a single car flashed in the distance, then rolled toward them. Everyone dove for cover, which in this area of the country was sorely lacking.

Once again, John pulled her close, tucking her head into his shoulder, pressing his face to the ground. Pale skin would stand out in the night.

Liz held her breath, too scared to move.

"Breathe, girl." John's voice was a thread of sound.

"Oh." She forced herself to pull oxygen into her aching lungs. She was still scared silly, but at least she wouldn't pass out now.

The car sped past. No one moved for a few minutes. When John rose and held a hand to Liz, she grabbed it and let him pull her to her feet. The team fell in line. They had crested another small hill when they saw a line of cars coming their way. Liz counted at least five pairs of headlights.

Rip fell back from his point position to stand beside John. "We're never going to get to the coast at this rate," he muttered.

John grunted. He raised his arm and pointed to the left. South. They dropped down into a slight ravine and walked away from the road. When the ravine turned left, they continued to fol-low it. East. Toward Syria and Jordan.

Fatigue hazed Liz's vision as they entered a small village. She read a sign posted by the road: Zebdine. The few houses were all dark, and not even a dog noticed their presence.

Liz looked at John's back hopefully. Maybe he'd call a halt and let them rest for a while. Her legs felt like jelly, and with every step her shins complained loudly about their abuse.

Lord, it certainly isn't an all-things-working-for-good thing if my lack of stamina endangers these men.

But there was to be no rest for the weary.

"Company behind," hissed Hogan.

Liz spun. In the distance was another line of approaching vehicles.

Rip, still on point, had rounded a bend in the road with his gun at the ready. He came hurrying back. "Cars. Several. Almost here."

They were going to be caught in a pincer movement.

The men melted into the shadows between the dwellings. John grabbed Liz's hand and pulled her after him to a large olive tree, its silver leaves black in the night.

"Up." He grabbed her around the waist and boosted.

With a surprised gulp, Liz grabbed the first fat branch she saw and pulled herself into a sitting position.

"Climb. Do not come down, no matter what happens." Then John disappeared into the shadows.

Liz stared after him in disbelief. He'd left her! All night he'd been watching out for her, and now that real danger was here, he was gone.

A column of six cars rounded the curve at the end of the village. The other column, five in all, pulled in from the opposite end of town. Every vehicle bristled with men and arms.

Liz began climbing. After stepping on her skirt twice and nearly catapulting herself to the ground, she paused. She reached down between her legs, grabbed the back hem, and pulled it through and up. She tucked it into her waistband, trapping the front of the skirt in the pouch the move created. Her car keys clunked against her thigh, but she didn't think they'd fall out of the pocket.

She nodded, satisfied. Not as tidy as slacks, but much safer than the fluttering gauzy material had been. She climbed as high as she safely could, then sat, clutching the trunk for security. She watched through the leaves as men jumped from the cars. All were shouting, and Liz listened carefully so she could tell John what they said.

There was no doubt about one thing: These men were searching for Valor and for her.

A couple of shots cracked the air. She jumped and grabbed at the tree's trunk more tightly.

Who had shot? Had they spotted one of the team?

An Arabic voice roared in the street below. "Hold your fire! Hold your fire! Save every bullet for the infidels!"

Thankful for the leaves that hid her, Liz noticed that not one house in the village had turned on a light. Surely the shots had wakened the people even if the noise of the cars and men hadn't. But no one acknowledged that their little town had become, at least for a few minutes, a terrorist stronghold.

Flashlight beams pierced the darkness. As Liz shifted a little, she caught sight through the leaves of a sign on one of the buildings. A beam played across the front window. A pharmacy. An idea took hold.

A man broke loose from the scrum in the road and headed straight for her tree. Liz thought she might throw up. She tried to hide her white face.

"Look!" the man called in Arabic. "See what I've found!"

H-5 Airfield, Jordan

MARY WALKER BURST through the door of the command center. She found Lou Williams hunched over a 1:200,000 scale topographical map of southern Lebanon, chewing on the plastic stick from a long-finished Tootsie Pop.

"Major Williams, I believe we have some good news."

The commander looked up and muttered, "I could use some good news."

"Come with me, then." She waved her arm in a this-way gesture.

They went outside, and Mary shoved her hands in the pockets of her sweatshirt to ward off the chill desert air. She led him across the blacked-out tarmac toward a cluster of vehicles, some military and some civilian.

"Is that what I think it is?" Williams quickened his pace to the point where Mary had to jog to keep up.

Two hundred yards later as they neared the vehicles, Mary felt more awake than she had. "You wouldn't believe what I had to go through to get it modified like you requested. They're just finishing up now."

The burly major maneuvered around a parked white box van and stopped. Mary almost bumped into him.

"Hot dog," he said. "Just look at that."

A red airplane sat in the center of the assorted vehicles, larger than a child's toy model but quite a bit smaller than a real plane, even a little Cessna. Men in desert tan flight suits hovered over it, working with screwdrivers and socket wrenches by the light of a van's headlamps.

"We had to bring it over from H-3 airbase in Iraq."

"Amazing. It looks like a sewing machine with wings."

"It's called an Arcturus T-15. The military doesn't have them yet, but we've got a few hanging around. Most of our Unmanned Aerial Vehicles are designed to operate at very high altitudes, but that wouldn't help us in this case, since your team's FM radios won't carry much more than a few miles. This one goes low and slow. It should be able to pick up their signal, and then bounce it via UHF to the command module that flies with it, then to us at base."

"What're they doing to it, rewinding the rubber band?"

She smiled. "They're finishing up the install of an FM module that will be able to link to your team's IC radios."

It had taken a call to the CIA division chief to get the thing here. She didn't bother saying that she hadn't actually gotten clearance to modify the avionics on the craft. Sometimes it was better to ask forgiveness than permission.

The major looked as happy as she had ever seen him. "Great. Absolutely great. Now let's get this thing in the air!"

Mary wished she shared his enthusiasm, but the chances of actually finding the lost team were lower than the odds on nickel slots in Atlantic City. For all they knew, Task Force Valor was already captured or worse. She hoped for the major's sake that her skepticism didn't show.

He crouched, inspecting the little plane. "Where does the...er, pilot go?"

"Pilots." She looked beyond him toward the other end of the runway. "Here they come now." She pointed toward the large gray cargo plane lumbering down the airstrip toward them.

"They control this unmanned thing from inside the C-130?"

Mary nodded, raising her voice to be heard over the sound of the approaching aircraft. "That's a DC-130 Echo, configured to launch and control drones and UAVs. I'll climb aboard and oversee the use of the T-15, then relay our findings back to you. The range on it is only 150 kilometers, which is just short of the distance between us and the coast, so it will cover most of Lebanon. If we fly up toward Jordan's northern border, toward Syria and launch it just this side of the Gaza Strip, we should have about ten hours of time on station. As soon as the T-15 makes Lebanese airspace, we'll begin broadcasting. Then we'll point the UAV toward the beach where the team should be and hope we can make contact."

She put up a hand to keep her red hair out of her eyes as the approaching craft turned and bathed them with its prop wash before the pilot shut down its engines. Sometimes, like now, she thought about how convenient the short military buzz cut was, but the thought was only momentary. In truth, she knew her hair, wild and unruly as it often was, was her glory. Good thing, too. Something had to make up for the millions of freckles that came with it.

Shouts went up from the men working on the UAV as they frantically tried to keep it from blowing away from the plane's inadvertent assault. She watched as they hustled the T-15 to one side of the DC-130 and began securing the small plane to hard points on the wing.

The major shook his head and turned to Mary. "Look, I know this is a long shot, Agent Walker. I appreciate your setting this up."

She nodded, afraid to look at him for fear he'd see the hopelessness she felt. For some reason the "German bikers" felt special to her.

"You know, Major, we risk getting ourselves in hot water with the Israelis over this whole thing. My boss has been on the phone with their intel folks and is trying to placate them while we get this done. But I wouldn't be surprised if the UAV never makes it out of the occupied territories."

"Please," Williams said. "No more happy thoughts."

The crew chief from the C-130 beckoned to her. She acknowledged him with a wave of her hand. Williams waved, too. Then he got that determined yet placid look she'd seen before, and she bet he was praying again, only this time to himself.

Once again she found that idea strangely comforting. "Time for you to go." With his jaw set purposefully, he added, "Godspeed, Agent Walker. I'll be here praying."

She grinned. She'd been right; he had been talking to God, and he planned to some more, this time on her behalf. How cool was that? She watched his oversized frame march back toward the clamshell and wondered what *Godspeed* really meant.

Zebdine

The terrorists finally drove off, half in each direction, and Liz climbed down the tree with her skirt tucked out of her way. John wanted to grab her and hold her. Of course, he didn't.

And now she wanted him to let her traipse across the street and knock on the door of the town pharmacy, alone and unprotected.

"Are you nuts?" John stared down into her beautiful brown eyes. Every time he looked at her, she was prettier, even with her black eye, dirty face, and messed-up hair. And she was gutsy, too, a quality he much admired.

So how could he let her do something that was, as far as he

could see, almost suicidal? His heart had nearly stopped when the terrorist shouted and raced straight toward the tree in which she hid. When the man picked up a small kitten cowering at the base of the trunk and walked back to his car with it, John had had to lean against the wall of the house beside him to hold himself up.

"You have to trust me, John. I'm 90 percent sure the owner will help us."

"And what about the other ten?"

She shrugged.

They stood with the rest of the team in the shadows of a vacant lot between two old cement buildings, scrutinizing a short line of dark storefronts across the one paved street that bisected the little village. As they watched, the second floor lights at the pharmacy came on.

John sighed. Granted, they'd escaped detection for the moment, but they were a long way from safe. He had to find some way to make contact with the major at H-5. A phone sounded like their best bet. They'd call the States and get the staff duty officer at their unit to radio H-5 and give Major Williams their coordinates. Then hopefully thirty minutes later he'd receive a message from the major via the States with his instructions.

The hope was that their commander had a better plan for getting them out of the country than the one they were currently looking at, which was to make their way on foot through hostile territory with one wounded man, one civilian, and very little food.

This was even assuming that once they made it to the beach, they'd be able to signal the offshore fleet. John still wasn't sure how they would do that with their only functional radios being their low-wattage FM units, carried only for communication within the team.

As soon as the terrorists drove away, Sweeney had located a public pay phone, only to find upon closer inspection that it wasn't connected to anything. Now Liz wanted to simply knock on the front door of an obviously closed pharmacy and ask the owner if they could use his phone. *Yeah, right.*

"I'm almost sure he'll help us," Liz repeated.

"What gives you that impression?" John was aware of the other men crouched around him in the shadows and thought he knew what they were thinking. *This girl is going to get us killed yet! Or herself.*

"Look, John. I've lived here. I know the culture. Most Lebanese are tired of the fighting and violence. They resent the terrorists for keeping things stirred up. We stand a good chance that this man will let us make our call for that reason alone."

Sweeney made a disbelieving growl, but John ignored him.

"He's an Arab," John said. "He has to live in this country. Helping us is very dangerous for him. And even if he does hate the violence and the terrorists, that doesn't guarantee he wouldn't call the local Hezbollah chief thirty seconds after slamming the door in our faces."

Maybe he was being overly cautious, but skepticism was part of what had kept him alive this long. He stared at the Hezbollah political party sign that hung across a shop front fifty yards to his left. A fist holding aloft an AK-47. Now that was a political statement.

"Ah, but I've got another reason why I think he'll help." Liz grinned like a kid who knows the right answer when no one else in the class does.

John raised an eyebrow.

"Shine your light on his window," she instructed.

He hesitated.

"Go ahead. If no one in the village responded to all those men and the gun shots, they aren't going to be upset by a lone beam."

John turned and shot a beam at the pharmacy window.

"See that decal?" Liz asked. "That's the seal of the American

University of Beirut. The pharmacist went to AUB. I'll just mention my father's name, and he'll let me in, at least to use his phone."

"Your father teaches pharmacology?"

"Well, no. He teaches sociology, but the pharmacist will undoubtedly recognize his name."

Again Sweeney made a small verbal sneer. Again John ignored him. For some reason, though, the other man's attitude annoyed him.

"I know it sounds crazy, John, but just trust me on this, please? I've been praying for God's leading the whole time we've been walking, and I really feel like this is what we should do."

"I thought you were having trouble with God."

"Well, yeah, but I haven't abandoned Him."

Oh, right. That was me.

"Okay, Liz, I tell you what. I'll write down a phone number to the shop at Bragg and a set of coordinates indicating our location."

She looked at him and nodded, eyes alert.

He reached into his pocket and pulled out some Lebanese livre notes. "You take this money over there and knock on the guy's door. Tell him your car broke down and offer him the money to let you use his phone. If he agrees, you call the number and tell the person who answers that you are with Task Force Valor at these coordinates and need to get that message to our commander at H-5. Then thank the pharmacist and come back here. We'll find somewhere to hole up and get some rest while we figure out what to do next."

"But John—" Liz started to argue, then stopped herself. Something about her face changed. He couldn't be sure, but he thought she was almost smiling. "Okay, give me the number."

John hastily produced a pad from a vest pocket and scribbled down the number. "You'll have to dial 011 from here, I think."

Rip leaned over to him. "Dude, better yet, give her this

calling card I picked up at the Moevenpick. It has the directions for calling the States right on the back."

John took the card. "You must have been a great Boy Scout, Rubio."

"No, but I think I beat up a Boy Scout once. Does that count?" The lanky sergeant's grin cut through the darkness.

"Don't worry, guys. I've called the States many times. I know what I'm doing." Liz took the calling card and piece of paper from John, then covered her head with her scarf . "I won't be long." She turned to go.

"Wait," Rubio hissed as he took a couple of steps after her. "Take my radio." He pulled the small unit from his vest and handed it to her. "If you get in trouble, just press this button twice and we'll be right there."

"Thanks, Rip." She slid the radio into one of the deep pockets in her skirt.

"Great idea, Rip." John felt much relieved. He wasn't sending her off completely helpless.

Liz threaded her way between two parked cars and onto the road. She looked both ways and quickly walked across. She rang the bell on the door of the pharmacy, then waited.

Nothing happened.

"This is a bad idea," Sweeney growled.

"This whole mission was a bad idea." John didn't take his eyes off of Liz. She stood hugging herself against the cool air, looking up and down the empty street. She rang again. The lights above the shop went out. Bad sign.

John stood. "I'm going to get her. Cover me."

"Hold up," Hogan hissed. "Car coming down the road!"

Sweeney swore under his breath. "That girl is bad luck!"

John craned his neck and saw a dark car rolling slowly toward them. It looked like whoever was in the vehicle was searching for something.

Or someone! John whistled softly, trying to get Liz's attention. He was about to throw caution away and charge across the street to her when the door to the shop opened. Liz talked to the paunchy, mustachioed man in rumpled khakis and a T-shirt. The man listened intently and then beckoned Liz inside.

John's heart almost stopped when she turned back toward where the team was hiding, smiled, and motioned for them to join her. Apparently she hadn't yet noticed the dark car, which was still about a hundred yards away. She beckoned again, waving happily toward the team's position.

Oh, God, please. Let her see the car! He forgot for the moment that he wasn't speaking to God anymore.

She didn't, but the pharmacist did. He drew her into the shop and closed the door.

Okay, God. You get a point for that one.

The men flattened themselves on the ground as the car came nearer. When it was close enough for John to smell the diesel exhaust fumes, he identified the vehicle as an old Mercedes. The driver sent flashlight beams probing the shadows on both sides of the street. John did his best to become one with the earth, hoping that the car hadn't been close enough for the occupants to see Liz waving.

Fortunately, a beat-up van parked between the team and the road shielded them from view as the car passed. When it had gone through town and sped off, the team got to their feet. John heard the soft clicks as his men returned their weapons to safe mode.

The pharmacy door opened. Liz's head poked out, and she beckoned to them once again.

"You gotta hand it to her," Doc said, chuckling. "The girl's got spunk."

John agreed. "I think she's found us a friend."

Sweeney snorted. "We're not home yet."

32

LIZ SAT ON ONE of the two single beds in the small room the pharmacist had given to Valor for their use. Doc, Rip, and Buzz lay on their backs on the floor, sound asleep. Frank was sprawled on the other single bed, dead to the world.

She couldn't stop smiling. She had done something right in getting them this safe spot. It was almost as if she were part of the team. Granted the four kids who slept in this bedroom weren't the world's happiest campers, but the exciting presence of a team of Special Operators should go a long way toward making things right in their eyes.

She pushed back until she rested against the wall. The smell of food being prepared drifted in the air, and her stomach growled its approval.

Aside from breathing and the occasional stomach growl from the sleeping men, the room was quiet. All the team had turned off their radios since batteries needed to be conserved. Liz leaned her head back, letting her eyes shut. She was almost asleep when the bed shook as John sat beside her.

"You're looking very pleased with yourself."

She grinned at him but didn't explain. "Did your call go through?"

He made a disgusted sound. "I'm going to try again in a few minutes."

"What happens if you can't get through?"

"We'll worry about that after we eat."

They were quiet a minute, and the silence was filled by Rip's gentle snores. Liz was very aware of John, aware that his shoulder was pressed against hers. When he was near, something shimmered in the air between them, a glimmer of possibilities barely seen but recognized, like a faint rainbow arcing over a lake.

What it all meant, she had no idea, but she wanted to find out in spite of the apprehension that she'd be hurt again. If she held back out of fear, she'd wonder all her life what might have been. All they needed to do was find Julie and get out of Lebanon alive. Then they could see what happened.

"How can they fall asleep so fast?"

"You live this life long enough, and you'd be surprised how your body adapts," John said.

She pushed her hair off her face, feeling tangles and leaves. How she'd love a brush. "You guys are amazing. You wouldn't let me write a story about you, would you?"

He just looked at her.

She sighed. "That's what I thought." Talk about the one that got away. "I'll just write the stories I was assigned and Julie's story." *Please, Lord, may it have a happy ending.*

"Who are you writing for? When we met, you had just finished graduate school and were waiting on a couple of job possibilities."

"I work for the *Philadelphia Inquirer*." She couldn't keep the pride from her voice.

He looked at her. "*The Enquirer*? Huh. Wouldn't have thought it of you."

Liz elbowed him in the side. "*In*quirer, not *En*quirer."

He grinned down at her, and she knew she'd been had. She

grinned back. "I might have upset my dad by becoming a Christian, but he's proud I can write. According to my mother, he brags about me to everyone in the English department."

John's grin faltered. "Must be nice."

There it was again, that sadness. "Your father must be proud of you." What father wouldn't be?

John shrugged. "He knows I'm an Operator, but in the general's mind it's not the same as carrying on family tradition at West Point."

Liz didn't think she liked the general.

"But the colonel's impressed." John gave a halfhearted smile.

"Who's the colonel?"

"My godfather: Colonel Michael LaFontaine, U.S. Army retired. A classmate of Dad's." John's smile turned bittersweet. "I've always gotten more encouragement from him than my father."

Liz pulled her knees up to her chest, her skirt pooling on the bed. She wrapped her arms around her legs. "It's amazing to me how we can love our fathers and yet be so at odds with them over such important things as our careers and our faith."

They were quiet for a few moments, thinking about fathers. At least Liz was. She pictured Charles when she had tried to explain why she had become a Christian. He had looked at Annabelle. "I thought we raised an intelligent daughter, not some naïve idiot who could be taken in by some snake-handling cult."

Liz stared, appalled at the viciousness of his comment. "It's not like that, Charles." How did she explain to him the impact of the highly intelligent and highly committed kids from the Christian fellowship group?

It all began when two girls from down the hall stopped at Liz's dorm room to invite her to a Bible study.

"A Bible study?" Liz had never heard of people studying the

Bible outside of a comparative religion class or Sunday school, not that she'd ever been to one. Curious to see what this group of college kids did at a "Bible study" and all too anxious to get away from reading *Beowulf,* she went. She found that they did just what they said—they studied the Bible, verse by verse no less. And most fascinating to her, Dr. Charles Fairchild's daughter, they believed in absolutes.

Jesus was THE way.

God was the God of Abraham, Isaac, and Jacob, not the Allah of Mohammed.

Jesus wasn't a victim; He let them take His life—for her.

You couldn't earn salvation. It was a gift from God paid for at great cost with the blood of His Son.

If that last was true, pity all the Islamist martyrs who thought they were earning heaven by blowing up innocents and themselves—though she never understood that mindset either.

When she first heard about the exclusivity of the Gospel claim, all she could think was that Charles would eat these passionate college students for breakfast. She could hear him say, "Whatever a person's heart tells him, that is his truth. To claim anything else is patently ridiculous."

But the longer she hung around with her new friends, the more she had to admit that, narrow though they were, there was a reality to their faith, a true kindness to their lives.

"You guys are so politically incorrect," she told them. "You're so exclusive."

"Hey, we didn't write the Bible; we just believe it," one answered, grinning unrepentantly. "We're not the ones who said Jesus was the Way, the Truth, and the Life. Jesus said it. So He either is what He said, or He's a liar."

Now there was a thought. What about all the Good Teacher stuff people said about Him, even Charles?

Over the course of several months, Liz returned again and

again to the Bible study, drawn by something she didn't comprehend. Slowly, slowly she began to understand that absolutes did exist, and they not only provided answers to some of the hard questions; they also gave life order. There was such a thing as Truth, and Jesus was at its center.

With a racing heart, she chose to believe. It gave her a feeling of stepping off into the unknown, but with that decision she found a peace she had never expected and a moral and ethical compass to guide her life.

"Charles, it's God reaching down and offering salvation, not us working like crazy, maybe even blowing ourselves up, to try and earn salvation," she told her father. "What a difference!"

After a warning glare from Annabelle, Charles had curbed his anger, but he still hadn't reconciled himself to his daughter's loving Jesus. Many days Liz wondered if he ever would.

John yawned again. "So what's your trouble with your father?"

"I disappoint him."

"I don't know why." John looked at her. "You seem pretty terrific to me."

Liz felt her cheeks flush. Wow! "He thinks I'm an idiot to be a Christian. Up until recently I've always felt strong enough and close enough to God to withstand his jibes, but now I don't know. I've had so many doubts lately, and he'll see that and assume I'm coming to my senses."

"As in throwing your faith away?"

"But I'm not! I'm just at a bad patch."

"Everyone has bad patches," John said quietly, and something in his voice made her realize he might be going through a hard time, too.

She studied the flowered bedspread. "Remember how we talked about that verse that says all things work for good?"

"I remember that I had just asked you how you defined good when that little girl appeared at the barn."

"Yeah, well, tonight I thought about what it meant whenever I wasn't too scared to think."

"And?" He gave her his full and focused attention.

"I think the only way that verse can be true is if God's idea of good is different from mine."

John looked away, his eyes staring at middle distance, seeing something she couldn't. "Back in basic training, we had a drill sergeant none of us could stand. Febus was his name. As we listened from the front-leaning-rest position, he used to tell us, 'Men, you might think that I'm making your life harder, but someday you'll realize that I made it better.'"

"Front leaning what?"

"You know, push-ups."

"Ah." She grinned. "So was he right?"

John nodded. "It sure didn't feel like it at the time, but he was. Everything they put us through was to make us better soldiers, better Rangers, better Special Operators."

Liz could hardly sit still. She felt as if she was on the edge of discovering something truly important. "In other words, God sometimes puts us in the front-leaning-whatever in order to actually make us better down the road? And not just better people, but better Christians, better image bearers of Jesus, better in the ways that really count."

John frowned. "But what about all those people who died at the hotel? What about Julie? Are you saying that God made them die or made her a hostage just so you could be better?"

Liz was horrified at the very idea. "No! I'd never say that."

"Okay. Neither would I. So what are you saying?"

She took a moment to get her thoughts in order. "Maybe it's that terrible things just happen because we live in a broken world. Evil men do evil things, but God can take those terrible things and somehow redeem them if we ask Him to. One way He redeems them is to use them to make us spiritually stronger." She looked at him. "What do you think?"

John smiled at her. "I think I've never before had a conversation like this with a pretty girl."

She flushed again. "No, really! This is great stuff, John! I can finally see that things going wrong can work for my good, but it's good as God sees it, good to make me better, even though it hurts, good to force me to rely on Him more."

John looked away, suddenly sad.

"What?"

He shook his head.

If whatever was between them was going any further, they had to talk to each other, even when it was difficult. "What is it, John?"

He shrugged, and Liz felt his shoulder rise and fall against hers. Had she leaned into him first or he into her? Who cared? She loved the feel of him resting against her, and she loved resting against him.

She merely sat and waited. The room was dim and quiet, conducive to shared intimacies. She watched him close his eyes and screw up his face, as if he hurt deep inside.

"I had a good friend, Vernon James," he finally said in little more than a whisper. "He was our medic. A big, black man who really loved Jesus. Last month when we were on a mission, he was trying to help a woman deliver a baby, and the car she was in turned out to be a suicide bomb." His voice dripped with pain.

"Oh, John, I'm sorry."

When he didn't say anything more, Liz said, "And that's what made you disappointed with God?"

"Worse. It made me want to stop believing in Him anymore." He looked at her, his face uncertain. "I'm finding it harder to put Him out of my life than I thought I would."

You've got to keep believing, John. You've got to. "I bet it is. How do you walk away from Someone who is everywhere?"

"Exactly. All kinds of things remind me of Him. Godly people like you who hang onto Jesus even when there's tragedy in your life. Gracious people like our hosts who remind me that all the world isn't bad. And the sky. Did you see that sky tonight when we were marching? Where did the stars and the planets and the clouds come from if not from God?"

He ran a hand through his hair. "It's driving me nuts. I don't like uncertainty and ambiguity. I want definite answers, definite proofs."

She rested her hand on his arm. "If we had all the answers, we wouldn't need faith. We wouldn't need God."

"I don't know, Liz. I really don't." He pushed up off the bed and sighed, turning to her. "But I'd better try again to make that call."

33

Washington, D.C.

THE PHONE BEEPED TWICE. "Mr. LaFontaine, General Cooper is on line one."

Michael raised an eyebrow. Little surprised him, but a call in the middle of the day from Buck Cooper did. Something was up. He smiled. Suddenly the day had extra spice.

"Thank you, Miss Davis. Oh, and while I have you, please call Senator Herger and tell him I won't be able to meet him at the Army Navy Club for lunch today."

Michael spun from his computer and snatched up the sleek brushed-aluminum telephone, which was the only other object on his massive mahogany desk. He pressed a button. "Recite the Corps, Maggot!"

There was chuckling on the other end of the line. "You always did treat me like a plebe, Michael."

Michael refrained from saying that he treated everyone that way. "Major General William Cooper. To what do I owe this great honor?"

"I have a problem, Michael. A big one."

The tone of Buck's voice told him this was no joke. He sat up in his black leather chair and grabbed his gold-plated Mont Blanc pen. He slid open the top drawer and extracted a tablet that read LaFontaine Industries across the top in a stylized logo.

"I'm prepared to copy, Buck."

"It's Johnnie. I just got a call; his team is missing."

Michael closed his eyes, allowing himself a brief moment of pain. He loved Johnnie like the son he never had. Then he pushed the hurt and fear away. Only weaklings allowed either pain or love to determine their lives. He was all business when he barked, "What? Where?"

"In the Middle East somewhere. They won't say exactly, of course."

"Not even to a two-star general at the Pentagon?"

"I'm not in the chain of command. You know that."

Michael did know. Buck was traditional Army. Johnnie was anything but. The boy had turned his back on family tradition, enlisted, and gone Special Forces. He'd always been his own man, much to Buck's distress. Their conflicts had never failed to amuse Michael, who went out of his way to get along with Johnnie, and not just to get Buck's goat. If he felt a genuine affection for anyone, it was Johnnie. Of course he liked Buck, too.

"Well, what can I do?"

"I don't know, Michael. You tell me. I know you've got some back-channel pull up there. What did they used to call it down in Central America?"

"*Palanca.*"

"That's it. Anyway, even my talking to you about this could lose me my job, so be discreet. But Johnnie's in trouble, and I couldn't live with myself if I didn't try to do something."

Michael was standing now. Getting things done was his specialty. "Buck, I'll do what I can. You have my word. Give me an hour to make some calls, then get back to me on my cell phone." He reeled off the number. "I can't promise anything, but I'll see what I can dig up for you. Unfortunately, I don't have many contacts in the Middle East, but I'll buy a C-130 and fly it over there myself if I have to."

"Thank you." Buck sounded momentarily hoarse. "You are a true friend and patriot."

Michael agreed with that assessment, but he didn't say so. "I'm glad you called, Buck. After all, the boy is my godson." He hung up and punched the intercom button again.

"Miss Davis!" One of his serious goals in life had become to fluster her. He'd been trying for six years and hadn't succeeded yet.

"Yes, Mr. LaFontaine?"

"Call the senator back. Ask him to meet me for lunch in twenty minutes."

"Yes, sir."

"Tell him—"

"I'll tell him the emergency smoothed itself out once you became involved, and you find yourself free after all. You are delighted because you had been looking forward to this lunch very much."

Some day. Some sweet day. But not today. It fascinated him how she took words out of his mouth, her lie always making him sound as good as or better than his own would have.

"Thank you." He punched the off button and reached for his suit coat. The good senator would be miffed, but he'd be there.

Michael smiled. The man would probably stand on the table and sing the theme song from *Hee Haw* if he asked him to. Six-figure campaign contributions would do that to a politician. More important, they would help him get an inside scoop from one of the senior members of the Defense Intelligence Committee.

He put on his suit coat and pulled a cell phone from his pocket. He stepped out onto the terrace overlooking the White House and the Ellipse. As always the sight made him proud to be an American.

Certain that his intensely sophisticated anti-surveillance technology protected him from listeners, he dialed an international number from memory and got a voice recording.

After the beep, Michael said, "We need to talk," and flipped the phone shut. He looked down onto 17th Street. Traffic was at a standstill as usual. Forget the limo. He'd walk. It would be faster, and the exercise would help him think.

Whatever it takes. Hadn't that always been his motto? It had served him well in the past, and he saw no reason to change his way of thinking now. What it took, in this case, was more information about what was happening with Task Force Valor. He'd been out of Military Intelligence for more than ten years, but he had learned the value of keeping up with old friends.

The phone in his hand chirped. He looked at the caller ID and smiled. There was one of the oldest now.

An hour later, sitting at Michael's regular table at the members' only dining area at the Army Navy Club in downtown Washington, Senator Dane Herger spread his hands in a conciliatory gesture. "Michael, you know I can't discuss defense department issues with you—even if you did have a top secret security clearance."

LaFontaine noticed that the senator hadn't touched his garden salad with buffalo mozzarella and red pepper vinaigrette. Neither had he yet had a bite of the beef medallions with shiitake mushrooms that were fast growing cold in front of him. The good senator had been too busy two-stepping, trying to tell him no without losing his campaign funding.

Politics was an intricate dance, one whose steps Michael had been practicing for years. And from the small beads of perspiration forming on Herger's brow, it was clear who was leading. But he was losing patience.

"I don't want you to discuss anything, Senator. I want you to listen. LaFontaine Industries' new pharmaceutical plant could bring a lot of jobs to your district—or not. I'm not asking you to do anything unethical or illegal. I'm simply saying that a unit very near and dear to my heart has been abandoned by this government in hostile territory in South Lebanon."

Herger looked as if he'd just swallowed his fork. "Where are you getting this information, Michael? Don't ask me to confirm anything because I…"

Michael held up a hand. "I don't need confirmation, Dane. I need action. My understanding is that somebody decided that their own backside was more important than some of our boys on the ground. That needs to change immediately."

The ruffled senator nodded, staring at his uneaten food. He appeared to have lost his appetite completely. "I'll see what I can do." He rose to leave.

Michael affected a smile and watched him go. "Pleasure doing business with you," he said quietly to the senator's retreating back.

His own meal was delicious.

Zebdine

There's no place like home. And this sure isn't it.

John fought to keep from ripping the telephone out of the wall. Another unsuccessful attempt to call out. Aside from the fact that the phone was probably older than he was, it seemed like the black ceramic instrument knew it was Valor's only hope and was toying with him because of it.

He reminded himself how generous it was for the pharmacist to have allowed them into his home at all. If he were in the man's shoes, risking his livelihood, his family, and his very life to take in a ragged bunch of armed strangers, John doubted if he'd be as willing. He was humbled by this man's generosity.

Still, they should have been back at H-5 long ago. He should be sitting in the Ops tent, sipping a cup of that nearly toxic swamp water they called coffee. Instead, he was about to eat in the tiny kitchen of a Lebanese druggist. Not that that was all bad. The smells wafting from the kitchen said that this family was preparing a veritable midnight feast, and his stomach rumbled in anticipation.

Unfortunately, good food would do little to quench the brooding sense of failure that had been building in him. No matter what he did, they kept getting farther and farther from their objective.

It wasn't just being out on their own or being attached to the CIA that made this operation feel different. Something was wrong inside, something he couldn't quite define, but neither could he ignore it. Something hadn't felt right about *John Cooper* since they'd landed in Jordan three nights before.

He didn't want to admit it, but maybe it did have something to do with how he'd felt since Doc James died. Then the talk with Liz had triggered the memory of Drill Sergeant Febus forcefully asserting that difficulty made one's life better.

To his military mind, that made sense. Soldiers chose to endure hardship all the time in order to be fit and competent to handle the rigors of the job. Hardship in training brings victory in battle. Sweat saves blood. Who had first said that? Patton?

But did God operate that way, too, allowing His children to face hardship in order to get better? Liz seemed taken with the idea. But better for what? So they could win some future battle? Doc sure didn't win. His life was cut off in its prime. Where was the victory there? Liz had said maybe they weren't meant to understand because then they wouldn't need faith. But John couldn't live with that. He needed something more.

Where's the victory, God?

He checked his watch. Almost 0100 hours. That meant it was nearly 8 P.M. back at Bragg. There probably wouldn't be anyone at the shop, but the 3rd Special Forces HQ would certainly have a staff duty officer around. All John had to do was make the phone system cooperate and actually connect with him! So far, all he'd gotten was a strange busy signal or a cranky French-speaking operator and then a busy signal.

As much as he hated to admit it, they would have to walk out of here, at least until they got a little closer to the coast, where there was more traffic and a vehicle wouldn't be so noticeable. The simple truth was, there were just too many Islamic extremists in the immediate area who would like nothing more than to have a collection of Task Force Valor hood ornaments. The fact that he felt increasingly powerless to save himself and his guys only added to the feeling of desperation rising within him.

The strange busy signal sounded again in his ear. With a supreme effort, he refrained from putting his fist through the wall and gently laid the receiver back in its cradle.

Liz sat quietly in the dark after John bolted. She rested her head against the wall once again, and this time when her eyes closed, she let herself fall asleep. It was easier than wondering about John and worrying about Julie.

She had no idea how much time passed before she became aware of John shaking her arm. She just knew it wasn't long enough.

"Wake up, Liz. Come on, Sleeping Beauty. Dinner's ready."

She batted at his hand. "Leave me alone!"

"Grumpy when you wake up, huh?"

"No! Ray of sunshine. Now go away!"

"Let her sleep," someone said. She thought it was Rip. "I'll eat her food for her."

She snorted, eyes still closed. "Don't you dare."

John grabbed her arm. "Doc, get her other arm." His voice was full of laughter.

"Hey!" she protested.

They pulled her off the bed and stood her on her feet. She swayed and slitted her eyes just a little. There in front of her with a disgusted look on his face was Alabama's favorite son, scowling at her.

She wrinkled her nose at Sweeney, forced her eyes all the way open, and grabbed John's arm for balance. She shook her head to clear the mists of slumber.

"I could sleep for a month," she mumbled, her diction slurred.

"Couldn't we all," John said. "Now let's eat."

Somehow she maneuvered her way to the overcrowded kitchen. People sat at the table, stood leaning against the wall, or collapsed on the floor. A steaming pot of rice appeared, then disappeared at an amazing rate. Large platters of *mankoushi* were passed, the stuffed zucchini as delicious as any meal Liz had ever eaten. Baklava, its delicate pastry swimming in golden honey, was dessert.

When she felt she'd no longer die of starvation, Liz paused long enough to ask John, "Did your call go through while I slept?"

He shook his head. "I'm going to try again in a few minutes."

Liz went back to her mankoushi as the pharmacist's wife sat beside her at the table. "I am Nazira," she said hesitantly in Arabic.

Liz smiled and answered in the same language. "I want to thank you again for letting us into your home. You and your family have been wonderful, and this meal is delicious."

Nazira returned Liz's smile shyly. "It is our honor to have you. We were afraid at first. We saw all those men in the street. There have been many robberies of pharmacies in this area recently, and we thought it was our turn. Even after they drove away, I was afraid."

"I'm sorry you were frightened. They scared me, too."

"So far they haven't hurt anyone, but you never know when that might change."

"You're right to be cautious." Liz found it curious that the small village pharmacies were being robbed. Why not electronics shops or banks?

"It is very strange," Nazira continued. "Apparently they only steal a certain kind of drugs—anti-inflammatories. This I do not understand. Morphine is worth much more, or several other drugs that bring a good street price, but they leave them alone. It makes no sense."

"Anti-inflammatories?" Liz felt her blood fizz. "My sister takes those for her rheumatoid arthritis."

Nazira nodded. "They are commonly used for such ailments."

Liz forced herself to stay calm. "Have any of the thieves been caught?"

Nazira batted the air with her hand. "Oh, they won't be punished. They are too powerful in this area."

"You know who the thieves are?"

"Of course. We all know. They do not try to conceal their identities. They are brutal people, ruthless people, and unfortunately they are invincible. It would do no good to complain. Who would we complain to? Hezbollah?"

"So the thieves are Hezbollah?" Liz asked, surprised. Such petty thefts didn't seem their style.

The woman clucked and shook her head. "No, no. Most of these terrible men I speak of are Islamic extremists who live in the refugee camps near Sidon. But they also use an old fortress near here. I think one of their leaders lives there. It is about five kilometers south of us on a high hill not far from the border with Israel."

Liz heard a buzzing in her ears. "Ansar Inshallah?"

Nazira blinked. "I am surprised you have heard of them."

Julie! She was at that fortress! Liz was absolutely certain. "How would you get to the fortress?"

"You wouldn't. No one goes near it. These are not nice people." With that pronouncement, Nazira rose and left to shoo her children off to bed.

Liz saw John standing in the hall near the telephone. She put her plate down, her baklava only half finished, and hurried to him. "John, I think I've found Julie!"

He was dialing a multidigit number. "Just a sec." He pressed the receiver to his ear, a hand held over the mouthpiece to block the noise of thirteen people in a very small apartment.

She put a hand on his arm. "John, I need to talk to you." Faintly, from the receiver there came the sound of a busy signal. John exhaled heavily, and his knuckles were white as he lowered the phone to its cradle.

He turned to look at her. "What do you want?"

His abrupt tone surprised and hurt, but she didn't back down. She knew his frustration wasn't really aimed at her. "I think my sister's near here. Really near. We can save her."

He looked into her eyes for a long moment, his gaze preoccupied. Then something in his face softened. He lifted a hand and stroked her cheek with the back of his knuckles.

"Look, Liz. I respect what you're trying to do, believe me. But it just doesn't work that way. I've been given a specific mission I must carry out, and right now that mission is to get my team out of this country safely. I can't decide to send my guys off on a different mission, no matter how noble, no matter how important, especially one that's likely to get us all killed."

"But…" She couldn't believe he was turning her down. This was *Julie!* Not only could she die because of his decision, but any budding relationship between her and John would die, too. The loss of Julie's life would always be between them.

He held a finger to her lips. "Shh. I wish it were different; I really do. When we get out of here, I'll do whatever I can to help you get help. You have my word. But right now I…"

She brushed his hand away. "By then it will be too late if it's not too late already. They said seventy-two hours, and seven this morning will be seventy-two hours since the tape was first shown on TV. Please, John!" Her voice was thick with desperation and tears.

"We can't, Liz." He was kind, but his words were final.

She turned away, struggling for control. She would not cry, especially with a sneering Sweeney watching her. She managed to stop her chin's quivering, though a lone tear slipped down the cheek John had brushed moments ago.

Even in her sorrow, she understood what he was saying. He had his orders and no choice but to follow them. He had to protect his men. Julie wasn't Valor's responsibility.

Julie was *her* responsibility.

She stepped past John without looking at him. She didn't want him to read her grief or her intentions in her eyes. "I'm going to lie down for a bit."

"Good idea. We still have quite a night ahead of us." He ran a hand over her bent head, lingering for a second at the nape of her neck. She knew he didn't like disappointing her any more than she liked being disappointed.

She walked slowly toward the bedroom. *Lord, come with me. Help me.*

She checked over her shoulder. No one was watching her at all. John was the only one in view, and he was once again trying the phone. She continued past the bedroom and down the back stairs. She let herself out into the yard and ran south until she was out of town.

Julie, I'm coming. Hang on. I'm coming!

34

Lebanese Countryside

THE NIGHT SEEMED so much darker when she was trying to find her way through it alone. And scarier. But she could see a light ahead, high on a hill to the south. She figured that was where she needed to go.

It had become visible as soon as she was out of the village, a pinpoint in the distance. She understood more fully now why John and Rip had gone to such extremes when they had to read their maps. Light showed a phenomenal distance.

The ground was rough and hilly, covered with low scrub brush that scratched her ankles. A quarter moon sat low in the sky, giving just enough illumination to make the landscape before her blur into a thousand indistinguishable shades of gray. If her feet didn't hurt so much, it wouldn't be a bad walk at all if she was careful where she stepped.

She looked at the light again. Julie was there. She was sure of it.

A little bell sounded off to her right. A wind chime? She looked but couldn't see a house, but that wasn't surprising. It was probably tucked just over the next ridge.

She trudged up a rise and froze in midstep. Someone was

standing in her path. When the dark silhouette didn't move, she approached it with caution. A few steps more and she realized that she almost had a heart attack over the trunk of a long-dead tree.

She shivered from the aftereffects of the adrenaline rush. *Get a grip, girl. Nobody's going to be out working in the fields this early in the morning. Just take it one step at a time.*

She concentrated on getting to the field of big rocks up ahead. When she reached that objective, she'd pick a new one. Taking a deep breath, she started down the gentle slope.

What she really wanted to do was sit down and cry. While she understood where John was coming from, she had been deeply hurt by his refusal to help. This was Julie, her sister, they were talking about. Surely a little side trip to free her from the radicals of Ansar Inshallah wouldn't have taxed Valor too much.

The chime tinkled again, much closer this time. As she wondered about it, one of the rocks in front of her moved.

She screamed and the adrenaline came rushing back. Then all the rocks stood up and moved away from her in unison, bleating in alarm.

Goats. There must be a hundred of them. Then she heard the sound of running footsteps. *Human* footsteps. Another shot of adrenaline.

Liz tried to whirl toward the sound and back away at the same time. She succeeded only in stepping on her long skirt. She sat down hard in the dewy grass.

"Deery baalek!"

She looked up to see who was warning her to be careful. She stared at a boy, short and skinny and dressed in the flowing garment of a bedouin.

"Are you hurt?" the boy inquired in Arabic.

"La, shukran," she said. *At least I don't think so.*

"Do not be afraid. My goats will not hurt you. They will not go near strangers. But be careful around Asal, my Honey." He patted the largest of the animals, the one with the bell. It was a donkey with a pair of the longest ears Liz had ever seen.

"That's Honey?" She pointed at the donkey.

"Asal. Yes. She protects the herd from danger. She is a very good guard donkey." He grinned at the donkey and stroked its scruffy mane.

Liz watched the goats press in close to the boy but keep a good six feet from her. "You care for all of these by yourself?"

The boy stood a bit taller. "Of course. I am Anwar. I am fifteen years old."

She smiled. "Of course. And I am Elizabeth." She didn't find the boy at all threatening. She had seen bedouin goatherds out in the country many times, and she knew that they spent the night with their animals.

She cast a glance toward the fortress. *Julie, I'm coming.*

"Why is a lady like you walking here in the middle of the night, Elizabeth?"

She looked again toward the fortress. Its walls loomed black in the wan moonlight, the silhouette faintly limned by an illumination within.

He followed her gaze. "That is an ancient Crusader castle, built in the eleventh century by Christian men to forcefully prevent the spread of Islam into Europe. If you could see it in the daylight, you would see that it is beautiful."

"That's why I'm here. That's where I'm going."

Anwar was shocked. Even Honey seemed to quiver at her words. "You cannot go there now. The fortress is being used by very bad men."

She nodded. "I know, but I must go. They have my sister." She began to walk, and Anwar and his flock followed.

"She is a hostage?"

"Yes."

"The one they show on television?"

Liz's heart caught. "You have seen her? Is she still all right?"

"She was last evening when we walked through the village." He pointed back the way Liz had come. "But how will you get her out without being caught or killed yourself?"

Liz hated to admit it, but she really hadn't thought that part out clearly. Her imagination stopped at the moment she and Julie wrapped their arms about one another, weeping in relief and joy. It was a picture haloed in gold, like the kissing scenes in the old comic books.

The reality of her situation, the sheer stupidity of thinking she could rescue her sister from the clutches of a heavily-armed band of terrorists, suddenly hit her full force. Futility washed through her in great waves, threatening to drown her determination. "I…I don't even know how I'm going to get in, let alone get her out."

The goatherd said nothing for a long moment. Honey's gently tinkling bell was the only sound. Then, "Perhaps we could help."

"We?"

"My goats and I."

She half sobbed, half laughed at the absurdity of the idea. "I don't see how your goats can be of much help, but I really appreciate the offer."

"I was thinking I could use the goats to distract the guards at the gate." He scratched his head thoughtfully. "But that wouldn't get you inside, would it? It is too bad we don't have some way to get you up the cliff on the far side."

Cliff? A spark of hope burst into flame. "I'm a good climber!"

"You are?"

She nodded. "I've even taken lessons."

"But we have no ropes." Anwar looked at her, distressed. "If you fell…"

Liz shrugged. "A bad plan is better than no plan. Besides, I won't fall."

The boy looked skeptical, but Liz didn't care. "If you would be willing to distract the men inside, I could at least try to make it up and over the wall."

"But, Elizabeth, it is very dangerous."

"Yes, it is. But I don't have a choice. I must try to free my sister."

As she and Anwar walked toward the fortress, there was no way Liz could believe their unexpected meeting was a coincidence. *Thank You, Father.*

She might have lost whatever help John could give—and that was not a heart pang she felt, at least not one over him; it was not—but she'd gained another ally. She glanced at the animals trailing them. Allies.

"God has sent you to me, Anwar."

He beamed at her. "You think so?"

Liz nodded. "I do, most definitely." They continued in silence for a few minutes. "Do you get lonely working out here alone?"

"Sometimes. Normally one of my brothers or even my older sister would help me, but…" he paused, and Liz thought she saw a painful sadness in his face, "…my family will no longer allow it. They will not send any of my siblings out with—" He hesitated again, as if he wasn't sure if he should say what he wanted to, "—an apostate."

"An apostate?" Fascinating. "What do you mean?"

"I chose to leave the faith of my father and become a Christian."

"Did you, now?" Liz knew he'd made a choice that had great ramifications for him. Conversion was the ultimate disloyalty. "Then we have something in common."

He brightened visibly. "You are a Christian, too? A true Christian, a believer in Jesus?"

"I am a true Christian," she assured him. "How did you become a believer?" She loved faith stories and listening would keep her mind off Julie and the idiocy of what she was trying to do.

The boy sighed. "I am the oldest son of my father. When I was born, as is our custom, he took the name Abu Anwar."

"The father of Anwar," Liz said. "I'm familiar with this custom."

"Yes, and even from a young age, I knew that I wanted to honor him. So I asked to go to school. I wanted to become a Muslim cleric and make my father proud to wear my name. So though we are poor, my father sent me to a *madrasah* in Sidon to study. We spent day after day there memorizing the holy Koran. I was the best student; I memorized my verses well. But one thing began to bother me. The Koran says that Jesus was sinless. But when Allah talks to Mohammed, He tells him to repent of his sins."

"How very interesting." Liz had never heard that before.

"It bothered me for many weeks. Why would we follow the example of Mohammed, who made mistakes, instead of following Jesus, who was perfect? Then one night I had a dream. I was standing before Allah, and I begged him to allow me into paradise. But he refused. I was crying and asking why, when I had been a good Muslim? He replied that I was not hairy enough."

"Not hairy enough?" That was another new one.

"Yes. We were taught that Mohammed said that God loves the hairy, strong man and the unhairy, sweet, soft woman. But I was not hairy. In my dream, I cried and cried and said, 'But why did you make me this way?' Then I turned and saw Jesus, wearing a white robe. He said, 'Come to me. I will love you just as you are.'

"When I woke up, I gathered my things and left the madrasah. I took a bus back home. I had decided to believe in Jesus. But as I expected, my family was very unhappy. My father stopped using my name, and I am not allowed in the tent. I only live with the animals."

"That's terrible!"

"No." Anwar shook his head. "I thank God every day for allowing me to know the truth. In my life is much hardship, and the people here treat me as an outcast, so now I must always trust God, because He is all that I have. And I have found that He is enough. I have a lot of time to pray out here." He spread his hands, taking in the flock and the valley.

All things working for good, Liz thought. *God's definition of good.* Anwar was being given a marvelous gift in the opportunity to get to know God in a deep way. God didn't make his family reject him, but He turned the rejection to Anwar's benefit.

That's how I should look at this, isn't it, Lord? For Julie and for me, this is an opportunity to develop our spiritual wings and take flight as never before. For us that is how You are redeeming Khalil's death and Julie's captivity.

Anwar was silent for a minute. Then he said, "God has put us together for a special reason, I think. Come, let us pray about it, and then we will finish our walk to the fortress. Perhaps He will show us a better solution."

Praying was the best idea she'd heard yet. With the goats pressing in on Anwar and Honey standing guard, Liz and the young goatherd bowed their heads and asked for God's help. When she finally raised her tear-streaked face again, somehow Liz felt better.

Zebdine

John held out a wad of Lebanese bank notes, offering them to the pharmacist. *"Permittez-vous me payez pour le telephone."* He was taxing his limited French to the hilt but still feared he was offering to buy the man's telephone instead of offering to pay for its use. He wished Liz were here to translate into Arabic, but he decided to let her sleep.

The pharmacist held up his hands and refused to take the money. *"Non, Dieu fornit. C'est mon honneur a servir."*

John shrugged and put the money back in his pocket. He understood the words about it being an honor to serve, and something about God. Clearly the pharmacist was a man of principle and didn't want the money. No matter. John would just hide it under the pillow in the kids' room before they left.

He reached out and put a hand on the man's shoulder. *"Merci bien. Vous avez la couer de lion."*

The man grinned broadly and went to join his now-sleeping wife and children in the bedroom.

John felt pleased as he wandered back to the living room. He'd finally connected with a duty officer at group headquarters. If Valor made it out of here, he'd probably get reprimanded by some armchair general for giving his grid coordinates over an open phone line, but at this point he didn't care. Whatever worked.

With any luck, his message had already been relayed to H-5, and the major now knew their plans to lie low until the following night. With a bit more luck they could evade their pursuers, and in little more than twenty-four hours be en route to an aircraft carrier in the Med with an escort of Navy SEALS. In the meantime they were fed and hidden, as safe as they could hope to be.

Thanks to Liz. He smiled at the thought of her. She was very unhappy with him at the moment, and he would have to do some fancy dancing to win back her favor. Waltz, two-step, fox-trot—it didn't matter. He looked forward to matching wits with her and being blessed by one of her wonderful smiles.

He glanced at the closed bedroom door. He'd better stop mooning and get some sleep himself. One look at Sweeney laid out asleep on the floor in front of him, cuddling his weapon like a kid cuddled a teddy bear, told John that for once they'd be well rested when it came time to move again.

Rip had been poring over the map on the kitchen table, and now he refolded it carefully. "I'm going to hit the rack, Coop. Wake me up if you need me."

John nodded. "Okay. We'll keep one man on the phone at all times, as I expect they'll be calling back shortly. I'll take the first hour and post a roster by the phone. Since Doc, Frank, and Hogan have already been out for a while, I'll put them on first. You should be able to get at least four hours solid."

"Shoot, that's more than I get at home." Rip headed down the hall. He entered the bedroom, then stuck his head back out. "Hey, you want me to sleep on the floor and save this last bed for Liz?"

John wrinkled his brow. "What do you mean? She's already in there asleep."

Rip shook his head. "I only see three bodies, and none of 'em is a hot mama."

"What?" John strode down the hall. When he reached the bedroom, he flipped on the light. Doc, Hogan, and Frank all sat up, shielding their eyes.

"Turn that thing off, Coop!" Doc ordered.

"It's not time to get up already, is it?" Hogan asked around a yawn.

"Just because you aren't sleeping, Cooper, doesn't mean the rest of us don't want to knit up our raveled sleeves of care," Frank muttered.

"What?" Hogan demanded as they all looked at Frank. All but John. He stared at the empty bed.

"Shakespeare, you unwashed pagans." Frank pulled his pillow over his head and immediately fell back to sleep.

John's stomach did a slow pitch and roll. He spun back into the hallway and flipped on the light in the small bathroom. Again, no Liz. It didn't take long to search the small apartment. No Liz anywhere.

Then it hit him. *Julie!*

"Why, you little…"

He ran to the window and searched the street. He saw no movement, but it was completely dark outside. If she stuck to the shadows, he might not see her.

"What'd you say?" Sweeney sat up behind him. "What's going on, Coop?"

John gripped the windowsill, willing Liz's figure to appear. It didn't. He imagined her out there in the darkness, alone, going to find Julie because he wouldn't. "It's Liz. She's taken off."

He heard Sweeney's contemptuous, "Pffff. I knew she was gonna git herself killed."

John glared at Sweeney. "Not if I can help it." He started for the bedroom to get his gear.

Sweeney caught up with him in the hallway. "Coop," he whispered in deference to the others sleeping, "what are you doing?"

"Going to find her."

Sweeney snorted. "That's what I was afraid of."

John put out a warning hand. "Stay out of my way, Bobby."

"Listen, man. You're the team sergeant, and you know I'd follow you to the gates of hell in gasoline-soaked underpants if you asked me to. But I gotta tell you, I think you're lettin' your feelings for this girl cloud your judgment."

John just stared at him.

"I know she's a friend of yours, and anyone can see she's a pretty thing. Anyone can also see you're taken with her."

John couldn't deny it.

"But we got a job to do, Coop! Right now that job is to get ourselves out of this country so we can track down the ITEB." Sweeney's face was hard, but his eyes told John that he sympathized.

John sighed. "What do you think I should do?"

"I say let her go off if she wants to. She's a big girl."

John sighed again, then shook his head. "I can't just leave her, Bobby. We brought her down here. She's our responsibility now. You stay here and man the phone, and I'll go look for her. She can't have gone far."

Sweeney scowled. "You're making a mistake, Master Sergeant."

"Maybe so, Sweeney. Maybe so." John hefted his rifle and turned toward the back door. "But sometimes there's no choice."

35

The Fortress, Southern Lebanon

LIZ AND ANWAR SEPARATED when the fortress was still a half mile away.

"It will take me at least thirty or forty minutes to move my herd around to the gate. That should give you plenty of time to get up the wall. When you hear the bell of my Honey, you'll know it's time to seek your sister."

Liz took a deep breath. "Okay. And thank you."

Anwar stopped and looked back at her. He smiled. "It is an honor to help a sister in need. I only wish that we were able to spend some time worshipping our great God. If not on this side of heaven's gates, then on the other." Then with a princely bow, he disappeared into the darkness, clucking and cooing at his flock.

While he and his herd moved up the hill that would lead them to the gate, Liz moved toward the shadows at the base of the cliff. The closer she got, the more terrified she became that someone would see or hear her, though it wasn't likely over the increasingly loud bleating of the goats. Whatever Anwar was doing to stir them up was working.

Static crackled, making her jump.

"Task Force Valor, this is Solo-Four-Four. Come in, Valor."

Liz spun, looking behind as her heart pounded. No one was there.

"Task Force Valor, this is Solo-Four-Four. Come in, Valor."

Liz blinked. The disembodied voice was coming from her skirt. The radio Rip had given her when she had crossed to the pharmacist's!

She reached into the pocket and pulled the radio free. At first she just stared at it. Should she say something? Shut it off so no one in the fortress would hear it?

"Task Force Valor, this is Solo-Four-Four. Come in, Valor. Please come in."

Liz heard an edge of desperation in the crackly voice. It was nice to know that Valor's people were as concerned about contacting Valor as Valor was about contacting them. This was the opportunity John had been hoping for. She remembered the button Rip had shown her and pushed. "Uh, this is Liz Fairchild speaking."

There was a moment of silence. Then the voice returned. "This is Solo-Four-Four. Please identify yourself, over."

"Uh, my name is Elizabeth Fairchild. I'm an American."

"Copy, you are American. What are you doing on this net, over?"

"I'm with your men, or at least I was. They gave me one of their radios. They are trying to telephone Fort Bragg from a house back in Zebdine. Uh, where are you?"

"Okay, say your name again, please."

"It's Elizabeth Fairchild." She thought she could hear a buzzing sound, like a gas-powered weed eater, somewhere high above her. Liz studied the sky for a moving light that meant a plane. "I can't see you. Are you in a plane?"

"Stand by." A moment passed, then the voice returned. "Listen, Elizabeth. We need your social security number, please. Over."

"What?" Then it dawned on her. They needed proof that she was who she claimed to be. That made sense. An American woman in the middle of the Lebanese countryside in the depths of night was probably the last thing they expected. As far as they were concerned, it could be a trap or a disinformation kind of thing.

She keyed the mike. "Okay, here it is." She recited the number.

"Thank you. Wait one."

Liz shivered in the cool night air as she felt the seconds tick past.

"Elizabeth, this is Solo-Four-Four. We've confirmed your identity, thank you. Now listen, we need you to get one of our operators on the radio right away, over."

"Sorry. Can't. I'm not with them anymore." No thanks to Team Sergeant John Cooper.

She climbed over a bunch of fallen stones that had tumbled from the walls sometime in the last several hundred years or so, using one hand for balance while the other held the radio.

A creature about the size of a house cat startled at her passing. She wasn't sure who jumped higher, the animal or her. She watched it scamper away and thought it might be a hyrax. No way was that little animal's closest relative an elephant, no matter what the zoologists said.

She pushed the radio button again. "I've got to get my sister."

"Say again, over?"

"Julie Assan."

The radio was silent for a moment, then, "I copy you said Julie Assan? She's the hostage they're showing on television?"

She tried mimicking the professional tone of the voice. "That is correct, over." It felt silly talking that way.

"Where did you say the team is?"

"They're in Zebdine."

"Zebdine, roger. Listen, Elizabeth. You should go back there now."

"Sorry, I can't. I...I won't. I'm going to go now. The goats will be at the front gate soon. I've got to climb the wall."

"Goats? Wall? Say again, over?"

"Look, I don't have time to explain. I hope you find your team, but I've got to go. So, uh...bye. Or 'over' or whatever you're supposed to say."

Liz turned the knob on the top of the radio until it clicked off, then dropped it back into her pocket. She moved close to the wall of the fortress. It towered above her.

Okay, girl. Let's do it.

Somewhere Over Lebanon

Mary Walker tore the headset off and let out a stream of words that would have made even her father scowl in disapproval. Immediately she cringed and her face flamed. She never talked like that. Hopefully the drone of the C-130 was loud enough to mask her outburst.

What just happened? No sooner did the UAV get over Lebanese airspace and start broadcasting than they got a reply from this...this girl? Elizabeth Fairchild? It had only taken a moment to radio her social security number back to Langley and verify her identity, but that still didn't explain how she happened to be in southern Lebanon with one of Task Force Valor's radios but without the team itself.

At first Mary had been sure it was some kind of trap. But the sheer improbability of the scenario told her it had to be true.

She looked down at the sergeant manning the radio. She had stood behind him listening while he spoke with the girl. To his credit, he had handled the exchange very well, considering there was no protocol for such a thing. Now the young soldier was still calmly trying to raise the girl again, but she had either shut off her radio or was simply ignoring them.

Mary replaced her headset, reached over to the console, and flipped the dial to the UAV pilot's channel. The T-15 was being controlled by a flight-suited captain, who was seated next to the sergeant at the radio.

"Take us to Zebdine, sir," she said into her microphone.

"Zebdine is only about three miles from where we were when we picked up the girl's signal." The man nudged the joystick that controlled the UAV's flight. "We're pretty much in range now."

"Then they should be hearing us, shouldn't they?"

"Roger that."

Mary frowned. "You think they have their radios turned off?"

The captain shook his head, keeping his eyes on the TV screen in front of him where the grainy video transmitted from the UAV flickered. "You've got me."

"If theirs are off, then why was hers on? Who would she talk to?"

The pilot shrugged. "So what do you want to do? You want me to head this thing to the beach and a possible exfil location, or should we do circles over Zebdine?"

"How much time do we have?"

The pilot punched some numbers into his console. "The plane could keep flying for another eight or nine hours. The only problem is that dawn comes in about three. The T-15 flies low enough that it'll be easy to spot once it's light, and even easier to shoot down. It'll take us another forty minutes to get from here to the beach, and an hour twenty to get out of Lebanon from there. That means if we go now, we'll have just about an hour to try and make contact with the team and arrange pickup at the beach. That's not much time."

Mary gripped the back of the pilot's seat and watched the grainy black-and-white infrared video. The few roads showed as black stripes on the ridges; the fields around them showed white.

She marveled that the pilot could keep the tiny plane from crashing with so little to work with visually.

Think, Mary! What would the major do?

The major would probably be praying.

Well, I hope you're praying now, Williams. I need all the help I can get!

The UAV pilot broke in on her thoughts. "We just passed Zebdine. We'll be out of range shortly."

The man on the radio spoke up again. "Ma'am, I've got something!"

36

The Fortress

IT'S JUST LIKE *the climbing wall at home,* Liz told herself. *Only it's the middle of the night in Lebanon instead of a well-lit gym in Pennsylvania. And there are people on the other side who will happily kill you.*

She never had been very good at giving herself pep talks.

Julie. Think of Julie.

That did it. She grabbed her back skirt hem and once again pulled it through and up, tucking it into her waist to get the material out of her way.

The frail moonlight was just strong enough for her to see the next handhold above her. In the flat colorlessness of night, depth perception was almost nonexistent. Crevices were just black, bottomless holes, who knew how deep, and she shuddered to think what might live in them.

Oh, God, nothing with teeth, please, she prayed as she slipped her hand into the next hold. She jammed her shoe into a crack. For the first time since she had run from the terrorists with Valor, she was glad she didn't have heavy hiking shoes on. Her flats weren't as pliant as her climbing shoes, and they had no stickiness to help hold her in place, but she could feel through them, and she could jam them into small openings.

The first thirty feet were the hardest, scaling the natural cliff face the fortress was built into. After that came centuries-old stonework that was much easier to climb. Slowly she stretched, held, jammed a foot, stood, stretched, held, jammed the other foot, stood.

A sudden fluttering, a blood-curdling screech, and a huge bird exploded out of one crevice just as she reached her hand in. She yelped and drew back instinctively. She felt that sickening pull as gravity began to exert its will on her.

Lord, help!

She grabbed desperately at the ledge the bird had just vacated. Her fingers flailed for a hold, found a knob of stone, and gripped. She pulled her body in and flattened herself against the rock.

She hung there and waited for her breathing to even out, her heart to slow, and her legs to stop trembling. When she was certain she had control of herself, she resumed her climb.

But no more birds, please, Lord!

Then she was finally at the top. Her fingers were bleeding, her nails broken, and her thighs and calves burned from the exertion. As she lay on the top of the wall, broad enough for two men to walk side by side, she whispered a fervent prayer of thanks. For a moment she just rested, watching the activity in the courtyard below. It was enough to make her wish she could turn around and climb back down.

Not that she could or would, of course. She had to find Julie. She had to! Still, the sight was terrifying.

Armed men scurried back and forth from a set of stairs leading underground to the back of a well-used black Mercedes. She counted at least twelve men. They were loading cases of something into the back of the car. She noticed that they treated these cases with the utmost respect, certainly not like the airport guys who threw your luggage onto the loading belt.

Two men emerged from somewhere beyond her view and walked over to inspect the cargo. The one on the left was older. He had a long white beard that hung down and blended with a flowing robe of the same color. He walked as if he owned the place, and he carried himself with an air of authority. He must be a cleric. She had no doubt that he was in charge.

One of the men took a bottle from one of the cases and handed it to the older man. He turned the bottle over in his hands. From her distant perch, Liz thought it looked like a bottle of Evian water.

The cleric turned to the younger, taller man at his side and handed him the bottle. The younger man called for the attention of the others. He held the bottle above his head like a trophy. Even from this distance, Liz could hear him shout out, "Naru Allah!"

The fire of God? In a water bottle?

All the men cheered. "Allah ak'bar!"

The tall man turned abruptly and threw the bottle in a long arc toward an empty corner of the courtyard.

The bottle erupted into an incredible fireball, like something out of a Bruce Willis movie. The concussion wave hit, nearly blasting her off the wall. She dug her fingers into the crevices between the stones and held tight.

She tried unsuccessfully to stifle a surprised yelp, but she wasn't worried about being heard. Any noise she made was drowned out by the roar of the writhing fire echoing off the ancient rock walls.

She stared, open-mouthed. What was it? Napalm in that little bottle?

She looked at the boxes visible in the open trunk of the car. How many boxes were there? And how many bottles in each box? The amount of damage all those bottles could do was terrifying.

With the fire's flash, Liz knew what had happened to the Hotel Rowena. How many bottles had it taken to produce that burned-out shell of a building? She now knew what John and his team were doing running around Lebanon.

The men in the courtyard cheered as they watched the conflagration, and a few fired their weapons in the air. The bearded man looked at the fire with great satisfaction before he turned and began barking out orders.

Liz reached for her radio. Whoever was flying around looking for John and his men needed to know what she had just seen. She fought with the clumsy harem pants and the uncooperative pocket until she finally pulled out Rip's radio.

As always, it reminded her of a kid's walkie-talkie with its short antenna and its push buttons. She turned it on, put it to her lips, and pressed the button. Whispering, she said, "Hello? This is Liz Fairchild again. Are you still there?"

She released the button and waited, praying they still could hear her.

The reply came back sooner but louder than she expected. "We read you, Elizabeth. Are you okay?" Liz fumbled to turn the volume down.

She didn't have time for pleasantries. "Listen, I'm at an old fortress on the hill south of Zebdine. There are some men loading a car with lots of bottles of something. It looks like water, but they just blew up one of the bottles. I think it must be what your team on the ground is looking for."

"Roger that. We just saw something light up the sky in the south. We'll let Valor know as soon as they establish contact. In the meantime, you get out of there as fast as you can."

She shook her head, remembered they couldn't see her, and pressed the button. "I wish I could, believe me, but I can't."

A woman's voice came over the radio. "That is not a suggestion, Miss Fairchild."

Liz hesitated a moment as tears started to well in her eyes. "When you do hear from Valor, please tell John that I'm sorry. Tell him Liz said she's sorry for messing things up. Tell him I know I'm being stupid, but I have to try. No one else is. And tell him I said good-bye."

"Listen, Elizabeth, we—"

Liz shut the radio off and put it back in her pocket. She didn't need it anymore.

That's when she heard another noise, the bleating of a hundred goats.

Zebdine

John was donning his vest and other gear as quietly as possible in the bedroom when Sweeney burst in the door. "John, you gotta come quick. Something just blew up near here!"

The other men sat up quickly, turning from sleeper to soldier in a matter of seconds.

John followed Sweeney into the living room, the others on his heels.

Sweeney pointed out the window. "There was this flash out there. At first I thought it was lightning. I went to the window to look and saw this fluctuating light, like a fire might make. Then I heard this muffled thump."

John shrugged. "So what makes you think it wasn't lightning and thunder?"

Sweeney looked positively hurt. "Come on, Coop. I know the difference between thunder and C-4!"

The man had a point. The shop at Bragg was so close to some of the live fire ranges that they had all learned to distinguish between the sound of a mortar round and an artillery shell, much less thunder.

Something in John's gut told him that whatever it was, wherever it was, Liz was there. He didn't like that thought one bit.

He checked his ammo supply. "I'm going to do a fast patrol around the village to make certain Liz isn't still somewhere near. Hogan, get your stuff on. You're coming with me. Sweeney, get your radio, and let's do a quick test to be certain they're still working.

Sweeney nodded and stalked off to get his radio. While John waited for Hogan to get his gear on, he reached down and turned his on.

Immediately, he heard a static-laced transmission through the headset. "…Four-Four, over."

At first he figured it was simply interference of some kind, maybe from the UNFIL observers that roamed this area. Then it came through again.

"This is Solo-Four-Four calling Task Force Valor. Come in, Valor."

The Fortress

Imad Hijazi watched the flames lick up the ancient stone wall and smiled. Tomorrow would be a wonderful day.

He turned to his leader and smiled. "What do you think?"

"Magnificent," Abu Shaaban said.

"I am glad you are pleased, sir. After tomorrow the names Ansar Inshallah and Abu Shaaban will be known throughout the world as defenders of Allah and Islam." And the name Imad Hijazi, too, if he had anything to say about it.

He looked at the old man. He still stood straight and moved with vigor. Imad smiled to himself. Such would not always be the case. Age and illness were no respecters of persons. Even Abu Shaaban would sicken and die. Given his age, that day couldn't be too far off.

And he would be waiting. After the success of Allah's Fire, it was merely a matter of time until he assumed his rightful position as the leader of The Followers of God's Will. Those who now commanded him would become his servants, obeying his instructions, following his orders.

There was also his coming marriage to Abu Shaaban's niece, which would make him family. Another link in the chain he was forging. Too bad Karima was such a sad little thing. He did not foresee much pleasure in his marriage bed.

But power was the great aphrodisiac, and power would be his, great power, thanks to Allah's Fire.

Of course there was one possible complication. They hadn't yet found the rogue commandos he was convinced were hiding somewhere nearby. He wasn't overly concerned. He knew they would eventually be found. They would never be able to outthink him.

When they were captured, he hoped they were taken alive. Then they could be subjected to the same fate the blond woman would soon face.

As far as he was concerned, she was fulfilling her purpose quite well. Misdirection. If only Abu Shaaban weren't so displeased with her kidnapping.

"You will have very powerful people looking for her, and by extension us," he had said the night she was taken, and he had said it in front of the rest of the leadership. "We are not extremists like those in Iraq. We do not execute women."

Imad stood tall and spoke clearly. "Not even a Westerner married to a Lebanese? Sir, she is one of the very ones we want to rid our land of."

Abu Shaaban stroked his long white beard. Imad, his contempt and ambition carefully concealed, watched along with the others as the old man thought. Finally he could stand the silence no longer.

"The Hotel Rowena showed our power." He spoke with

much force. "The woman will divert them from finding out what our next target will be. They will concentrate on locating her, not Allah's Fire."

"Then you will care for her," Abu Shaaban said. "You are responsible to see she is fed and kept well. Whether we behead her or not is yet to be decided."

So Imad had seen to her, using the meek and foolish woman he was to marry as the caregiver. He would be happier, though, when her death sentence was carried out, for no matter what Abu Shaaban said, she would die.

He frowned. What was that terrible noise? Animals?

37

The Fortress

LIZ BLINKED IN SURPRISE. The courtyard was suddenly empty. The men had all run off in different directions, some to the front gate to protect the fortress from the marauding goats, some back down the stairs at the far corner of the courtyard. The old man and his assistant had gone into the castle tunnels.

She could see that this unexpected opportunity would be her only chance to get inside the fortress, but how? She sat up and looked over the edge of the wall. Could she downclimb that?

At the gym, climbing down had always been harder than going up. In truth, she'd usually tried to just lie back into the safety of the rope and let the belay guy lower her to the ground. A wave of dizziness swept over her, and she flattened herself on the top of the wall once again.

Come on, girl. You can do this. Just take it one hold at a time. From the climb up Liz knew there were plenty of cracks and crevices to provide holds for her. She was more concerned about turning her back to the courtyard as she climbed—she'd be unable to see if someone was coming.

Looking around, she chose a corner to her left where the

shadows reached highest on the wall and would give her the best chance of climbing undetected until she could drop the rest of the way without hurting herself. The last thing she wanted was a broken leg.

She searched all the darkened corners of the courtyard just to be certain no one was skulking about, waiting to grab her as soon as she was on the ground. She saw no one. She could hear the men shouting at Anwar and his goats, and it brought her a brief smile.

She scooted carefully to the chosen corner, keeping herself as low as possible, then peered over the edge, searching for a foothold. In the rapidly dimming flare from the explosion and the weak light from the fixture mounted on one of the sheds, she saw a promising crevice and another below it.

She rolled to her stomach and lowered her legs, her toe finding and jamming into the opening between two massive stones. She let that foot take her weight and began the nerve-wracking business of feeling for a way down. Spread-eagled against the fortress wall, she had never felt so vulnerable.

And I used to feel like I'd get swatted climbing in the gym!

All she needed was one man to decide the goats weren't a grave threat after all and return to the courtyard.

Keep 'em bleating, Anwar!

She had gone about halfway down the wall when she saw movement above her out of the corner of her eye, something black moving against the lesser black of the sky. She looked, then froze.

A guard! Walking the top of the wall! Had he just climbed up, or had he been there all along? His leisurely pace proved he hadn't seen her. He seemed more interested in what was happening at the front gate than in his patrol duty.

All he had to do was look down, and she was toast. He walked steadily toward her, his rifle held casually in his hands. She could hear the crunch of his footsteps and the rattle of little stones that he disturbed as they fell from the wall.

When he stopped right above her, she turned her face down, hoping the top of her dark head would provide some limited camouflage. She squeezed her eyes shut, as if that would make her more invisible. She opened them quickly as a weird feeling of vertigo swept over her.

Then she couldn't help it; she had to look up, compelled to see where the guard was. She swallowed hard when she saw the tips of his shoes hanging over the edge of the wall directly above her. The flare of a match and the scent of tobacco came to her. He was lighting a cigarette, taking a break, at the worst possible place!

How long could she hang here? Her legs were already getting rubbery from the exertion of holding on, and her arms begged for a break, but she dared not move.

The guard shifted position slightly, and the pebbles his foot displaced rained down on Liz's face. A little rock struck her cheek, and she jerked her head away as grit fell in her eyes. That flinch was all it took. With a disbelieving gasp, she lost her hold. She made a desperate grab for a rock, a ledge, anything, and missed.

Back at the gym when this happened, she would cry "falling" and the handsome instructor, Greg, would clamp down on the belay rope, and she'd swing free in her climbing harness, shake it off, and try again.

But here there was no harness, no rope, no Greg.

With a sickening feeling of weightlessness she half slid, half fell, rolling until she hit the ground.

The force of the impact knocked the wind out of her. She lay there looking at the black silhouette of the fortress wall against the starry sky directly above her. She was sure some of the dancing stars hadn't been there before. She gasped for breath and rolled into a fetal position, all too aware of the fiery pain in her hands, forearms, and knees where she had scraped them as she fell.

She looked up and stopped breathing again, this time by choice. The sentry had stooped and was looking down directly at her. He must have heard her fall.

For a long moment the man squinted into the shadows where she lay frozen. Would he sound the alarm or simply shoot her himself? She closed her eyes and shuddered. A shot rang out, and she braced herself for the impact before she realized the sound didn't come from above but from the front gate.

Liz glanced up again. The guard now stood, distracted from his search for noises in the night. He glanced quickly down once more, then hurried off to investigate the shot, the occasional red glow as he drew on his cigarette showing his location. Relief left her limp.

Very carefully she sat up. She ached all over, but nothing seemed broken, just badly jarred. Gratitude washed through her. She rolled to her knees and put her left foot forward, preparing to stand. A searing pain shot through her ankle.

Putting her weight on her right foot, she stood carefully, cautiously, her spine protesting vigorously as she straightened. She tried the left ankle again and sighed. Walking was going to be a challenge.

Lord, wasn't Julie's RA enough of a problem?

But she had done it. She was inside. Step one was accomplished with relatively little ado. Now all she had to do was find a hiding place before the guard on the wall returned. And find out where Julie was being held. And figure out how to get her safely out.

Piece of cake. Not.

From the bleating and shouting that filled the air, it was clear Anwar was having a very successful run as her diversion. Since there were no screams of pain, the shot that had captured the sentry's interest must have been fired into the air in the vain hope of moving the goats along. A raucous hee-haw sounded, and Liz smiled. Honey was doing her part, too.

But the goats would be effective only so long. A door in the side of one of the two sheds beckoned, and she limped to it. The shed had no windows and looked like a good place to hold someone captive. The padlock on the door drew her up short. She knocked softly. "Julie? Julie, are you in here?"

Nothing.

She hobbled to the second shed. Another padlock greeted her. Again she knocked and called out for her sister. Again nothing.

She stood in the shadows of the shed, trying to determine her next move. It came to her that she could barely hear the goats. At the same time she realized this, the men began filtering back into the courtyard, calling to each other, laughing over the fiasco with the shepherd boy and his animals.

Anwar seemed to have gotten away safely, and for that Liz was thankful. But how could she find Julie if she couldn't move freely? She sank to the ground, hugging the deepest shadows behind the shed.

Lord, You can't have brought me this far only to fail! Help me find Julie. Please!

She watched as the men finished loading the car. The leader in his white robes and his assistant with his haughty step emerged from the cellar. In surprise Liz noticed that a young woman trailed behind them, taking care to remain hidden in the shadows of the cellar doorway.

"Tonight with your trip to Beirut we take another step in our great plan," the assistant shouted. "For the glory of Allah, may his name be praised!"

The men cheered and shot their rifles into the air. The white-haired man held up his hands in what looked like a blessing. "Allah ak'bar!"

With more shouts and cheers, five of the men climbed into the dented old black Mercedes, four of them holding briefcases.

"Be careful with my car, Mamoud," the assistant called.

"I will be back by midmorning," Mamoud assured him as the vehicle began to move. He drove it across the courtyard and out through the main gate.

All those not in the car ran beside it, cheering their comrades on. Even the old man went toward the gate.

Once again the courtyard fell silent, and Liz knew she had another chance. The only other place to search was underground.

Her stomach pitched at the thought of going into the cellars and maybe being trapped down there, but she had no choice. Julie might be there. She looked once more around the empty courtyard, then at the cellar doorway. The young woman had disappeared. It was now or never.

Liz hobbled to the doorway and ducked inside. She found steep steps that led down into gloom, and with her back against the wall, she slowly descended. The stairwell was lit by a forty-watt bulb at the top and another at the bottom where a hallway disappeared into darkness.

When she reached the bottom, she slid along the corridor, peering cautiously into a pair of musty rooms whose doors had long since rotted away. The first was dark and empty, its earthen floor smelling of urine and blood. The next room was hazy with acrid smoke and held a table and two battered aluminum folding chairs. A kerosene lantern cast a dim light on the papers spread helter-skelter across the table. Obviously an office of some kind, but no Julie.

She continued down the corridor and came to a third darkened room where she could just make out several thin woven rugs spread on the floor. A prayer room in which the men of Ansar Inshallah could face Mecca for their five-times-a-day prayers?

Voices echoing in the stairwell froze Liz's blood. People were coming!

Terrified, she stepped into the prayer room and hugged the wall shared with the corridor so she couldn't be seen by whoever walked by. Straining to hear, she cocked her head toward the doorway. It seemed to her the conversation paused, and she got the impression that one or all had entered the messy office.

In less than a minute, the movement in the corridor resumed, coming closer to her hiding place with every step.

Oh, Lord, don't let it be prayer time!

It wasn't. The men walked briskly past, and Liz let out the breath she'd been holding. They didn't go far, however. She heard keys jangling and the click of a lock opening. A gruff voice yelled, "Now!" Then she heard the men coming back toward her.

Once again Liz pushed back against the wall, trying to become one with it as the men moved past the open door. Soon she heard them climb the steps, returning to the courtyard.

Now that she was safe, at least for the moment, Liz's knees gave out. She slid down the wall until she was sitting on a rug. She rested her elbows on her raised knees and dropped her head into her trembling hands. She was definitely not made for clandestine operations. Every instinct she had screamed for her to get out of this terrible place and hurry home where it was safe.

Oh, Lord, You've got to get us out of here because I sure can't.

38

The Fortress

JULIE FELT HER WHOLE BODY GO WEAK when three men in black masks stormed into her room. If she hadn't been lying on her cot, she would have fallen.

"Now!" The leader pointed to the door.

Somehow she had convinced herself that this moment would never come. In spite of her captivity, in spite of the video, in spite of the seventy-two-hour deadline they'd announced, the very idea of being killed by terrorists was so extraordinary, so action movie, so it-happens-to-people-you-don't-know, that she felt ambushed, taken by surprise as they grabbed her and pulled her off her bed.

Of course it could have been plain old denial.

Like last time, the men dragged her by the arms, putting terrible stress on her shoulders and neck. All she wanted to do was fight them, but her physical limitations overwhelmed her. The pain was so intense that her vision began to go black.

"Let me walk," she managed. "Please."

Try as she would, she couldn't stifle her groans, and in the circumstances, they embarrassed her. These men would misinterpret her involuntary response to her pain as fear. Not that she wasn't afraid. She was terrified. It was just that her spirit wanted to fight, to spit in their eyes, but her body couldn't cooperate.

For all the attention they paid to her request, she might have been a carpet they were carrying or a load of dirty clothes. They pulled her up the stairs and across the courtyard where she had a quick sense of fresh air and a brief view of the starry heavens before they dragged her down another set of stairs on the other side of the fortress.

Her last time to breathe clear air and be under God's majestic nighttime sky.

They didn't let go of Julie until they pulled her into a small, dark room much like her cell. Then they released her so suddenly that she fell. She landed on her knees, and once again her vision dimmed as shooting pain enveloped her.

After a moment to get her breath, she forced herself to rise, ignoring the urge to throw up, fighting it, refusing to yield to the nausea. She would not humiliate herself in front of these people.

She braced herself with a hand against the wall. One of the masked men stood beside her, watching her every move. Not that he needed to worry. There was no way she could try to escape.

When she felt in control, she lifted her head. Her eyes fixed on the video camera set on a tripod in the middle of the room. She couldn't pull her gaze from it, as mesmerized as a person hypnotized by a gently swinging object. The same crude handpainted sign hung on the wall in front of the camera. Slay the Infidel!

I don't want to die, Lord!

Hard on the heels of this prayer, she asked, *Does that make me a weak Christian? Should I be rejoicing that I'll see You soon?*

A verse came to her mind. "*Even though you walk through the valley of the shadow of death, you will fear no evil for I am with you.*"

She sighed and felt a bit braver.

"You!" One of the terrorists pointed at Julie. "Over there." He indicated the wall. "Now!" He gave her a push.

Julie stumbled and cried out. Making a disgusted growl, the terrorist dragged her to the wall, placing her in front of the sign.

This is what's meant by the shadow of death, isn't it, Lord? It's not the dying itself, but the darkness surrounding it. It's the process of dying, whether in a bed with some illness or in an unholy circumstance like mine.

"Face the camera!" He grabbed her arm and turned her.

The world was going to watch her die, and that fact filled her with a strange sense of sadness. She especially regretted that Charles, Annabelle, and Liz would see this terrible thing.

She saw her father, his face alight with the stimulation of a good debate, surrounded by his students during one of the open houses he and Annabelle frequently held.

She saw her mother standing in front of one of her canvases filled with wild swathes of color and joy.

And she saw her sister, dark eyes serious, as she said, "You can do it, Julie. I know you can do anything you set your mind to."

Lord, I love them all so much. Don't let me make it harder for them. Help me die with dignity.

She looked beyond the camera and into the eyes of the boy who had videotaped her before. He was the only one without a mask, which she assumed meant he wouldn't be in the video. As before she thought she saw a flash of sympathy, but he turned away so quickly that she wasn't sure.

"Why do you do this?" she asked him in Arabic.

He glanced at her quickly, then at the masked man who was obviously the leader. He said nothing but became engrossed in checking his equipment.

In that instant Julie realized that he had no choice, and her heart broke for him.

A generator roared to life, and the room flooded with bright light. Julie blinked and looked away, the intensity of the illumination stabbing at eyes used to a dark cell.

I am the light of the world, and in Me is no darkness at all.

"Kneel!" A hand pushed on her shoulder, and Julie folded. She couldn't help it. The masked leader came toward her with a knife in one hand and a blindfold in the other.

Lebanese Countryside

"Okay, Bobby. Heads up." Rip sat in the passenger seat of the pharmacist's delivery van, holding the map he illuminated with a tiny red LED flashlight. "The turnoff to the fortress should be about a half mile ahead on your right."

The men of Task Force Valor sped south on a winding mountain road toward the place where the UAV pilot had said they'd find the terrorists' compound and, *please, Lord,* Liz still in one piece.

The pharmacist's minivan was smaller than the van they'd used in their run from the refugee camp, but at least this one had seats in the back. John sat behind Sweeney, who was driving again. Frank and Doc were crammed in next to John, and Hogan was sitting on the floor in the back. With all of their gear, it was a little like trying to stuff a basketball team into a golf cart, but they didn't have far to go.

"How far is the fortress off the road?" Hogan called.

"About one klick," Rip shot back. "Sweeney, it looks here like the road leading to it is probably gravel or just…"

"Car!" Frank yelled.

Sweeney jerked the wheel hard to the right to avoid a black Mercedes that came careening around the bend in their lane.

John closed his eyes and braced for the impact. *I tried, Liz.*

Somehow Sweeney wrestled their minivan onto the sandy shoulder while keeping the vehicle from plunging off the ridge into the valley below. They shuddered to a halt.

For a moment everyone was too stunned to speak.

Doc spoke first. "For a minute there, I was looking about two hundred feet straight down the mountain. Don't these guys know about guardrails?"

"Well, one thing's for sure. They don't know about staying in their own lane." Sweeney sounded grumpy rather than scared.

"Good piece of driving, Bobby!" John slapped him on the shoulder. He just might make it to Liz after all.

"Valor One, this is Solo Four-Four, over." It was the radio in John's ear. "Was that you who almost went in the ditch?"

John keyed his mike. "Ditch, Four-Four? That was a canyon! Where are you?"

"Look out your rear window, over."

John turned to look. "Here comes the UAV, boys."

They all craned their necks to look up at the dark sky.

"I don't see nothin' but stars," Hogan said. Then a very large hornet buzzed right over their vehicle. "But I hear it!"

Sweeney pulled back onto the road. He pushed the pedal to the floor. "Do you think that car came from the compound?"

"Probably." John frowned. "I wonder where they're off to in such a hurry." *And does it have anything to do with Liz?*

John's radio beeped again. "Valor One, this is Phoenix. Be advised, we are working on getting you out of the country this morning, over."

"That would be great, Phoenix, but you'll have to let me know the details later. We're getting ready to go extravehicular, over."

"Our turn is coming up, gentlemen," Rip announced. "Prepare to bail!"

"Roger that, One. Contact me once you've secured the fortress," she said.

That's assuming we'll be able to take the fortress.

According to the information Liz had relayed to the UAV pilot, there were at least a dozen men in the compound, maybe

more. He thought of the car that had just flown past. Maybe
fewer. John patted his vest to check his ammo supply one last
time. Hopefully among the team, they had enough to do the
job.

When Sweeney cut the lights and coasted to a stop on the
sandy shoulder, Doc slid open the side door and jumped out.

"Rally up one hundred meters to the west of the road." John
said. "Go, go, go!"

Within seconds, the team was out of the vehicle. The men
followed John as he sprinted away from the van down the brush-
covered hill. About thirty seconds later, he took a knee behind a
large rock. One by one, the other men joined him, panting.

John counted noses, then said, "Sweeney, you, Frank, and
Hogan take the south side of this dirt road. The rest of us will stay
on this side. We'll coordinate by radio when we're ready to execute. You guys will be the support element, so on my signal, take
out anybody you can see outside who might be hostile. Then
cover us while we go in. Once we're inside, leave Frank as outside
security and come on in. We don't have time to rehearse, but the
plan is pretty straightforward. Any questions?"

"We're all going to have to be very careful where we shoot,"
Frank reminded them. "If they've got a stockpile of ITEB in there
someplace, one stray bullet could send all of us out in a blaze of
glory."

"Good point," John said. "So no flash-bangs, no demo. Hit
what you aim at."

"That's my motto in life, bro." Rip grinned. "Hit what I
aim at."

Six minutes later they had moved to within fifty yards of the
fortress. John saw that it really wasn't as medieval looking as he
had expected. The old outer wall was mostly intact, but some
money had obviously been invested in a more modern front gate,
which now sat partially open. Inside, a couple of low, contempo-

rary looking buildings had been built in what once must have
been the courtyard.

"Valor One, this is Valor Three, over."

Sweeney. John hit his push-to-talk button. "Go, Three."

"We've run into a large herd of goats. Gotta be a hundred of
them at least, all baaing like crazy."

Bleating, Bobby. Goats bleat. Sheep baa.

"Anyway, we're having a hard time getting up there to provide
support. Give us another five minutes, and we'll try to be in place,
over."

We don't have five minutes! John's internal alarm clock was
already ringing off the bedside table and doing a jitterbug across
the floor. He just hoped they weren't too late. He refused to think
about what might have happened to Liz and her sister by now.

And it would all be his fault.

Not now, man. You can do guilt after the party's over.

He left his night-vision goggles flipped up on his helmet
because the light above the front gate would make them all but
useless. Strangely, he could see no guards of any kind on the outside.

John turned to Rip, keeping his voice to the faintest whisper.
"Okay, we've got to do this, and do it now. You cover Doc and me
as we run up to the wall next to the gate. If it's clear, I'll wave you
on up. Take Doc's radio so we can communicate."

"You got it, bro." Rip reached up and flipped the bipod legs
out on his heavy-barreled rifle and then dropped to the prone
position. He crawled forward until he had a clear view of the gate
about thirty yards away.

When Rip gave the okay signal and waved them forward,
John tapped Doc. The two of them ran to the wall of the fortress
just outside the circle of light given off by the mercury vapor bulb
above the gate. Back to back, with John facing the gate and Doc
Kelly facing away, they moved down the wall into the light until

John could look around the corner into the compound.

He saw nothing. No movement whatsoever. *This can't be right. There has to be a...* Tiny bits of stone exploded as bullets smacked into the corner of the gatepost, sending a few stinging shards into his face as he heard the heavy stuttering sound of an AK-47. John jerked his head back just as another weapon boomed from outside the compound.

His radio crackled in his ear. "You okay, Coop?"

"Yeah, Rip."

"The shooter was up on the wall. He's not anymore, though."

"Good." John turned to Doc, knowing the shots would have alerted anyone else in the compound to their presence. "Let's move!"

The two of them charged up to the partially opened gate and slipped through. They scanned the courtyard with weapons poised and ready.

Nothing.

39

The Fortress

LIZ FORCED HERSELF to stay still for several minutes. She needed to be sure that no one was down here with her. As she waited and listened, her trembling slowly eased until it was gone.

She got to her feet, stifling a groan as her ankle and spine protested. She moved silently over the rugs to the doorway. She listened a bit longer until she was as sure as she could be that she was alone.

For a moment longer, she stood just inside the room, eyes squeezed shut, trying to get up the nerve to look out. Last time she'd looked to see what was happening, she fell off the fortress wall. What could happen this time that was any worse? She gave a mirthless laugh. How about a bullet? She glanced down at the beige handwoven rug with its brown, blue, and gold pattern and imagined her red blood marring its beauty.

Taking a deep breath, she stuck her head out, looking toward the steps. She pulled it back immediately as she registered that no one was there. Just as quickly she looked the other way. No one.

With a sigh of relief she entered the hall and crept toward the fourth room, the one with the door she'd heard the men open.

The door remained ajar, and a shiny new padlock hung from the hasp attached to it. The room was dark, but she thought she heard something. She stilled and strained to hear. With a sense of shock, she realized it was the sound of a woman weeping.

Her heartbeat quickened as she rushed toward the open door. "Julie?" she whispered even as she realized that the door wouldn't be hanging open if this was where her sister was being held prisoner.

A gasp sounded, and the young woman Liz had seen lurking in the doorway appeared out of the gloom. They stared at each other. Liz was uncertain who had scared who more.

"Julie?" Liz asked. "Where is she?"

The young woman's tears flowed, her cheeks like the face of an overflowing dam after a great storm. She stuffed a fist in her mouth in a futile attempt to contain the sobs.

"You are too late," she managed. "They have taken her already."

Liz stared at the young woman in horror. A roaring filled her ears, and she thought she would pass out.

God, how can this be? You brought me here against all odds, You got me inside this horrible place when I should have been discovered, and You kept me safe even here in the tunnel. And Julie's already dead?

I keep those in peace whose mind is stayed on Me.

Liz blinked. Where had those words come from? She looked at the young Muslim woman who gave no sign of hearing anyone but Liz herself. She glanced up and down the corridor and reconfirmed that no one was here except the two of them.

That left one possibility, didn't it? She had just heard God's voice. She shivered. She'd never in her whole life heard Him speak like that. And He hadn't said, *Precious in the sight of the Lord is the death of his saints.* Did that mean that Julie was still alive?

Okay, Lord. I'm trusting. It makes no sense, but that's what trust is, right?

"Where have they taken her?" Liz asked. "How long ago?"

The woman waved vaguely toward the stairs. "Only a few minutes."

Liz thought of the men who had just been down here, only to go back upstairs almost immediately. She had undoubtedly been within feet of her sister, separated only by the rough-hewn wall of the prayer room—well, that and several armed men.

"Show me," Liz ordered.

The woman merely cried harder.

Liz let out an exasperated sound and turned to leave. She would have to find Julie on her own.

"Wait." The woman, still crying, looked at her now, an almost angry expression on her face. "I will show you. They should not do this thing."

She brushed past Liz and headed for the stairs. Liz followed, anxiety and desperation eating at her. *Oh, Lord, help me know what to do when I find her—and don't let us be too late!*

As they approached the room with the table, an old cleric suddenly stepped into the corridor, blocking their way. Cold, black eyes swept over Liz and turned to the young woman. "Karima!"

With shaking hands, the woman stepped between Liz and the cleric. "Uncle," she managed in a strangled voice.

"Where are you going? Who is this woman?"

Karima opened her mouth, but nothing came out.

He took a menacing step toward them, his white robes billowing. "Who is this woman? How did she get in here?"

"Please, Uncle." Karima spread her hands in supplication. "Don't let them kill Julie. She has done nothing to you, to any of us."

Rage radiated from him like a fever. "That is none of your concern!"

"But you can—" Karima's protest was cut short by a vicious backhand from the old man.

"Hey!" Liz blurted in English, anger rising in her chest. "Leave her alone!"

The man whirled to look at her. "You...you are an American!" It was half question, half epithet.

The cleric lunged at her. Liz gave a shocked yelp and took an automatic step backward. In her hurry, she trod on the hem of her skirt, lost her balance, and fell. She tried to skitter away, but the old man caught her and dragged her to her feet.

He tore off her head scarf and grabbed her dark hair, looking more closely at her face in the dim light. A wicked smile spread across his face. "You resemble our captive. A sister perhaps?"

He wasn't much taller than she, and he was much older. He was fit for an old man, but she was fit, too, and much younger. Liz struggled, trying to twist away.

Lord, give me a chance and the courage to take it.

When he wrapped his hand more tightly in her hair and yanked, she couldn't stifle a cry. Fighting him was not working. She forced herself to go limp, and he smiled, thinking her defeated, just as she wanted. He turned to his niece. "Karima, go to your room. I will deal with you later."

Karima blanched and turned to go.

He released his grip on Liz's hair and shoved her toward the faintly-lit stairwell leading to the courtyard. "Allah, may his name be praised, has sent us another infidel woman. Today is indeed a great day."

Liz spun to face him, her anger overcoming her fear. "Would that be Allah the Merciful?"

She never saw his fist fly. Stars burst on her vision as the crushing blow connected with the left side of her face. She stumbled backward, hand to her jaw, and fell. Landing on her right side, she cried out as a fist-sized rock bruised her thigh.

"Stop it, Uncle!" Karima's hands shook almost as much as her voice as she darted forward, but her chin rose in spite of her obvious fright. "Rashid would not want you to do this thing!"

The cleric was panting and red-faced as he rushed at Karima and grabbed her about the neck. "Rashid was a fool who wasted his life!" He began to squeeze. "Imad is our future!"

"Uncle!" Karima clawed at his hands. "Stop! Stop!"

Liz reached for the rock that was still digging into her thigh and discovered it wasn't a rock at all but Rip's radio, still in her pocket.

As she clambered to her feet, she pulled at the radio, struggling to free it from the folds of material that insisted on wrapping around it. With a mighty yank and a tearing sound, she got the radio free.

She launched herself at the cleric's back, swinging the heavy plastic radio like a club. With all her strength she brought the radio down on his head. He cried out and turned to defend himself. As he did so, Liz brought the radio down on his temple. She flinched at the sickening hollow sound.

For a second she thought nothing had changed. All she'd done was break Rip's radio. She lifted her arm for a third swing with the shattered plastic when the man toppled like a falling tree. He hit the floor with a thud and didn't move.

Liz stared down at him. Had she killed him? Though the thought made her nauseous, she knew she'd had no choice. He was going to kill Karima and Julie and wanted to kill her, too.

As Karima's rasping breaths filled the corridor, Liz turned her back on the old man. "Let's go." She reached a hand to help Karima who had fallen when the old man fell.

Karima seemed not to hear. She stared at the crumpled figure of her uncle.

"Karima!"

The girl blinked, then took Liz's hand. Liz saw the fear in her eyes and knew she had to be the strong one.

"Show me where they took her, please. Help me. Help Julie!"

Karima looked again at her fallen uncle, then at Liz. "There are many of them."

Exactly what I'm afraid of. She pulled Karima toward the stairs. "We've got to try!"

Shots sounded in the courtyard outside, and Liz's heart turned over.

The Fortress

Seeing no movement in the courtyard, John raced to the corner of a shed about four feet away from the stone fortress wall, Doc on his heels.

Then came the sound of running footsteps. A shout. John peeked around the corner of the building and saw two armed men emerge from a stairway that looked like it led underground. He snapped his weapon up and fired a long burst, sweeping both terrorists off their feet.

His headset beeped. "One, this is Five, I'm coming in."

"Make it snappy, Rip. Sweeney, you copy?"

"Stand by, One." He could hear Sweeney breathing like he was running a footrace. "Be advised, we are being chased by a really mean donkey, over."

John blinked. "Whatever. Just get in here!"

"Roger, be right there."

John heard Rip approaching the gate. Then a bullet snapped by John's head. He flinched and dropped to the prone. He knew the sound of a near miss.

"Did you see where that came from?" Doc scanned the area.

"Nope." John keyed his mike. "Hold up, Rip! I think we've got a sniper."

Too late. Rip was already rounding the corner, coming through the gate. A volley greeted him, some rounds sparking against the ages-old rock. Rip hit the brakes and tried to retrace his steps, but a round found him, knocking him off his feet. He went down hard on his back and lay still.

"No!" Rage roared through John. *Lord, not again!* He jumped to his feet, ready to charge around the corner and annihilate the enemy.

"No, John!" Doc grabbed his vest and pulled him back down. "Don't!"

He struggled to pull from Doc's grasp. The need for revenge burned white hot.

Doc stuck his face in John's. "Cooper! Remember the ITEB. We can't fire back unless we know what we're shooting at!"

Anger threatened to consume John from the inside out. Doc was right, of course, but that did nothing to quell the shock of seeing his friend gunned down. He looked again at Rip's motionless body, then back at Doc. Slowly training kicked in, and the red haze cleared, at least for the moment.

He nodded and said through clenched teeth. "Okay. Let's find our target."

His radio crackled. "Valor One, Valor Three. Is it safe to come on in?"

He hit the transmit button. "Negative, Three. Rip is down. We have a sniper. Stand fast while we deal with it."

John slapped a fresh magazine into his carbine, then turned to Doc. "You stay here. I'm going to see if I can flank the sniper from the far corner of this building. When I engage him, you go get Rip."

"Hooah." Doc gave him a sweaty thumbs-up.

John moved quietly to the far corner of the long wooden shed where they had taken cover. Doc again followed close behind. A ten-foot gap stood between the building and an identical one right next to it.

Before charging around the corner, John stuck his head out to find his next cover and concealment. When he did, the machine gun opened up again. He jerked his head back to keep from losing it to a hail of bullets.

He dropped to the ground and returned fire around the corner on full automatic, hoping to keep the gunner's head down long enough for Doc to get to Rip. Seconds later, his magazine was empty, and John rolled back behind cover just as the machine gunner opened up again, punching holes in the shed above John's prostrate form. Then another weapon joined the fight from John's right. The enemy fire stopped abruptly.

"That was one of ours!" John turned and sprinted back toward their original position. As he ran, he heard shouting, but it wasn't in English.

It was in Spanish.

Rip?

John rounded the corner just in time to see the skinny Latino limping toward him with one arm around Doc Kelly. He was muttering in Spanish all the way. John didn't understand what he was saying, but he got the drift. Rip was mad.

John was so relieved he wanted to hug Rubio. "Are you okay?"

"No! I'm not! That *chango* shot me, man!" He dropped to one knee.

"So you took him out?" John asked.

"Doc did."

The medic looked smugly satisfied.

John shook his head. "I thought you were done, Rubio."

"Good. Because so did he." Rip jerked his head in the direction the sniper had been. "Why do you think I wasn't moving? I wasn't going to advertise that I was okay, or he'd have finished the job. But *hijo de la mañana* that hurt!" He rotated his arm and pulled his vest out to look under it. "Man, that's gonna leave a mark!"

John's radio squawked. "Valor One, this is Three. Everything's clear out here. Need some help in there?"

"Roger that, Three. Bring it on in."

"Be right there."

A moment later, Sweeney, Frank, and Hogan swept into the compound. John nodded to them as they hunkered with him, Doc, and Rip behind the storage shed. The six gathered in a tight half-circle, facing toward the courtyard with the wall at their backs.

John scanned the courtyard, then spoke quietly. "We need to clear the two arched tunnels at the far end. We can't see the one on the left from here, but I think I saw a truck parked in it. The other is where the resistance has come from. Sweeney, cover the right side tunnel with your element while Rip, Doc, and I clear the left one."

Faint voices sounded in the courtyard. Six weapons snapped up and prepared to fire. Rip put a finger to his lips and stepped to the corner of the shed that shielded them. Keeping low, he looked around the corner, then frowned and made a low growl of disbelief. "Coop, you've got to see this."

John stepped forward and looked around the corner with his weapon at the ready.

Two figures were hurrying from one tunnel stairwell to another, trying to keep to the shadows, which were receding as the eastern sky began to lighten.

Two *women!*

"Liz," John muttered, relief surging over him like high tide over a jetty. *She's alive!*

John let out a whistle. The two women froze and looked toward the sound. John stepped out from behind the shed and waved.

Liz beckoned frantically.

He waved back, then turned to the others. "Bobby, you guys cover us. Rip, Doc, let's go!" Before Sweeney could protest, and John was sure he wanted to protest, he took off at a run across the courtyard, Rip and Doc close on his heels. He kept his weapon trained on the stairwell to the right. Six seconds later they reached Liz, who was accompanied by a younger Palestinian woman.

"We've got to quit meeting like this." John couldn't quite swallow his smile.

Her quick smile disappeared into a look of desperation. "Karima says Julie is in one of the three rooms down that staircase." She pointed to the opening on the right. "John, they took her there to kill her." She grabbed his arm, as if to pull him toward it. "We have to hurry!"

"Not *we* as in you and me, Liz. Rip, Doc, and I will take care of it. You stay here, with Sweeney and the others, both of you."

"But, John, I want—"

John held up a hand. "No."

Liz swallowed, and John saw tears in her eyes. She nodded and let go of his sleeve. She might be proud and desperate, but she wasn't stupid.

"Go!" John moved quickly toward the stairwell, followed by Rip and the medic. *God, please don't let us be too late.*

Above Lebanon

VALOR HAD BEEN QUIET for too long.

Mary stood behind the UAV pilot and stared at the grainy black and white video feed being sent by the tiny remote-controlled aircraft. It was doing a slow circular pattern above the fort. Much to Mary's frustration, the high walls only allowed a momentary glimpse inside the compound on each pass.

"If I take it up to about six hundred feet AGL, ma'am, we might get a better view," said the flight-suited captain.

"Do it."

They had followed the radio traffic during the assault on the compound, and Mary had breathed a sigh of relief when she heard the report that though Rip Rubio had been hit, he was uninjured. The last thing she'd heard was John Cooper's voice saying, "We're going in."

She turned to the radio operator. "Call for a situation report, Sergeant."

"Yes, ma'am." He flipped a switch. "Valor One, this is Solo Four-Four, over."

Static.

"Valor One, we need a sitrep, over."

Mercifully, the radio beeped a reply, and Mary's shoulders relaxed a bit.

"Solo Four-Four, this is Valor Three, over."

Mary looked at the notebook in her hand. "Sweeney. Good." The sergeant just shrugged. "Go ahead, Valor Three."

"Buzz, Frank, and I are out in the courtyard pulling security. Be advised, we have secured Miss Fairchild and a Palestinian woman. Valor One went inside with Doc and Rip to attempt to secure the American hostage. I'm going to give them another minute and then go in after them."

"Keep us posted, Valor Three."

"Roger, Four-Four. But we have another problem. Miss Fairchild reports seeing men loading the ITEB into the back of a black Mercedes. It must be the same vehicle that almost ran us off the road on the way in here, over."

Mary flipped the switch so she could speak directly to Sweeney. "Valor Three, this is Phoenix. Does Miss Fairchild have any idea where they might be headed? Over."

"Roger, Phoenix. She believes they are headed to Beirut International. Please advise, over."

"Stand by." Mary's mind raced. It didn't take much imagination to see what the terrorists had in mind. In fact, it was the very scenario they feared.

The UAV pilot turned to her. "Valor has a vehicle, don't they? Can't they go after the car?"

Mary checked her watch. "It has at least a five-minute head start. Valor would never catch them." She held up a finger for silence and narrowed her eyes as an idea slowly took root. Excitement made her heart beat a breakneck tattoo. *This is going to get me in trouble.* But the alternative, doing nothing, had terrifying consequences.

She looked at the pilot. "How fast will this thing go?"

The man's eyes went wide. "Wait a minute. What are you thinking?"

A smile spread across her face. "I'm thinking that ITEB explodes on contact with air."

The Fortress

Julie held her head up proudly as she watched the leader approach with a very large and very sharp knife. She would not whimper even though her heart was racing so hard she felt lightheaded.

Give me strength, Father. Let my death somehow bring You the glory that my life did not.

"A minute, Imad." The young cameraman stood frowning at his equipment. "Let me put in another battery. I am afraid this one hasn't much time left on it."

Julie could feel the intense disapproval of the leader, and so did the boy though he didn't back down.

"Be quick!" the leader snapped, leaving Julie kneeling before the Slay the Infidel! sign.

The boy nodded and began fiddling with the camera. He shot a quick look at Julie, and when their eyes met, she realized with a start that nothing was wrong with his camera. He was stalling, purposely holding up her execution. Because he didn't want her to die? Because he didn't want to be part of the murder?

Who cared why? She had been given several more minutes to live. She gave him a little nod of acknowledgment. He turned away quickly and concentrated on pretending to fix his camera.

What would his life have been if he'd been born into a family of wealth and privilege like Khalil's? It was obvious the boy was intelligent. Might he have become an economist too, a man who could make a difference in the mixed culture of Lebanon?

The loss of her marriage and her husband pressed on Julie. What a sad, sad thing it was when two people as educated as she and Khalil hadn't cared enough to make the necessary compromises that would have saved their marriage. Somehow they had allowed themselves to get to the point where there were only greater demands, greater damage, and greater pain.

She watched the terrorists conversing in the corner, probably rehearsing what they were about to do. The tall black-haired man produced a Palestinian kaffiyeh and, with his back to Julie, began slowly winding the scarf around his head and face while giving orders to the other two, whose faces were hidden by ski masks.

"What about the commandos?" one of the masked men asked Imad. "They're still at large."

"I have ordered one hundred men of Ansar Inshallah to search for them and not stop until they are captured." He raised a fist. "They will not live!"

Shouts of "Allah ak'bar" filled the room, terrifying in their intensity. Julie squeezed her eyes shut.

I will never leave you or forsake you.

The door to the room burst open. A wild-eyed terrorist who looked to be no more than fifteen entered. "Imad! We are under attack!"

"What? Where?"

"Fighters are attacking the front gate! I think it is the Americans!"

Imad swore, then turned to the two masked men. "Go find Abu Shaaban! Take him to the cellar where *naru Allah* is stored. It must be safeguarded at all costs!"

The masked terrorists sprinted from the room.

"You!" Imad pointed at a young man wearing a gaudy red and yellow shirt. "Go into the corridor and guard the door. If the Americans come, defend it with your life." He looked at Julie. "If they are here to rescue the girl, they will find that they are too late."

The leader stalked toward the camera. "Roll tape! Now!"

The boy slid the original, perfectly fine battery into place. "All ready." Imad strode toward Julie, and their eyes met. She willed herself not to look away.

He pulled a plastic restraint from his pocket and tied her hands behind her back. Then when he dropped the blindfold over her eyes, she knew time had run out.

In a cocoon of shock, she heard Imad read a statement that ranted about imperialistic Westerners, evil infidels, and extremist Palestinian xenophobia.

Julie's tears saturated the blindfold. They weren't tears of fear as much as tears of regret. There was so much that she wanted to do, so many dreams that would now go unfulfilled! She wanted to float around Venice in a gondola, see the Taj Majal, buy a house in the mountains. She wanted to have babies and learn how to knit tiny sweaters. She wanted to take art lessons from Annabelle. She wanted to finish her degree and—

Shots echoed in the hallway outside. Imad hesitated for a moment. When he began speaking again, his voice betrayed a renewed sense of urgency. "You have ignored our demands long enough!" He spat at the camera. "Now you will see what happens when you do not take us seriously!"

With that pronouncement, he grabbed Julie by the hair and jerked her head backward, exposing her throat.

John sprinted down the dark passageway with Rip and Doc close on his heels. He vaulted over the body of a young man in an ugly red and yellow shirt who seconds before had been shooting at him and, without breaking stride, dropped his shoulder and hit the door at a dead run.

His momentum splintered the aging wooden door frame so easily that it threw him off balance, and he stumbled into the room, pulling his weapon up to bear with his right hand and throwing out his left to break his fall.

A man with his face obscured by a black-and-white kaffiyeh stood in the middle of the room. At the sight of the knife in the man's upraised hand, John jerked the trigger instinctively. With a scream of pain the man fell.

Rip raced into the room behind John and held his fire as another terrorist, more boy than man, raised his arms in surrender from his position behind a video camera.

John executed a quick combat roll and was immediately back on his feet. Only then did he notice the third person, kneeling in the center of the room blindfolded with arms bound.

Julie! She must be terrified, not knowing what was happening around her.

"It's okay, Julie. We're Americans, and we're going to get you out of here."

Julie sobbed all the harder.

"Doc! Take care of her, would you?"

The medic knelt next to Julie and removed her blindfold. "It's okay, Julie. The good guys have arrived." He produced a pair of medic's scissors and began cutting the plastic zip-ties that held her wrists.

"Clear," Rip called, rifle still trained on the cameraman.

"Clear," John echoed, speaking into his radio as he approached the man who had been about to execute Julie. He was facedown on the floor behind her, moaning.

John held the man in his gunsight and nudged him with a boot, rolling him onto his back away from Julie. The terrorist's eyes flashed not with hatred as John expected but fear. He began to babble in Arabic, whimpering like a six-year-old with a bee sting. John was filled with revulsion. This was no soldier. He was little more than a street punk who thrived on hurting innocent people. People like Julie.

People like Vernon James.

John looked down his gunsight at the whiny coward before him, and it was all he could do not to pull the trigger. Men like this were responsible for most of the chaos and hurt he had seen and endured around the world. Such men appeared tough on camera when they had some hapless victim cowering at their feet, but stick a gun in their faces, and they turned into sniveling little girls.

Some called them religious zealots or nationalistic patriots, but John had always felt that if they really believed in the legitimacy of their cause, they wouldn't feel the need to force it on others. No, men like these were the lowest form of cowards, little power-hungry barbarians bent on ruling the world.

And it was because of them that truly good men like Doc James died early. John turned away in disgust.

"Look out, Coop!" shouted Rip.

John swung back just in time to see the terrorist roll, scoop up his knife, and with a desperate scream, lunge for Julie.

John stepped between her and the terrorist as Doc pulled her from the danger. John aimed a swift kick at the man's wrist, his leg arcing high. A searing pain in his shin told him that while the knife missed its intended target, it found flesh nonetheless—his.

Using the downward arc and his forward momentum, John stepped onto the terrorist's arm, pinning the man's hand to the stone floor with his full weight.

The Palestinian screamed and dropped the knife once again. John bent and tossed the knife away, and it clattered against the wall out of the terrorist's reach.

"Nice try, skippy." John aimed his carbine at the terrorist's head. "Let's hope that Allah shows you the same compassion you showed to this defenseless woman."

The man's eyes flicked to Julie, who was being helped to her feet by Doc. He tried to sneer through his tears.

John's finger tightened on the trigger. He had every reason to give this coward a terminal case of lead poisoning, and nobody would question it if he did.

For some reason, though, he couldn't pull the trigger.

The Palestinian began screaming in Arabic, whether at Julie or at him, John didn't know. A dark pool was forming near the man's right leg, which he clutched with both hands.

"You okay, Coop?" Doc had his arm around Julie's waist, supporting her.

"Yeah." John ignored the warm sticky feeling on his left trouser leg. He looked at Rip who was covering the cameraman and at the camera, which was still rolling.

"Turn that thing off," John ordered brusquely.

Rip stopped speaking into his radio and motioned with his rifle at the young Arab. "You heard him, *ese.*"

The young man looked confused. Julie said something in Arabic, and understanding dawned on the boy's face. He slowly reached to turn off the camera.

"How did you find me?" Julie asked. Her eyes were still red from her tears, but though she was pale, she was composed. John couldn't help thinking that the Fairchild women were quite something.

"Liz found you," Doc said.

"Liz?" Julie's head jerked up.

Doc nodded. "We followed her here."

"She's here?"

"Right outside with the rest of our team."

Tears once again spilled from Julie's eyes as she took an unsteady step toward the door.

"Hold up a minute, Julie." John gestured to the man on the floor. "Do you know who he is?"

"They call him Imad," she said. "He's one of the leaders here, and one of the men responsible for bombing the Hotel Rowena."

For killing her husband. One more reason to cap him. So why was he hesitating?

Rip secured the videographer's hands behind his back with a pair of flex cuffs. "What are we going to do with these two, bro?"

John took his finger off the trigger and shook his head. "We don't know how we're getting out of here yet, but if we're walking, we sure can't bring them with us."

"Well, if we leave them alive, you and I both know they'll be blowing stuff up again before long."

John nodded. "Want to bet that if the tables were reversed, we'd have been strung up and set on fire already? And in my opinion, that would be too good a fate for this loser." He looked at the writhing man on the floor. "But the truth is, he may be worth more to us alive than dead. He may be able to help us track down who's making the ITEB."

"I agree," Doc said. "Cover me while I get some flex cuffs on him, and then I'll see to his wounds."

Rip shook his head. "You're a bigger man than I am, bato. Where I come from, this homie would have already been roasting in hell."

John didn't mention Vernon James's words echoing in his head while Doc Kelly bound Imad's hands and feet. "*We can't complain about what the evil men do if we act just like the bad guys.*"

Footfalls sounded in the hall, and John brought his rifle up. Liz raced into the room, her heart in her eyes as she scanned the room. Lowering his gun, John watched with a smile as she located her sister. "Julie!" With a joyful sob, she raced to embrace her.

"Liz!"

To his surprise John had to clear the lump in his throat as the sisters clung to each other. He saw Rip and Doc exchange satisfied glances as well.

Liz stepped back and studied her sister. "I was so afraid we'd be too late! Are you all right? Really all right?"

Sweeney burst through the door. "We got ourselves a problem, Coop."

41

On the Road to Beirut

IT WON'T BE LONG NOW.

Mamoud prayed for the aging Mercedes as it labored up a steep hill leading northwest toward Beirut. The other four men in the car were quiet, immersed in their own thoughts, much as he imagined he would be if it were his turn to be martyred. But today the glory went to others. Still, he was fulfilling a noble purpose, taking them to their targets.

When Allah's Fire ripped four fully-loaded passenger planes from the sky over Europe and the United States, he would be so proud of his part in the operation. Because of him, air traffic would effectively shut down for weeks, maybe even months, while the authorities scrambled to update their security mechanisms.

He downshifted, and the car jerked as the tortured engine groaned toward the top of the incline. His gut tightened as he hit a pothole. *Be careful!* He must not let anything happen to cause Allah's Fire to detonate prematurely.

The men in the car with him each carried two bottles of the explosive, one in his suitcase and another in his carryon. More was stored in the trunk. That made for enough of the volatile substance to ensure that the Mercedes would virtually evaporate. Mamoud shook himself. That would not happen. Allah was watching over him in approval.

The air inside the car grew stale. He rolled down his window and breathed deeply of the crisp Lebanese morning. Its invigorating coolness filled him with a powerful sense of purpose. He was risking his life to take these men to their assignments. Imad had not even done that.

The sun was just rising over the Anti-Lebanon Mountains behind him, and even with his dark sunglasses, its rays reflected painfully off the rearview mirror. As he reached to adjust it, he heard a faint buzzing sound. At the same time, a silhouette of something passed between him and the red orb of the sun, breaking the sun's intense beam. At first he thought it was a bird, but it seemed too rigid, and it was moving far too fast. The strange object grew larger and larger as it flew straight toward the Mercedes.

He turned in his seat to glance out the rear window, involuntarily easing off the accelerator. His eyes went wide at what appeared to be a very small aircraft.

The plane rammed his rear window, and the resulting impact tore the wheel from Mamoud Shaka's hand. As he screamed, the car veered off the road and tumbled into a valley. Allah's Fire blazed brighter than the sun.

Inside the Fortress

"What's wrong now, Sweeney?" John asked.

"Vehicles coming this way—lots of 'em."

John grimaced. "Any idea who?"

"Nope. But they don't look friendly. Hogan saw a coupla

armored personnel carriers. They're already near the road to the
fortress, so we've probably got less than three minutes. Oh, and
there was a large explosion on the side of a hilltop a few miles
from here just a minute ago."

"Wonderful." John reached down and grabbed the still-
whimpering Imad under one arm. "Doc, help Liz with Julie. Rip,
take charge of camera-boy, and Sweeney, help me with snapper-
head here."

"No problem." Sweeney quickly slung his carbine behind
him and grabbed Imad's other arm. Doc picked Julie up in his
arms and carried her out of the room, Liz tailing them. Rip and
the camera boy followed with John and Sweeney bringing up the
rear, half dragging, half carrying the blubbering terrorist leader
between them.

"You think we can hold 'em off from inside the fortress?"
John asked as they emerged into the courtyard.

Sweeney gave him a grave look. "Not for long. Buzz says
there's at least a hundred men."

In the light of the rising sun John saw Hogan lying on top of
the wall, looking through his scope toward the road. "Buzz! How
long?"

Without taking his eye off the scope, Hogan held up two
fingers.

John and Sweeney dropped Imad in a heap in the center of the
courtyard. The young cameraman sat to the side, his back against
one of the sheds. Doc set Julie on her feet near the second shed, and
Liz moved to her side. She slid an arm about her sister's waist.

"I've got her. Go help John."

"Karima." Julie held out a hand. "Come stand with us. We'll
be out of the way here."

John pointed to Imad and the cameraman. "Doc, keep an eye
on them." He turned to Frank. "Do we still have communication
with the UAV?"

Frank shook his head. "I haven't been able to raise them for a couple of minutes. I'll keep trying."

"Don't bother. They won't be able to help us in two minutes. What other assets do we have?"

"We found some RPGs in that shed over there." Sweeney pointed to the far end of the courtyard. "And there's a truck parked—"

"John, behind you!"

He whirled as the terror in Liz's voice shot adrenaline through him. Emerging from one of the tunnel stairwells was a grizzled old man with a long beard that had once been white but was now matted with blood. His robed arm was already in midswing, and John recognized the water bottle in his hand just as he let it fly.

"Incoming!" Sweeney yelled.

The men dropped and rolled out of the way. Liz grabbed Julie and pulled her down even as Julie pulled Karima to the ground. The women huddled like three teaspoons curled on one another, Liz's back exposed.

John dove at them, wrapping his arms around them and covering Liz with his body just as the bottle hit the ground and shattered, instantaneously transforming into a ball of flame. He pressed his face into Liz's neck as the concussion and the flames washed over him, then slowly subsided.

He lifted his head and looked at Liz, her eyes squeezed shut. "You okay?"

She turned her head and smiled at him. "I'm fine."

The other two women seemed fine, too.

His ears ringing with screams and the percussion of weapons' fire, he scrambled to his feet. Multiple 5.56 millimeter rifle rounds had knocked the cleric off his feet. He landed on his back and lay still.

The terrible screaming continued. Imad.

The man writhed and rolled, but there was no escaping the fire. Then a weapon fired once more, and the screaming stopped.

John turned right to see Doc holstering his nine-millimeter pistol. He looked at John and shook his head. "No one should suffer like that."

John was about to mention that Imad most likely would know an eternity of that sort of death when Hogan whistled from the top of the wall. "We're out of time, boss!"

Just then the front gate was flattened by an olive-drab tracked vehicle. Its fifty-caliber machine gun swiveled toward John as the vehicle ground to a halt in the center of the court-yard. Immediately behind it, two jeeps full of soldiers entered and took up positions on either side of the armored personnel carrier. Green-uniformed soldiers jumped out, bristling with American-made M-16 assault rifles—all pointing at Task Force Valor.

Disgusted with himself and the outcome of his mission, John dropped his weapon and slowly raised his hands in surrender. The other men followed his lead. So did Liz and Julie. For a full sixty seconds, nobody said anything as more vehicles pulled into the courtyard until it was nearly full. John counted at least fifty guns pointed at him.

The hatch opened on the top of the APC, and a sunburned older man emerged, smoking a cigarette. Today he wore a military uniform instead of an ill-fitting suit.

Zothgar?

"Gentlemen," the Lebanese operative said. "By order of the government of Lebanon, you are under arrest."

What? "You can't—"

The man held up a hand to silence John. "You will leave your weapons here, please. We will escort you back to Beirut for ques-tioning. Then you will be turned over to your embassy and asked to leave Lebanon immediately."

John was speechless. Rip, his arms raised, said, "You're kidding, man, right?"

Zothgar ignored him. "We have reason to believe that the American hostage, Julie Assan, is being held somewhere near here. Our men will—"

Julie stepped forward, assisted by Liz. "I'm Julie Assan. These men just freed me. They are to be honored, not arrested."

Now it was Zothgar's turn to be speechless.

John, who now realized what was happening, had to smile at Julie's unsubtle reprimand. Without lowering his arms, he nodded toward the tunnel entrance behind the body of the old cleric. "I believe you will find the explosives you're looking for inside that tunnel. But I must warn you, some of the men left to carry out another attack before we arrived."

"Were they driving a black Mercedes?" Zothgar asked.

John looked at Liz, who nodded. He winked at her, and he saw her relax a fraction.

"Not to worry then." Zothgar flicked his cigarette butt away. "The threat has been neutralized."

"That explosion we saw?" Sweeney asked.

Zothgar gave an abrupt nod as he shook another cigarette from a crushed package he'd pulled from his shirt pocket. The rear hatch on the APC whined open. "We do not have much time. Please get in. We must leave for Beirut immediately."

"What about the women?" John cast a glance toward Liz, feeling something stab at his gut. She stood beside Julie, her hands at her shoulders. All she had known from him was trouble, and that ate at him.

Julie suddenly staggered, and both Liz and Karima reached for her. Rifles swiveled, and the women froze.

John took a step forward to draw attention, and the rifles swiveled back. "Mrs. Assan has had a terrible few weeks. She needs medical care immediately."

Zothgar signaled, and several soldiers stepped toward Julie. "She will be taken to the hospital in Beirut, and then returned to her family. Have no fear for her."

"The other two will be returned safely home also?"

"Of course."

Liz looked at John. "You have the addresses. Please use them."

He smiled. "You have my word of honor."

Zothgar issued some curt orders in Arabic. Then he turned back to John. "We will secure the explosives now. We will shortly issue a press release detailing the demise of those who were responsible for the Hotel Rowena bombing—and the rescue of the American hostage—all at the hands of our highly trained Lebanese commandos."

John's mouth curved sardonically. "Fine. Just tell your highly-trained commandos not to drink the water."

To: reprtrgrl
From: jcman
I saw you on TV yesterday. You and Julie did a great job.
It couldn't have been easy to play dumb before the
massed newsmen of the world. I was proud of you.
John
P.S. You clean up very nicely.

To: jcman
From: reprtrgrl
You're right about how hard it was. I'm not good at
playing dumb. Acting like Julie's release was the work of
the Lebanese army was galling, even though I'm sure
you had no problem letting them take the credit. You
don't seem like the kind of guy who would get along
with the international press. I'm sure Julie and I sounded
like idiots, but the ambassador helped, and having
Charles and Annabelle there to hug us and cry helped,
too.
Are you guys back at Bragg?

To: reprtrgrl
From: jcman
We got back to Bragg just before your press conference
yesterday. Zothgar was glad to see our backs. I don't
know all the details, but I have a sneaking suspicion that
my godfather had a role in getting us out of the country.
I'll tell you more about it when I see you. Sweeney and I
went to McDonald's last night and got two orders
super-sized. Each.

To: jcman
From: reprtrgrl
I never thought I'd say I was jealous of Sweeney, but his
getting dinner at McD's with you turns me green. I
won't be back in the States for a couple of more weeks.

To: reprtrgrl
From: jcman
Are you jealous of Sweeney over dinner at McD's or
dinner with me? I'm sure I saw some golden arches
when we were in Beirut…

Liz laughed as she read John's e-mail and knew there was no
way she would answer that last question.

"Let me tell you about last night's dinner," she wrote instead.
"Julie told our parents that she had survived her imprisonment so
well because she knew the Lord was there with her."

Liz had rarely been prouder of Julie. Her sister was feeling
better physically now that she was home and on her infusion
treatments for her RA once again. She was slowly regaining the
weight she'd lost. Liz could only imagine her emotional chaos, on
one hand being glad to be free and in possession of her head and
on the other mourning Khalil and her marriage.

"You have done so well, Julie." Charles, pompous and clueless as ever but kind in heart, reached over from his place at the head of the table and patted her hand. "Such courage. You have made your mother and me very proud."

Julie turned her hand over and held her father's. "God gave me strength, Charles. I never would have made it without Him. *He* enabled me to survive."

Charles blinked, straightened, then pulled his hand back. "Yes, yes, of course."

Julie persisted. "I was afraid to tell you that I had become a Christian. I know how you feel about religion and people of faith, but I have learned that it's total commitment to Christ that makes life worth living."

Charles was clearly torn. He had just praised Julie for her courage. He couldn't turn around and criticize the very thing she said gave her that courage.

Annabelle surprised all of them by saying, "I must admit, it was prayer that carried me through these past weeks. I'm not even certain who I was praying to, but if it was God, He was gracious enough to help me."

"Annabelle!" Charles stared at his wife with more horror than if she'd confessed to bombing the Rowena.

"Oh, hush, Charles." Annabelle waved her hand at her husband. "It's not the end of the world to think about God, even talk about Him. Many intelligent people do."

"None that I know."

She shook her head in loving frustration. "What a terrible thing to say about your wife and daughters."

Charles was shocked to speechlessness.

Liz thought of the day she had heard her mother pray outside the Assans' home and her skeptical reaction to Annabelle's words of despair. *Shows how much I know.* "Oh, Annabelle, the same God who helped Julie is the One who helped you. The Bible says that God is gracious and blesses both the just and the unjust."

Her father was so insulted he all but sputtered. "Are you saying your mother is unjust?"

"No, no," Liz said hastily, relieved to see that Annabelle nodded as if she understood what she'd meant. "I'm saying that God listens to all of us, and out of His mercy and goodness answers even those who don't yet know Him well or even who He is."

"Humph." Charles clearly wasn't satisfied, but he was momentarily placated.

"It's going to be very interesting to see how things develop over the next few months," Liz wrote John. "Very interesting."

From: jcman
To: reprtrgrl
Julie's story is wonderful, and it's just one more thing that's soothing my doubts about God's goodness. You can't push Him away, can you? No matter how hard I tried in my anger at Him over Doc James's death, He always kept showing Himself in some way.
Your faith.
Julie's faith.
Vernon's faith—showing compassion, even in the act that took his life.
Even the glory of a night sky over the desert. Somehow it just speaks to me of order, of God's plan.
I don't know if I'll ever understand why God allows evil and suffering in this world, and maybe that's not even the right question to ask. Perhaps I should be focused instead on how I can be a part of the solution—showing God's compassion and grace through my own life, in my chosen profession. If I can focus on that, then maybe I won't have to be in control of everything

myself. I get too task-saturated that way anyhow. Even in
the evil of the Rowena bombing I can see His hand in
so many ways. I don't think I can fight it—or Him—
anymore.
Even writing that loosens the knot that's been tied in my
gut for the past weeks.

From: reprtrgrl
To: jcman
Welcome home, soldier.

From: jcman
To: reprtrgrl
It's good to be home. Speaking of which, when will you
get back on U.S. soil? I'd like to invite you to stop here
for a few days on your way to Philly. (Do you have any
idea how many times I typed and deleted that last line?)

From: reprtrgrl
To: jcman
Another week, John. There are two more things to do
before I can leave. Today Julie and I are going to visit Dr.
and Mrs. Assan. The day after tomorrow I'm going to
try and get back into Sainiq to talk with some more
friends of Hanan, Nabila's cousin, for my articles.

From: jcman
To: reprtrgrl
You be careful in that camp, Liz! I don't like you going
there at all. Last time was a bit of a disaster, wouldn't
you say?
I don't envy you the visit with the Assans. Can you say
emotional overload?

And what about an answer to the question I sweated over in the last message?

From: reprtrgrl
To: jcman
The visit with Dr. and Mrs. Assan wasn't as bad as I expected. They were genuinely glad to see Julie, but it hurt them too. She's alive and Khalil isn't. I'm glad I don't have to go again.
And I'd love to visit you and the guys. (Do you have any idea how many times I wrote and deleted this answer?)

From: jcman
To: reprtrgrl
Glad things went so well with the Assans. Whatever happened to the Palestinian girl who was Julie's nurse? Oh, and thanks for the answer. It's the right one, but did you have to add "and the guys"?

From: reprtrgrl
To: jcman
Our embassy people talked fast and got Karima released with us. We brought her home where Nabila took her under her wing. We all had visions of another Nabila success story, but it was soon obvious that Karima hasn't the intellectual curiosity or the self-confidence to deal with Beirut.
"But I don't want to go back to the camp," she told us, tears filling her eyes. "My father will just marry me off to another without concerning himself about my heart. I don't know what to do."
Nabila contacted the family who had cared for her cousin Zahra when she was pregnant. Was there a

place for Karima with them? Work for her? Yes, yes, they
said. Send her to us. We will care for her.
Last week Julie and I drove her to these people who
warmly welcomed her. It was easy to see that she
would feel more at home there than with us. She will
be free of the restrictions forced on her by her father
and her culture but still surrounded by those who
understand her, her upbringing, and her thought
patterns. They'll help her find as much or as little
independence as she wants.
Why wouldn't I want to see the guys again?

When Liz tried to write to John about her trip back to the
refugee camp, she struggled with the words to convey what she
felt about the interviews. At her request Hanan arranged for her
to meet other women, ones who ardently supported the extremist
Muslim position on women.

Liz had been both fascinated and upset by these women who
were obviously very intelligent. They made Liz think of the strong
Iraqi women who wanted to use their country's new democratic
process to overturn the family status laws that gave freedoms to
women, laws that had been passed when the less religiously
extreme regime of Saddam Hussein ruled.

"You believe a husband has the right to beat his wife?" Liz
asked after several minutes of preliminary conversation.

A woman wearing a chadar nodded, only her eyes visible.
"She is his property. He may do with her as he chooses."

Everything Western in Liz shuddered. She fought to keep her
voice nonjudgmental. "Even kill her?"

"If she dishonors him."

"You believe that if there is a divorce, she should lose the right
to her children?"

"If she has been immoral, yes."

"But if the husband has been immoral, he never loses custody, does he?"

"Allah has made the man superior."

All the way back to Beirut Liz kept thinking of the gracious way Jesus treated women, elevating them above the views held by the society in which He lived. And St. Paul taught equal respect of husband and wife for each other's needs as well as mutual submission, respect, and love.

From: reprtrgrl
To: jcman
I don't think I can begin to express what a gift it is to know the freedom found in being a Christian woman. Sure, as a believer I put myself under the authority of the Word of God, but its purpose is to help me develop to my fullest potential, not to imprison me and limit me. The Bible tells me God has given me special gifts and abilities. It tells me that God has planned a life of useful service for me and that God loves me and delights over me. How great is all of that?

From: jcman
To: reprtrgrl
I hope you noticed that all of those wonderful biblical promises are for us guys, too.

From: reprtrgrl
To: jcman
I noticed. Just goes to prove how wonderfully loving and accepting God is. Smile.
I leave tomorrow. Can't wait.

* * *

Liz didn't know what to expect when she moved toward the security exit at the Fayetteville Regional Airport. John said he would meet her if he could, but he couldn't promise.

"My life is never certain," he'd said in an e-mail two days ago. "But if I have anything to say about it, I'll be there."

She didn't want to think how disappointed—make that devastated—she'd be if he didn't meet her. It scared her how he had engaged her heart so thoroughly and so quickly, but she couldn't be happier.

Wait. She would be happier if John were waiting.

And he was. She walked out of the secure area, and there he was in jeans and a dark T-shirt, looking much as he had when running around the Lebanese countryside, but better all cleaned up, shaven, and smiling.

Suddenly she was self-conscious and tongue-tied. It was so easy to talk to him in her e-mails, but what should she do now? She smiled shyly as the heat rose in her cheeks. No two ways about it. She had it bad.

He took a step toward her and opened his arms. She stepped into them and burrowed close. She shut her eyes and held on tight.

"I've wanted to do this since I dragged you out of the warehouse," he muttered in her ear.

"Mmm. Me, too." They walked hand in hand to baggage claim, John carrying her computer case.

"I have three days," he said.

"Guaranteed?"

He gave her a crooked smile. "I wish."

She pointed out her suitcase, and he pulled it off the carousel. He stacked the computer on the case and wheeled it out to his car, his other hand still gripping hers. He popped the trunk and put the luggage in.

Liz stood between his car and the next, waiting for him to unlock the passenger door. When he slid into the narrow space beside her, it suddenly felt as private and intimate as a darkened room. Her mouth went dry, and she looked at him, only to find him staring back.

He reached out and ran a finger over the brow above the eye that had been battered by Frank's scope. "Looks a lot better."

"Feels a lot better."

They looked at each other for long seconds. Then he leaned down and kissed her, a sweet, somewhat tentative kiss. When he drew back, she smiled. "Nice."

He laughed and kissed her again, this time with total concentration. She wrapped her arms around him and enjoyed the ride.

"I've got to warn you," he said when he pulled back. He looked so serious that Liz felt afraid. "For all kinds of reasons, both personal and professional, I make a lousy love interest."

Her heart kicked. He'd said the *L* word. No, he'd said two *L* words. She had to laugh. "Lousy, huh?"

He looked a little disconcerted, as if he hadn't meant to say the second *L* word. "Yeah, lousy. Gone at any time day or night and for weeks or months at a time without contact. Everything secret. I already told you how I came home to find Kim married to someone else."

"Kim was a woman of poor character, no doubt about it. I, on the other hand, have guts."

"I've noticed." He grinned. "Does that mean you're willing to see where this thing between us goes?"

She kissed him in answer. He held her close.

They talked easily on the drive to John's cottage, and Liz needed only one glance to fall in love with the lake. She felt like a princess when John took her for a ride in the canoe, and she laughed when he took her to McDonald's for dinner.

"Can't have you be jealous of Sweeney," John said.

When he dropped her at her motel for the night, John gave her a kiss that kept her warm all night.

The next day was spent getting ready for a cookout at the cottage with the men of Task Force Valor.

"They're all coming," John told her. "To see you."

As Liz set the meat from Omaha Steaks out to thaw, she eyed John. "They're coming for the food, and you know it."

But when they came, Liz recognized a genuine delight on their parts as they hugged her. Even Sweeney seemed almost pleased.

The food was plentiful and delicious, the conversation non-stop, and Liz thought she'd never had a better time. She smiled at John across the lawn, and he smiled back, a special private smile that lit her heart.

St. Paul really did know what he was talking about, she thought. All things definitely worked together for good, and sometimes she and God actually defined "good" exactly the same.

After dinner Liz and John were sitting in lawn chairs talking to Rip and his date for the evening when John reached for his cell phone vibrating on his waist.

"Hello, Major Williams."

All conversation stopped. Liz's heart plummeted.

John sighed. "Roger that. We'll be there immediately."

The party exploded in groans and complaints as the men gathered their belongings and began to leave.

"I warned you," John said as he hugged Liz good-bye. "A lousy love interest."

She thought of the next day, the third day of his leave, stretching empty without him. Then she thought of something much worse—her whole future stretching empty without him.

"Just promise me one thing." She stood on tiptoe to kiss him. "Call me as soon as you get back."

He nodded. "If you promise me one thing in return. No insurance salesmen."

Now there was a promise easy to keep.

Report to your nearest bookstore in spring 2007 for
Task Force Valor's next mission.

Authors' Note

Explosives Ordnance Disposal units began in the United States around 1940 when the need was recognized for a specially trained force of men who could deactivate and defuse explosives used in warfare. Over the next five decades, bomb disposal units and their successors, EOD teams, racked up an impressive track record of successful missions worldwide, both in wartime and in peace.

Today, Explosives Ordnance Disposal units are in such high demand that the Army is recalling Vietnam-era EOD technicians to help meet the need. At the outset of the war in Iraq, Special Operations forces found the ad-hoc nature of their relationships to the EOD teams lacking. The global war on terror also highlighted the need to make changes in those relationships.

Part of the difficulty has been that Army EOD soldiers are more technicians than combat soldiers. They are well trained in their military occupational specialties but are considered by the Army's top brass to be support elements for frontline combat troops. By and large, they don't train on things like close quarters battle or hand-to-hand combat, leaving those tasks to other units.

The Army has reportedly discussed the idea of instituting an operational EOD unit—a completely self-sufficient group of Special Forces soldiers who are cross-trained to be explosives experts. The Navy has added an EOD cell to its super-secret DEVGRU, or Development Group, which was part of the Navy Special Warfare Group. Delta Force, the Army's elite and reclusive counterterrorist group, also has a special EOD section, but it is believed that they focus mostly on the really big missions, like hunting down nuclear threats around the globe.

The idea for Task Force Valor was built from a mixture of these real-life units and circumstances. Our team is fictional; its mission is a figment of the authors' imaginations, based on the reality of the current world situation.

Our explosive—Iso-Triethyl Borane, or ITEB—actually exists as a liquid compound that reacts explosively with air, but we have fictionalized a few important details so as not to give anybody ideas. For the same reasons, while we have endeavored to portray the U.S. military and the Special Forces in a realistic and positive light, some realism has been intentionally distorted to avoid encroaching upon the tactical profile currently in use by the troops who are doing these kinds of missions for real.

Our Palestinian refugee camp Sainiq is fictitious. Named after a river south of Sidon, Sainiq presents many of the realities of the twelve camps that exist in Lebanon—lack of infrastructure, extremely crowded quarters, limited educational opportunities, poor health facilities, little or no sewerage, massive unemployment, and virulent unrest. Hopelessness.

The United Nations has been involved for years in trying to open up opportunities to those in the camps through education and training in fields like automobile mechanics, one of the few occupations open to Palestinians under Lebanese law. As we complete this book, Lebanon is making moves that the government pledges will ease the plight of the refugees. One step is the promise to open up more of the forbidden seventy occupations to Palestinians.

The fascinating thing to us as Americans living in the great melting pot where everyone, no matter their ethnic origin, becomes an American is that neither the Lebanese nor the Palestinians want those living in the camps assimilated into Lebanon. The Lebanese see Lebanon as a sovereign nation merely hosting those in the camps, and the Palestinians do not want to be Lebanese. To the fourth generation, they only want to go back to their homeland.

Do not think harshly of Lebanon though. Similar conditions exist in the refugee camps in Jordan and Syria and the rest of the Middle East. For many Christians, used to thinking of the establishment of Israel as the fulfillment of biblical prophecy, it is easy to forget the plight of these refugees, many our brothers and sisters in Christ.

As we pray for the peace of Jerusalem, we must also pray God's redemption on the children of Ishmael.

Dear Reader,

The day after Pearl Harbor, my father and all the male teachers at the high school where he taught went to the recruiting office to enlist. Dad was not accepted because he was married and had a child. To do his part for the war effort, he left teaching and went to work as an inspector at New York Ship in Gloucester, NJ. He claimed he got the job because he knew what the dotted lines on a blueprint meant, not because he knew what he was doing.

Later when men with wives and children were being gladly accepted by the military, Dad was again refused because he now had a defense-sensitive job. I remember going with my mother to watch the launching of one of the ships he had worked on. To my great surprise the boat slid down the skids into the water sideways.

War always brings sorrow and death. In Dad's case, it took thirty-five years before the war got him and ten years of suffering before it claimed him.

"Asbestosis," the doctor had said. "I'll give you all the documentation you need to sue."

"Why sue?" Dad asked. "First New York Ship no longer exists, but even if I could find some entity to hold accountable, why attack people who had no idea they were dealing in death? We thought asbestos was the greatest thing ever."

There is no doubt that the asbestos that lined the bowels of the ships, the asbestos through which Dad walked regularly as he inspected the ships' progress, saved many lives through its fire-retardant properties. No one knew then that it, like much in life, would prove to be a two-edged sword.

Those of us who live in peace owe much to those who serve, those on the battlefield blatantly in harm's way, and those who, like Dad, more quietly offer their lives.

> May He command His angels concerning you
> To guard you in all your ways;
> May they lift you up in their hands,
> So that you will not strike your foot against a stone.

May He be with you in trouble,
May He deliver you and honor you.
—A prayer based on Psalm 91:11–12, 15

Gayle Roper

The authors would love to receive your comments on this book. Please send your thoughts to:

Both authors: authors@TFValor.com

Chuck Holton: chuck@TFValor.com

Gayle Roper: gayle@TFValor.com

Or visit the authors' websites at: www.livefire.us and www.gayleroper.com.

To Everything There Is a Season

Seaside Seasons by RITA Award-Winner GAYLE ROPER

Spring Rain, book one

Leigh Spenser is thrown into conflict when her boy's estranged father comes home to Seaside. A lesson on God's forgiveness shines through this emotionally gripping read about a modern-day family.

> "Gayle Roper is in top form with *Spring Rain*. Her storytelling skills make this one a page-turning experience readers will love."
> —James Scott Bell, author of *Blind Justice* and *Final Witness*

Summer Shadows, book two

Abby Patterson investigates two mysteries: Who is responsible for the hit-and-run, and who is Marsh Winslow? The first endangers her life, the second, her heart, in this story of mystery, humor, and romance.

Autumn Dreams, book three

Cassandra Merton, who just turned forty, has her hands full with aging parents, a teenage niece and nephew, and a rich bachelor who arrives at her bed-and-breakfast to contemplate his future.

Winter Winds, book four

As Dori and Trev face physical and spiritual danger together, their marriage of convenience becomes one of love and commitment.

Available in stores now!

Find Peace of Mind in Today's Uncertain World

More Life-changing Messages from CHUCK HOLTON

✺✺✺✺✺✺✺✺✺✺✺✺✺✺✺✺✺✺✺

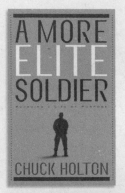

A More Elite Soldier

Former U.S. Army Ranger Chuck Holton shows how God oversees our training and gives each of us specific skills to accomplish the mission He has for us. Riveting action and powerful vignettes offer potent spiritual ammunition for the battles of every Christian serving in God's army. Find out what it takes to be a more elite soldier.

✺✺✺✺✺✺✺✺✺✺✺✺✺✺✺✺✺✺✺

Bulletproof

Would you like to have the confidence, the kind of driving purpose that shuts out all fear? Do you want your life to be filled with adventure? *Bulletproof* is a field manual that addresses the issues of fear and risk from a Christian perspective, using primarily military examples and analogies. Chuck Holton teaches believers how to overcome fear and join the ranks of the army of God.

✺✺✺✺✺✺✺✺✺✺✺✺✺✺✺✺✺✺✺

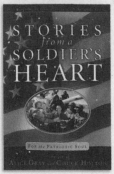

Stories from a Soldier's Heart

To preserve our peace of mind and our way of life, the men and women of the United States military often sacrifice their youth—and sometimes even their lives. Now more than seventy-five riveting stories bring to life these heroes and the loved ones for whom they have fought. *Stories from a Soldier's Heart* honors those who carry in their warrior hearts the world's hope for freedom.